About the author

Katie Hetherington is a young northern writer from Bolton who studied Journalism at Sheffield Hallam University.

After graduating, Katie began writing in numerous industries, whilst penning her first novel, *The Soul Watcher*.

Inspired by many authors over the years, particularly the likes of J.R.R. Tolkien and J.K. Rowling, she began to develop a strange dream she had, drawing on her imagination to create the storyline of *The Soul Watcher*.

THE SOUL WATCHER

KATIE HETHERINGTON

THE SOUL WATCHER

Vanguard Press

A CIP catalogue record for this title is
available from the British Library.

ISBN 978 1 80016 260 0

Vanguard Press is an imprint of
Pegasus Elliot MacKenzie Publishers Ltd.
www.pegasuspublishers.com

First Published in 2022

Vanguard Press
Sheraton House Castle Park
Cambridge England

Printed & Bound in Great Britain

Dedication

For all my family, in particular my mum, who spent hours reading the first drafts, and for Matthew, for unwavering support.

The path we travel on is a long one, but as you know, it eventually ends. Whether you die, give up, or you stand stock still and refuse to go any further. Either way, you hit a dead end, a paradise, a haven. But what happens when it ends? Who will be there to greet you? Friend or foe? And if you meet a foe, does it really matter? In the grand scheme of things, it doesn't, does it?

All we know is Jonah Heizium (the protagonist) would find out that fate one way or another. Now let's just pause there for a bit. I've skipped the best parts; forgive me for that. You see, I often get confused with past, present, future, beginning and end.

I have a lot on. My mind gets somewhat muddled with these human perspectives. You're a lot more complicated than what you seem.

Alas! I've just realised a key fact, one I must apologise for. My introduction, how rude.

Dear reader, I'm the Watcher; it's nice to meet you. You see, I have a specific and peculiar job, a requirement as such. Simply put, I'm Death's right-hand man.

I watch (as you may have guessed) the souls of the Earth who have got lost in death. I protect souls and guide them away from the Hollow, the world between life and death. It's no man's land and a place, ideally, nobody should linger too long. For it's not only me who lurks in that place, but many disturbing and evil creatures, ones that are forever trying to break into the land of the living. I shan't go into any more detail; it's not wise to dwell on such matters.

There are many reasons a soul gets lost: love, pain, sorrow and heartache are often the reason. Some are easier to coax onto the right path than others; it solely comes down to the life they live.

My purpose in life or death, depending on how you see it, is to get the souls to their rightful place and, depending on the person, the place they desire. There are many variations: heaven, hell, paradise and even reincarnation, to name a few.

I'll have you know this is a significant job, for a lingering or lost soul can soon turn into a tormented one, and that is no way to end. A tormented soul wreaks havoc, especially to those they love. The bond to those they care for helps souls to linger, but they become angry, resentful and a nuisance. They're an unseen, undefeatable parasite that infects and destroys those they once cherished. Their presence changes the fabric of time, a new path is woven, and the consequences can be disastrous, which is precisely why a Watcher is needed.

Now, before I start I want it to be known there are few blunders that have led to anything as disastrous as the tale I intend to tell, but nevertheless, there is a tale that must be told.

It began in Manchester, 1883. I'm not entirely sure if that's the past, present or future for you, so I shall provide a description anyway.

Manchester was the working man's city. It was rife with squalor, poverty and disease. Streets clumped together, filled with men, women and children staggering through life, trying to get whatever pennies they could to survive. It was a town where nobody knew when or where their next meal would come from. It was a collective stomach, rumbling day and night. The people were slowly decaying, emancipation saw the bones take over the flesh.

Together they fought for survival, taking the worst jobs, taking to the ever-impending doom of the mills, or worst, the workhouse. Both hideous options that were, in effect, the first shovels of dirt towards their grave. Whilst those jobs, kept many fed and housed, the days were long, the work dangerous and the conditions inhumane.

I've seen many souls come out of there, most too young to realise they'd even died. It was a sad state to see, but they were the last places of survival, or so many thought.

Jonah, for better or worse, managed to avoid the workhouse, but he still resided in one of the worst areas. It was an area festering with beggars who stumbled through the cobbled streets among the stalls, the fabric shops, run-down pubs, decaying bookstores and apothecaries. For a short while, Jonah lived above one said apothecary. It was overpriced, damp and hideous, but was a roof over his head nevertheless.

Life for Jonah and his mother wouldn't have been so hard had it not been for the untimely death of Frank Heizium. It was ten years before our tale starts when Frank succumbed to the winter chill and died. He was barely thirty when he met his inevitable end, but that he did. He quite literally worked himself into a grave, and he didn't save enough to pay for it, either.

His funeral wasn't cheap, and it wiped out all of their savings but for a few coins. If it wasn't for the sympathy of others, the workhouse would have been Jonah and his mother's final destination.

While our story is primarily about Jonah, there are others along the way who have gotten tangled up in his cursed life. Remember what I said? A tormented soul has the ability to not only affect the one it clings to, but to those around that person, too.

The tormented soul was that of Frank. He couldn't leave his family behind, especially his son, who he'd desperately tried to protect and shield from the poverty they lived in. His love for his son was like no other; it never is when a child is born from that of a soulmate.

You see, Jonah's mother, Theresa, was one of the lucky ones: she found the person she was destined for. It's a rare occurrence, and I must admit it's something that I very rarely see myself, which could explain my crucial mistake.

A person with a soulmate has a bond so strong it's hard to let go of the living, the ones left behind. Frank had barely got to know his son, and he wasn't ready to leave the love of his life behind, and vice versa for Theresa.

If each soulmate holds onto their memories and wishes for them to be real once again, the bond, the lifeline between the two, never truly breaks. True love sounds nice, but it can be a deadly thing if one leaves without the other.

Now, dear reader, I do not deny my mistakes because I slipped up. I dropped the ball, as you would say. I neglected the strength of Theresa's and Frank's bond, of the strong, compelling love for Jonah. I've seen it before, but the souls usually realise it's time to move on again, believing one day they would see their soulmate again. But it was Jonah; he was the factor I forgot to acknowledge. This soulmate business is far more severe and complex than what I anticipated, and with my gaze turned elsewhere, I failed to see the brewing creatures of the Hollow sneakily descending on Frank's grasp to the living world.

There are many, many hideous creatures, some which have become legends, others that still remain hidden myths — and let's just keep it that way. From the dawn of time, you humans have created stories that feature weird and wonderful creatures, some of which are eerily accurate. They're entertaining to us in the Hollow, but they're hardly comparable to the truth.

Some are worse than others, and it's with deep regret that Jonah and his family were tricked by the most powerful and dangerous creatures in the Hollow. Dear reader, have you heard of the seven deadly sins?

Lust, Wrath, Gluttony, Greed, Pride, Sloth and Envy. Seven mischievous, in the worst sense, creatures that have one collective goal: destruction. They feed off people's misery. They use a person's desires, and they manipulate it for their own amusement.

The Sins are a force of disaster, and they revel in the pain and death of innocent people. They cling to one person and cause as much damage as possible, until, they cannot stay on Earth; they've drained that emotion from the soul they clung to, and with no soul, the Hollow is the only place they can survive. The worst of the seven, the leader as such is Anger for it is such an overpowering emotion. The Sin is fuelled by pure rage, constantly wanting to infect the unsuspecting souls on Earth.

Collectively, the Sins should never have escaped, but I was naïve. I underestimated the power of love, and for that, Jonah paid the price.

You might think it's simple enough to bring escaped creatures back, but I can tell you that once the Sins are released, I cannot reverse their presence in the world. The Sins cling to the souls of the living, and they are what keeps a person connected to the living realm, and I do not have one. I'm not a physical creature. I may take the form of a man when needed, but my true form is nothing of the like. I had no connection, no way to cross the Hollow and drag them back. Dear reader, if I could, I would have done, trust me on that.

I had no other option but to let the Sins run their course; they simply cannot be tamed.

Because of this, their crossing the natural timeline, the one laid out before Jonah, was altered. Of course, such timelines are never entirely truthful — decisions, actions, war, death and wealth can divert a path and cause another to be rewritten. But that isn't what the Sins do; their presence wipes out the potential future ahead, and they rewrite it for their own entertainment. As soon as they appeared in the living world, the future became unknown, and the lives of many were in peril.

It's a terrible story and a dark mark on history, one that went unknown to those unaffected. To such people, it was a string of events put down to bad luck and a terrible human being. The fact of the matter is that the Sins were on a rampage.

Here is where I leave you. Now is the time you learn about the depressing life of Jonah Heizium. Like many, it starts from the beginning, and for that, we must delve into the past before the Sins had taken their victim, back when the path for the future was vaguely written. Back when everything seemed normal, when evil didn't loom in the distance. For there are key moments that date back to decisions made by Jonah's ancestors that led to these unfortunate events.

Dear reader, please don't judge me too harshly. I may not be human, but everybody makes mistakes…

The Heiziums' Plight

It was 1830 when the Heiziums first arrived in London. It wasn't a family affair, and it certainly wasn't meant to be a permanent move. It was a trip for business, not pleasure, for the great, great-grandfather of Jonah, Heinrich Heizium, who was a rich and highly regarded man within the political hemisphere. He was the German negotiator, and he often spent time travelling to different countries to maintain peace yet still prosper under the restraints, especially that from Britain, who were leading figures across the globe.

It was a hard and difficult task, but it had brought many riches, a lavish lifestyle and two darling girls, and eventually a son. Heinrich and his wife had tried many years to conceive a boy, but he'd only managed to produce girls, three of which didn't see it to their first birthday, much to the dismay of his wife and himself, too. Alas, in 1815, Anna, his wife, gave birth to a boy, Jonah, and it was a blessing and a miracle for both of them. Heinrich couldn't have been any prouder that day, but sadly this pride declined with each year the boy grew.

Heinrich was a harsh man who didn't tolerate the liberal and naïve views of his growing boy. Jonah's childhood was a trying one that had one clear path that fell in line behind his father's. Yet that wasn't Jonah at all; he was far more interested in the arts. Literature, music and theatre were his true passions in life, and his father did not approve, not one bit. In a bid to teach and develop his child, he took Jonah on the journey to England. There he could teach him how to act, how to hold a role similar to him with dignity.

At the time, Jonah was just fifteen years old, and they'd planned to stay for a year, but politics isn't as straightforward as that; there is no timescale accurate for an official agreement. Which inevitably meant they were to remain for much longer than anticipated. It was hard learning for Jonah, who wanted nothing to do with it, especially not the kind that favoured the rich over the poor. He only ever mentioned his views the once and in return, he received the biggest beating of his life. That was not the viewpoint of a respectable Heizium; the poor were vermin, and that is how it was to stay for the likes of their family to retain their status.

After that, Jonah kept his mouth shut and his head down for the next four years. He worked tirelessly to please his father, doing what was necessary, learning how to act, how to be a good son. It was a hard task to not only learn but to pretend he enjoyed it, that he fitted in with the likes of his father's friends and colleagues. He felt defeated and was very close to giving up on his dreams of becoming a philanthropist. It looked like his future was set in stone, and that was the life he was due to live. His father had already begun arranging his future wife setting him up with suitable women, and he'd practically secured him a job within the English government as a translator for the foreign diplomats.

It was around that time that he met Mary. She was a young, slight thing and worked as a scullery maid. Jonah was the only one that saw her beauty and he fell hard and fast for the girl, and she for him.

They talked daily and met secretly as they cemented their friendship and then their courtship. It wasn't long before he was talking about marriage; he felt a bond with a woman that oozed joy.

At last, plucked up the courage to ask his father for his blessing to marry the scullery maid.

Over the four years, they'd formed a bond, and they surprisingly got on well enough that he decided she would make him very happy. His father, whilst harsh at times, was growing in pride at his son's success, his hard work to follow in his footsteps.

Heinrich had begun to talk with his son more frequently and with kindness, and Jonah felt his father would come to accept and support his decision.

The philanthropist inside him still remained; he thought love would outweigh the position that his beau carried. How wrong he was; as soon as the words tumbled out, Heinrich became enraged. He bellowed in his native tongue, shaming him, his name, values and the disappointment he brought upon their family as a son. In a fit of rage, he punched Jonah in the nose, causing it to erupt with blood — and that was the last time Jonah ever saw his father.

He packed his things up, grabbed Mary and, with the blessing of her father, he asked her to marry him. He had a fair number of valuable possessions that he sold to support their new life, but London was expensive, and it wasn't possible to live a good life down there.

The prospect of a career in politics disappeared the moment he left his father's side. The little friends he'd made disowned him, he was viewed as a joke and no government body would touch him with a barge pole. Even his fellow liberals wouldn't take him; they didn't trust or believe that he'd suddenly become interested in their values. They thought it was a play to piece together what career he had — or worse, to spy for the opposing party. Either way, he was rejected and now faced a jobless and impoverished life.

Although dejected, Jonah was a fighter and he wasn't going to let Mary down, and he decided to live a more sustainable and cheaper life up North, in Manchester. There, he could establish himself as something new, build a life in an upcoming city that wasn't nearly as expensive as the capital.

They each found work and were able to make ends meet, but it was hard work they endured. For Jonah, it was a breath of fresh air; there were no airs or graces, everyone worked together, people laughed and seemingly enjoyed their lives. Even with all the riches, he'd never experienced this; it was a liberating feeling, and he never wanted to return to his old life.

Soon after, Mary, who he'd since wed following the move, gave birth to a baby boy. They named him Frank, after Mary's father. He, too, settled up North, not long after they made the move, and he taught Jonah how to survive and was pleasantly surprised by his willingness to learn and ability to do it fast.

For the most part, the Heiziums lived a happy life with good memories and plenty of laughter. Sadly, they never lived to a grand age. They died from cholera when Frank was in his mid-teens — leaving him to find his own way in the world. It was tough for Frank, but he was a hard worker like his father, and he had the potential to survive, even become someone.

The Watcher

Love, my dear reader, is a beautiful thing that has the ability to rip worlds apart. Jonah was a remarkable man and would have proved himself to be a great one if he'd followed his destiny; but, alas, he changed his path and instead chose love.

I personally don't understand it, because I have never experienced it. I once asked Death what love was, and he simply said it was human. I cannot fathom what that means, but it is possibly the biggest and most unpredictable emotion that can change the future.

Do remember, dear reader, the future isn't entirely written. Imagine a path that's covered with fog and every step you take it gets a little clearer. This path is a straight one, but every now and then another path appears, creating a fork in the road. You can choose either to continue on the original path or divert from it and take an even more mysterious one. The paths represent your decisions: if you take a risk, a big, life-changing risk, then you're no longer on the original path.

So, when Jonah made his decision to leave his family, his career and his home, he diverted from the path, and he headed towards a new future. Does that make sense?

I should have been attuned to these happenings, but I wasn't. As I recall, I was dealing with a Shaman on the other side of the globe — funny fellow, always torn between reincarnation and the aftermath of death. He's been a familiar soul that I've met many times, but he always lingers in the Hollow and, having lived so many lives, he was vulnerable. Reincarnated souls are ideal hosts for creatures in the Hollow; that soul has touched many lives that span far and wide. You couldn't imagine the damage a creature could do if they stole it, the terrible influence they could have on the world.

A reincarnated soul carries much power; if absorbed, a creature could become the master of the Hollow, an entity that could break the unknown, let the Hollow merge with the living land, releasing evil upon the innocent.

Sorry, I digress. Where was I?

Ah, yes, Jonah the first had made the life-altering decision — one that I was unaware of. A new path had been created; quite suddenly, I may add, too. Such happenings typically send a ripple through the Hollow; they're exciting as it means unpredictability and possibly the chance of freedom on Earth. Something that the Sins quickly realised.

However, this isn't the end; there is a lot more to come. This is simply the catalyst of events that were destined to bring heartache, untimely death and bitterness to many.

For now, you must follow the journey of Frank, our protagonist's father, for he plays an integral part in this story.

Frank Heizium's Final Act

Frank Heizium was a relatively normal man. He was tall, over six foot, with thick, wavy blond hair with a chiselled face made up of high cheekbones and a strong jawline. The most distinctive feature was his bright blue eyes that illuminated his face and twinkled every time he smiled. As a young man, he was desired by many; even the richer ladies turned their heads when he walked past. He was the pauper's heart-throb.

Frank was the spitting image of his father, and a lot of his looks were inherited from his German ancestors; but that was where the similarities ended. He may be the descendant of the rich and mighty, but he was nowhere near rich nor mighty — not in the eyes of those in power.

Like his father, Frank never received a penny from his German ancestors; he wasn't entirely sure whether they knew of his existence. His father rarely talked of his past or his family, for that matter. Over the years, Frank pieced together the story of how he came to be.

Life had been tough for them, his mother had scandalously left her employee without a reference, and it took weeks until she found a cleaning position in a small townhouse. His father, a man of few skills except the gift of a good conversation, that secured him an apprenticeship at a local factory.

Neither were on good pay, but it was enough to raise a child and be happy. Frank was very much like his father: if he had the love of a good woman, in life the other things would be a bonus.

By the time he'd reached twenty-one, he had the love of his life on his arm, Theresa, a roof over his head and a beautiful baby boy that he cherished. It seemed like a promising future ahead, but this soon turned sour.

Frank had terrible luck securing a job or a steady income. He was close to inheriting his father-in-law's butchers' shop, but that dream was crushed when he suddenly sold it. He wasn't a huge supporter of their marriage, and he'd seen that Frank was limited in his skills. While Frank saw Theresa as a glimmer of hope in a stagnated town, Theresa's father thought there were more suitable husbands out there.

'Theresa, listen to me, that boy is no good,' Theresa's father spat and pointed at Frank. 'He doesn't have a job, he's unskilled, he can't run my butchers, he'd ruin it!'

It had caused many arguments, and cracks appeared between Theresa and her father. Frank was disheartened, but decided bitterness would be wasted energy.

After a particularly trying day, Frank sat Theresa down and said, 'My love, I know this is hard, and I cannot lie I'm hurt by your father's reluctance to accept me into the family or trust me with his business, but this isn't the end. You mark my words, I'll prove your father wrong.'

Through watery eyes, Theresa grasped Frank's hand and sobbed. 'I'll be proud no matter what,' she said, crying. 'My father is a mean and bitter man, but I know you'll provide for me.'

Theresa's words gave him strength, and he wasn't going to let her down. Despite his lack of skills, he'd always had luck picking up odd jobs, so he took to the streets, searching for any work that would pay the bills. It wasn't steady work, nor was it well paid, but he managed.

He became a familiar face around town, known as the cheap labourer that could get the job done.

At the beginning of the marriage, it worked out well, but when Theresa became pregnant, the pressure was on. He was ecstatic to become a father, but he was determined that his son or daughter would have a decent life, one that wasn't filled with work or hardship. That was his job. He wanted a child that grew up strong, skilled and brainy, knowing that they had two loving parents. He might not have been able to provide nice new things, but their child would know what love is.

Many people thought Frank mad for not encouraging his child to work, but he held liberal views for a working man in need of money. His focus on being a good father and being actively involved in his child seemed so alien to other men.

'Frank,' they'd say, 'you're best getting your boy in work as soon as you can; start him in the mills, teach him a trade, bring in some more money for you and Theresa.'

Each time he'd laugh and protest, 'Now, now, fellas, this is my business. My boy will have skills and brains, but he won't be put to work like a dog.'

He didn't want him to have the life he had: his parents died when he was young, old enough to work but young enough to still need his parents. That was when he was tested; he was an orphan and a borderline pauper. Which is around the time he began job-hopping in a bid to survive.

When Theresa gave birth, Frank was overwhelmed by the tiny thing that was so soft and gentle. Frank wanted nothing more than to name him after his father, which Theresa willingly agreed to. Thus, Jonah Heizium II was born. Frank wasted no time boasting about his darling son, which helped him get more work, as men took pity on a man trying to support a family without a job. He was big and handy for the odd labour job, and over the years he'd collected a handful of friends who spoke highly of him. While it never led to a steady job, Frank wasn't often left without work; it might only be a couple of months at a time and the work on occasion was hideous, but he provided for his family.

'Oh, my dear,' Frank groaned after a particularly long and hard day. 'It's a hard life if you don't weaken. I've got some work sorted for the next few months; it's not great, but it will do.' He breathed a heavy sigh and fell into bed, asleep.

The majority of conversations started and ended that way, as Frank left before dawn and returned after dusk. Sometimes money in hand, other times glum and disappointed in himself.

For ten years, Frank had worked like this; he was almost a stranger to his son, but a hero nevertheless. He often wondered out loud how other families did it: keep a solid job, a roof over their head whilst raising half a dozen children as well.

'I suppose the more children they have, the extra wages they bring home. Extended families often take care of one another, but me and you, we're in this together, and we do just fine,' Theresa always replied.

It was a sore point for Frank, because he did have a large family. He knew the story about his kin, and he wondered where they were now. Were they happy? Sad? Did they have families of their own? Were they still rich? These questions whirled in his mind, but he didn't have the opportunity to find out. He was a nobody, constantly looking for a lucky break.

Throughout the years he spent a lot of time walking, waiting and working. He ate scraps, for that was all he could afford, and he slept uneasy in fear of disappointing his wife and growing child, but he never gave up. It wasn't in his nature.

I

Before they knew it, a new decade had arrived. It was 1870 and life was as tough as ever. The bitter chill of the winters were the worst and inevitably turned into the deadliest. Frank had been job-hopping for many years, and his body was showing it. Jonah had just turned six. He was tall for his age, just like his father and grandfather. He was smart, smarter than most, and he filled Frank with so much joy. It had been a fun six years raising him, and with every day he felt prouder and more determined to go out there to be a strong breadwinner for his family.

Sadly, the turn of the decade didn't bring a great deal of hope; work was sparse, with many employers fully staffed or without the need for extra short-term workers. Even his regular employers turned him away, much to his dismay.

Over the past few months, they had been living on watered-down cabbage soup and had fallen behind on their rent. Luckily, their landlord, Mr Burke, was a kind man; he'd known Frank's father well, and he had enough money to not rely on their rent. He was practically letting them live there for free.

Their home wasn't massive; in fact, it wasn't really a home, but a room in a tiny house just off Nelson Street. There was a bed squeezed into the left-hand corner; it was old and haggard with a thin mattress. It bore the signs of age, with yellow stains and dips from where Frank had lain. Each night, all three of them piled in, with Jonah being firmly squashed in the middle; not that he ever complained, especially during the winter months.

Over the years, Theresa had made the room more homely. In the centre of the room was a small fireplace where most of their meals were prepared. She'd laid out a rug, passed down from her mother, and surrounding the fire was a wooden stool, a small chair and a comfy armchair they'd found dumped in an alley behind the house. That was Frank's chair, and after a long day he'd sink into it and put his feet in front of the fire, and Jonah would crawl into his lap and tell him stories of his day. On how he'd helped Theresa sell potatoes in the streets that she had graciously been given by pitiful neighbours, or how he'd been next door and played with the little boy. The neighbours were friendly enough and often dropped by during the hard times with leftovers or hand-me-down clothing for Jonah.

They were always too big for the skinny lad, but Theresa was a whizz with a needle and thread, and she could make the largest of garments fit the boy. She could easily mend patches in worn-out shirts, and when they could afford material, which was rare, Theresa could fashion a dress for herself that fitted her bountiful curves.

Frank often thought she could have entered the trade with her quick fingers and eye for detail, but she suffered from aches and pains. Strenuous stitching left her hand curled, unyielding and painful. He understood and accepted the fact, but he always wondered. He did a lot of wondering about life, his in particular. There are so many what-ifs in this life, but you can't live on if, could, would, should or maybes, or you'd never step through the front door.

Despite the seemingly bad luck and lack of a steady job, they had a roof over their heads, clothes on their backs, occasionally damp, and food on the table, most of the time. It was a pleasant enough place to live, though it was small.

They didn't have much when they moved in, and they hadn't bought much in the time they lived there. They had a rickety table in the right-hand corner that had even fewer stable chairs which Frank had saved from his old home. That, too, was on its last legs, with him having to hammer them back in every now and then.

Theresa had brought with her an old closet which they shared; in the drawers went the plates, pots and cutlery, for they had nothing else to fill it with. In the other corner was a frayed curtain and behind it was a small basin and chamber pot that Theresa emptied each morning. There was a communal tap downstairs where they could get water. Each morning, Frank would take a bucket down, fill it to the top and lug it back up the stairs for Theresa to use.

It was home, it wasn't fancy and it wasn't big, but it was where they shared their time, ate and slept, and, most of all, it was better than the workhouse. The rent was cheap with the landlord Mr Burke charging very little for their board.

He was a good man with a kind heart, and he often stopped by to see how they were doing. When there was a lull in work, he made sure they had enough to eat, coal for the fire and clothes on their backs. Frank appreciated the help, but he hated taking things from others. It made him feel like a beggar and thief and each time it motivated him to seek work. Even on the worst days, he headed out onto the streets in search of work.

The winter months were always the worst, and as October approached, so did the worst winter they'd experienced in their lifetime. The bitter chill of winter whipped at people's faces, and the snow began to fall. Thick, heavy snowflakes flurried down, burying the streets and turning the town into a white bliss. It looked beautiful, but that white sheet was deceitful. Walking became impossible as people slid on the ground like a deer on ice. The cold was impossible to escape, and the roads became treacherous. Even the horses were struggling to stay upright A thick layer of ice was causing the horses and consequently the carriages and carts of goods to veer off course, ploughing into unfortunate passers-by. It was pandemonium as the streets became a dangerous place to venture.

Local authorities issued health notices and warnings as more incidents started to happen. Restrictions were placed on the numerous carriages carrying goods in and out of Manchester. It began affecting businesses, and many people were let go as the demand for their services declined.

The snow had caused more damage than anticipated, the townsfolk were worried as work ceased and food supplies ran short, and it wasn't long before people began demanding action. To combat the uproar and decline in trade, the officials issued a plea for workers to clear the streets by shovel and hand.

It was hard work, in freezing conditions, but Frank didn't care: it was good pay. Many men applied, but few had Frank's build — he was tall and strong, ideal for chipping away at the ice and shovelling for hours on end. Plus, he knew the roads, the layout, and in the thick snow that was plummeting to the ground, his navigation skills were next to none.

For the first time in months, Frank felt he'd got his lucky break, and he was ecstatic, as was Theresa. They finally had pay, finally had money to put food on the table.

II

The bright light of the wintery morning muffled by snow streamed onto Frank's face as he woke on the frosty Monday morning. He yawned and stretched his arms out, his bones cracking as he did so.

Jonah was perfectly snuggled between them both, sound asleep and snoring gently. He seemed so peaceful, and Frank looked upon him and smiled. He was the reason behind every decision he made; he was the reason to keep on looking for work, to be a success for his family.

As he groaned and began to climb out of bed, Theresa woke up, turning around in a sleepy haze.

'Frank,' she croaked, and rubbed her eyes, before she gasped and quickly scrambled out of bed. 'Frank, oh, Frank, today you start your new job.' She was so horrified after realising she had overslept that she jumped out of bed and ran to the half-kitchen, half-storage area and began piecing together food for the day. She grabbed a loaf of bread and began slicing into it, cutting thick pieces and layering it with butter donated from the Smiths across the way.

Frank smiled as he watched his wife in her nightdress, rushing to feed him before his long day ahead. He slowly climbed out of bed, trying not to wake up his darling son. He tiptoed across the floor and put his arms around Theresa. She was thicker than when they met, but he liked that. She felt like home, like love, like happiness. He sighed and laid his head on her back, breathing in her scent. It was familiar and relaxing.

For a moment they paused in their embrace, Theresa leaning on him, holding his hands and pressing her head against his arms. They stayed this way for a few moments, before Jonah launched himself at them both. He waded in and, clinging to their sides, his arm reached across Theresa's stomach and Frank's back. They all chuckled as they felt the love. Theresa turned and, once again, Jonah was in the middle, with both parents embracing him.

Frank didn't want to let go, but this was a fleeting and memorable moment, one to be cherished. He kissed Theresa on the lips and Jonah on the head, before letting them go.

'I've got to go,' he sighed. 'Work is waiting for me, and this is a good thing. I'll be home before you know it.' He smiled, clasping Theresa's chin and squeezing it, before pulling away to get ready. He walked to the fireplace and picked up his clothes, building up the layers for the chill of winter was already biting.

As he got ready, Theresa returned to buttering the bread and placing it on a plate, whilst Jonah jumped about excitedly. She handed him the plate as Frank finished buttoning his shirt up. He looked down lovingly and picked up the bread, taking a huge bite. It was stale and crunchy, but the butter helped the food slide down his throat and into his empty stomach. He didn't realise how hungry he was until he took that first bite, and despite its texture, he savoured every moment. By all means, it was delicious, but he only ate the one, giving Jonah and Theresa the remaining slice, despite their protests.

He waved their comments away, pulled his jacket on and left. He came out of the room and made his way down the stairs, trying to avoid the ones that creaked. It was early, and he didn't want to wake the entire house. He closed the front door behind him and embraced the bitter chill of the morning, wincing as the wind whipped at his cheeks. Turning his collar up, he started to walk towards the town hall, where he would be given the tools and told where he would be working that day.

A new layer of snow had fallen overnight, leaving an untouched sheet that covered the entire road. It seemed a shame to disrupt the flakes with his heavy boots, but needs must. In a child-like manner, he jumped into the street, creating two large footprints, and he smiled as he blessed the snow that gave him work, and then he sloped in the direction of the rising sun.

The walk to the town hall was well over half an hour, and that was at a hurried speed, but with the snow weighing him down, it took almost double the time. When he finally arrived, he was dripping with sweat, his feet were soaked, and he was panting heavily. He was due to be there at seven a.m., and he was just about on time. A crowd of men stood around him, some shivering in the freezing cold with nothing but a shirt on and looked to be half-starved; others were like him, with layers of clothing that were drenched in sweat and snow.

The one thing they had in common was the need for work; this was a job only the most desperate of men would take. For they all knew this wasn't going to be easy. This was going to be tough work that required muscle and stamina. He recognised a lot of the men around him; he'd seen them in the work yards when he'd been searching for work, and they must have been the unlucky ones that were let go following the lack of trade because of the snow. On the plus side, this meant when the snow had cleared up there would be a demand for the workers they'd let go, which meant he might have a chance at securing something permanent.

It was just another bonus, another treat that came with the snow that so many hated. Unlike the rest of the men, he had a smile on his face and had a joyful outlook on the day's work ahead.

As they were waiting in the chill, nodding towards the men around him, a large pot-bellied man opened the doors of the town hall and began slowly walking down the stairs, his belly wobbling with each step. He had a thick black jacket on that hung to the floor. It was a tad too small as the buttons were almost popping off. His cheeks were bloated and red from the chill, despite his top hat shading his face.

He loudly cleared his throat, getting the attention of the men, and shouted 'Listen up! You've got a long day ahead of you. We need the snow and ice clearing from the major roads. As you know, trade has almost ceased, and some of you might be here for that. I'm going to split you up into groups and then send you on your way.'

The man proceeded to order the men, placing Frank with a scrawny selection of workers. The pot bellied man ordered them to Chapel Street and Frank groaned internally. The street was over an hour's walk and they each had to carry a large, metal shovel that had been handed to them.

Frank decided to take charge considering he was inevitably going to be doing most of the work, he figured he had a right to leadership. He looked upon the group of men: there were seven in total. Three of which were elderly and frail — a strong gust of wind would have easily knocked them over. Two were practically children — they were skinny, spotty and looked as if they didn't have a day's work in them or even a muscle either. The remaining two were of regular build, and around Frank's age. He knew their faces but not their names; at some point he'd worked with both of them, one at the docks and another in a loading bay. He'd seen them work before; they weren't half bad workers and would be an asset if partnered with the rest of the group.

'So, fellas, Chapel Street is a fair walk away and, in this snow, it's going to be a tough walk. Balance the weight of your shovel wisely, because today isn't going to be easy. One last thing, keep up; the faster we get there, the quicker we'll get the road clear, hopefully before the snow starts falling again.' He moved through the crowd, paving the way towards Chapel Street. He knew a few short-cuts that would shave some time off their journey. The men he partly knew fell side by side with Frank as they slowly made their way forward.

As they walked, Frank found out about the men beside him, Jack and Sam. Jack was a tall man, with broad shoulders, he was slender but strong, his muscles could be seen under his jacket. Tufts of brown hair stuck out from under his cap, hiding part of his face, he had grey eyes that looked like they had seen a lot in this world, and he talked like he did, too. Sam was as sharp as they came and fairly tall, but had more fat than muscle to him, but was nevertheless strong. He had deep brown eyes, a flat nose that looked like it had taken a punch, and chubby red cheeks. His face had a few wrinkles around his eyes and mouth, but they looked like they had come from laughter, not age.

They both had families; Sam had two daughters and a doting wife, Jack had two boys and two girls and a wife not so loving.

His daughters both worked: the younger one helped his wife wash clothes for the middle-class ladies who didn't do their own washing. The elder worked in a nearby mill, working on the machines and producing cotton. It was hard and dangerous work that came with many terrible stories. Sam didn't like her doing the work, but they needed the money, especially now.

Both of the men had lost their jobs following the lack of work and seemed grateful for the snow

They continued their walk, chatting away, exchanging stories and cursing yet blessing the snow. The rest of the group fell behind them, staggering under the weight of their shovels. Every now and then, Frank called back words of encouragement to keep spirits high, not that it did much. They were half-starved, too old to do a decent day's work or too young to know what an honest day's work was.

'Today is going to be hard,' Sam sighed.

'Yes, it is, and it's not going to be easy with them lot slowing us down,' Jack whispered.

'Agreed,' Frank said, turning his gaze back and seeing the men lagging behind, sweat dripping from their foreheads. He heaved a deep sigh and marched on, hoping the men would keep pace and still be up for the long day before them.

After walking for what seemed like forever, the men reached Chapel Street, half of which were panting like rabid dogs.

'I say we spread out along the road, taking on one section at a time,' Frank proposed. Jack and Sam nodded in agreement; the remainder of the men looked weary but reluctantly agreed. Splitting up, the men aligned side by side with a good five foot between each man, covering the majority of the road. Frank was next to Jack and a frail old man. The three men had tried to position themselves between the weaker men, which meant they'd do more than their stretch. It was an unfair deal, but it was the quickest way to get the work done.

Frank stamped his foot on the ground; it was rock solid with ice and was covered with a deceiving layer of fluffy snow. It would take some muscle to chip away at that. Nevertheless, he raised his shovel and struck the ice fast and hard, Jack and Sam following his motions. It barely made a dent, with a few pieces of ice chipping away. Again, he raised his shovel, both hands grasping at the wooden handle, and struck the same spot.

The iron spade collided with a thud and sent vibrations through the stick. This time he made more of an impact as the ice cracked. He smiled triumphantly and again he raised his shovel and hit the ground. He'd disturbed enough of the ice to start shovelling it to the kerb. Jack and Sam had similar successes, encouraging the other men to pick up their shovels and hack away at the ice.

In a short space of time, all seven of the men were in rhythm, hacking away simultaneously. They went at the snow hard, some seemingly attacking it as if to take their anger and frustration out on it, digging away in vengeance at these white, delicate flakes thathad stolen their jobs, forcing them into hard labour.

As the day went by, more people started to emerge from their homes, braving the slippery streets of Manchester. Some brought food and drink to the men, which they happily indulged in.

By midday, they'd cleared a fair amount of the ice. Frank's plan had paid off; it was a faster method of clearing the road, but that didn't mean it was any less tiring. His arms ached from repeated stabbing at the ground and he could see the other men were feeling it, too. He was surprised by the old man next to him: he'd hardly stopped and made good progress on his section of the road.

Turning to him, Frank said, 'You're a dark horse, you are, sir. I didn't think you'd have the strength to do such manual work, but I must say I'm impressed.'

The old man looked up, cupping his ear that had white tufts of hair poking out, and smiled at Frank's words. He was a funny-looking man with a face full of wrinkles. He had a long hook nose, thin wispy hair and deep green eyes. His arms were slim and tender-looking, but when he bashed at the floor, his muscles appeared out of nowhere, making a huge impact. He was much tougher than what he seemed. At first, Frank thought him mad, for he only wore cotton trousers and a vest that was stained with yellowing patches, yet the cold didn't seem to bother him.

'Yes, yes, I am. I've spent all my life doing work like this, and I'm not done yet,' he said in a surprisingly deep and gruff voice.

Frank simply nodded his head, watching the man as he returned to his work. He looked over at Sam and Jack, who both looked weary. They hadn't been as lucky as him: they were both stuck next to weak boys that had barely scratched the surface, which inevitably meant the pair of them had taken on a larger stretch of the road than they anticipated.

Frank looked on at them in pity and shook his head. For the rest of the day, he vigorously worked, trying to shift as much snow and ice as possible in a bid to help the other men. His joints ached, his hands were full of calluses, and his clothes were soaked

Dusk was beginning to approach, and the men had cleared most of their own patches and had descended on the last remaining stretch of road. The old man, Sam, Jack and Frank were the only ones doing any work. The remainder of the men were feebly clawing at the road.

Frank could see the other men were weary and annoyed at the others. It didn't help that the snow had begun to fall again; it was a weak shower, but it was still covering what they'd already dug up. By the time they'd cleared the road, a layer of snow was re-covering the surface, but night had almost fallen, and their workday was up. They were to return to the town hall to hand in their shovels.

There was a sigh of relief and dismay when they'd finished. It was the first day of a tough job, and the men had yet to complete the tiresome walk back. Frank hoped some of the roads were cleared and that they could have a nice walk back, but the snow had begun to fall faster, and it was turning into a blizzard. Once again, Frank, Jack and Sam were leading the group. Frank had lent his jacket to the old man, after taking pity on him.

He was now staggering through the snow in nothing but a cotton shirt. The wind stung his bare skin, and he slowly began to lose feeling in his hands and feet. His shovel weighed heavy in his arms, and he prayed for the day to be over, to be back in his home with his wife and son. His longing kept him going, giving him the strength to power through.

They felt as if they were walking for a lifetime before they finally reached the town hall. The man who greeted them in the morning was pacing back and forth, his arms clasped behind his back. Their sodden footsteps turned his gaze.

'You're late,' he gruffed, anger piercing his eyes. 'Put your shovels in that cart over there.' He nodded in the direction of the road where a cart was stationed. 'Same time tomorrow, men; don't be late again or else.' He left on a threatening note and marched towards the cart. One by one, the men dumped their shovels down, muttered their goodbyes and stumbled in the directions of their homes.

It was yet another dire walk for Frank, halfway home, he realised he hadn't got his jacket back and he cursed the night's sky. Freezing and disheartened, Frank finally returned home, his spirits lifting as he climbed the stairs and opened the door.

He'd barely taken a step inside when Jonah hurled at him, jumping up and almost falling backwards as he did so.

'Jonah, get down,' Theresa chastised. 'Your father has had a long day; let him settle in before you start jumping on him.'

Frank merely smiled and placed him down, rubbing his hair and breathing deeply. He turned to his wife, who immediately wrapped her arms around him.

'Frank! You're soaking wet and freezing. What on Earth! Where is your jacket?' Theresa talked in a similar tone in which she had addressed Jonah. It was a caring, condescending tone and one he didn't care for; he was tired, and he just wanted to sit down.

Before he could speak, she had pulled his shirt off and sat him down in front of the fire. She bustled around and reappeared at Frank's side with a plate full of food and a pint of ale. He smiled from ear to ear in joy as he wolfed down the food. Jonah sat at his feet, asking question after question about his day.

Frank moaned and Theresa nodded sympathetically before suggesting they head to bed, for it was going to be just as hard a day as today. He barely made it to the bed before collapsing, breathing in a wheezy huff. Jonah snuggled in beside him, and Theresa continued to potter around. She was worried. Frank looked drained, peaky and shattered, but she put it down to Frank's first real day back at work. He'd been out of work for so long that he wasn't used to it; it must have been a shock to his system and hit him hard. She looked at him lovingly as he slept and she stroked his hair, before kissing him on the head and then she, too, cosied up to him.

Dawn came around too quickly as Frank rose the next morning. His bones were stiff, and he ached all over. He tried to leave the bed quietly, but failed miserably, for when he stood, he suddenly felt faint. The cold air rushed to his head, and he stumbled into the wall, grasping his heart as he fell with a loud thud, waking the entire household.

Theresa shot up and lunged at Frank.

'Frank, Frank, are you all right? What happened?' she screeched hysterically as she crouched over him, helping him up and sitting him on the bed.

'What's happening?' Jonah groggily said, rubbing his eyes and staring at his mother and father.

'Nothing, Jonah, go back to sleep,' Frank gasped, rubbing Jonah's leg reassuringly.

'Frank,' Theresa whispered urgently, 'you're not well; you have a fever brewing and it knocked you down. You can't go in today, you're sick.'

Frank waved her away before saying, 'Don't be a silly woman. I'm fine; it was just a stumble is all. I don't have a fever, and there is no way I'm missing work; it's only the second day, and we need the money. I refuse to keep living off our neighbours. Now shift — I need to get ready.'

He moved Theresa out of the way and stood up carefully. Once again, the faintness washed over him, but he gained control, refusing to succumb to the darkness.

He shook his head hard and fast, then began pulling his clothes on; all the while, Theresa was staring at him, worried. He tried to ignore her as he went downstairs with the bucket to get water to wash his face. He was out of breath before he even reached the bottom of the stairs. Gulping for air, he filled the bucket halfway up and dragged it back upstairs. By the time he reached his home, he was panting and covered in sweat. Theresa edged towards him, but didn't say anything. The look in his eyes was clear: he was going to work whether she liked it or not.

While he finished getting ready in slow, staggering movements, Theresa fixed him his breakfast. Unlike yesterday, Jonah remained in bed asleep, unaware of the silent argument between his mother and father or his father's failing health.

Frank left him that way, as he picked up his food and headed out into the cold streets, merely pecking Theresa on the cheek as he went. Tears welled in her eyes, but he ignored them.

She called after him, 'Frank, wait, what about your jacket? Where is it? You can't go out without one, not in the snow; you'll catch your death.'

'I don't have it. I lent it to an old fella yesterday, and he forgot to give it back. Don't worry, I'll get it back; the walk won't kill me,' he called back, and left without turning to face her.

He sighed in the doorway. He contemplated going back, but he could see outside that the night sky was getting lighter. If he was late, they'd send the men off and he would miss a day's wage and would have walked all that way for nothing. Against his better judgement, he headed down the stairs, hating that he hadn't made up with Theresa.

He pulled the door open, and once again the cold air stung at his face and snow caked the streets, but today he wasn't as jubilant; today he was moody, and he wasn't looking forward to the hard work with lazy men unable to lift a shovel. He was angry and cold, the hairs on his arms stuck up, goosebumps prickling his skin.

He stomped through the fresh snow, marching steadily towards the town hall, his arms wrapped around himself in a bid to retain some heat. He slowly began to warm up as he fought through the snow, but the wind continued to sting his skin.

Frank had been walking for a good while when he heard someone calling his name; the streets were empty at this time, with many not bothering to wake for they either had no work or money to buy anything. They were reliant on the men who dug up the paths for trade, for food and for warmth.

Turning in the direction of the voice, Frank saw the outline of a tall, broad man, who was running and waving his arms. Frank paused, waiting, before he realised it was Jack.

'Frank,' he panted as he reached him, placing his hand on Frank's shoulder and one on his knee as he gasped for air. 'Morning. I tell you, I'm aching after yesterday. I feel it in my legs and arms.'

'Tell me about it,' Frank sighed, looking at his new friend He hoisted him up and they set off together. They weren't too far off the town hall, and as they walked, they wondered where they'd be off to today. They each hoped it wouldn't be another long journey coupled with back breaking work.

Like yesterday, there was a huddle of men waiting outside of the town hall — fewer than the day before, but still a decent number of men to get the job done. Sam was readily waiting for his friends and caught their attention with a wave.

'Frank, are you feeling well?' Sam asked, concern plastered on his face.

'I'm fine, I'm fine, just have a bit of a chill is all. I lent that old fella my coat yesterday, and he walked off in it,' Frank replied.

'Right, is that fella here now? He might have it with him, and you can get it back. This is no weather to be walking around without a coat,' Sam said, scanning the crowd in the hope of spotting him.

It seemed he was one of the few that failed to show up, and Frank kicked the ground in frustration; it was just his luck, and now he was going to freeze to death in the chill.

Shivering away, Frank waited, watching as a slender man descended the town hall stairs. He was much older than the man yesterday; his back arched forward and he relied on a cane for aid. He wore small circular glasses and had a thin wispy moustache.

'Hello, hello,' he said cheerily, 'good morning, everyone. I can't say how proud I am that we have such wonderful men willing to help their city get back on its feet. Good on you. You did a fantastic job yesterday, but alas the snow has fallen again, so off you must go — but today will be different.'

He paused in thought, wondering how to continue. Opening and closing his mouth, he said, motioning his hands, 'Well, the thing is, we've realised clearing the snow by day doesn't increase trade; the night is when we need you to clear the roads.'

The men began muttering among themselves, calling out insults and demanding answers.

'I know, I know,' the man replied. 'What we're suggesting is that you work through the day and then through the night. You can have tomorrow off, and then you can work the night shift.'

More noise erupted from the crowd as the men shouted out complaints and the injustice of this request.

'Wait, wait,' the man said, holding his hands up in defence. 'You will be paid in plenty for doing this.' As he spoke, he withdrew a pouch full of coins and tossed it with surprising force at the closest man.

The man caught it in bewilderment and fumbled with the strings, pulling it open. His eyes widened, and he said in awe, 'Gold, gold coins; there must be over ten pieces of gold in 'ere.'

'That's right, my dear fellows, you'll be paid triple what you would usually earn; we won't let you go empty-handed now,' he ended with a smile.

The men looked at one another, exchanging words with a gleam in their eye and nodding excitedly at one another. The money was worth an entire day's work. Even Frank agreed as he smiled and raised his eyebrows at Sam and Jack.

After everyone got their money, the man pointed them towards the shovels and gave them directions of where to go. They'd settled in the same groups as yesterday, and nearly everyone had a man short — this work wasn't for everyone.

Frank's group was directed to the mill quarter. It was a short walk away, unlike the previous day's work. It pleased each of them as they headed off in high spirits, their pockets heavy with coins, and even the shovels didn't seem as weighty nor the chill of the cold air.

They marched in defiance, trudging through the snow with power and determination, reaching their patch in no time. They began their work hard and fast, slipping into a line and defeating the snow as a team. They hacked away hard and fast, going at a pace that quickly cleared the ice; but it was tiring, and before long the men had to stop and rest, panting and gasping for air. The thought of money kept them going, but the lack of energy was defeating them.

'I don't know if I can do this,' Sam said wearily.

'Yes, yes, we can,' Frank replied breathlessly Despite his words, he was weak, weaker than he'd ever been.

He was burning inside and out, every movement required all of his energy, and he was constantly fighting the light-headedness that kept impairing his vision.

Nevertheless, he powered on, along with the men, trying to keep up but failing miserably. He soon became a liability and was now being carried by Sam and Jack. They'd barely finished the day shift when Frank's blows to the ice had become futile.

His breathing was deep and dense, almost desperate for air, his head was spinning, and he was in a daze. It was like he was there, but not there; he saw himself through his eyes, but it was as if he wasn't in control.

Sam and Jack sensed something was wrong, and despite their constant concern, Frank waved away their questions.

'I'm fine, I'm fine,' he shouted, before grasping his chest and slowly sinking to the ground. Sam and Jack ran to his aid, slapping him in the face, trying to wake him.

'He's warm, and it's not from the work; he's ill, he is,' Sam said seriously. He was worried he'd seen this sickness before.

It was what many called the winter chill, a cold made worse by the horrid weather. It had taken the lives over many within just a few days.

With worried glances, Sam and Jack hoisted him up and half-dragged, half-carried him. Jack had a vague idea of where he lived, and they headed in that direction. It was a difficult walk, but the streets were empty with many hiding in their homes from the bitter cold.

In silence they stumbled down the streets, quickly reaching the spot that Jack had met Frank that very morning. It was with luck that they came upon a woman, she, too was stumbling and fighting against the snow.

'Frank, Frank,' she screeched hysterically. 'Is he all right? What's happened? Is he alive?' she continued.

'We need to get him home now,' Sam said. 'He's not well.'

With fear in her eyes, Theresa led the way. It was a struggle, and all three felt it. Theresa was shivering in fear as she led the men through the streets to her home. It seemed like a lifetime before they arrived. Theresa fumbled with the key, before pushing the door open. Together, they helped Frank up the stairs, who was beaded in sweat and muttering nonsense. She grabbed his legs as they pulled him up the stairs and into their home.

Jonah jumped out of his father's chair, eyes wide in shock.

'Father,' he proclaimed, 'what's happened? What's going on? Is he all right? Is he alive?' He spoke fast and with urgency, his voice full of fear.

All three ignored his words as they struggled to get Frank into bed. He lay there, sinking into the worn mattress, his arms flung over the bed.

Theresa stood back, her hands pressed to her mouth as she sobbed. 'What happened?' she forced out.

Sam looked at Theresa and placed his hand on her shoulder. 'He's not well, Theresa,' he said softly. 'It looks to be the winter chill.'

He stumbled over the words; he couldn't complete the sentence and truly tell Theresa the extent of his fate.

She was shuddering, clasping her hands together, with her head bowed. Even without Sam saying it, she knew the fate, she knew that Frank would be lucky to live out the night. She was going to lose the love of her life, and there was nothing she could do.

Calling out a doctor would be pointless; there wasn't any medicine to give, not that they could afford it anyhow. She caught her tears and suppressed her sobs in front of Jonah; she didn't have the heart or soul to tell him he was sure to lose his father that night.

Sam put his arms around her as Jack began positioning Frank on the bed in the most comfortable way he could. Their eyes were filled with sorrow, but there was nothing either could do. Before departing, they each left their bag of gold coins with Theresa, dismissing any protests. 'Use it for doctors, use it to avoid the workhouse, use it to survive,' they said.

The outlook was grim, and Theresa was struggling to cope. She dragged herself to Frank's chair and fell into it, his musk scent rising and filling her nostrils. She turned away from Frank, not daring to look at him. Jonah rushed to her side, holding her hand and laying his head on her shoulder. She hastily wiped her tears away before turning to him.

'My sweet boy, my sweet, sweet boy,' she said, stroking his hair.

Jonah's blue eyes looked into hers, and she felt like it was piercing her soul. He closed them in sorrow before asking, 'He's dying, isn't he?'

Theresa couldn't look at him, she couldn't meet his eyes, but she tried anyway. 'No, don't be silly; he's fine,' she said feebly.

'Mother,' he said gravely, 'he's dying. He'll be lucky to live out the night.' He looked back at his father in the darkness. 'I don't want him to go,' he uttered so sadly.

'Me neither,' Theresa replied, as she pulled him into her chest, resting her head on his, her tears freely running into Jonah's hair.

They stayed like that for some time, listening to Frank's wheezing breath. It was getting weaker and fainter with every passing moment. They could hear the life fading from him, from a man who had brought so much happiness into their lives, who'd been so strong and solid throughout his entire life.

The night was fading, and Frank simply lay still, his chest becoming almost motionless. Theresa had moved Jonah to his father's chair and placed a blanket over him. He slept motionlessly, and she envied him for that, his sweet innocence and ability to shut out this nightmare whilst she stood around, numb.

She wanted to be near Frank, but couldn't bear to look at him. The dry wheeze of his breath was tormenting her. She knew she had to be there for him, but she couldn't make her legs move to his side.

It was only when a hideous cough erupted from Frank that she moved. 'Frank,' she croaked hysterically. Running to his side, she grasped his hand and sat next to him, dabbing at his brow. A small trickle of blood oozed out of his mouth, and she swatted it away as a sob burst out. Jonah bounced into sight, his eyes wide with fear as he looked upon the frail specimen that once was his father.

Frank's eyes opened, he looked and attempted to move, but Theresa pushed him back, telling him to keep still. She grasped his hand, lifting his fingers to her mouth and kissing them gently.

'Theresa, Jonah,' he croaked, 'I love you.'

And with that, Frank Heizium died. With his last breath, he imparted with them the most important message he could — love.

Upon his death, Theresa let out a howl, a blood-curdling howl that screeched deep into the night. Jonah looked on in horror, completely terrified: it was so sudden, too sudden. Jonah's mother lay over Frank's chest, sobbing, pleading with bated breath for him to come back.

Jonah was numb. Time seemed to freeze as he eerily looked on at the corpse on the bed. In the distance he heard a faint rumble, a clatter of footsteps and finally the door bursting open, shattering Jonah's dazed state.

It was the family from upstairs. Jonah couldn't remember their names, but knew their faces. The woman dashed through first, her curled hair crushed under her nightcap. She wore a grubby nightgown with a worn shawl draped over her shoulders. She hurried forward, grabbing Theresa by the shoulders and dragging her up.

'Come now, deary, come on, he's gone now, you need to let him go and let him rest in peace like the good Lord would want,' she said, shushing her gently and lifting her off the lifeless body of Frank.

Theresa slumped into the woman as she half-carried, half-dragged her to the chair by the fire — Frank's chair. As she placed the crumpled body down she turned and nodded at the man by the door. He wasn't quite a man, but he had surpassed childhood. He hung in the doorway, his forehead wrinkled, his dark brown eyes drowned in sadness as he looked at the sorry sight. He had his hand raised to his head, rubbing his short brown hair; as he averted his gaze from the young boy who appeared lost in a sea of disaster.

His mother nodded at him, and he made his way out of the room and towards the front door. He was dressed in his trousers and shoes, his braces hung over his vest, and he had a thick coat on; his mother insisted he put that on when she awoke to the cry of the dead.

The boy wasn't gone long, but he returned with a gaggle of men, including the doctor, a police officer and a man in a long, dark overcoat. Jonah was pulled to the side by the unknown woman, who hugged him close to her, shielding him from the ghastly sight in front.

'It's the winter chill that's got him,' she said to the men.

The doctor, a small man with a thick head of white hair, looked back at her, then his wrinkled face whipped around and his piercing blue eyes landed on the boy she hugged, before circling the room and finally spotting Theresa. He looked desperately sad and nodded.

'Indeed, it is, my good woman. This winter has taken too many good people, and I believe it is only going to get worse,' he said in a room full of silence.

The police officer gruffed and nodded to both men, turning to Theresa and stating his condolences before leaving. It wasn't a matter for the police; it was a matter for the undertaker who had come with the doctor. It seemed like the doctor and undertaker were a package deal during these hard times.

'Right, I'm going to get Theresa and the boy out of here,' said the woman, lifting Jonah into her arms and nodding for her son to get Theresa. 'We're just upstairs. Please let us know when everything is done with.'

With that, she left, the boy staggering under Theresa's weight, who was limp and heavy. She made feeble attempts to stay behind. She didn't want to leave him, but it was not appropriate, and in the end the boy forcibly removed from her.

That was the last time Theresa and Jonah saw Frank. They left him stone cold and dead in their home with two strangers. It tore through Theresa's heart; her life had just crumbled in a matter of hours, and for what? Money, survival? Why was this world so cruel and bitter? Why did it take all that is good and destroy it? Theresa was at a loss at the whats, the maybes and the mights, that were swirling around her head as she tried to absorb and accept the day's events.

Frank

It was dark. Unnaturally dark. Frank couldn't even see his hand in front of his face. He lay face down on a hard, dry surface, but the smell was rancid: it stank of rotten eggs. He scrunched his face in disgust and slowly slapped his hand against his face, covering his nose to stifle the smell.

Everything around him seemed alien. He wasn't home, he was in an obscure place, and nothing in his memory could conjure an area that he'd know. The last memory he remembered was lying in his bed: he had been cold but warm to the touch, and he remembered looking up and seeing the worried faces of his beloved wife and son.

He jerked forward, clawing at the ground. His legs felt numb, his body heavy, and he barely had the strength to drag himself forward or even lift his torso off the ground. He began patting at the floor, hoping to feel something that indicated where he was. He could feel the dirt and grit beneath his fingers, but the lack of a breeze made him believe he was in some sort of shelter.

Every moment drained what little energy he had, and he swayed as his head filled with fog. It was a thick and dense fog that was dulling his thoughts. He shook his head fervently, trying to regain a presence. He was crouched down on the floor, in the dark, with no pain, no chill and no fever. It was weird; it wasn't right or natural, for that matter.

To combat the fogginess, he took a deep breath, inhaling the stale air. It wasn't refreshing or pleasant, just a natural action. His face contorted with horror as he realised the dark, harrowing truth. He was dead. It had to be that, he thought; how else would he explain his whereabouts, the lack of life left in him?

But surely this couldn't be it. This couldn't be the afterlife — it's either heaven or hell. He presumed both would be more extravagant, have a bit more to them, but seemingly not. He thought maybe it was limbo, but then again, he'd been baptised.

Squinting, Frank held a hand over his eyes and peered around. He was in a room, one that looked as if it belonged in a mill, but it was empty. He looked down and saw a small pile of dirt under his shoes. How strange, he thought; dirt from his grave, perhaps, he wondered morbidly. By this point, he was sure he was dead. Mills aren't empty or abandoned, not in this town — there's too much money to be made off them.

The sheer thought of death caused a beaming light to appear to the left of him. It was a warming, reassuring light that filled him, that lightened his burden. That light was far too bright to be the sun, especially in the thick winter's morning.

He was dead. It was as simple as that. He was dead, and he was in an empty mill; but why? What's the purpose of this? As if someone was reading his mind, the doors on either end of the room opened. The one facing was illuminating that bright light. It was welcoming and pleasant, but what lay beyond could not be seen.

He turned, half expecting to see flames and fire from the other door, but there wasn't. Instead, there was a soft light; the light of a candle or fire was streaming into the room. He looked, perplexed, and hesitantly began walking towards the light, his legs moving effortlessly towards it, and he could see it was streaming through a door. It was wide open and beckoning him in. It was a light, one filled with happiness, the type that washed away all the woes in the world, the hardship and the pain. He basked in it, enjoying the pleasantness of the golden light.

He was almost there when the door behind him creaked; he whirled around fast and saw the other door nudge open. The soft light ebbed through; it was a natural welcoming, not beautiful and alluring, and there was a noise: it was a faint voice that was echoing through the open door, it was a voice full of pain and sorrow. Frank's heart sank in pity for whoever stood on the other side. When, suddenly, a second voice drifted through, it was a child's voice, a boy who hadn't hit puberty yet. It was Jonah, his son, and the broken voice, the fractured soul, was Theresa.

His head snapped fast in the direction, as he heard the murmurs of his family; the connection between them was a vine to his leg, dragging him back. He turned from the compelling light, despite its drawing gaze and empowering lull, and the trance was broken by the fragile voice of his son.

He began walking slowly towards the darkened room; a creak sounded behind him, the door streaming out the light was closing slowly, but Frank paid no attention. It wasn't important; the things that kept him alive, those who made it bearable were calling his name lovingly. How could he not resist?

The light seemed a minuscule factor when the drawing call of his loved ones came. Their pain, sorrow and heartache penetrated him with such sadness that he couldn't turn away; the love for these people couldn't sway his mind even from the beauty of the wholesome, loving light.

As he walked away from the light, he swore it began to dim, as if fading away, but his heart wouldn't let him turn towards it.

He moved slowly, his body dragging behind him as if fighting against the darkness, but he persisted. Hauling his body forward, Frank finally grasped the edge of the door and, with all his weight, pulled it open to see who was making that heart-wrenching sound.

Frank peered into the room, shouldering the weight of the door, and was surprised to see that it wasn't an extension of the mill — it was his home, the small room he shared with his family. The fire, the tiny stove and his chair were laid out in front of him. The flames of the fire danced to their own tune, casting light into the room. A shadow lay on his chair, his favourite chair that he'd perfectly moulded to his shape. He loved coming home after a long day of work and resting by the fire. At this moment in time, it was inhabited by a curled-up figure that was sobbing uncontrollably.

Upon closer inspection, Frank realised it was Theresa, the love of his life, his soulmate. She'd contorted her body to encompass the entire chair as if to mould herself into his shape also. She looked pitiful. Such sadness radiated through the room. It physically hurt Frank's heart to see her like that, so broken and feeble. His heart ached and longed to hold her one more time. But something was telling him, urging him not to take that step into the room, to turn, break the soulmate bond and return to the first door. This was not the path he was supposed to take, and his gut was practically screaming this to him.

Yet, Frank stood there at a crossroads. Unable to move, unable to make a decision. His wife, his loving wife, how could he leave her behind when she was so defeated? Who would support her, be there for her, help raise their son?

Jonah, Frank thought with a sigh. My boy, my only child, my legacy, he thought longingly. There was so much he'd wanted to teach him, so much he wanted to show him, and now he'd never have that opportunity. Frank held on to the door frame and leaned into the room. Craning his neck, he desperately searched the room in hope to get one glance at his son.

He was leaning in far, almost crossing the doorway, when the opposite creaked loudly. His gaze turned as he edged his way back into the room, turning his body to look at the light. He made sure to keep his old life wedged open, because he wasn't ready to leave it behind just yet.

The door was creeping itself shut, and the light was dulling with every passing moment, but one more look, one more glance was all he desired. Despite the light fading, it still pulled him in; but the gentle sounds of his home, the crackle of the fire, the soft crying of his wife and the sound of small feet stepping across a wooden floor were still there. Home was where he was meant to be; not here, not in a desolate room, in the dark. With no regret, he looked away from the light and back into his old life.

It was light out; the night had passed in the fleeting moment he looked away. It horrified him to think that time passed so fast. How much had he missed in those few seconds? He had no idea, but he was sad. Sad to see the scene he had left remained the same. Theresa was still in his chair, and a small bundle was wiggling in her. It was Jonah: he was curled up into her, asleep with tear-stained cheeks. He looked tiny and exhausted. He looked like he needed his father. The timing was all wrong, Frank thought angrily.

He wasn't ready to say his goodbyes, and why should he? It was as if something or someone was whispering, encouraging and building up his emotions. Everything in his gut was telling him to turn and leave; he was dead, he accepted that, and now he needed to move on. But everything in his heart said to stay, and his thoughts, his emotions echoed that, but Frank wasn't entirely sure they were his own. However, the power to resist was becoming increasingly difficult.

Hands grasped to the doorframe, his body angled towards his family, he bit his lip in thought. Maybe he could stay a while just to see that they were well, that they came to be happy and managed to survive.

After all, it was his job to look after them. Again, the creak of the other door echoed across the empty room and he turned, still biting his lip. The light had almost disappeared in the time he spent absorbed in his family, the allure had all but disappeared. The pure whiteness had faded to a subtle light, similar to that of the first light on a cold winter's morning.

His gut told him that if he stepped over the threshold and into his home, there'd be no going back. He'd be trapped. His safest bet was to wait, watch and hope that his family survived the tragedy of his death.

Theresa

It had been weeks since Frank had died, yet nothing had changed. Theresa remained her lonely self, cascaded on the chair of her husband, barely rising to wash, eat or drink, totally dismissing her son in her heartache.

While she lay crushed Jonah began picking up the pieces of their fragmented lives; while he was young, he knew sitting by would do little for them.

He'd been out in the streets, looking for work like his father did, earning a few coins each day as people took pity on the small child. It was enough to keep them going but Jonah really needed his mother. He tried and unsuccessfully failed to make cabbage soup, but Mrs Fairhurst upstairs had helped him. She'd been quite the helping hand since Frank had died, what with Theresa barely being there at all.

Theresa was living a dead man's life. She sat half a world away questioning everything that had happened. She could see her son and neighbours working to keep the room clean and him fed. They made her food, but she didn't have the energy to eat. The only time she ate was when Mrs Fairhurst poured cabbage soup down her throat. Even the pain of scalding soup didn't awaken any feelings. She was numb, everything ached, her head throbbed, and her heart was non-existent.

Their home was quickly becoming unbearable; to Theresa it was an empty cell and no matter the efforts of Jonah and Mrs Fairhurst, Theresa couldn't move.

Theresa didn't realise the toxic environment she was creating. She barely even noticed that Jonah left during the day, or listened to his stories of getting work in dribs and drabs. He'd come home with money and food, placing the remaining pennies in a small pouch saved for rent, just like she used to do with Frank's wage. Theresa was watching this through a solid pane of glass, unable to speak her praise or thank him for his help, so underway he went.

She was trying to fight the impending doom that was crushing her, but whenever she attempted to focus on her son, an overwhelming sadness hit her like a deadly wave in the worst storm imaginable. Jonah was a replica of her husband; his blue eyes and ruffled blond hair reminded her of him so much that it knocked her for six, but she had no focus or impending obligations that she considered worthy.

Jonah seemed fine; he was being taken care of by Mrs Fairhurst. She knew deep down it was wrong, but she was physically and emotionally broken; the closest connection she had to Frank was the mould he'd left in the chair. It was his lasting impression on the world before he died, it was what little she had or thought she had.

This went on for weeks, and nothing seemed to get better. It was the power of kind strangers that helped her survive. She was rationally processing everything, but wasn't taking any action. It was spiralling out of control, and nothing was scaring her enough to get into motion.

It had been about a month and a half, and Theresa had gotten no better. She'd lost weight and had barely felt anything since her husband had died. She'd taken no responsibility, she just sat there, motionless.

It was only when Mr Burke, their landlord, came to visit on a late Thursday evening that Theresa awakened.

Mr Burke was an average-sized, skinny man with short brown hair, a big bushy moustache and eyebrows that were speckled with grey hair. He had gentle brown eyes that oozed kindness, and he often wore a black bowler hat, pin-striped trousers, white shirt, waistcoat and a long black overcoat. It was the upper-end middle-class attire that often earned the nod of respect from the working class and peers in similar dress.

Despite his status, Mr Burke was nervous about facing the poor Heiziums, but he'd always given them the benefit of the doubt. He was an old romantic, always fantasising that a true love would sweep him off his feet. One that would cherish him as much as he'd cherish her. He had a big heart and couldn't resist the urge to help when he could, and his benefit of the doubt was his weakness.

He couldn't help but feel the guilt of a thousand men as he stood looking at the broken home

He'd liked Frank a lot, admired his work ethic and determination; but even before his death, he was just shy of being late for two months' rent. It was only because Frank had secured work that he hadn't tossed them out into the street. .

He was sympathetic, and he didn't like to do this. He knew the hardships of the working man, but he, too, had to earn a living — he wasn't a charity, and he couldn't give rooms out for free, despite his sympathetic heart.

Mr Burke had liked the family, but they'd been living too long with delayed payments, and his wife wasn't a tolerant woman she wouldn't stand for a person living rent free.

One time, Mr Burke had seen his wife as a breath of fresh air that made the rest of the world dull, but she'd since grown into a mean and bitter woman who was money-obsessed. Her status was far more important, and with money came status. She was constantly urging and nagging him to take a stand before other tenants that failed to make a payment. Her brutality to reduce others to the poor house was harrowing, and they all knew it was secretly a death sentence for the poor.

Despite the hate of his wife's views, he did happen to agree with her on this occasion. Of course, he was deeply saddened by Frank's death and felt for Theresa, but this couldn't continue. He felt dreadful, but unless the rent was paid within the next week, he would have no other option but to kick them out, or at least tell them to find cheaper accommodation.

While the house wasn't his sole business, it was a good earner, and had sentimental value. Originally, the house was Billy's family home, one left to him in his father's will. While he had moved away from this life, he liked the nostalgia of the home and the people.

It was because of this that Billy kept the house and rented it fairly to those in need, often lowering the rate or accepting late payments.

Sadly, the Heiziums' situation had spiralled, which left him standing outside their home, head bowed. He closed his eyes, took a deep breath and raised his fist to the door and knocked three times. He then proceeded to place his hands behind his back and gently rock back and forth on the balls of his feet, contemplating how he was going to address the situation.

Slowly, the door began to open, and the blond curls of Jonah Heizium came into view, his pale face and brilliant blue eyes stared up at him, mouth slightly open, eyes slightly red.

With a cough, Mr Burke said, 'Ah, Jonah, you, you. How are you?' He stumbled on his words, unsure of what to say to this small, innocent child.

Jonah bit his lip, shrugged and turned his head, looking into the apartment, presumably at his mother.

'I'm really sorry, Jonah, but I do need to speak with your mother. I know it's not a pleasant time, but this is rather urgent,' Mr Burke said uneasily.

'Mr Burke? Billy, is that you?' croaked a voice from within the apartment.

'Yes, Theresa, it is me. Sorry to bother you, but we need to discuss the rent, I'm afraid,' he replied with defiance as he peered through the crack that Jonah had left for him, his body still wedged between the door and the frame.

'Jonah, shift. Open the door fully and let Mr Burke in,' Theresa said. She didn't sound angry, just defeated. Jonah turned his head, pushed the door fully open and pressed his back up against the wall, before sliding down to the floor.

The apartment, which was usually well kept, was caked in thick dust. It hadn't been cleaned in weeks. Plates mounted up in the sink and ash from the fire decorated a severely singed rug. The bed was unmade, but looked like it hadn't been slept in. The last person to lay their head there never woke up, Billy thought grimly as a shiver soared down his spine.

In front of the fire that was glowing with embers was Theresa. She was slumped in Frank's chair. Every time he visited, he found Frank happily smiling in that thing. It was old and frayed, but he was always assured it was the best seat in the house. Today was different; today it was occupied by a very frail-looking widow.

Theresa sat there, limp. Her black dress was crumpled and lined with dust as if she hadn't moved in weeks.

She looked haggard, her eyes bulging out of her pale gaunt face, her lips cracked and dry. She was exhausted.

Mr Burke looked around, panic-stricken at having to tell this woman she would either have to pay up quickly or leave.

The likeliness of having regular rent wasn't promising. If both her and Jonah worked, they could scrape it together; but given the state of

Theresa, there was little hope that it would happen. Plus, they'd then have to pay for food on top of that, and he couldn't lower the rent any more; he'd been generous enough with Frank as it was. Their lease was one of the lowest in the building, and their room was of good size, too. No, it was definitely time he put his foot in the door, he thought.

Clearing his throat, Mr Burke said sternly, 'Theresa, I'm here for the rent. I know with everything that's happened, and I'm truly sorry. You know I liked Frank, but even before his passing, you were in debt. I cannot condone nor can I...'

Before he could finish, Theresa cut in with a throaty cackle, 'Oh, Billy, dear Billy. I don't care right now. I know we owe the rent, but I cannot fathom a worse time. And I cannot give you a time when it will be good for the money. You know as well as I do, this place is far too expensive, even if I and Jonah both got jobs.'

She stopped in thought. Theresa had received a small pay out for Frank's death; well, it was the remainder of his pay and then some from his sympathetic friends. Most of what they had, had gone on the pauper's funeral, and she only had a few coins left, plus whatever Jonah had managed to collect in his attempt to earn whilst she was grieving. It wasn't much, but it could help if she were to start her new life — but she felt terrible. It would be dishonest of her to lie, but she couldn't risk him taking what little she had.

Lowering her gaze to the floor, she said, 'I think it's time for a change of scenery. This place now holds far too many tainted memories. While there were plenty of laughs, I feel Frank's death will always darken this door.'

With every word Theresa seemed to gather strength and determination, as if she knew that this was the end of an era and the start of a lesser one.

The omission of truth plagued her, but there was a hole in this family now, and that angered Theresa. Her son was now to grow up without a father and her without the love of her husband. It was time to move, to attempt to start anew and to be both mother and father to Jonah.

With a heavy sigh, she placed both hands on the arms of the chair, stood up and stared a rather stunned-looking Billy in the eyes.

'Mrs Heizium,' Billy stuttered, 'I… Are you…? How can I help?' He finally settled on a question, one which would make this rather peculiar and confusing situation go away.

Theresa looked into his eyes, the innocent and friendly man that had been so lenient with her throughout her mourning. She decided that he deserved to be told about the money. At the very least, it would relieve her ill feelings.

'Well, Billy, I'm going to need some time to find a place, find Jonah a job, myself some part-time work and get all the affairs in order. I've had a pitiful number of coins come in from dear friends of Frank's — not much for a life, I must say, but what I have should cover some of the rent owed. Once I've got Jonah into work, I shall begin paying you back and hopefully save some for the move, if you wouldn't mind?' Theresa said, her voice wavering. She was being bold in asking so much, but this was her chance to take control and look after her family.

To her happiness, Mr Burke bowed to her request; she knew him to be a kind man and hoped his pity would give them some time. However, that was limited: he had tenants waiting to move in at the end of the month — having realised Theresa would never have enough to rent again, he'd made arrangements.

With his apologies, Mr Burke stepped out of the door, bowing his head, refusing to make eye contact, not even to the little boy slumped by the door.

Theresa watched as the door clicked shut behind him, then took a deep breath, before lowering herself back into Frank's chair. She was very much aware of the situation. Frank had died, but she must live on for their son. She couldn't live like this: she had to get her life together and get Jonah into work.

This was the first time Theresa had thought rationally, and it was the first time she realised she would swim and not sink. It was a daunting task she faced, but one she must accomplish.

I

The next morning, Theresa awoke in the same chair she'd been sitting in for weeks. Her neck was stiff from lying crooked and her knees numb from Jonah's weight. Neither could face the bed, the final resting place of their beloved husband and father.

Her movement woke Jonah, who ducked from under her armpit and looked her straight in the eyes.

'Today is going to be different, young man. I'm getting up, and we're getting sorted,' Theresa said with determination, her finger under Jonah's chin, lifting his face to hers.

'We can't stay here, Jonah. We're going to have to look for something smaller, I'm afraid, but without your father, we haven't got much choice. So, come on, up you get, we've got work to do, little man,' she continued, lifting Jonah to his feet and standing up herself. With a slight wobble, she made for the sink. It was then she realised the mess.

All of their pots, plates and spoons were stacked up in the small basin. Food was decaying on the sides, and a layer of dust and dirt had formed on all the surfaces. An unimaginable amount of guilt filled her. She had abandoned her post as a mother.

She looked around, to see Jonah gazing at her with a shameful smile that said, I tried my best. Theresa bent down, ruffled his wild blond locks and pecked him on his forehead, before starting her first chore: cleaning the house. She methodically wiped down each surface, before washing the crockery in the sink and stacking it neatly on the side.

She then got out the brush and swept the floors and dusted the mantel. Theresa was a dab hand at this, and within no time the place looked spick and span.

After cleaning the house, she addressed the next task: herself and Jonah. They both needed to look presentable if they were to find suitable jobs and a place to stay. She began with Jonah, scrubbing every inch of his body, much to his protest. She then beat the dust and mud off his clothes and had him scrub his shoes, which were a little too small, but clean. Now that Jonah was looking presentable, she turned to herself.

She looked pale and gaunt, and her hair was wiry in the tight bun she had scraped it into. Taking a deep breath, she started the cleaning process all over again, scrubbing like mad in the hope of removing the grief that consumed her. At the end of the process, she looked human — a damaged human, but one that was at least presentable to the world.

It was past lunchtime when they set out, much later than anticipated, but at least they had the afternoon to make a start on the next chapter of their lives. Heading out onto the cobbled streets, Theresa and Jonah headed east, towards the industrial side of town. It wasn't a far walk, and the cold air wasn't biting.

Familiar faces passed by; some even stopped to say hello, others avoided eye-contact, afraid of the widow and her son.

Widows can be unpredictable at best; the raw emotion could mean hysterical crying or euphoria at getting rid of a horrible husband, leading to awkward happiness or even worse — the flirty widow who is on the prowl for another husband.

Theresa was glad of the lack of interaction; she had far too much to do without the pleasantries, plus tears wouldn't help her situation. She needed to get work and get it fast. Starting with Jonah, she headed towards the mills, where they could train him up and give him a proper job, one that she hoped he could have for life. The first one she came to was a dismal-looking place. High brick walls encased the building and thick metal gates that were locked at night.

Now they stood wide open, and the yard was filled with men running around carrying various heavy-looking boxes from one end of the courtyard to the other. They disappeared around the corner and quickly returned empty-handed and ready to collect more. It was organised chaos, and the work looked tiring. However, beggars couldn't be choosers.

Standing a little taller, Theresa wrapped her shawl around her, grabbed Jonah by the elbow and marched forward, stopping the first man in sight and demanding to speak to someone in charge.

'Er, down there, love,' a rough-looking man in a grubby white vest responded, pointing towards the main entrance of the mill. 'You're after an old fella, grey curly hair, named Peter I suppose you're here for some work?' he asked.

'Yes. Well, work for my son actually. My husband has just passed, and we need to work.' Theresa wavered as she spoke.

'Ah. I see. Ask the gaffer; 'e might have summert, but don't hold your breath. Finding a steady job ain't easy right now, but good luck, and I'm sorry for your loss,' he responded solemnly, before heading off back to work.

With a nod of her head, she managed a slight smile and watched him saunter back to work. Looking down at Jonah, she raised her eyebrows and jerked her head towards the mill in a silent motion to walk. He took the hint and took the lead. Theresa trotted behind him as he reached the steps and clambered up towards the open wooden door. Their feet echoed against the concrete floor as they made their way down the hallway and towards two barred doors.

As they approached, they heard the sound of talking, laughter and the clatter of the cotton spinning machinery. It was loud and frightening to those not used to it, but that was the modern world they lived in.

Jonah and Theresa made their way to the end of the room in the right-hand corner, where a small table and chair were placed. Papers were lined up in neat piles, all organised, and light from the windows streamed through onto them; but Theresa wasn't too sure what they said, as her reading was limited. As she was looking, a woman in a long, fitted, navy dress teetered through the double doors. The working sounds rose, but quickly quietened with its closure.

The woman was young, mid- to late-twenties at the most. She was pretty, with a pale complexion and chocolate brown hair that was fashioned in a modest but smart bun. She wore spectacles that framed her face wonderfully and widened her luscious brown eyes. Her nose was tiny and curved at the tip. She was nothing shy of cute.

Theresa started forward and said, 'Excuse me, I'm here for work, or work for my son at the very least. We're desperate, and we need this. I recently lost my husband, and if I'm to put a roof over our heads and food on the table, then I'm going to need a steady income.'

The woman looked up, seeing Theresa and Jonah, her eyes scanning them, taking into account the frail duo.

Nodding at Theresa, she pursed her lips and said in a sharp tone, 'I'll see what I can do, but I can't make any promises. I know the boss is looking for an errand boy — it's not great pay, the hours are long, and he can be a bit of a brute. I'll fetch him now, shall I?'

She didn't wait for an answer, but turned sharply and headed back through the door she'd just come through. Theresa stood there, twisting her fingers together. It was a nervous habit of hers.

Neither she nor Jonah had had a job or even attempted to get one before. Together, they decided that Jonah shouldn't have to work, and before that, she worked for her father, and once she got married and had her son, she no longer worked. They seemed unlikely candidates for this job, but she had to try something.

A few minutes passed before the docile sounds of a man's voice could be heard, slightly muffled by the thick doors and machinery.

'Out there, are they? Any good? Are they worth my time? Be honest now. I'm a busy man, and I don't need some bored housewife bothering me,' the voice impudently stated.

'The woman, no. She looks old and tired. I doubt she'd be much use. She's past her time for laborious work. The boy, on the other hand — well, he's young, he could be moulded into a good worker, and at the very least he could be a general dogsbody, depending on what you're after,' the woman replied.

Slightly hurt by the brutal comments, Theresa looked on in anticipation at the closed doors. She was ashamed to admit that the kind-looking girl's comments were accurate. Even before Frank's death, Theresa had felt the pains of old age. Arthritis in her hands started at a young age; it wasn't a terrible affliction, but strenuous work was limited due to her hands seizing up, leaving her fingers clasped together like a claw. Combine this with the aftermath of Frank's death, and Theresa wasn't the picture of a hard worker. She might have left the house feeling strong and determined, but now she felt weak, a burden, a waste of space.

The door swung open, and a bulbous man strode through. He was a large man, a large wealthy man. You could tell from his smart long black overcoat that just about fastened over his large stomach. The button was slightly strained, as if it was going to pop off at any given moment.

In essence, he looked like a walrus, with his thick white hair and a bushy grey moustache that covered his mouth. His eyes, a dull brown, were small in size but very determined. The beady look gave a sense that he could see straight into your soul. His most prominent feature was his chin that was so large it rolled into his neck. Gluttony had turned this man to a hideous creature.

'Boy!' he gruffed, looking Jonah up and down. 'You'll do. I'm not promising full-time work, but I do need someone to do general tasks. The days are long, but I pay decent wages, and for that I expect hard-working men. I don't take any nonsense, do you hear me, boy?'

Wide-eyed, Jonah looked at his mother and then back at the man, and he nodded curtly, knowing how important this was. Theresa beamed at her son's bravery, his willingness to commit to her and what was left of their family.

'Right, you start in two days' time, just before sunrise. It's six days a week, seven while five, pay eight shillings and sixpence. Don't be late and be prepared for a hard day's work, boy. Playtime is over,' he barked, as he turned on his heels and clattered back through the door, passing the girl who had fetched him.

The girl in the navy dress gave a small smile as she looked at the two haggard beings in front of her and said softly, 'So I take it you do want the job, don't you?'

With pained eyes, Theresa grasped her hands together and looked at her sweet son. Could she do this to him, could she leave him at the mercy of a man without any? She'd have to if they were to survive together. Jonah stared back, clinging to her dress and swaying slightly in a child-like manner.

'He'll take it,' she said, resigned.

'Oh, good, I'd hate to go back with bad news. I'm sorry about him, he's not the friendliest of bosses, but he's good to those who work hard. Remember that,' she said, looking Jonah in the eyes, before collecting some papers off the table and walking back through the doors and into the heart of the mill.

Theresa bent down towards Jonah and put his hand to her lips, kissing as she did so, and said, 'That's one job down; just somewhere to live and a small job for me and we'll be sorted. Come on, little man, we'll get this sorted before the day is out, just you see.'

Jonah took his mother's face into his hands and said in the most grown-up manner he could, 'Ma, I'm going to take care of you, just you see. I'll work the hardest I can. I won't let you down, I promise.'

Eyes streaming from his gallant statement, Theresa nodded her head towards the main door, and together they set off in the direction of town, where she'd be able to find information on any rooms looking for tenants.

As they began trudging towards town, a strong breeze started to blow, pushing them back with each step they took over the uneven cobbled courtyard. The next fifteen minutes were a constant battle as they walked towards the main high street. The closer they got to the main street, the more congested it became, and they constantly had to weave in between women in bright coloured dresses and ostentatious hats as they went about their daily shopping spree.

Jonah lagged behind, trying to keep up with his mother, who had bowed her head in a bid to hide from the bitter wind. She was cold and wanted the day to come to a close, but securing housing was a priority task that needed sorting that same day.

Mr Burke had recommended she try asking about the town. Many shop owners owned houses on the outskirts, and some even let out rooms above the shops. Although they'd be a few bob, Theresa reckoned she had enough money from Frank's death and income for Jonah to afford a small room. She also lived in hope that she might be able to get a bit of work from whoever she resided with. Cleaning, sewing or even running errands was within her capabilities, somewhat limited but doable.

She was nervous; she'd never been faced with such a task, and it suddenly hit her just how much she was reliant on Frank. She'd always thought herself strong, but she wasn't, she merely fed off Frank's strength. He'd taken care of everything, and before that, her father took care of her. She had never been unsupported or by herself in all of her life, and now she was expected to survive, even thrive in a world that was tiresome and heavy with gloom.

It was without choice that she swallowed her fear as she grasped the handle of a second-hand bookstore and marched in, head held high, hands quivering. It was a medium-sized room that was dim in light. All around were piles of books, some in better condition than others. The stench of musk and damp lingered in the air. It was a mixture of damp from some of the water-stained books and the ageing paper. In a strange way, it had a comforting and welcoming smell.

The shop itself was quite dark, despite the six candles hanging on the walls and which had clearly been burning for a long time. Wax dripped down the side of the candle holder and ran down the walls as they burned through the day. Each candle was nearly burnt out, with the flame barely casting any light in the room. The large bay window cast a dark shadow on the room, the grime caking the windows clouding the light into the room.

At the far end of the store was a high wooden counter that ran from one end of the store to the other. To the right was a moth-eaten cloth that hid the stairs that presumably led to the rooms up above. Theresa made her way towards the counter, careful not to knock anything over.

Hidden in a dark corner was a man who sat with his back to Theresa. He was slightly bent over, with his nose in a book. He was quite oblivious to the fact that Theresa and Jonah stood in his presence.

'Ahem.' Theresa gently cleared her throat. The man's head jolted, and for a second, he peered at the wall in front of him as if wondering whether he'd imagined the sound. Again, Theresa cleared her throat.

This time he was sure he'd heard a noise, and he spun himself around on the chair rather a little too fast and almost fell off. His leg flew to the side, almost dragging him in a full circle, and he just caught his hand on the desk and managed to steady himself.

For the first time in ages, Theresa laughed. It was tiny, and she tried her best to stifle it, but the sight of the tall, scrawny man with fluffy brown hair and small circular wire-framed glasses almost falling off his chair was funny. It was the look of shock by his own admission that made her chuckle the most.

'I'm sorry, I don't mean to laugh,' she said, pressing her hand to her mouth as if to stop the laughter by force.

'No, no. That's quite all right, I'm fine. It's just that I haven't had many visitors, well, ever really,' he said, scratching his head. He had a London accent that was fairly high pitched, and he talked eloquently. 'So, how can I help you? Are you here for a book?' he inquired.

Without hesitation, Theresa replied, 'No, I'm here to find a place to live. I've heard some of the shop owners around here let out rooms at a fair rate. I can't afford a home and the outskirts are too far away for my son to get to work. I myself am also looking for work as well. I want to know if you could help with either.'

Adjusting his spectacles and squinting his eyes in thought, the man said, 'Well, I suppose I could do with a cleaner, but it wouldn't be full-time, and I'd only be able to give you half of a normal paid job. As you can see, my business isn't booming, but I do find myself neglecting the place. In regards to the room, I sadly don't have a place to offer; the room upstairs is my own, and I'm quite positive everywhere else is out of your price range.'

'I'll take the job,' Theresa beamed, her hands clasped together. 'Now, are you sure there aren't any rooms going? Anything would do for the time being. With two jobs we could have a roof over our heads and steadily save for something proper,' she added.

'Oh, excellent, I guess I could give you a job,' the man replied, flummoxed and taken aback by her joy. 'Well, Mr Welts might have something. He owns the apothecary down the street, and he runs it with his wife; nasty woman, but he's a good chap. If anyone was to know or have a place to stay, it would be him,' he said, picking at the chipped desk.

'Great, excellent. I shall head there now; but before I leave, we should iron out some details. Firstly, my name is Theresa Heizium, and this,' she said, grasping her son by the shoulders and placing him in front of her, 'is my son, Jonah.'

'A pleasure, I'm sure. My name is Marcus Jonathan Leary the second. I was named after my father; he was a writer, and a good one at that. He passed a few years back, and I bought this place with my inheritance. It's not much, but I enjoy it, and I get to read at my pleasure.'

The long name and posh accent suddenly fitted — he was a wannabe aristocrat with a flair for the arts and, most likely, the dramatics, Theresa thought. 'Well, it's lovely to meet you, and I'm looking forward to working for you, kind sir. When will I be starting, may I ask?' she responded politely, and in the classiest voice she could muster.

'Oh, next Monday, I should think, and we're on.' He paused, thinking. 'Wednesday, mid-week. Yes, Monday should be absolutely fine; it'll give me a chance to dig out the cleaning supplies,' he said with a sheepish smile.

'What about pay? How much will you be willing to give me?' she added, knowing full well it wouldn't be much, but she hoped he'd take pity on her.

'Ah, pay, yes, let me think,' he replied, placing his finger on his chin and looking up towards the ceiling. 'How does five shillings per day you're here, which is likely only to be the one? I don't think I'd need you every day, and I'd have to see how it goes.'

'That sounds reasonable, I suppose,' she said, not entirely sure it was, as she'd never dealt with wages. Frank took work where he could, and his pay varied on the type of work he ended up doing.

She guessed it was reasonable, and, besides, it was five shillings more than what she started with, and she supposed she could get another job alongside the cleaning one if she was only working one day a week.

After pausing for a moment, Theresa nodded sharply and took Jonah by his shoulders and steered him through the shop and back out onto the street. The light of the sun caused both of them to step back and shield their eyes from the glare Neither had realised just how dimly lit that bookshop was.

'I think my first job will be cleaning those windows,' Theresa said, looking at the milky white panes of the large window. It was so bad that she couldn't even see Mr Leary in his own store; no wonder it was always empty — ordinary folk wouldn't venture in there unless lost or desperate.

Turning her gaze from the bookstore, she raised her hand to her eyes as she searched up and down the street, looking for the apothecary. It had been a while since she'd been down this neck of the woods and she couldn't quite remember where it was. She perched on her tiptoes and eventually saw a sign with a mortar and pestle. That was it, that was the one.

Hitching up her skirt and grabbing Jonah by the hand, she began a quick trot down the street, making haste for the apothecary. It was the last piece in the jigsaw, and if she got the piece she needed, she'd have done it. She would have accomplished something without needing Frank at her side. It was a step towards independence, towards survival.

Slightly out of breath, Theresa arrived at the apothecary. It was much cleaner than the bookstore, with the windows gleaming in the sun. The wood around the shop was a wine purple colour, and in the centre above the door a sign read 'Mr & Mrs Welts' Apothecary'.

Looking at her reflection in the window, she could see her hair had come loose and her cheeks were rosy. Her dress had speckles of mud from her day's walking. This was not the impression she wanted to make. She immediately began swatting at her dress in a bid to whack the water-dirt marks off herself.

After satisfactory success, she moved onto her hair and began running her fingers through it. She tugged at the knots that fought back, but after some persistence, they untangled, making her look slightly more presentable.

She looked down at Jonah: he had muck and dust on his face and his white shirt. With a lick of her finger and thumb, she began wiping at Jonah's face. He put up a struggle trying to get her to leave him alone, but he wasn't fast enough to stop his mother.

With persistence, she managed to get most of the grime off his face, and with a quick brush of her hand down his torso, dislodged most of the dirt. It fell away like crumbs, leaving a small brown stain, but still left him looking sort of presentable. Well, it was as good as it was going to get.

Theresa stood up, shoulders back and headed into the apothecary. The chime of a bell announced her presence to the semi-occupied shop. A plump, kind-looking woman stood behind the counter. She had brown curls, chubby red cheeks and hazelnut-coloured eyes. She was just finishing up serving an elderly man who was practically bent over, clinging to his walking stick. He slowly made his way to the door and Theresa headed to the counter.

'Hello, hello, hello,' the woman happily said in an Irish twang, 'are you new in town? I don't believe I've seen you around here.'

'No, not new, old but not been around much. I'm here because I need a room. I've recently lost my home and my husband, and Mr Leary at the bookshop thought Mr Welts would have a room or know somebody with a cheap room to rent.

'I've got a part-time job, Jonah' — she squeezed his shoulders — 'has a full-time one, so we can pay our way.' She sped through her rehearsed speech at lightning speed to avoid being interrupted.

With sympathetic eyes, the Irish woman patted her hand and said, 'Let me fetch Mr Welts for you and see what he says.'

She shuffled off towards a velvety curtain that was the same wine colour as the outside wood. As she pulled the curtain aside, a short, frail man with wispy brown hair, circled spectacles and brown goatee stepped through, almost bumping into the large Irish woman.

'Oh, June, I didn't see you there,' he said, raising his hand to his heart in surprise. He really was a tiny, thin man. So much so that the strings on his apron were wrapped around him twice, only to be tied in an untidy bow at the back. Although the apron hid most of his clothing, you could see his shirt around the shoulders and neck hung loose.

'Oh, sorry, sir, I didn't hear you. I was just coming to fetch you,' June said, lowering her voice to a whisper as she started to relay Theresa's story.

Theresa looked on wide-eyed as June turned her back and began talking into the man's ear. Every so often he would glance over, each time his expression becoming more pained and sympathetic.

After what seemed like a lifetime, the man shuffled to the front counter and beckoned Theresa and Jonah towards him. As they approached, he lifted the latch and opened the counter up to them, ushering them through the curtain he'd just come out of.

A couple of the customers looked up and stared as Theresa scuttled into the back with Jonah tailing behind her.

Behind the curtain was a large parlour that was overly decorated in different shades of lavender. To the right was a small dresser with a basin bowl and a vase of precious lilies. There was another door which Theresa presumed led to the kitchen and a corridor that led to a set of stairs.

The room itself was beautiful. Wooden bookcases took up the outer edges, each one stuffed with well-read books — she could tell by the aged look and cracked spines. It looked far more superior than Mr Leary and his bookstore. In the middle of the room, a medium-sized fireplace divided the bookcases. At the present time, the embers were glowing and crackling, keeping the room nice and toasty.

To the side was a basket filled with little coal pebbles; it was almost empty, not surprising, considering the cold winter that had blown its way through the city. The basket sat on an aged rug that was slightly burnt and frayed at the edges. The rug covered the majority of the floor and was a musty colour, patterned with faded lavender flowers.

At one time it would have been a pretty, elegant thing, but through the many years it had been owned it had aged badly. A large sofa sat a few feet away from the fire and, with this, two armchairs flanked the sofa, creating a welcoming parlour room. Like the rug, they had aged and were stained with various marks of living. In between the sofa and armchairs were small tables, and on both was a neat stack of rusted silver coasters. It was clean, but the furniture had clearly seen better days.

Mr Welts had silently followed and was waving his hands towards the sofa, motioning Theresa and Jonah to take a seat.

Her host chose to sit in the armchair closest to the curtain. He placed his hands on his bony knees and slowly lowered himself down to the chair, his bones creaking as he did so. He positioned himself so that he was facing the pair of them. Reaching forward, he grabbed his pipe and lit it. It looked to have been prepared beforehand, as if ready for when serious conversations took place. From what others had said, maybe that was more frequent than one would expect.

He slowly inhaled and puffed out a stream of smoke, before stating, 'You need somewhere to live.'

'Yes, we do, but we need a room is all. I can make do with that. I've got some part-time work, Jonah here' — she motioned her hands towards her son — 'has a full-time job at the mill not too far down the road. Of course, I'm happy to pick up extra work when I can, or at least look for something more permanent.'

In wild panic, she threw herself at Mr Welts's feet. 'Please, sir, I can't leave here not knowing I don't have a roof over my head. I can't face the workhouse. I've heard the stories and the screams.' She shuddered as she mentioned the workhouse howl.

At night-time, if you are close enough, you can hear the screeching howls of the workers who pray to sleep and never awaken. It was blood-curdling, and even as a last resort she'd be reluctant to enter. She'd be split up from Jonah and forced to work long hours for very little food in return. In the beginning, the workhouses were considered a godsend that gave the poor food, shelter and work, but not long after the stories began to emerge from the very few that managed to escape that trepid life.

'My dear woman, up, up with you!' Mr Welts gripped her wrists surprisingly tightly and hoisted her back onto the sofa and looked her in the eyes, before finally saying, 'My wife is going to kill me.'

He sighed and settled back into his seat. He sat there licking his lips and then wiping the saliva off for a few minutes before starting again. 'There is a room upstairs.' He pointed his hand towards the ceiling just above the fireplace.

'It's nothing spectacular, and there is no bed or anything like that. It's more of a storage cupboard. It's decent in size and has a small fireplace, and I suppose I could give you that to stay in, but it'll have to be temporary. The wife's going to kill me as it is, but you leave her to me,' he said, rolling his eyes to the ceiling and saying a silent prayer.

A jubilant giggle escaped from Theresa's mouth as she squeezed Jonah's arm in excitement. Jonah, too, was smiling at his mother's success. It seemed they'd achieved everything they set out to do.

'Right, come this way, let me show you where you'll be staying,' Mr Welts said, as he walked back out through the shop.

Theresa followed, a little perplexed. It was only when they stepped back into the shop that she noticed a set of rickety stairs. Slowly, Mr Welts began climbing them, gripping at the banister.

Jonah and Theresa followed, passing June, who was on the other side of the counter. She was in deep discussion with a small woman, but that didn't stop her from quickly glancing at the widow and son heading towards the storage areas.

The staircase was narrow, meaning they had to walk single file. It was covered in dust, with faint footprint marks showing signs of not so recent trips up this end of the shop. At the top of the stairs was a corridor. There was a door at either end; both were covered in dust, and the doorknobs had all but rusted off.

Mr Welts began motioning towards the door closest to the window that peered out onto the main street. Below the window was a bay seat which had a thick layer of dust on it. The panes were milky white around the edges, just leaving a small section to view the streets below, the sounds of shoppers idling by echoed through the room.

What little light pooled in, shone upon the decaying door that was to be their new home.

Gasping a little, the man turned and said, 'Right, here we are. I've brought you up this way, well, because my wife doesn't like visitors upstairs in our apartment. The door over there' — he pointed to the right-hand side — 'leads to our bedrooms, you see.'

'I will put you in this one.' He waved his hand in the opposite direction and towards the more deteriorated door.

Theresa took a step towards it and glanced back at the old man. He gave a small smile and waved his hand forward, as if to say 'go ahead, this is yours now'. With every step, dust sprang up as her delicate feet impressed upon them. This side of the house was clearly neglected, and it appeared nobody had been up in months. As she approached the window, she could see right across Manchester and could even see the factory Jonah would be working at in the distance.

Turning her gaze away, she grasped the rusted doorknob and pushed. It was stiff and required a strong push. The door creaked and whined on its hinges as it opened into a large room. It was caked in dust and cobwebs that clustered in the corners of the walls. It was practically empty, apart from a few boxes. At the far end, facing the door, was a modest-size fireplace. Two windows looked out onto the street below; they were small in size and had a thick rim of grime. Theresa gazed upon the room: it wasn't a bad size and, once cleaned up, it could be very nice indeed.

Jonah stuck his head in and clung to the door, slowly drawing his finger across the wood, the dust clumping on his hand and turning his finger black. He scrunched his nose up in disgust, before wiping it on his clean shirt.

Pursing her lips at her son, Theresa bobbed her head out and faced Mr Welts.

'We'll take it. How much will you be charging? My son will be earning eight shillings and sixpence per week. It's not much, I know, and I've got a bit of a job with Mr Leary down the road... it's only one day a week, but I'll be on five shillings... it's not much, but I really need this, we really need this.' She spoke quickly, talking too much as her eyes widened and filled with tears.

This was the last piece to her puzzle; if she did this, she could manage, she could survive and do Frank proud.

'Right, well, you've got more than what I expected, and I think I can work with you. Mr Flemming over the road rents his room at five shillings and sixpence, and I think that's fair enough, don't you?'

She was quickly trying to do the maths; and with both wages she'd have enough to live on and pay the rent. 'That's more than fair. I think we can live off what is left,' she replied happily.

'Excellent! Well, that's good enough for me. Of course, now I'll have to tell the wife; she isn't going to be pleased, but I'm hoping the money might persuade her. When did you want to move in again?' Mr Welts peered over his spectacles as he absent-mindedly asked the question.

'Well, as soon as possible, really. I'm not too sure how this works, but I was hoping to get settled in and ready for when I and Jonah start work,' Theresa replied.

Mr Welts looked deep into her eyes; he could see the worry and stress that rested on her shoulders.

Chewing his lip, he finally said, 'My wife isn't back until next week. She's gone visiting family down south. Ideally, I would have liked to have told her before you moved in, but I can see that you're desperate. Move in tomorrow, get settled, and I'll just have to deal with her when she returns.'

Theresa got the impression that Mr Welts wasn't overly fond of his wife, and from what she'd heard in passing, it didn't seem that many people were. This worried her. The fears of being thrown out of another home and onto the street plagued her mind. It could be disastrous, but what other option did they have?

Despite her doubts, Theresa took Mr Welts up on his offer. Tomorrow was soon, but given their lack of possessions, she figured she could be ready in time. With yet another deadline approaching, Theresa said her quick goodbyes and headed out onto the street.

It was raining slightly when they both left and Theresa lifted her shawl over their heads and prayed the rain would ease off, for they had a long walk ahead. The journey there, although longer in distance, seemed shorter. This trail was a straight mission that had no rests along the way. Unlike before, the streets had become more crowded as people left work. She hadn't realised how late it had got, and this stampede of people made their journey home all the more laborious.

When they finally returned, their clothes were sodden, and they were filthy. Mud had been flicked all over them from the neighbouring people rushing by and splashing bystanders in their haste.

Theresa's hair was a mess: it poked out from under her hat and was all scraggly. Jonah wasn't much better either: his hair was in all directions, and he had mud smeared all over his face.

It had been a long day, and the chair by the fire had never looked so welcoming, but alas she had far too much to do. She was moving house tomorrow and, looking at the state of the pair of them, they'll need to wash their faces at the very least.

Taking her shawl off and wrapping it around Jonah, she set about gathering their possessions up. They had so few things that it barely took Theresa one hour to do. Their entire life sat in two bags, one with garments and blankets whilst taking the furniture would be helpful, she had promised it to Mr Burke as part payment. Her eyes lingered on Frank's chair, it would have been nice to take it, but the cost of removal was just not in their budget and somehow, moving it didn't seem right. Without Frank, the chair didn't belong, it no longer had its owner.

The bags sat next to the door; they were worn and aged, but very sturdy and of good quality. They'd been the bags Jonah's grandfather had packed his stuff up in when he turned on his life and left. Funny really, here they were not two decades later, using the same bags to pack their lives up and leave once again.

She sighed — it's all she seemed to do these days — and then she ruffled Jonah's blond locks as he looked up and smiled.

'What now, maw?' he asked innocently.

Theresa paused for thought and then said, 'We get on with life: we work, we earn, and we live. And right now, at this moment, we go to bed.

We have another long day ahead tomorrow, and we need all the strength we can get.'

For the first time since Frank died, the pair of them crawled into bed for one last time. It seemed that they weren't asleep that long when the crows began cawing.

The morning sun beamed through the windows and Theresa awoke squinting at the bright light. She groaned, before staggering out of bed and heading for the kitchen, only to realise she had packed everything away.

She yawned and scratched her head, undecided as to whether to unpack and make something or leave it be. Before deciding, a sharp rap came at the door. Theresa's head turned, and Jonah slowly peaked out from under the pillow. They each turned to one another in surprise, only for the sharp rap to come a second time. With a start, she rushed towards the door and flung it open, to find Mr Burke stood there.

'Billy?' Theresa quizzed breathlessly.

'Mrs Heizium, I'm sorry to intrude, but I've got some rather urgent and pressing news,' he said, twiddling his bowler hat in between his thumbs. 'You're going to have to leave, well, now… and I will need some of the rent owed from what you were given after Frank's death.'

Theresa stood there with her mouth open as Billy looked at her with urgent eyes. Without a word, she walked to her bag and pulled out her purse. There was a handful of coins, not an overly lot for a life, but she handed them over to him all the same.

She reached down and grabbed the bags by the door, just next to Billy's feet, and she heaved them onto her shoulder. She let out a sharp whistle and nodded her head Confused and dishevelled, Jonah quickly got out of bed and ran outside. Theresa took one last look around; it was sudden — she'd planned a day dedicated to remembering and saying goodbye to the times with her family, but the fast upheaval meant she couldn't do that. All she got was a sad glance and no explanation.

With a firm grasp she grabbed Jonah's hand and marched him outside. They had an entire day to kill, zero money and two bags full of everything they owned. Theresa's shoulders slumped in anguish as she let her head drop into her hands, letting out a little scream as she did so.

People on the street quickly skirted around her, and Jonah clung to her arm, gently pulling her to the side of the road and soothing her woes.

They spent the entire day like that, before making the long trek to their new home. It was no easy feat with two huge bags, but as dusk was approaching, they arrived at a dimly lit store.

Ignoring the 'closed' sign, Theresa knocked. The large Irish woman from the day before peered over the counter with a scowl until she recognised the pair of them.

'Ah, I'm ever so sorry,' she said in her perky Irish twang as she unlocked the door and ushered the pair of them through. 'Right, Mr Welts said you'd be coming by; he's just gone for a wee little lie-down — it's been a long day for him.'

The apothecary was very dark, with only the beam of the moon and a small candlestick casting any light. June shut the door, turned the lock and smiled, before nodding her head towards the stairs.

They each followed in suit as she stomped up the stairs. Gasping for air, June walked them towards the end of the corridor and into their designated room. Again, she ushered them in.

'Wait, wait, what's going on? Why are you rushing us, June?' Theresa said, throwing her bags on the floor and turning to face her.

'Theresa, listen, Mr Welts isn't so well at the moment; he's resting up, and his wife is due back sooner than we anticipated. His wife isn't the nicest person, and Mr Welts is ill. I've just... I've got a lot on,' June responded in panic.

'When is his wife back? Maybe I can help.'

Theresa was cut short by June, who spoke quickly, 'No, you've got to let him deal with this. I suggest you go to bed. He's left a few things for you: a washbowl, some coal, an old chair and table from out back. He's a good man, and I just hope this good deed isn't going to be the death of him.' She left, closing the door behind her, leaving Jonah and Theresa in the dark room.

Outside, the laughter of men floated through the air from the nearby pub, The Crow, just a few doors down. Theresa dropped her bags and wandered to the fireplace. Kneeling down, she grabbed a couple of pieces of coal and threw them in. Mr Welts had been kind enough to leave some paper and matches, so she set about starting a fire. Once it was lit, she

71

took out the blanket she'd brought with her and rolled it out in front of the fire. That night, both her and Jonah curled up together and soundlessly slept.

II

Theresa awoke feeling stiff. She'd slept all night on the floor, but it was the most decent night's sleep she'd had since Frank passed. She was idly lying there, playing with Jonah's hair while he slept silently.

For the first time, she felt relaxed and at ease, but it was a fleeting moment. She hadn't had time to enjoy her contentment before the door to their room flew open with a crash as it ricocheted off the opposing wall. Theresa sat up fast, knocking Jonah over with a thud.

Standing in front of her was a short woman, with murky brown hair that was collected into a tight bun. The skin of her head was stretched tight, making her dark, almost black eyes bulge, pulling her dainty nose into a point, and revealing her wrinkled prune-like lips. She was a plump woman, so much so that her wine-coloured dress stretched across her wide stomach. Her hands rested on her hips as she glared angrily at Theresa and her son.

'So, this is the woman my husband has kindly given a room to,' she said vehemently.

She paused, taking in the scene, eyeing every inch of the room, before stating, 'Rent will be paid on time, no noise is permitted, I need my beauty sleep, and you've to move in the other room down the hall. This one is more suited for storage, and the other one is smaller, ideal for you and your son,' the woman spoke in a sharp and commanding voice.

Theresa guessed this was the famous Mrs Welts. This woman must be sleep-deprived, for there was nothing beautiful about her. Theresa smiled at her private joke, before saying, 'Mr Welts said that you wouldn't rent the other room because the door led to your bedroom.'

Looking a little shocked, the woman said haughtily, 'This is just as much my house as his, and I say you're to move into the next room — or would you like to pay more for the larger space? As for the door, it will be sealed. I don't want any riff-raff coming into my space.' She glared at Jonah when she said that, as if accusing him of something he hadn't even thought of doing.

Anger bubbled up inside Theresa as she gazed upon the odious woman. She opened her mouth to argue back, but quickly shut it; they'd been lucky enough to get what they had, and any arguments could quickly crush their chances at survival.

Scowling, Theresa rose from her slumber, cracking as she did so, and began gathering their things up, back into her bags. The woman kept her beady eyes on her the entire time, watching every precise move.

When everything was packed away, she led them out of the room, down the hall and to at the end of the corridor. She produced a key from the cuff of her dress and inserted it into the lock. With a click, the door opened, revealing a worn and tiny space that was dirty and hideous.

It was a third smaller than the one they were in, and it was in terrible condition. The floor was warped and thick with dust, much thicker than the previous one creating a dirty layer that puffed upwards with every step. Two dirty windows revealed the desolate sites of Manchester, tainted slightly by the green slime-like substance that coated the window panes. In the centre of the room was a table and two chairs.

The table was crooked, so much so that one of its legs hovered a good inch off the floor. The chairs didn't look stable either; they looked old and brittle. Behind the door was a stack of broken pallets; they were riddled with mould and rested uneasily on the warped floor.

At the back of the room was a small fireplace; it was tiny, and Theresa knew it would take forever to heat the room. Unlike the other room, there was a small counter which again was slightly rotted, and a basin.

This shop had clearly been a large townhouse that had been converted decades ago, yet some features still remained. Theresa guessed this room was quite possibly a small powder room that had since been left to decay.

Towards the other side of the room was the door that presumably led to their rooms. Two wooden blocks had been nailed across the door to stop anyone from entering.

Theresa observed the room and her heart sank. It was nothing short of grim. She looked wide-eyed and gulped. Mrs Welts's lips curled as she saw the horrified look on the dishevelled face of the woman before her.

In the sweetest voice she could muster, she said, 'Right, I'll leave you here, then. You can have a table and two chairs for free if you like, and I'm willing to sell you some curtains and a bed for, say, a sixpence?'

To her horror, Theresa realised the pallets were a bed and the rest of the furniture was the little she was to have.

Glancing at the room she knew they desperately needed, she replied with the same sweet voice, 'Thank you for your generosity. I'd be happy to buy those items from you, but I'll have to wait a couple of paydays until I can get the money to you.'

'Hmm, I'll add it to your rent, shall I?' she replied with the sarcastic smile. Before she could say anything, the woman shut the door and scurried away.

It wasn't long before footsteps could be heard. Theresa sighed and wondered what that woman could want now.

To her surprise, it was June, and she came holding a bundle of items. Some food, blankets and coal. . She held her fingers to her lips, beckoning Theresa to keep quiet, she nodded and placed them gently on the floor.

June looked at her with sad eyes as she gazed upon the room.

Theresa laid her head into her hands, before angrily saying, 'Have you seen this?' She waved at the room before continuing. 'And that bed,' she said in disbelief. 'It's not a bed, it's a piece of wood.'

'Shhh, quiet,' June quickly said, pushing her hand over Theresa's mouth. 'Just take it. I know this isn't the best of places, but like you said, you're desperate, miss.

'For now, it will have to do. Just keep your head down and get on with it. Any chance she gets, she'll have you out on the street. The promise of money and a stern talking from Mr Welts is the only thing keeping you here.' She slowly withdrew her hand, glancing at the door as she did.

A little shocked, Theresa whispered, 'You're right, I'm sorry. I am grateful. It's just…' She hesitated, before deciding against bad-mouthing

Mrs Welts just in case she did hear her. She turned her ill thoughts from Mrs Welts to Mr Welts, asking about his health.

As it turned out, he hadn't improved; in fact, he'd gotten worse. It wasn't looking good at all. Mr Welts's health had been deteriorating for months. He'd lost a lot of weight and had taken to coughing deep into the night.

June told her about Mr Welts's reluctance to see a proper doctor. Over the years he'd developed some understanding of the body and simply refused to seek specialist advice. His wife was more than happy with this decision, for it meant she didn't have to waste any of her precious money. June ended her tale bitterly, and her face was scrunched in a defiant scowl.

Theresa could tell June had a soft spot for her employer. He did seem an incredibly kind man, so it was a shame. She smiled at June sympathetically and reached out, placing her bony hand on her meaty shoulder. June ducked her head and repressed a small sob as she patted Theresa on the arm and slowly pulled away and out of the door.

Raising her hands to her hips, Theresa turned around the room and internally groaned; it was a mess, and it was far too small. She looked down at Jonah, who stared back, shrugged and began grabbing items out of the bags as if to unpack.

But he didn't. Instead, he pulled out an old rag and the small brush and pan that she'd liberated from the old house. Jonah raised his eyebrows and cocked his head to the side and grinned a wicked grin. She couldn't help but smile back. He tossed the cloth to her and then set about sweeping the floor.

All day long they worked, and about mid-day June popped up with a cup of tea and cake for the both of them to share. She came bearing bad news: Mr Welts was getting worse, he'd gone a deathly pale colour and could barely lift himself into a sitting position.

Theresa was deeply saddened by this, death was seemingly following her and it was only the distractions of life that was keeping her going. She wanted to visit Mr Welts, just to express how grateful she was but was also glad to hear he was sleeping and unable to see him.

Repressing the grief seemed easier than accepting it and busy hands made it more manageable – and with that she focused on the room they were to call a home.

By the time they had finished, the place looked spotless and rather nice. She unpacked all their items and made the bed up and was in the process of wiping Jonah and herself to look presentable for Mr Welts for possibly the last time.

Together they trundled out of their room and down the rickety stairwell. The noise had aroused Mrs Welts, causing her to quickly appear, a sinister glare on her face as she raised her finger to her lips.

In a whisper, suppressing her own grief, said, 'I'm sorry, we've come to see Mr Welts and pay our respects.'

Mrs Welts's beady eyes squinted into a scowl, before she hissed back, 'He's dead, deary he can't hear your pathetic sympathies… and what was that awful racket upstairs? It's been going on for hours.'

After realising her intrusion was a mistake, Theresa began apologising profusely, fighting back her own tears before stuttering her excuse of cleaning the small room.

'You can clean, can you? Hmm, that's useful — I could do with a cleaner around here,' she said, running her finger through a line of dust. 'You know that room is ridiculously cheap, considering the prime location and size.

'Yes, you've been quite lucky. I suppose some could say you took advantage of my poor dying husband with your sad little story,' she mused, as she leaned on the counter, rubbing her finger and thumb and watching the dust sprinkle at her feet.

Jonah could feel his mother's tremors, and he knew it wasn't fear or shock; it was anger, and he was worried. He'd never seen his mother like this before.

'How dare you,' Theresa hissed. 'I had no idea your husband was ill or that he was dying. I wouldn't, I couldn't. Do not lower me to your standards,' she spat defiantly.

Mrs Welts's eyes momentarily widened, as her lips curled into a fearsome smile, and she gave a short snort. She looked Theresa in the eyes and boldly said, 'Your rent has since gone up by sixpence. That room is in a prime location and has far more to offer than the one you were originally placed in.'

Theresa's jaw dropped as she gasped in horror. They could never afford that, not even with both wages, or they'd have nothing to live on. Before she could plead and beg for the rent to stay the same, Jonah interjected and said, 'That's not fair! We had an agreement; that room at the front was ours at the price we'd confirmed with your husband.'

Mrs Welts let out a shrill laugh, before maliciously saying, 'Life isn't fair, get over it — and my husband's dead, so this place is mine. Of course, the apothecary will go to my husband's brother, but that spineless swine won't come near here. I'm in charge now, I dictate the rules.'

Pointing her finger at Theresa, she spat, 'These are your options: either pay the extra rent or clean my shop free of charge. If you don't like either option, then pack your bags and get out.'

She was mad, outraged, and, in order to stay, Theresa would have to put her hopes of a secondary job on hold so that she could clean this place. Not only did this mean they'd have to scrape by, but that they'd be confined to this place unless they could save money.

It was a difficult decision. Just as everything seemed to be going right, a dark cloud had begun crawling overhead; but they had no choice, they had to survive. Which meant they had to live under the stern eye of Mrs Welts.

With shame, she swallowed her pride and exhaled her anger, before replying, 'Fine, I could lend a hand to clean the place, but I have a one-day cleaning job that I must do, if you are to get your rent on time.'

With a triumphant smirk, Mrs Welts nodded. 'You can have that day off, and the rest of the week you can spend tidying and cleaning my store and my home. I'll be keeping a keen eye on you.' With that said, she strolled into her back room, sliding the curtain closed behind her.

Jonah watched as she disappeared into the back, before whispering, the tears welling in his eyes, 'What is wrong with her? She's so mean, her husband is dead, and she doesn't care.'

Theresa wasn't sure how to reply; she truly didn't have an answer. Instead, she grabbed Jonah by the shoulders and led him towards the door and out into the street. Halfway down, they came across June, her eyes red raw from crying.

The death of Mr Welts had massively impacted her life. She had been close to him: he'd given her employment when she was desperate for money, and she, too, had even lived above the shop before securing a better place to live.

His death meant that she was now out of a job, and her woes of paying for rent and food were plaguing her mind.

Between sobs, Theresa and Jonah learned that Mr Welts had been an incredibly kind man. He'd lent his ear, hand and even money to those in need, much to his wife's dismay, which in turn was another funny story. Mr Welts had been a bachelor for many years before she came along, and, like many, she approached in need of help, which he willingly obliged.

June steadied herself on Theresa and took her hand, dragging her past the apothecary and into the pub, The Crow. The pub was packed inside with working men and women. It was hard to move, but June pushed her way through, squeezing Jonah and Theresa between the many people until reaching the far corner.

As they sat, a tall man set down three glasses and a bottle. He was easily as tall as Frank, if not taller, and he had a big round bald head that was gleaming in sweat. His hazelnut eyes twinkled as he caught Jonah's gaze and a smile could just about be made out under his thick bristled moustache.

'Kept the table clear for ya, June; thought you'd be popping in after what happened to the quack shop,' the man gruffed.

June sniffed, 'Thanks, Tom. It's terrible news, isn't it?'

'For the likes of you and me, yes; for Robert, it's most likely a blessing — he can get away from that wife of his!' he replied with a smile.

June let out a snort as she cried and nodded to herself. Tom, the barman, squeezed her shoulder and left all three of them in silence.

They sat like that for some time, drinking in synchronisation. After a couple of drinks, June began talking about Mrs Welts, who had slimed her way into Robert Welts's life. It turned out she had at first appeared to be a genuine, kind person, but not long after the 'I do's', things changed.

Everything became about money: only the finest of things brought joy to her, and what truly made her happy was others' misery. She enjoyed comparing her wealth with that of the poor. It had been both shocking and heart-breaking for Mr Welts, which is when his health started to decline.

By this point, the entire pub was lending an ear to their conversation, with some throwing in comments when they could. Mr Welts had been very popular, and his death had caused much turmoil. This wasn't just the usual afternoon pub crowd — this was a solemn gathering in mourning for their good friend.

They talked deep into the night, with many curious about the two strangers with June. It wasn't long before Theresa, too, told her terrible tales, with the help of Jonah. Many sympathised as they understood the dangers of living.

As the sun started to set, Theresa began gathering her things together to leave. Tom the barman had been kind enough to give her the drinks for free and even made up a small parcel of food that they could live on until their wages began coming in. Theresa was overwhelmed by the community she'd stumbled into; it seemed they'd found their footing on this rocky road.

III

It had been a few days since Mr Welts's wake, and not much had changed. Mrs Welts continued to be as horrible as always, and demanded Theresa's services at all times of the day. She'd bark orders and have Theresa running around trying to keep the shop neat and tidy to her desires.

Jonah watched as his mother was slowly drained of her energy. He, too, was tired; the hardness of the floor on his back and the sobs of his mother, combined with his fear of starting a job, were taking their toll. He was to start work the next day, and he wasn't entirely sure what to expect.

For the past few days, he'd been walking to and from the mill, getting to know the route that he was going to be taking twice daily. It was a good few miles away, and he was determined so wouldn't get lost. Being late would make a poor impression and could very well get him fired.

He knew this job was the main source of income that would pay the bills and put food on the table. Jonah was the man of the house, and having a steady job with decent pay was an added bonus.

He was nervous; it was a big world he was stepping into. Until that point, he had been in the shadows of his mother and father's love, but that had changed now — he was the leader of the pack.

The night before starting work, he scrubbed himself and his clothes whilst listening to the horrible woman downstairs shout out tasks and criticism to his mother. It was late, and his mother had still not returned. With nothing else to do, Jonah unfolded a sheet and laid it on the floor, making a makeshift bed. It was no comfier than the box mother slept on, but it was better than nothing.

He lay under the window, looking up into the sky and at the bright light of the moon. He was mesmerised, and before long he fell into a deep sleep and didn't even wake when his mother eventually climbed into bed in the early hours.

IV

Jonah woke before sunrise and began pulling his clothes on, ready for the hard day to come. Not wanting to wake his mother, he gave her a peck on the cheek, grabbed a stale piece of bread and left quietly. He slowly descended the stairs and entered the dark shop below.

He was making sure to be extra careful so that he wouldn't run into Mrs Welts. As he silently crept towards the door, turning the lock and quietly closing it behind him, before trotting in the familiar route towards the mill.

The streets were busier than they'd been when he'd taken his walk. They were filled with half-asleep men and women staggering towards their jobs. Jonah joined the crowd and began the long walk to work. It was a cold morning that had many bowing their heads downwards to avoid the chill.

The walk seemed more tiring today. His feet unwillingly dragged him towards the mill. With every step the mill came into sight, the stoic walls and iron gates looked frighteningly tall, whilst the large mill loomed overhead. It looked bigger than Jonah remembered, and he was ashamed to admit that he wanted his mother there.

He watched as men, women and children dragged their weary bones into the mill; they looked haggard and filthy, and yet many had smiles on their faces. They were exuberant, chatting and greeting one another in friendship. This lifted some tension, but it didn't make Jonah feel any taller. He gulped, taking in the full presence of the place, before joining the crowd through the gates and down the cobbled path. Workers branched off and idled in all directions of the mill to their stations.

Some men dressed smartly; others wore trousers that were thick with grime. The men in suits were clearly the bosses, as they carried themselves with more poise, whilst the men in trousers joked around, laughing as if they had no care in the world. They were in two completely different worlds in the very same place. The working dynamics of a mill seemed confusing to Jonah, and he wasn't entirely sure where he would fit in or how he would cope for that matter.

As he stumbled his way into the courtyard, he was pushed and shoved into numerous bodies, each reeking of sweat. He gagged in disgust as he tried to make his way to the building he'd first entered with his mother. It took some fighting to bypass the masses, but he eventually managed to escape the thick of the crowd while he gathered his bearings.

Looking around wildly, Jonah noticed the entrance, which also happened to be where the crowd was hustling towards. He slapped his hand to his forehead, before re-entering the crowd. Pushing his way in, Jonah knocked heads with a bright red-haired girl, just managing to catch her from falling as she staggered sideways from the blow.

She gave him the filthiest of looks, before snatching her arm back and marching into the thick of the crowd. Jonah was still a little shocked, but was abruptly shunted into the person in front. Grumblings of annoyance were echoed as he disrupted the flow. Eventually, he was rushed over the threshold, and his attempts to dislodge himself from the crowd proved fruitless. To his dismay, he was dragged through the large double doors and into the mill.

It was massive, much bigger than he anticipated. The entire floor was filled with contraptions, boxes and cotton. It was strangely quiet, unlike his previous experience where the sounds erupted throughout the mill. He supposed these noises would arise once the machines were powered up.

The crowd continued to file in behind him and disperse to their various sections. Big, burly men headed to the end of the room, past the machines, and disappeared through a door. The women took to the machines, standing and waiting for them to be turned on.

Jonah could see the red-haired girl he'd bumped into just a short distance away; she was still rubbing her head from the blow. The girl was around Jonah's age, but was shorter and slimmer than him and wore a ragged dress that was stained in various places. Smudges of dirt were caked on her face, and her hair was wild and untamed. She didn't look well-kept or cared for. Just as Jonah was turning his gaze from the girl, she caught his eye and glared at him in hatred. Today was not starting well! He went to take a step towards her, when a steady hand grasped his shoulders.

'And who are you?' a deep voice asked inquisitively. Jonah turned to see a tall, chubby man. He was bent over, peering into Jonah's face. He was a well-kept man; his round face was cleanly shaven, and his hair was slickly combed to the right with a pronounced parting.

The man was relatively nice as he demanded answers and marched him back to the main doors and into the care of Anna, while chastising Jonah for running away and ignoring his protests.

Jonah knew Anna; she was the woman who had helped him when he first visited. As she got on with her morning duties, she hollered advice. She began with names and descriptions of people: Rhys Mighty was the man that brought him, he was the floor monitor, as was Jason Files, a short, tubby man with a pencil moustache; Ralf Hinders was the scrawny, spotty floor monitor, who enjoyed catching the slackers and punishing them. Jason Hunter was the man who ran the floor: he was a relaxed man with a dry sense of humour, but Jonah was reassured that he didn't take any messing and was happy to hand out the punishment.

The main man who Jonah originally met was Peter Samson; he was a name most knew, as he was one of the biggest traders in the North West. Jonah learnt that he was a well-travelled man who did deals all over the world, but was currently stationed in Manchester for the next few months.

During this time Jonah would have to prove himself, as Peter would be the man who would decide Jonah's fate. Anna made it clear that he was to prove himself capable during that time if he was to keep his job.

Peter was set to arrive any moment, and Anna looked at Jonah apprehensively. She shrugged, deciding he looked ready for the work at hand.

The boss man arrived, his stomach looking as if it had grown in the last week. He was biting into a pastry as he entered, the flakes spraying everywhere. He saw Jonah and looked confused, before Anna explained he'd hired him the week before.

The man nodded, took a bite of his pastry and then said, 'Yes, yes, of course, I remember now.' Pieces of pastry landed on Anna's face, and her eyes froze wide, before she swatted the food away in horror.

He pointed at the boy and then at the door. Jonah looked at Anna and then at Peter, who frowned at his hesitance. Jonah began walking towards the door when he felt a sharp blow hit his backside. He'd kicked Jonah quite literally through the door.

Jonah had never been hit before, and this came as a shock. Blood rushed to his cheeks and tears filled his eyes in pain and embarrassment. The man laughed and told him to move it, which he did slowly, blinking back the tears.

Peter led Jonah around the mill; he barely noticed the boy as he went around the mill, but Jonah overheard the names of men that Anna had described to him.

He was left with the man he'd first met, Rhys, who set him about collecting stray wool from the floor for the meantime. From there, he bounced between floor monitors, doing the worst jobs that often got neglected. That night he was to stay and help clean the machines. It was terrible work that was painful, dirty and dangerous.

Any mistake was received with a backhander, the kind that bludgeons the skin and leaves huge round marks. It was his first day, and he made a lot of mistakes; by mid-afternoon, Jonah ached.

The day proved to be a horrendous one that saw Jonah hit more times in a day than he had in his entire life. His skin was red and cracked from the beatings of the day, but the day was coming to an end.

The feeling of freedom was fleeting, as Jonah was made to stay behind watching, as the workers dispersed into the night. He was to stay late and help the workmen outside clean the machines.

Drained, he set about the work, putting in as much effort as he could. The men mainly ignored him, except one, one man Jonah recognised — it was the man they'd met on the first day who had pointed him and his mother to the entrance. When he spotted Jonah, he gave him a small smile and moved next to Jonah.

The man was nice; he talked with Jonah and even shared his food with him. They discussed one another's predicaments. Not a single one of them had an easy life, but some knew of Jonah's father as they'd worked with him on odd jobs. Nick, who had helped them at first, said he'd mentioned it to the gaffer: they might ease up on you if they know that. The bruises of the day were visible, and the men felt sad for him.

It was a friendlier atmosphere in the evening, but they still worked long into the night, ensuring the machines were spotless.

At the end of it, the men left, and Nick and a man named Paddy walked Jonah back to the apothecary. After finding out he lived with Mrs Welts, they again stated how rough Jonah had it, but both agreed they would do what they could to make it easier. They said they'd be waiting for him the next morning and they'd all walk to work together.

When he finally got in, he was confronted by Mrs Welts, who demanded an explanation for his early departure and late arrival. Jonah was drained and, without thinking, laid it out in front of her.

Although shocked, she held her tongue and simply pointed at the stairs for Jonah to take. He was once again struck as he turned his back on her. Hitting his head on the stairs, Jonah growled in anger, before wearily getting to his knees and crawling to the top and into his mother's arms.

She looked at him in horror, embracing him in a hug, before exclaiming, 'Where have you been? What time do you call this? I was worried.' She gasped in shock as she saw the marks and bruises on her son.

She lay him down and rushed to the countertop, grabbed a bowl and cloth, before returning to dab at his various sores and bruises. He winced with each touch, before wriggling free.

He described his day and the hardships, but also told of the friendships forged. His mother looked at him worryingly, but before she could say a word, Jonah spoke wisely, stating the obvious facts and that he was the man of the house now and it was time for him to bear the hardships.

He held her face, kissed her cheeks. They were warm and soft. Her eyes were too weary and tired from another hard day. Jonah looked at her in pity and said, hand on heart, that things would get better. He then went and unrolled his bed under the window just below the stars. His head had barely touched the floor, and he was already asleep.

The next day came much quicker than it ended, and Jonah was up at first light. This time his mother was awake and had a small piece of food awaiting him. She kissed him goodbye and sent him on his way, her eyes filled with fear of what the day would bring for her poor boy.

Outside, Jonah was met by Nick and Paddy, just as they said they would. Paddy graciously gave Jonah some bread that had a thin layer of butter on it. Jonah was surprised and grateful; at first he refused, but Paddy cut him off and forced the bread into his hands. As he watched Jonah eat, he said, 'Your father once did that for me; it's a small way to repay the man.'

Jonah smiled as they marched their way down to the mill. They spoke of many things and people, most of which Jonah didn't understand, but he enjoyed the conversation and deep laughter from the pair of them.

When they arrived at the mill, they said their goodbyes as they sauntered off towards the delivery yard. Jonah headed into the main building, this time keeping to the outer right side of the crowd so that he'd end up at the front desk, where Anna was sitting. He successfully made it in and was waiting for instruction when the red-haired girl pinched his arm, before running off into the heart of the mill.

Anna ignored the girl and turned to Jonah and said, 'Well, you impressed the men yesterday; most little ones would have folded, but you didn't. Today you will be working for Fred Miller; he will be your gaffer now.'

She stood up promptly before leading him outside, over the cobbles and towards the delivery area. It was there that he was introduced to the gaffer, who was a tall, bear-like man with warm brown eyes. His jet-black hair was pulled into a messy ponytail.

He looked at Jonah and smiled. 'You're your father's son, that's for sure,' he mused, before continuing, 'He was a good man, your father, and a hard worker, too. I'm going to be expecting the same from you.'

It turned out that Nick and Paddy had managed to get to him before Jonah could and had given him a glowing report on last night's work and who his father was. This gaffer was interested in Jonah; he, too, had started out in the delivery room and wouldn't be where he was if it wasn't for his father, who encouraged him to go for a promotion.

Despite his interest in Jonah, the other men didn't care for his father or his work ethos; they only cared for a good job and a harsh beating. Jonah was again subjected to another hard day that lasted long into the evening as he and the men set to cleaning the machines again. This was his life now as he grew up into this new world. It became a routine, as it did to walk home and to work with Nick and Paddy, who had become the brothers he never had.

V

The next day both Theresa and Jonah rose for work. Although Theresa had spent the last few days cleaning the apothecary to the unsatisfactory needs of Mrs Welts, despite her continued efforts, she was about to start her first real paying job.

Jonah left, whilst Theresa was cross-examined by Mrs Welts, who was annoyed that her lackey wouldn't be around to carry out every task she desired. Theresa left feeling beaten as she headed up the street to the bookstore.

She was banging on the door for a fair few minutes before Mr Leary answered. He'd clearly pulled his breaches over his nightshirt as he stood in front of her with bare feet and lopsided spectacles. He was deeply confused by Theresa's early calling, and it hit them both that they'd never agreed on a time. Rolling her eyes, Theresa pushed her way in, 'Point me in the direction of the cleaning supplies and I'll make a start. You head back to bed if you want to.'

'Oh, cleaning supplies' Mr Leary sighed, wiping sleep from his eyes. 'I forgot to get those.'

Theresa breathed deeply, the anger rising within her. 'Right, well I'll go out and get those but you will have to give me the money to do so.'

'Yes, that could work,' the man replied as he searched his pockets, pulling out a handful of coins.'

Turning on her heel, Theresa headed out, purchasing cloths brooms, lotions and potions that would make the dirtiest of places gleam. When she returned, Mr Leary was nowhere to be seen, so she began to clean the store, and she was making good progress when he finally rose and came downstairs.

To the surprise of both of them, the shop was getting attention: people were peering in. Mr Leary cheered with joy, hugging, grabbing and spinning Theresa around the store. However, when the day came to a close, he had no pay package in hand.

'Your wage, yes, well, I think I'll be paying you monthly,' he stammered as Theresa's scowled at him.

'Monthly,' she replied hotly. 'That was not what we agreed on, that money is to pay for food and necessities.'

Mr Leary bowed his head, ashamed, before darting upstairs. He returned with a satchel full of food and grog and gave it over willingly.

Reluctantly, she took the food, an odd sensation rising in her as she prayed that her wage wouldn't be replaced with satchels of food. That evening, she went home to be greeted by Mrs Welts. She was angry at Theresa's late arrival, despite her constant reminders of her paid cleaning work. Before Theresa had made it to the counter, she was barking orders, demanding that she immediately set to work.

She even attempted to snatch the satchel from her hands, but Theresa's reactions were quicker than both women suspected. This outraged Mrs Welts beyond belief, and she even attempted to snatch it back; but again, Theresa pulled it away, claiming it was given to her instead of her wages.

Despite Mrs Welts's attempts and protests, Theresa refused to hand over the satchel; instead, she tucked it within her shawl and skirted around her and straight up the stairs. She quickly closed the door behind her and sorted through the items. She chose a select few bits to make a solid meal for Jonah and herself. The rest she tucked away out of sight.

She began tapping at the floor, looking to find a loose board. Finally, she found one and pressed her heel to the end, popping it open She bent down and fought until it came out, before stashing the satchel away and then placing the board back on top, ensuring it was fully sealed.

Before returning to Mrs Welts, she lit the fire and headed downstairs with a pot, in the hope of getting some water from the basin sink. Mrs Welts looked at her with rage. 'Please, Mrs Welts, it's been such a long day. Let me sort out my home before cleaning yours.'

Mrs Welts sniffed loudly, 'Fine, if you must but hurry or else.'

Theresa nodded and scurried upstairs. She placed the water on the side and quickly built a fire before returning to the shop to clean for a second time.

Just as she finished, Jonah came through the door and together they walked up the stairs, turning their backs on the lurking gaze from Mrs Welts. Jonah rolled his eyes at his mother, and she quickly pressed her fingers to her lips, mimicking a shushing sound. She led Jonah up the stairs to a warm room, and they both smiled. She lifted the pot of water over the fire to boil. In the time it took, Jonah had laid his bed out. He was telling her about the nice day he had, but she could see the bruises building on the ones he'd sustained the other day.

She told Jonah of her day, and he wasn't too pleased about the lack of pay. It appeared the masculine environment had rubbed off on Jonah, as he said, 'No pay, that's it, I shall go down there myself and have a word with him.'

Theresa laughed, 'Oh Jonah, please. Let's not forget that we wouldn't be eating if it wasn't for the food that Mr Leary has given us.'

Jonah pouted and lay his head down on the floor, frowning as he pondered her words.

Once the water was boiled, she made up some gruel and eventually they sat down to a small but warm meal that satisfied their stomachs. That night they went to bed feeling happier than they had in months.

This was the life they lived now, and they got into a routine. The days for each of them varied, some less abusive and tiring than others. Jonah's pay didn't stretch as far as Theresa had hoped. Mrs Welts had a habit of wrestling it out of his hands and leaving but a few pennies behind.

As for Theresa, it wasn't getting any better. Mr Leary had yet to supply a proper pay package, but was happy to keep giving her food. Sadly, that wasn't the only worry she had, though: Mr Leary over the weeks had made some advancements.

It started with hugs of welcome, followed by grasping at her hands as the custom filled into more handsy interactions. Theresa was beginning to feel uncomfortable when she voiced her concerns and he laughed them off. From then on, her wages began to be paid, but the touching got worse: he'd pinch her bum and press himself awkwardly upon her. It was creepy and disturbing, but the money was far too precious to pass up.

For both Heiziums, the days were becoming too hard to bear. They each had their demons, Jonah more so as he endured the brutality of the mills and he very much relied on how the bosses were feeling.

The majority of the time, they revelled in punishing Jonah, making him do the toughest of jobs, as if testing his ability to work. One of the worst days he was to endure happened not a week into his employment, and that was the scalping of another child. The girl was a small, slight thing, who had been running under the contraptions all morning like a professional.

Jonah had been stationed on that section and was about to run under, before she beat him. It was a game to her: she'd been beating him all morning, but this time was different. She ran under so suddenly and jumped up to show her triumph when she let out a mighty blood-curdling scream. The girl's hair had come loose and got caught by a piece of machinery, spinning with immense force and ripping the hair, the roots and her scalp with it. Blood gushed on the floor, and it spread far and wide as the mill turned into pandemonium.

The women tried to retrieve the hysterical child, while the floor monitor rushed to shut the machine down. They eventually dragged the girl out, and Nick appeared, dividing the crowd as he marched through. He scooped the girl up in his arms and walked off towards the exit, presumably to the doctor.

Jonah was designated the task of unpicking and removing the hair and scalp from the machine. The smell of blood knocked his senses and churned his stomach as his hands poised at the cold, wet blood and skin that was entwined with the fine string that was used on the machinery.

He gagged with every tug and heaved as he collected the scalp in chunks. During this time, he was constantly being shouted at by the floor monitor, demanding he worked harder, faster and got the machines working.

Surprisingly, he withstood it all and came out stronger, but the hours were long, pay barely satisfactory and conditions horrendous. He never did forget the piercing scream that had deafened his ears, or the intense pain that etched itself upon the poor girl, or the sickly feel of a human scalp. But he survived, he lived another day, another experience, and he thanked the Lord it wasn't his scalp that was ripped from his skull.

They were both slowly dying through their survival, taking each day and each hardship with limited energy. They had a roof over their heads and steady wages that put food on the table. Still, the hatred and desolate conditions were worse; they were barely making it, surviving it, and they certainly weren't living — they were existing for a very expensive trade-off.

Frank

It had been weeks since Frank had died, and all he did was watch helplessly as his family tried to piece their life back together.

He was in limbo, in a room that was hollow, empty and lonely. With every second, the drawing appeal of the white light that was shimmering through a tiny crack in the door was becoming less appealing. The life of his family that his eyes clasped on felt more human and natural; it kept him waiting, undecided on his next move.

'Theresa, please, can you hear me?' he said, frozen in the doorway, watching as Theresa momentarily froze, a shiver running down her.

They couldn't hear him, but the world before him looked fuzzy. It was hard to explain, but he didn't fit into it any more, yet every fibre of his being was pushing him forwards.

It was calling and enticing him into the world, whispering in his ears; but when he turned, nothing was there.

'That's your family, your legacy and you're going to abandon them in this cruel world,' a seductive voice whispered in Frank's ear, and he shuffled sideways, recoiling from the sound. It carried the same feeling of a person dragging their fingers across a chalkboard, the noise squirming within him.

After scanning the room for the owner of the voice, he returned his gaze to his family, only to find that in that fleeting moment, dawn had come and time had passed at an alarming rate.

'The longer you look away, the more you miss. Soon you won't even remember them,' the unseen voice oozed in his mind, causing his skin to crawl as he looked on at the contorted bodies of his family.

'No, I won't let that happen. I won't forget them. I can't,' Frank said firmly into the darkness, his eyes fixated on his family.

'That's what they all say,' a gruff voice from behind muttered, while several others laughed mockingly.

'No,' Frank shouted, tears welling in his eyes as anger, love and guilt swirled within him.

'You could always stay with them,' a gentle tone sounded to his left, and Frank gulped.

He grasped the doorframe and angled his body in further, his mind racing as the heightened emotions of his family ricocheted around his body. He was yearning to be with them again, but he knew that if he stepped over the threshold then there was no going back.

'No, it's not right,' Frank whispered, as he bowed his head, allowing his tears to run freely down his face. With a huge intake of stale air, Frank moved his leg back, retreating from his home with every intention of leaving them.

'Sorry, we can't let you do that,' the gentle voice wafted through the air, a sinister threat layered within its tone.

Frank shook his head and tried to move, but his body was pushed back, the claws of a rancid creature snapping at him as he howled in pain.

The light he tried to escape to had dimmed to a low glow, the warmth draining away as strips of black fog whipped and cracked at Frank's body. He stomped his feet into the ground, pushing with all his might as he was struck from all angles.

His body was aching, the feeling of pain spurting through him as the voices of unseen creatures infected his mind.

'Come now, Frank, or do you want to abandon your family?' they would utter, as the fear within him grew.

'Leave me alone,' Frank screamed, as he collapsed to the ground, his body trembling as the black fog began to transform into human shapes. There were seven in total, all of them surrounding him as he curled up on the ground, whimpering.

In the distance, he could still hear the whining cries of his loved ones as time elapsed, their lives rushing forwards whilst he was afraid and alone.

The faceless creatures stood menacingly, their claw-like hands dashing at him and peeling away his soul.

'Stop!' Frank screamed. 'Please stop. I beg you, I beg...'

A chorus of laughter erupted as a vicious hand slashed at Frank's face, causing him to slump to the ground as the remaining six creatures lunged on top of him like a pack of rabid dogs.

The ghoulish screams of Frank Heizium pierced the room as the fabric of his soul was ripped into seven pieces. The agony exploded throughout his body as his very being was stretched, torn and pulled apart.

He begged over and over, his cries ignored as his soul was devoured until nothing else remained.

The Sins

The seven Sins struck hard and fast, ripping the soul to shreds as the feeble human within withered and cried in pain.

Their claws unrelenting as the soul broke beneath their grasp, the final whispers of Frank fading into nothing.

'For a moment there, I thought we weren't going to succeed,' Gluttony muttered, holding a thin veil of soul within his claws as the seven stood in unity, each holding a piece of soul

'Ye of little faith, Gluttony,' Anger responded, chuckling at the thought of a Sin possessing faith. Soon the caws of laughter filled the room as they basked in their glory.

After a few moments, the screeching sounds died down and Pride faced Anger, the leader of the Sins, and said, 'Now, how do we do this? We're still shadows of ourselves.'

'Patience is a virtu—' Anger began.

'Will you stop with the incessant similes and get on with it,' Greed retorted frustratedly.

Anger snarled, a ripple of evil emitting from him, causing the Sins to recoil, before Anger gained control of his emotion.

'Don't test me, Greed; this is my plan and if you want passage into the human world then you'd better listen. For too long we have been imprisoned in the Hollow, and it has taken many years for these events to line up. Now we need to take it.' Anger stepped into the circle and enclosed his hand around the whisper of soul within his claw.

The soul retracted within the shadow as the form of a human began to develop around the shadow. Surging within the body, Anger could feel the pain from the human, the untimely death and the abandoned faces of Frank's family finally sealing it to the human world.

One by one, the Sins stepped up, taking hold of their own soul and cementing their shadow with a human form. Greed absorbed Frank's desire for wealth and to provide for his family. Envy took control of the human's desires for another life and the daily annoyance of seeing the rich walk freely among those in poverty. Gluttony sucked up Frank's stabbing pains of hunger and the pitiful wish of a lavish banquet.

Sloth inhabited the desire for rest and freedom to do as a person wished; it was strong, and the Sin lapped it up, infusing the bond to the world.

'Oh,' Sloth gushed, 'this is good, this is a suppressed desire, a desire to do nothing. One that led to this human never getting a proper job.' The Sin laughed as he patted the body he had been bestowed with.

'Move over, Sloth,' Lust said, as she entered the circle giddily.

Lust pinched the soul, the overwhelming love of his wife and child surging into the shadow, the medley of sin and soul shot together, the elements feeding off one another. The power cracked and rippled through the room and the other Sins retreated slightly, a gleam of excitement in their now human eyes.

The Sins warped the desires of the soul, fuelling them for evil as they became a physical plague, ready to seek destruction in the human world.

'Now,' Anger said, slapping his hands together, the noise echoing as he paused with a smile at the sound, 'we need to enter the human world through the portal into Frank's life.'

The Watcher

Dear reader, forgive me.

As you can see, I underestimated Frank and his inability to abandon his family. I naively assumed he'd move on once he'd peeked into their lives, as most do. Alas, I was wrong, so very wrong, and now I can do nothing more than wait and watch for this terrible story to unfold.

Remember dear reader, the Sin's need a soul to have a presence and only once that soul dies will they return to the Hollow.

On the outside, they look like any other ordinary person with some questionable traits, but what human doesn't have those?

The Sins are deceptive people who have a way of being likeable. They hide in the crowds and are the puppet masters of life. They dictate even the smallest of decisions. You see a left or right turn could very well flip the world upside down. They're opposite directions with different destinations. Those rights, those lefts, could be the path to a different life, but the Sins always manage to direct those who are lost in a dangerous and detrimental place.

You'll soon see that the Sins manipulate themselves into Jonah's life. I can't tell you how; they're an unpredictable force, but they'll be there. The Sins picked this trick up many moons ago; they quickly grasped, that humans are willing to open their hearts and souls to one another. It was the perfect disguise, and one they use every time they manage to escape into the world of the living. Sadly, it's also one that never fails.

I'm not human, but today I made a mistake. I seemed to have become more complacent than what I was. I underestimated the emotions and powerful sentiment that you humans possess. You're far more complex beings than one would expect.

You're never the same. Each one is unique to the other, yet each one perfectly matches with another. Not that you all meet the other half to you. Some leave the Earth a piece missing without even knowing, but that never stops you from fighting or from being any less complex.

You're a confusing bunch, and the Sins know they can use it to their advantage. It's what makes them so dangerous, the ability to control and manipulate your fragile minds.

Please, don't be offended, dear reader, but you are fragile, you feel too much, you care too much, and you hate too much, which is why the Sins love you so much. There's so much to feed on that they can't deny your precious bodily functions. You're fragile, dear reader, which is why we aim to protect — but we, too, fail.

Frank had succumbed to the Sins, and now Jonah's fate lies with them. It cannot be foretold, and it cannot be re-written; we can do nothing but wait and see.

All we know is that Jonah's life has now been altered; his course, his destination has been changed, and all I can say, dear reader, is that it is not for the better. I fear this could be rather disastrous, but there is nothing you or I can do. We must await the future and see what will come true.

Jonah

It was a Tuesday morning in Mid-November 1883. The sun was peeking out from its slumber. For Jonah, it seemed the sun had set just as quickly as it rose. He was tired, and he was hungry, but the day's work had to be done; he needed to provide for his mother as she had done for him.

Wiping the sleep out of his eyes, he slowly looked around, taking in the tiny room he called home. Over the years he'd come to realise that the world wasn't fair, and no matter how hard he worked he'd never have it easy.

Ever since his father died, he and his mother had worked long, tiresome days, yet had little to show for it. They lived in a decaying room, less fit for the strays than humans. It was disgusting in all manners, yet the cost was extortionate. There were too many times that he woke up hungry and aching all over from a long day's work and a rough sleep on uneven wooden planks.

It was in those periods that his mind wandered to the time that his father was alive. It was easier then; he and his mother lived a simple life.

The memories of his father were fleeting, with his funeral being the most vivid memory he held onto. The lowering of his coffin into the ground, while his mother wept, was the most piercing memory Jonah had retained.

He often thought as to whether life would be better or worse. He knew his father's wage would have been useful, but he always got the impression that his father had minimal skills and earned very little. So, maybe not; maybe it would have been worse. Three people in this tiny hole, three people to feed with the already watered-down gruel and extra on the rent.

It was often these thoughts that consumed him, that kept him day-dreaming, imagining a life so different.

A sudden crash brought Jonah out of his deep thoughts. Theresa, his mother, had dropped a bowl in her haste to make what little food she could.

'Oh, no! I'm sorry, Jonah, that was the only bowl without a crack in it,' Theresa said, with tears in her eyes.

'Well, not any more. It smashed to pieces. I say, mother, your hands are getting worse. That old bat downstairs will have something to say about this. The noise alone will have her raging,' Jonah replied, whilst groggily rubbing his eyes and sighing. 'Now I'll have to work double shifts or skip a few meals so we can get some new plates, new bowls, new everything.'

The irony of skipping a meal to buy a bowl was too much, he thought with a weary heart. Standing up, he stretched, and his young bones cracked. The wooden flooring was plaguing his back, but he could hardly ask his elderly mother to surrender her bed now, could he?

So, he did what he did every morning: he threw his clothes on, which were stiff with grime and mud from work. He slipped on his shoes that were at least a size too small, and bent down to kiss his mother on the cheek.

She was in the midst of cleaning up the broken bowl and minuscule gruel that had resided within. She looked weary and sad. He wiped a tear away that had escaped and picked her up off the floor.

In a quiet whisper, she said, 'I'm sorry. Sorry for everything, for the unfair life you've endured, and now you have to put up with my ageing. I didn't mean to break the bowl and drop your breakfast. I don't have anything else to give you.'

'Don't worry. One day, everything will change. I'll get the money somehow, and I wasn't that hungry anyway,' Jonah lied.

He hated seeing his mother like this, for it was not her fault, it was a life they'd been handed, and they had to make the most out of the worst. He wasn't hopeful that things would change, but that didn't stop him from dreaming of a better life.

Trying to repress his stomach from grumbling, he headed for the door. It wasn't unusual for him to leave the house hungry, but with no food inside him, he was ravenous. He felt within his pocket and found a coin he'd been saving, and decided to pick something up on the way to work; but even thinking about it, he felt guilty. The little money they had needed to be put into the rent and food for himself and his mother.

Maybe just this once he thought that he could have something warm and filling before the exhausting day ahead. He thought about how nourishing that would be and smiled; he couldn't resist.

Jonah's happy thoughts soon ended as he slowly climbed down the rickety staircase. The old bat downstairs, Mrs Welts, the woman whose last name was just as hideous as herself, screeched, 'You! What are you doing up there? In case you haven't noticed, I am trying to run a business down here. You and that mother of yours are lucky that I even rent that room to you both. All you ever do is make noise and disrupt my customers. Explain yourself now.'

Jonah, who was still in the process of waking up and dreaming of a warm meal, was swiftly slapped back to reality. There were so many things he wanted to say. For starters, the shop was empty, which wasn't unusual, and no wonder — it was a dump.

A fine line of dirt had settled on every single jar that sat on the counter, and the contents were murky at best. Shelves reached all the way to the ceiling, with each one managing to hold large glass jars filled with all kinds of concoctions, many of which Jonah suspected were simply water.

A ladder was placed on the shelves so Welts could crawl to the top and get the medicine for the poor beggars that were one foot in the grave. A counter ran from one end of the room to the other, and a hatch was located towards the left-hand side for when Welts needed to inspect the customer's health. Surprisingly, they all needed the most expensive medicine. Her dramatics left many in a state of hysteria; not surprising, as she'd made out, they wouldn't make it to the next hour.

In between the shelves, there was a grimy emerald green curtain that when pushed aside, led to her abode. She had an entire back room, separate bedroom and a small kitchen area. Everything was nicely decorated, probably from the overpriced rent she charges us, he thought bitterly.

Jonah had only been in once or twice in all the years he'd lived there, but it was nice, especially in comparison to the shoebox of a room she made them rent.

He never forgot or forgave the hideous woman for cheating them out of a larger room that was slightly more homely. For one night they held that room before she shoved them into the damp and dingy room.

To both Theresa and Jonah's annoyance, Welts never actually rented the larger one, instead, claiming to use it for storage — but they both knew it was as empty as the day they vacated it. It was another rotten piece of his life that infuriated him.

It was tough living in that space, but it was a roof over their heads, even if there was a constant guard present. Welts was forever around, scrutinising their every movement.

Even leaving, they had to pass down into the shop, and no matter how quiet they moved, she always heard the noise, and she always commented.

She'd stand there poised and ready to attack. Over the years, Welts had aged to become a plump woman with thick black hair that was always scraped into a bun on top of her head. Her hair was so tightly pulled back the skin on her forehead stretched, making her dirt brown eye bulge, giving her a crazy and mean-looking gaze.

When angered, her eyes would stare with menace and horror, while her pruned, wrinkled mouth wavered as she thought of the cruellest words to throw in their direction. Behind closed doors, Jonah and his mother would laugh, commenting that she would have a lot fewer wrinkles if she smiled once in a while.

She stood in front of him, pure rage ebbing out of her in the same dress she wore every day, a plum floor-length one that was stretching at the seams, her white apron strapped to her and covered in an array of colourful stains.

Sometimes, Jonah would look at her, wondering whether she could have been pretty; in a previous life maybe, but her hideous personality made her ugly as hell. There was a rumour around town that her husband simply died to get away from her. That was over ten years ago now. Jonah briefly remembered their encounter. He was nice; well, nicer than she was.

He wouldn't be stood there glaring and attempting to look hateful towards him. Over the years he'd been terrified, but now, at over six foot tall, with big broad shoulders, unruly yellow hair that stuck up in odd areas and brilliantly blue eyes and chiselled cheekbones, it didn't bother him as much.

He was a handsome man, considering his poverty. Yet, despite his strong stature, he was still a little scared of Welts. She could shout bloody murder when she liked; plus, she had the ability to kick them out at a moment's notice. Keeping her happy was key, so it was a case of abiding by her rules and trying to keep calm when she came at you with rage.

Which was most days, and today was just like the rest. She stood there, trying to look mighty with a deathly glare in her eyes.

'Well, I'm waiting, what was that racket?' she hissed at Jonah.

Taking a breath and trying to sound defiant, Jonah replied, 'My mother dropped a bowl. Her hands are getting worse, it couldn't be helped. We're sorry, but these things happen. It won't happen again, I promise.' He tried to dodge around her, but she moved quickly and blocked his path again.

'Oh, really, and how do you expect to do that? You tell me every time something happens, it won't happen again, and yet it does. You two are more trouble than you're worth,' she spat at him.

In defence, Jonah replied, 'Well, for starters, that was our last bowl, so it really won't happen again. We do try to be good tenants, but sometimes it can't be helped. Now, if you don't mind, I've got to get to the mill, otherwise the gaffer will have my guts for garters.' He hastily pushed past her and headed for the door onto the cobbled streets.

Outside, he exhaled and embraced the morning chill. The streets were beginning to come to life. Shop owners were opening up, and men, children and women were all trundling out towards their various workplaces.

It was a bitter morning, and Jonah's stomach was yearning, aching and dreaming of that breakfast he'd almost indulged himself in.

He caved. Life was hard, even tougher on those who were determined to look after their loved ones. But the fresh smell oozing out of Bakery Bank, the hotspot for pastry goodness at a fair price, filled his nostrils. It brought with it a tingle of happiness, for the bakery was notorious for the light, soft, cloud-like interior and the crisp crust of a roll. They sold separate small rolls that could easily fit in a pocket.

Although few lasted that long, it was the only place where the bread wasn't dry or stale.

The bakery lay further down the street, and despite the distance, the smell of baked goods infiltrated the streets. The sweet yet gentle smell of the pastry mixed with warming mince was a refreshing and soothing smell that far outweighed the damp, mould and sewage stench that hung in the air of Manchester.

Typically, bakeries opened a little later, when the housewives had finished their duties and were off to collect the shopping. However, Bakery Bank was always open at the crack of dawn, welcoming the hard workers in.

The owner, Rose, was a kind-hearted, sweet woman who, like Jonah, had lost her father to a stoic life. It was her and her mother that ran and owned the place. Rose had been definite in keeping the business within the family. It caused quite a stir at the time, but nobody could say it wasn't a good decision.

Rose wasn't like any other woman. She was strong and beautiful. Her chocolate brown hair that was always pulled into a loose bun, contrasted with her pale complexion. Her skin was soft and silk-like and enhanced her big hazelnut eyes. Her eyes pierced the soul with kindness and happiness, and many speculated that's why the bakery thrived so well. Her love for baking and her drawing eyes had many people return time and time again.

Jonah thought her perfect: her striking features, her little button nose and small, plump lips that made the most infectious smile that melted his heart. He'd dream of the days that she would be his, but deep down he knew she'd never really laid her eyes on him.

He walked with a lightness in his step, eventually arriving at the bustling bakery. It was packed with a mixture of people from rich to poor to fat to thin, all crowded within. Like sardines, everyone pinned together. It was quite comical really, as people were pushing and shoving their way towards the counter.

Joining the pack, Jonah entered the shop and was immediately squished into the back of a very large man who was slowly going redder and redder in the face. To his left was a small child who was clearly from a more well-off family than his.

He was jumping up and down, coins and blond curls bouncing with him. The little boy had on a clean pair of trousers and a white shirt. Definitely better off than himself, Jonah thought, as he looked down at his grubby rags. He looked out into the street, where the boy's mother was waiting. She looked nice, not just in appearance but on her face also. It was sweet, round and the colour of a snowdrop. It was so pure. She stood there, her blonde curls swaying as she slowly moved side to side.

He smiled at her oblivious nature. Imagine being that rich that you didn't need or have to have a care in the world. He turned, shaking his head, the little smirk still in place, and he shuffled forward as people began fighting their way out of the shop, food raised above them in protection of the pack below.

The space between the door and him was filling up, and he was thrown once again into the large man in front. His face pressed into his suit jacket, and the smell of tobacco and musk filled his nose. Pulling away, he stuttered an apology, only for the man to wave him away, grunting in discomfort. It was a familiar sensation, and everyone knew of the stifling conditions in exchange for worthy and delicious baked goods.

As Jonah squirmed forward, he glanced at the counter and spotted the stacks of warm food that were prepared and ready for sale.

The big man in front was leaning over the counter, his chubby hands eagerly grabbing at a massive pie that looked hot to the touch but nevertheless tasty. He turned with a huge smile on his face, his beady eyes bulging in delight as he pushed through the crowd, biting into his pie, sending a flurry of flakes of pastry in the air. The crowd parted hastily as the man thrust them into one another as he made his way to the exit.

Turning back to the counter, Jonah's eyes connected with Rose, and for a moment, time seemed to stop as her lips curled into a welcoming smile. He smirked and was about to make his request when the little boy beside him tugged at his trousers and pointed upwards.

He wasn't quite tall enough to reach, but he was undoubtedly a determined little fella. Jonah bent down, scooped the child up and presented him to Rose. With a high-pitched giggle, the boy said, 'Pie, please.'

'Just the one?' Rose responded.

The boy looked up at Jonah and asked with such innocence, 'Do you want a pie, too? For your help?'

Jonah raised his eyebrows in surprise and stutteringly declined. The little boy shrugged, turned to Rose, lifted two fingers, indicating how many pies he wanted. She smiled, picked out two decent-sized pies and handed them over.

The boy gave her his coins, and Jonah was left juggling the pies and the boy as he reached for his change. The crowd around him were rolling their eyes in annoyance, but Jonah tried to shield the boy from the towering bodies.

Placing the child down, he motioned a silent apology with a grimace to those around. He attempted to hand the pies over, but the boy grabbed one and shoved the other back into his hand. Before he could protest, the boy ran through the mass of people, ducking between legs in his haste, as if he was expecting Jonah to chase him.

Outside, he waved the pie at his mother, handed over the change and hugged her tightly as they turned down the street and went on their way. Jonah turned back to Rose, who stood there with a big grin on her face.

Jonah let out a laugh in disbelief as Rose said, 'Well, you don't see that every day. You best be on your way, or you're going to be late for work. Oh, and enjoy the pie.'

He momentarily stood there, his mouth open, slightly; he was about to say something, something wonderful, but was quickly cut short by aggressive customers who shunted him out of the bakery. The impatient gaggle moved forward as the fight for pies started to turn into a frenzy.

Outside on the street, Jonah rubbed his head, mulling over the events, the boy's kindness and Rose's sweet voice. He smiled, taking a bite of the pie.

Delicious, buttery pastry melted into his mouth, and the meaty filling slithered down his throat. It was hot, but he was too impatient to wait, the taste was far too good. Chewing with joy, he made his way down the street towards the mill.

It was a ghastly place that reeked of depression. The high stone walls and thick steel gates reminded Jonah of a prison. It was early in the morning, which meant the doors were wide open, awaiting its workers or, more accurately, slaves. The pay was little, and the dangerous conditions meant the place was rife with injuries.

Inhaling the last bite of the pie, Jonah brushed the crumbs from his shirt, wiped his mouth and headed in, greeting fellow workers as he made his way forward. All around, people were chatting and wishing one another a good morning, and together they climbed the steps and headed towards their various stations.

Over the years, Jonah had many jobs: he'd been a dogsbody, a machine worker, and, most recently, a labourer, which seemed a permanent fixture. He was in charge of moving the cotton from the machines to the loading bay. It was hard work that was tough on the body, but it paid the bills, just about.

The gaffer gave him a nod as he walked by and he gave the obligatory 'good morning'. Markus was his name. He was a good man, a bit of a tyrant at times, but he was kind to Jonah as he knew he could rely on him, and he worked hard, but that was as far as their relationship went.

Mutual respect was what they had, and that in itself was a rarity; most gaffers tended to treat their workers as slaves that could easily be replaced, which wasn't wrong. There were many men on the streets begging for work, yet jobs were sparse.

As a child, Jonah was useful for jobs adults couldn't get to; as a man, he was useful for lifting and hard labour, his height and muscular build keeping him employed. His skills were replaceable, but his stature not so much.

It was a job for life if he didn't get injured or weakened, and he hoped that one day his hard work would earn him a promotion. One that would give him a respectable place in the mill and in society.

It was that dream that gave him hope and strength, the kind of strength that made sleeping on the hard wooden floor bearable, the pain in his stomach manageable and the ache in his bones worth it. The thought of being better — but, of course, to be better you must start at the bottom and work up.

Tucking his hands into his pockets and lowering his head, he made for the back end of the mill.

No cotton had been produced yet, so he wasn't needed on the floor; he had other morning duties to fulfil first. He was to get clearing the back and checking what deliveries were required to go out that day.

He dodged in between the giggling mill girls who seemed to look his way but never met his gaze, except for Myra Luster who was a bold girl, a mischievous one whose reputation had long since been disputed. She had a thing for him, he knew it, and he hated it.

He met Myra the first day he started at the mill; he'd bumped into her accidentally, and for a long time, she'd held a grudge. She was always in the right place to get Jonah in enough trouble that he came close to losing his job, but somehow never did. Then one day she changed, as if noticing Jonah becoming a man and not a scrawny child, but that wasn't enough. The thought of Myra disgusted him and made his skin crawl.

While Jonah had grown to become a strong, tall man, Myra had barely changed in those years. She was still small and thin, and her bright red hair was still tied messily on her head. In some lights, she was pretty, as her brilliantly blue eyes and English rose skin gave a doe-like impression when her face wasn't contorted into a grimace or snarl, which was a rare occurrence.

Despite all of this, that wasn't what deterred Jonah; it was something else he couldn't stand. He couldn't quite put his finger on it, but his gut told him that she was someone to avoid. She was cheap, and she was desperate.

'Jonah,' she purred as she stood in front of him, her finger jabbing at his chest, 'how are you on this fine morning?'

Trying to squirm away, he said politely, 'Morning, Myra. I'm very well, thank you, but I've got plenty to do and so do you, so I'll be on my way if you please.'

Before she could protest, he'd sidestepped around her and quickly made for the doorway at the back of the room.

Stepping through, he saw Larry. He'd been working with Larry for years, and he was an infectious man that made the long days easier; it was just the way he was, his tongue-in-cheek humour that only he could get away with.

Larry was the complete opposite of Jonah. He was a short but broad man with a gleaming bald head, a large red nose and a thick black moustache that curled at either end. He had slight wrinkles around his eyes and lips that bunched together every time he smiled or laughed, which was often with Larry.

As Jonah entered, he could see Larry had something to say — he never missed a chance, did Larry. He looked up, a little twinkle in his eyes, and chuckled, 'See you dodge the tart there, mate.'

Repressing a smile, Jonah replied, 'Now, now, Larry, be nice. Myra is… well, Myra is Myra. I don't know why she has such an obsession with me. Always me. Wherever I go in this place, she's there.'

'Yeah, tell me about it. She's like your shadow. Avoid that bitch like the plague. She's the type that'd fake a pregnancy to trap you forever. Sure, she's a pretty thing to look at, but can you say where she's been? I reckon she's had half of Manchester myself. Old Bill down the pub was only saying the other night that she'd been in there, throwing herself at everyone. Dressing like a whore. Wished I'd been there, but the wife's got me on house arrest, hasn't she, now she's got a bun in the oven,' Larry responded.

'Well, Larry, you were the one that did that to her, not me, friend,' Jonah said with a smile.

'Anyway, I've had enough of talking about that Myra; she's nobody to me and has no importance, and we need to get on. Looking at the board, we've got a fair few deliveries that need going out today, and there's only you and me to load everything into the crates and have it loaded onto the carts.'

Looking back into the mill, Jonah could see Myra twirling her hair and talking to another carter; his name was Anthony, but most called him Ant, due to his uncanny ability to lift heavy objects despite his weak-looking frame. Usually, he worked at the other end of the mill, bringing in the materials needed to make the cotton. He and Myra always seemed to be together; that's where the non-virtuous rumours soared from, but neither cared.

For shame on them, Jonah thought to lower his gaze in disgust, but not quickly enough, as Myra had peeked over her shoulder and noticed his gaze. Her eyes lit up, and her mouth curled as she etched her body into a seductive pose. He shuddered with uneasiness.

He often tried his best to avoid her; she was either presenting herself as a tart or bombarding him with questions about his love life, and he hated it more than anything.

It was like Larry always used to say, dodge a tart and dodge a life of infinite pain; he'd know — he's married. He said that most days and laughed, and deep-down Larry knew he loved his wife, but he hadn't planned on such an early marriage; it had been very sudden, and Larry had a lot of regrets, but that's how we live, how it is. The poor live with regrets because they can't afford to live without them.

Turning back to the board which was nailed to the wall, Jonah attempted to memorise the daily schedule of what needed to go out, when and where to. Most days were busy, but this one, in particular, was hectic. The writing on the board had become cramped towards the end as more deliveries had been added.

He stood there, staring at it, rubbing his chin and thinking of how he was supposed to manage all this. He looked to Larry and gave him a nod, a nod that signalled it was time to get on. Without a beat, he went to the far side of the room, where a dozen crates were stacked. They needed to be placed in the centre of the room, and Larry was starting to lift them down in preparation.

As Larry moved, Jonah walked to the opposite end of the room and unlatched the door, sliding it sideways with the might of his body. Sunlight streamed in, and the cobbled courtyard lay before him. It was a large space that was big enough for horse-drawn carts to enter easily enough.

Stepping out into the chilly morning once again, Jonah made his way to the top end of the courtyard, where massive metal-clad gates stood, the second set that led towards Sunderland Street.

This was the business road where men of trade made the deliveries to various companies. It was notoriously treacherous, for many rushed to complete the day's work, which often led to sloppiness.

The high amount of traffic and large orders meant those manning the carts didn't always see everything around them. Thankfully, there hadn't been a fatality for some time, but that didn't mean it wouldn't happen again.

Jonah held onto the bars, his face pressed in between them as he closed his eyes and let the morning breeze tickle his face. It was a pleasant feeling that made him smile. His mother always said that it's the little things in life that make it truly enjoyable. His smile grew bigger as he gripped the lock and pulled, his muscles bulging, and he began pulling the gate towards him.

It ached and creaked as he shoved each half to the brick walls and dropped the bolts into the ground to keep them secure. Standing back, hands on his hips, he took in Sunderland Street. It wasn't glorious, but it was home.

With reluctance and a sigh, he turned on his heel and headed back into the loading bay. Larry had made a good start, and Jonah wandered back into the room, slapped him on the shoulder and went to the rear, grabbing two crates and bringing them into the courtyard.

Back and forth, they did this until all the crates were nicely laid out and ready to be stocked with cotton. Together, they would collect the cotton to be placed in the crates before being sealed and stacked on the carts as they arrived. The physical work was tiring, but with Larry by his side, they'd easily get it done, with a few laughs thrown in as well.

By late afternoon, both Larry and Jonah had worked up a sweat; their hands were coarse, and their arms ached.

'It's a tough life if you don't weaken, eh, Jonah, what do you say?' Larry puffed out as he leant against a somewhat unstable-looking stack of crates.

Jonah doubled over, breathing hard as he replied, 'It certainly is, Larry, it certainly is.'

It was the first breather they'd had since the crack of dawn. They hadn't even stopped for lunch, and the noises from their stomach reflected that. Jonah was really thankful that he'd had a warm breakfast. He smiled, remembering the kindness of the boy who had bought it for him; it was so unusual that it was precious.

That day, Larry pulled out a feast of a lunch that his wife had packed him. It contained half a pork pie and a ham sandwich. Jonah looked on in awe, his stomach yearning for just a bite. Instead, he pulled out a stale cob of bread and sighed as he munched away. It wasn't much, but it kept him going as he continued to work into the afternoon.

As usual, Myra paid them a visit, lingering in the doorway as Larry flirted with her as she made alluring remarks towards Jonah.

Each time he sighed and made blunt comments to deter her, but to no avail. Eventually, the boss stopped by, doing his daily rounds, and in seeing Myra, he gave each of them a grilling, going as far as to threaten Jonah with his job. Seething, Jonah persisted throughout the day, barely saying two words to Larry. When the bell signalled the end of a long day, Jonah bypassed Larry and headed home alone, dust flying up behind him.

Theresa

The day stretched on as Theresa awaited her Jonah's arrival. The bell below echoed upstairs and she could hear the berating words from Mrs Welts.

Her heart ached at the sound of harsh hatred followed by thunderous footsteps and a loud bang as the door flew open. She jumped and breathed deeply.

Worry crossed her face as she watched Jonah slump into one of the weakening chairs at the table. She bided her time, moving quietly around the room, waiting for Jonah to calm down. Finally, he let out a sigh, his breathing steadied, and his fists unclenched.

With small steps, Theresa approached her son, before timidly saying, 'Jonah, I have some good news.'

He looked inquisitively at his mother as she smiled sheepishly.

'I've got a new job, the rich widow Mrs Hughes offered me one,' she said excitedly. 'I'll be getting more money, which means more food!' she exclaimed.

Not long after they'd moved in, Mr Leary fired Theresa, once he realised that Theresa would not accept his advancements. It was a harsh lesson to learn, and Theresa had to work tirelessly for Mrs Welts to cover the rent. After a while, Theresa had given up and continued to be berated day in and day out by Welts.

The news of a new job shocked Jonah, but it did immediately change his mood, and he now realised why Welts had been so unhappy. She had lost the slave she had been berating for years.

Mrs Hughes, the woman she was to work for, was a rich widow, and it was rumoured that she was harsh on the staff and demanding of the duties she set. Nevertheless, Theresa was excited. Mrs Hughes had been in the shop this morning and noticed how hard she worked; and when Welts wasn't looking, she offered Theresa the job, provided she started the following day.

The news lightened both their hearts as they lay in their respective beds, awaiting a new day and the very first job Theresa had ever really had.

Dawn came too soon, especially for Theresa, who had been tossing and turning all night. The light shocked as she realised her mistake. She rushed out of bed, pottering away and getting herself presentable as Jonah stirred from his slumber.

There was no breakfast for either of them today, and with them setting out at the same time, Jonah couldn't plan a sneaky trip to the bakery. That morning, they both left with gurgling stomachs.

It was a typical day for Jonah: he went about his duties like always, greeting the familiar faces and dodging others. For Theresa, it was an entirely new routine.

I

Theresa was set to work on Richman Street, the more affluent side of town that so happened to be a five-mile walk away.

As she quickly walked, she noticed the drastic differences as the streets became cleaner and the air thinner, with fewer smog clouds. The closer she got, the more it changed; everything looked pristine, like a glorious painting, rather than run-down housing with streets overflowing with dirty people.

The streets seemed less congested as she moved with speed, searching for number 67, her new workplace. It was one of the larger properties on the row of houses, having a three-storey space plus a basement and attic. Mrs Hughes had briefly mentioned the size, and Jonah had told her what the houses were like on Richman Street, and it had wowed her — but the sight terrified her.

There was so much to be done, and the giant home loomed in front of her as she gazed at the enormousness of it.

Thick black gates surrounded the front garden, accompanied by a shiny one that was crafted with roses and cherry blossoms.

With shaking hands, she reached forward, grasping the handle and tugging gently to unlatch the gate and go down the slim pathway that led directly to the large front door. It stood tall, shimmering as the sun glanced off the black paint.

Timidly, Theresa banged on the door, avoiding putting her hands on the shiny door knocker. It echoed loudly as her fist hit into the solid wood. She withdrew quickly, pulling her arms into her chest and waited, drawing a small breath as the door swung open.

Facing her was a small man with white-grey hair and moustache, both equally groomed. He was an older gentleman with a wrinkled face that almost hid his deep blue eyes. He peered curiously, his lips pursing, causing his moustache to rise into his nose.

Theresa stuttered, 'I'm, I'm the new maid, sir.' She threw the 'sir' in last, unwilling to seem rude or demanding.

He smiled and nodded, stepping aside and allowing Theresa to step through the doorway. She gasped as she took in the grand interior. Everything was marble, including the spiralling staircase and glimmering floor. The ceiling rose upwards towards the sky, and Theresa clearly counted the three floors.

Furniture, trinkets and pieces of art decorated the room, filling each surface. Theresa had never seen a place as beautiful as this.

The butler watched her as she turned in a circle, taking it all in, with her mouth hung slightly open. He cleared his throat loudly, making Theresa jump.

'Come,' he said in a sharp voice. 'We've got a lot to do. Mrs Hughes has high expectations.'

He began listing quickly what Theresa was to do that day. She was to clean the fireplaces in every room, ranging from tiny to large, some of which Theresa could easily stand in. From there she was to change the sheets, dust the rooms, sweep the floors, dust the curtains and wash the windows.

The list itself made Theresa tired, and she was wondering how on Earth she was to get it done. She'd barely put her handbag and wrap down, when she was handed her supplies and told to get on. The remaining staff all but ignored her, judging her poor exterior as they, too, rushed in circles, prepping for the day to come.

It felt such a strange atmosphere, each person fighting for their own good, not working together as Theresa had imagined. It was a disappointment, but this amount of work that faced her kept her busy as she moved from room to room doing her duties.

She started slowly to be thorough, ensuring every surface, every fireplace and every floor gleamed. By the time it reached lunchtime, she'd completed two rooms, and she was proud. That was until Mrs Hughes arrived back from a luncheon with her neighbours.

'You're here and working, how nice. I see you've done a good job. How many rooms left? Not many, I presume,' Mrs Hughes said pleasantly.

Theresa looked surprised, before stuttering, 'I... I... this is my second room. I've been sure to give everything a proper clean, which does take time.' With every word, her voice became fainter as she realised the high expectations set out before her.

Mrs Hughes's voice suddenly changed. 'Two! Two! Is that it? I don't pay good money for laziness; get it cleaned!' she yelled.

Wide-eyed, Theresa picked up her pace, rushing into each room, barely dusting, wiping, sweeping or cleaning anything with great effort. After each departure, the rooms looked barely touched, despite her efforts.

The rushed job was finished, but everything was untidy and nothing was thoroughly cleaned. Theresa was drained, and her hands ached as her arthritis flared. The pain was so bad that she wanted to cry.

The day passed quickly and her heart sang as she crossed over the threshold. She was hungry and tired, but the first day was done. The journey home was long and with every step, her body felt heavier, but eventually she made it home.

Welts was nowhere to be seen, to her relief, allowing her to get to her room with ease. She pushed the door forward and was glad to see Jonah sitting there waiting. He jumped to his feet immediately, having seen the state Theresa was in.

She began relaying her day to Jonah, who nodded sympathetically while secretly thinking that is what working life is about. It's relentless and painful. He understood how his mother had been so misled. She saw a job as freedom and independence, while many viewed it as a prison in which they were trapped for life.

The following days, Theresa only relayed her problems to Jonah, the piling jobs that Mrs Hughes continued to put on her. She demanded Theresa restore and fix her clothes and she didn't mind but for her arthritis. Her frail hands would cramp and crumple after a few garments of a growing pile, most of the time she carted home.

It had been a relief when Jonah offered to help and she readily welcomed it, but he wasn't a patch on her neat stitches.

The pain of trying became so painful for the poor widow, and she practically begged for Mrs Hughes to seek help.

'Fine,' she spat, 'I'll grant your wish, but it's with luck that a new tailor has come to town. You'll take your items to be viewed by Baxter, he offers a fair price for pathetic workers like you.'

Theresa had been crestfallen by the comments of her employer, her failings weighing on her deeply, but she couldn't deny the help.

Baxter, the newcomer, turned out to be a charming man who all but adored Theresa, seemingly pitying her poor plight. Together they agreed that Baxter would complete a few items whilst she would mend the rest under his scrutiny.

For a while, the agreement and job worked well. The additional wage helped enormously, with her finally having money to spare at the end of the month. In her younger days it would have gone towards practical things, but now, lost and sad, Theresa was more than happy to treat herself.

It started with an evening at the pub. She'd been there once or twice and was familiar with Tom. That freedom of extra money gave her a wonderful, inspiring feeling, one that gave her air to breath, to laugh, smile and drink merrily.

One night soon turned into a habit, a desire. Before long, she became a regular that everyone knew, a face associated with the rotten wood. More often than not, she arrived home drunk, laughing at her childish ways, much to Jonah's dismay.

It was a break, a small relief that eased the work, and it wasn't long before she began craving the drink more and more throughout the day.

The continuous cleaning and scrubbing of a large house weakened her bones, cracked her nails and drained her body, her energy.

The evenings became a solace, a place to relieve herself, but it was one that made her neglect her duties. The cruelty of Mrs Hughes often left her taking work home, work she shared with the local tailor. Work that she needed to sit in and prevail against, but the temptation was too high, and, coming home drunk, attempting such tasks was impossible.

It was on those nights that Jonah would come home to find her half asleep with clothes draped in her hands, with very little mended. Having previously spent his time watching his mother's fine hand, he eventually began taking up the task, sewing deep into the night, waking early and continuing on to do a hard and laborious job by day.

He was beginning to feel the effects and see his mother slowly turn into something he had never known.

It broke his heart, but he didn't want her to fail; he wanted to appease her and keep her mistress happy. He'd sew as neatly as possible, but would always stop by the tailors, like his mother did, to check the work.

Despite Jonah's efforts, his stitching wasn't superior to his mother, and her reputation had Baxter questioning the skills at hand.

Mere weeks had passed, and Jonah was once again doing his typical run with garments when Baxter said, 'It's you, you who is doing this work?

'It's good,' he said, pausing. 'If you would permit your evenings to me, I would gladly teach you my ways.'

Jonah had been perplexed by his offer, even tried to dismiss it, but Baxter cut him off before he could speak, the sheer look on his face signalling that he had heard the drunken nature of Theresa.

Baxter's offer wasn't optional, his evenings were now to be occupied with sewing lessons. Anger surged through him, but soon the feeling settled as the thought of an apprenticeship with an established tailor settled in. It was a skill that could change his life and the promise of four evenings away from his mother and Mrs Welts was enough for him.

Theresa was more than happy with the agreement, her excitement at even more freedom bubbling and it consumed her. Getting drunk was her new hobby, one that had her dismissing her duties in favour of the numbing sensation of drink.

The weeks tumbled by, and Theresa was taking more liberties, her actions barely posing as a consequence and Jonah, so present in her life, was the one to quickly notice the drunk she was becoming and how little he could do.

It was getting worse. Theresa was far too content with drinking and soon took to the odd gin in the morning and a quick tipple through the day.

With the added confidence of alcohol, Theresa was becoming more careless as the weeks passed, with not just Jonah noticing. Both workers and Mrs Hughes began to see the slow decline, even directing the scullery maids to watch her drink.

It wasn't long before she was caught topping her drink with grog and it took Mrs Hughes no time to humiliate and dismiss her in front of those who would witness it.

The rumours of Theresa's dismissal spread wide and fast. The shameful drunk was exposed and the pitiful being was tarnished against all future employers. She was a mess, neglected and rejected.

She had no wage, yet a thirst that demanded a price. Her life was escaping her, yet the solace of an empty bottle enticed her more. At one time she awaited her son's presence and now she was left lonely as he avoided her at all costs.

She was a drunk, revelling in pain, a pain she had long since thought was a memory. She was no longer Theresa Heizium. She was a shell of that woman.

Jonah

It was a Tuesday, it was dark and miserable, Jonah had just left work. He'd had the worst few months of his life, watching his mother go from a loving woman to that of a disgrace. The stories he'd heard, the pain he felt was unbearable. Everything had changed; the world he knew had since gone.

He yearned for the evenings, to have an excuse not to see Welts or his mother, but instead see Baxter, who was training him with a skill, an intricate skill that would transform his life into one of riches.

It gave him hope and made the work easier to do, despite the hardships and the people that surrounded him.

This particular Tuesday had been tough; there was a lot to be done, and he'd had very little sleep due to his mother crashing into the room drunk in the early hours of the morning.

Tuesdays and Thursdays always proved difficult, as these were the days, Baxter wouldn't teach, and now he had to contend with a dreary evening with his mean and abusive mother.

With a heavy heart he walked slowly, his hands in his pockets, his shoulders slumped.

Jonah had barely begun his journey when he heard a loud yet familiar voice calling his name. He frowned and turned slightly, looking over his shoulder and seeing a large man gently running towards him.

It was Sam, an old friend of his father's. It had been years since he'd seen him; he'd moved on not long after he'd started at the mill, and Jonah had missed his presence dearly.

'Sam!' Jonah said with a smile on his face. 'It's been too long! How are you?' he said, grasping Sam's hand firmly.

Sam shook his hand hard, before pulling Jonah into a hug. He smiled, placing his hands on Jonah's face, and said, 'Jonah, my boy, how are you? Have you got time for a catch-up, a quick trip to the pub?' he posed with an eyebrow raised.

Jonah smiled and nodded fiercely, happy that he could avoid his mother and Mrs Welts. He was joyful at the prospect of an evening out, and together they marched with speed, passing conversation, to the Roaring Dragon, a small pub that crossed their paths on the way to the busy street on which he lived.

They wandered in, desperate to wet their lips and have a good night. The pub was barely filled as they went to the bar, ordering a drink and taking a table of their choice, which they settled into with ease.

Jonah and Sam sat drinking in silence, enjoying one another's company. Jonah was thankful for the quiet; he had grown bored of constantly hearing his mother's complaints and drunken rants.

As of late he had been doing everything he could to avoid her. He despised the woman she had become.

It troubled him that he forcefully neglected his mother, but he'd put up with it for so long, his evenings should be used to relax and not to hear the troubles of others.

He knew the source of this was due to his mother's lack of friends. Before working for Mrs Hughes, she had barely left the apothecary for anything other than errands for Welts.

Sure, she greeted familiar faces on the street when she was out, but she never made an effort to make friends. Not even June, who had been so kind; it was Jonah who stayed in contact with her. Theresa had never truly got over losing her husband, his father. It was a tragedy, and he, too, wished he was alive; but it doesn't work like that, and sooner or later you have to move on. No matter how difficult it may seem.

While she had frequented the local pub, she never made friends, simply acquaintances that she used to pass the time with. Even then, those people distanced themselves from her as they watched her slowly succumb to drink.

Jonah was mulling this over while he drank, when Sam nudged him.

'What you thinking about, son?' he asked inquiringly.

Jonah smirked and said, 'Nothing. It's just sometimes I wish my life was different. I wish my mother would move on. I wish I was someone different.'

Sam looked at him sympathetically and signalled the barman for two more drinks.

Tom, the master at Jonah's local, came over with three pints and joined them.

'Men,' he said with a nod, 'I'm glad today is over. Is it me, or are the weeks getting rougher?' he sighed.

They both sniggered into their drinks as they nodded in agreement.

They exchanged pleasantries, talking about one another's lives, how each had changed. Tom had been running errands when he bobbed into the Roaring Dragon to see old friends and had spotted Jonah.

It had been a while since they'd seen one another, and Jonah couldn't help but notice that Tom had aged over the years since their first meeting; but he was a good friend to him offering help and advice to him whenever he'd had a tough day at work.

It was always nice seeing him, and he had a ready smile for Jonah; in some ways he'd stepped in as a father figure. Jonah looked up to him, and even in silence, it was a pleasant time.

The night was getting on, and the pub was slowly filling up. As Jonah looked around, he spotted Rose from the bakery, who was enjoying a drink and laughing with Myra, of all people. His eyes lingered on her, and he smiled at her beauty.

Sam sat watching him and then he laughed. Jonah turned to him, his eyes widening.

'Don't try to deny it, son she's a looker, you have good taste,' he said with a glint in his eye. 'She's the baker's daughter, isn't she, from that place where they make those delightful pastries?' he asked, looking at her.

Jonah turned again and said quietly, 'Yes, that's her. She's lovely,' he admitted reluctantly.

Right at that moment, Rose looked up and straight into his eyes. He blushed and quickly turned away.

'Ey-up, she's smiling,' Sam said with a huge grin. 'Come on, you, let's go over there,' he said excitedly.

Sam lifted his drink to his lips, took a huge gulp and stood up. Jonah's eyes widened, and he tried to protest Sam's advances.

Despite his age, Sam knocked him out of his way and grabbed his shoulder in an embrace, before saying, 'Listen here, life is too short for regrets; it's now or never, and the not knowing is far worse than rejection.

Don't be a fool — the love of a good woman is something worth chasing.'

Jonah bit his lip, contemplating the situation. Sam was right: it was now or never. He gulped, and with a shaking hand, he reached for his glass and drank the lot. He then turned and grabbed Tom's, necking his drink also, before placing his hand on Sam's chest, pushing him out of the way as he sauntered over to Rose.

Tom and Sam looked at the bottom of his empty glass, laughed and cheered as Jonah marched forward with his head held high.

Rose

Rose was far more than a precious flower that her name had many believe. She'd endured a painful life. As a teenager, she watched her father die of a brutal illness. It killed her to watch the man she loved the most, transform into a weak shell and in response, she's thrown herself into her work, pulling her mother along with her as they built the best bakery in town.

Baking was an escape for the pair of them, and it was a saviour; they'd managed to create something special in a rotting town.

People travelled all over Manchester to buy their food, and the rich often demanded delivery of freshly baked bread and pies for their pantry.

They both shared an equal love for the place, but love was something Rose had never experienced, although it was something she craved so desperately.

Despite being well liked, Rose found herself closed off to the world. Her friends had moved on and she always found herself working late into the night, that was until the last few weeks when she befriended a bold red head, Myra Luster.

She had no intention of meeting Myra, but it seemed fate brought them together. They had both been shopping and in passing exchanged light comments, before Myra decided they should have afternoon tea together. Rose found her to have a suspicious character, but she was good company, and she had become fond of their friendship.

They often met at the Roaring Dragon, a pub halfway between each other's work.

It was there that they sat and giggled about the people they came to see each day. Myra could be brutal, but Rose laughed all the same, for she had a shameful agenda. Rose liked Myra, but she also liked a man who worked at the mill.

He was a gentle giant, and, like her, had experienced the pain of the death of a parent so young. She understood his troubles; not only did he succumb to the woes of being raised by a heartbroken widow, but he also had a woman who was driven by drink. She was wealthier than him and didn't struggle half as much, but she did inherit a broken family, shattered by love.

His name was Jonah Heizium, and she'd seen him in passing many times but never dared to approach and talk to him.

Rose was being tactical with their friendship, trying to bring love and men into the conversation. Myra would often dominate these questions, and Rose struggled to get Jonah's name mentioned, except for on this day. Opportunity had struck. She hadn't seen Myra in a few days, days in which Jonah made an infrequent stop at her bakery.

She relayed the story to her friend in hushed tones despite the loud crowd of the pub. Of the young caring boy and the kindness of Jonah and disbelief that someone showed kindness.

'Jonah, you say? I've seen him around, I suppose I could get to know him for you, if you like him.,' Myra said with a twinkle in her eye.

Rose's eyes widened and her cheeks reddened, before she stuttered, 'No, that's not what I meant. I simply meant that, that…'

Myra wiggled her finger at Rose with a painfully forced smile on her face. 'Rose,' she said delicately, 'if you like Jonah, speak now. Like you said, he's kind — those men get snapped up quickly.' For emphasis, she snapped her fingers and slammed her drink down.

Rose was wide-eyed, unsure how to proceed, when Myra put a sweetened smile on her face, as if forgetting the conversation. Her eyes twinkled, and her smile became a cunning one as she strolled to the bar, ordering more drinks.

The conversation soon turned to frivolous chatter as the pub began to fill as it usually did. Rose was confused, but played along, ignoring her surroundings in a bid to please her newfound friend.

That was until she noticed Jonah – who never frequented the place – sitting with Tom and a man she'd never seen before.

All night she spent staring, turning her gaze when he felt hers upon him. She didn't want to draw attention, but couldn't help but gaze at the handsome, forlorn look on his face. Myra twisted, her eyes resting on Jonah before she peered at Rose with a smirk who swallowed nervously.

At first, a large unknown man stood, drinking quickly, before Jonah rose apprehensively, quickly following suit, drinking heavily, before the pair headed her way.

Jonah

'Hello, Rose, don't mind if I sit here, do you?' he asked, his blue eyes gently boring into hers. She blushed, nodded and took a sip of her drink.

It was a little awkward as they sat staring at one another. Rose simply looked at him before quietly asking, 'So, Jonah, do you come here often?'

With a look of relief, he quickly replied, 'No, actually this is the first time I've ever been here. My friend Sam' — he nodded towards his friend — 'we haven't seen each other in years, and he suggested the Roaring Dragon. I'd never heard of it before, but it seems like a nice place and reasonable prices,' he finished with a smile.

Sam coughed loudly as he approached, taking a seat next to his friend, who smiled. 'This is Sam, he's an old friend of my father's; and Sam, this is Rose,' he introduced them. Sam gleefully winked at her, causing her cheeks to darken once more.

With a giggle, she said, 'Hello, this is my friend Myra. She works at the mill like you.' She pointed at Myra, who glared at Jonah.

'Yes, me and Myra are good friends,' Jonah said spitefully, realising this was the first mention of their acquaintance.

Rose raised her eyebrows in shock, quickly glancing at Myra, who pretended she hadn't heard the comment. She had clearly lied to Rose, something which deeply irked her.

Turning from Myra, she looked deeply into Jonah's eyes and began talking in a seductive voice; anything and everything she could think of, she said. Jonah happily lapped up the conversation, eagerly replying and slowly becoming more confident.

As the drinks flowed, Jonah found himself smiling and laughing at the peculiar situation he had found himself in. The last bell rang, and Jonah offered to walk Rose home. She smiled and headed towards the door, completely ignoring Myra, much to Jonah's amusement.

As the cold air whipped around them, Jonah slipped his jacket off and draped it over Rose's shoulders. The drink and the merriment of the evening had Jonah in high spirits, and as he dropped Rose off, he turned unexpectedly.

Looking deep into Rose's eyes, he said, 'You're a true beauty, Rose, you really are, inside and out, and I'd be honoured to get to know you more and maybe even work to courtship.'

He said it so formally that Rose began to giggle, but before long she was howling with laughter and Jonah stood there feeling like a fool. Just as he went to turn and leave, her hand caught his arm.

'Wait, don't leave,' she said, wiping a tear away, a firm grasp on his arm. 'I'm sorry, I don't mean to laugh, but that was just so formal. You're as nervous as I am,' she said with a giggle.

Jonah smiled and went to speak, before Rose perched on her tip toes and kissed him. Wide-eyed, he lent in, a huge smile appearing on his face. She pulled away gently and said, 'Tomorrow evening, come to mine and introduce yourself to my mother; then we can take it from there.'

Nodding furiously in agreement, he promised he'd be straight there after work. He was ecstatic and merrily skipped back to the place he'd been hiding from all evening.

He didn't even care; the one thing he'd dreamed of was finally coming true, and he couldn't be happier. He strolled through the apothecary door, quietly closing it behind him, before walking with a bounce in his footsteps to his home. He half expected Welts to come shouting the odds, but she didn't. Tonight, was a winning night for him, and he smiled in bliss as he turned the handle of his home.

I

Jonah stepped through the door and was immediately met with a cold breeze that hit him sharply. He watched his mother sway drunkenly, clutching a bottle of gin, tears streaming from her eyes.

His smile turned to a frown as he began rolling his bed out, completely ignoring his mother, despite her efforts. He shut his eyes and angrily slept into the night.

When he awoke the next day, anger still coursed through his body. His mother had stumbled into bed not long after he returned, sobbing deep into the night as she failed to get his attention.

He sauntered down the stairs and for once he and Mrs Welts held the same frustrated gaze, and for a brief moment he thought he saw softness and sorrow in her eyes.

Squinting slightly, he stepped into the bright chill of the morning and turned in the direction of the mill, when last night's events drifted into his mind. His anger dispersed as he doubled back, running towards the bakery to get a sweet glance at Rose.

He stood like a child staring into a sweet shop and was delightfully rewarded with Rose's gaze as if she was waiting for his face to appear. Her face erupted in the largest smile, and his cheeks blushed a deep red as she tried to hide her excitement.

Jonah stuck his hands in his pockets, biting his lips in shy joy. He quickly ran his hands through his hair, walking towards the mill, a small bounce in his step.

For Jonah, the day passed quickly as he anticipated the evening when he was supposed to meet with Rose's mother. He didn't know what to expect, but he was excited nevertheless. All day, his smile remained plastered on his face, much to the annoyance of those higher above.

The lead runner, William, had never liked Jonah. He was a small shell of a man that many made fun of, but Jonah was big, strong and well-liked by many. William had been brewing for a fight, but today was not that day. Jonah waved his remarks away, choosing to disregard the hard and hateful comments.

Even at the end of a tiresome day of brutal work, unlawful working conditions and the ever-so-seductive glances made by Myra.

The day ended much to Jonah's relief, and he headed out, darting in between the crowd, when a hand grabbed his shoulder. It was Sam.

Sam looked at Jonah with a smirk on his face, before he said, 'Let me guess — off to see that Rose again?'

Jonah looked at him before replying, 'I'm going to meet her mother; we're to have tea and talk, I think.'

Sam's brow furrowed. 'Wait, don't you think this is moving too fast? You've barely met the girl, and now you're meeting her mother. What's next? Marriage?' he asked inquisitively.

'Would that be a bad thing?' Jonah said, eyes wide, before continuing, 'I've been lusting after this girl for so long. I know in my heart she is the one. Like you said, Sam, it's not often you find a good woman like that.'

Sam thought momentarily and raised his eyebrow. 'Well, that I did, but it's sudden, very sudden. But she is a looker, and I if I were you I'd want to marry her as fast as possible.'

The blessing given by Sam made him grin from ear to ear, and he patted him on the chest before stating, 'I've got to go; don't want to be late — it'll make a bad impression.'

With that, he dashed down the cobbled streets, leaving Sam standing, looking perplexed but with a smile on his face. Jonah had very little in his life, and this was the best thing that had happened to him in years.

Without a second glance, Jonah's quick steps soon turned into a jog as the excitement bubbled inside him. In no time he was rounding the corner to the bakery. Rose was patiently waiting for him, a bright smile reaching her eyes as she saw him running to her.

'Jonah!' she exclaimed. 'My, look at you; you look all hot and bothered.'

'Yes,' he panted, 'I didn't want to be late.' His hands dropped to his knees as he inhaled deeply.

Rose laughed and dragged the rather tired-looking Jonah through the bakery and up the back stairs, where her mother was setting out teacups and a small plate of freshly baked scones.

At the sound of their clattering footsteps, Lucinda, Rose's mother paused.

She stood barely four feet off the ground, one hand pressing to her hip, the strings of her apron digging into her fat.

Lucinda was a plump woman with strawberry blonde hair that stuck out in a frizz under her cap. She had a sweet face with big round cheeks and brown eyes.

After peering at their joyous faces, she rolled her eyes, amused at their youth before ushering them into the parlour, pointing at them to take their seats as she arranged the four teacups.

Once the table was set, she smiled, took her seat and turned to Jonah, her eyes burning into his.

'Well, let me take a look at you,' she said with a sweet smile.

Jonah beamed at her as she looked him up and down, before casting her gaze at Rose and gently winking at her.

'Well, you're a looker, I'll give you that,' Lucinda said, patting him on the knee. 'So, m'dear, when will your mother be arriving?'

Jonah looked stunned. 'My mother?' he asked, his voice rising in pitch. 'I... I didn't think to invite her; she's not been well, you see, not well at all,' he stuttered.

'Ahhh, not to worry, dear, I'm sure the three of us will have a good time,' she said sympathetically, patting his knee gently as she pressed her lips together, knowing only too well the rumours that followed Mrs Heizium.

With relief, the evening proceeded with much tea, scones, cake and eventually a hearty stew. Throughout it all, they laughed and talked, Rose and Jonah seemingly becoming more comfortable with one another.

Night had fallen when Jonah left, and between plans to see Rose and meet with Baxter for his lessons, he was bound to be away for most evening. It pleased him to have his evenings filled with something other than dread.

II

Weeks passed, and Jonah had fallen into a routine, one which had him yearning for the evenings

It was one of those mindless days at work that he paused, thinking about how much had changed.

He was now a tailor's apprentice, stitching by candlelight with a man who he cherished.

Jonah smiled as he thought back to the first evening, how dubious he was, to now when he looked forward to every lesson.

Baxter was a dark horse. He sniggered at the thought, his mind wandering to the ludicrous stories Baxter told. Of him bartering for rare material in the foreign lands, getting cursed out by French maids in overseas pubs and fighting roughens in the dark alleys of Ireland.

'You have lived, Baxter,' he would laugh, rolling his eyes as he hung on every word, delicately piecing material together as he did so.

Baxter chuckled. 'It's the life we get given, friend, but don't worry, under my influence you'll get to experience life, the good the bad, the ugly.' He winked as they carried on with their duties.

Then there were the other days. He smiled, the blood rushing to his cheeks as the loving face of Rose surged into his mind.

For every spare moment he got, he would wander to the bakery, patiently waiting for customers to leave before drawing Rose in close.

Naturally, Lucinda was never too far away, but he didn't mind. She had become a warm presence in his life; he smiled again with her sweet chubby face coming into view.

A lot had changed for the pair of them in those weeks. He stayed true to his word with Sam, proposing to Rose just a few days later. It was the most confident decision he had ever made.

It wasn't an important moment for either of them. They were at the bakery, sharing a delicious cake that Rose had stowed away when he got down on one knee and proposed. The squeal of excitement rung in his ears, the yes pierced his heart as he felt her embrace that almost knocked him to the ground.

'Yes, a thousand times yes, you fool,' she laughed, tears of joy streaming down her face. Lucinda had rushed down at the sound of their voices.

'She said yes,' Jonah cheered at her entrance.

Lucinda was not overly surprised by the gesture but the worry of how fast everything was going was painstakingly written on her face.

They didn't have a ring yet, but they knew and that was all that mattered. It had become a hot topic among the workers, how quickly it was moving, with rumours of an out of wedlock baby spreading. Jonah huffed at the thought; he had an inkling it was Myra who had started that vicious tale but no evidence to prove it.

Shaking his head at the thought, he let his mind continue to wander, bored of the mundane work day. He let the love and happiness wash over him again as a life that he craved was becoming true. Everything seemed to be falling into place at a time when he needed it.

It pleased him, but still, a dark and brooding problem still gnawed at him. His mother. He exhaled at the thought of her, the disgrace she had become. Her drinking had become a necessity, or so she believed. Day and night she would let the liquid flow, squandering their money to numb the pain that had reared its ugly head.

She was too incoherent to even know of Baxter and Rose. She didn't even know her only child was due to be married and he didn't care.

He knew Rose desperately wanted to meet her, but the shame of his home, the rotting stench and drunken nature of his mother was too much. It was the first time they came close to arguing, the memory of the previous night swimming before him.

'Jonah, we're due to be married, surely I should meet your mother,' Rose pleaded, her dainty frame swaying around the counter as she tidied after a long day.

'She's unwell, she won't understand.' He waved his hand, peering into the glass shelves.

'Jonah, please, this is…' Rose said firmly.

'No, Rose.' His nostrils flared, the anger rising in him and he shuddered at the thought, how hurt Rose looked.

He tried to find the words to explain but couldn't, eventually leaving with a feeble goodbye. Guilt racked him but he was sure he could fix it, he could find the words to explain.

It was hard, finding her passed out was just expected these days and he was thankful that Baxter would let him curl up in front of the burning embers of his fire most nights.

A loud clatter sounded and Jonah jumped as he looked around the dispatch room. He was pulled from his day dream as his eyes landed on one of the gaffers, Jimmy, who, under the order of Myra had been keeping a close eye on him.

'Nothing to do, have we, Jonah,' Jimmy snarled, his feet clattering along the floor.

Jonah straightened up, his tall frame towering over Jimmy who paused at the sheer height. Just as he readied himself, the door leading from the side room to the loading bay opened, revealing Sam and Larry. They stopped, taking in the angry stances of the men.

Sam paused momentarily, his mind racing. 'Jimmy, have you got that order yet? It's just we've all been told to wait and it's not like us three don't have any other work to be getting on with.' The lies tumbled out of his mouth as he looked firmly at Jimmy who recoiled, confusion washing over his face.

'Come on, Jonah,' Larry called. 'If the order is late, then that's on you, Jimmy.'

Together they stomped out into the cobbled loading bay, Sam slamming the door behind him before doubling over, laughing.

Jonah breathed heavily, a sigh of relief washing over him. 'Thanks,' he laughed. 'I thought I was sure to be fired then.'

Larry chuckled. 'Well, that's love for you.'

He nudged Jonah sharply in the ribs as the three began walking to the gate, their spirits high.

Rose

Life for Rose was going by as quickly as it was for Jonah. She had found herself happily in love with what she believed to be the most handsome of men.

Marriage, she thought, usually one that brought desire and most recently hope, but today was different. She was confused as she mundanely went about her work. The argument between her and Jonah repeated in her mind; the anger that had flared scared her.

'Rose,' a familiar voice called.

'Hmm,' she looked up, her eyes focusing on her friend, Myra. 'What are you doing here?' she asked, confused, her eyes darting outside, wondering where the day had gone.

'Here to see you, silly, it's been too long and I want to hear about you and that handsome boy of yours. Come on, let's go to the pub and talk like old times.' She smiled sweetly, her tone light and caring.

'I don't, I… yes, yes, I will.' She paused slightly; it was what she needed and without thought she tossed her apron down and headed out the door, turning the lock as she went.

Linking together, the ladies walked towards the Roaring Dragon, ducking into the warmth of the pub that they once frequented.

Myra called for two drinks as they sought a table in the dark corner, hidden from view. Rose immediately slumped into the chair. 'I'm so glad this day is over,' she sighed.

A chuckle escaped Myra's thin lips. 'Not quite over, how distracted are you,' she pointed out and laughed again. 'It's midday, silly. I managed to convince the gaffer, Jimmy, to let me go home and clearly you've just abandoned your post.' She smiled wickedly as the horror washed over Rose.

'Myra, are you serious, my mother is going to kill me,' she groaned as slapped her hand to her forehead.

'Please, what's one afternoon, besides, you look horrid, now talk,' she responded, grabbing the two drinks from the barman and pushing one towards Rose.

Within moments Rose had drunk her gin and the words tumbled from her mouth, the horrible fight with Jonah, how angry he had become and how annoyed she was that he refused to introduce him to his own mother.

'It's so frustrating, how can he think we can get married and I not meet his mother,' she ranted, her voice rising.

Myra nodded, quietly sipping her drink as she listened intently. 'Not surprising, Jonah is known for being overly aggressive. Rumour had it his father was the same, which is why he never got a proper job.' Myra spoke her words slowly, her lies clearly hitting Rose's ears who hung on every word. 'Of course, you know how his mother is. She's the town drunk, can't go a moment without the grog,' she nodded wisely.

'That's awful...' Rose began.

'Yes, I heard it was because of him she started drinking. People say that he would go home so angry and just treat her like dirt, to the point that she took up drink to drown her sorrows,' Myra interjected with more lies, her voice firm.

Gasping, Rose looked at her friend in horror, the words biting into her. 'I don't know this man at all. I can't marry him.' She uttered the words breathlessly, the daunting realisation knocking the wind out of her.

'It's not surprising, you two moved so quickly. I thought the big brute had forced you into it.' Myra paused. 'If I was you, I would march to the mill and tell him straight.'

Rose looked up, tears welling in her eyes and spilling onto her cheeks. She sobbed and pursed her lips before standing up.

'You're right.' With a nod, she marched outside, her heels clicking against the cobbles as she quickly carried herself towards the mill, wiping her tears away as she did so.

Nerves wriggled inside her as she walked on determinedly, through the iron gates. She paused, unsure of where to go, when Jonah's face loomed in the distance. His head cocked to the side upon seeing her and slowly he began to walk, leaving the two men beside him behind.

'Rose,' he smiled, his soft voice echoing around her mind.

She breathed deeply, shaking as a tear rolled down her cheek. Jonah moved to brush it away and Rose jolted backwards, stumbling out of reach.

'No.' She pointed at him.

'Rose?' he looked at her, confused.

'No.' She shook her head firmly. 'Jonah, we're done. I don't know you, not who you are. This, us, it's all too quick and I can't marry you. We are done.' She spoke solemnly, her voice growing in confidence.

Jonah recoiled in pain. 'No, Rose. If this is about last night, I can explain,' he said feebly, his voice wavering as he whimpered.

'No, it's because we don't know one another. I've made my decision.' She turned and Jonah grasped her hand.

'This isn't happening,' he said, the anger rising within him.

Rose pulled hard, her arm releasing as she ran from him. He made to go after her when the strong arms of Sam pulled at Jonah.

'Let her go, Jonah, let her go.' He patted his shoulder, pulling him tightly as Rose ran away.

With haste she scurried down the streets, her legs moving as quickly as they could until she was home. Panting and out of breath, she collapsed on the hearth of her parlour, her sobs filling the room as Lucinda hastened to comfort her.

Jonah

Jonah's world fell silent, his body numb as he watched Rose flee. Sam's strong arms embraced him, restraining him before he finally shook free.

Without a word he left, his hands stuck deeply into his pockets, his head hung in shame as he aimlessly walked away, ignoring the faint cries of Sam and Larry.

Jonah's heart ached worse than ever, the pain weighing him down as his feet pounded the streets. The glimmer of joy had disappeared in mere seconds, with Rose's words repeating in his mind.

The night wound on, the darkened sky turning light as the orange rays dashed across the clouds. He dragged his aching feet over the hard cobbled ground, his body weary. Dark purple rings etched around his red eyes as he tiredly wandered through the empty streets. More than once he had dared to pass the bakery, desperate to get a glimpse of Rose, yet she never came.

Eventually, dawn struck and the rumblings of people began to sound. People began to emerge, their cheery deposition echoing throughout the city. Jonah sighed, his nostrils flaring at the joy that was piercing him.

Turning his back on the world, Jonah marched away from the street where Bakery Bank lay. Anger and pain throbbed within him as he quickly paced towards the mill.

'A poor person's prison,' he muttered wearily as he passed through the iron gates, already open and beckoning the broken workers in.

Skilfully, Jonah wound through the mill, avoiding the glares and gossiping women until he was safely tucked out of sight. Larry was awaiting him, sheepishly smiling at him. Jonah nodded, wearily smiled and set to work with Larry following him. The silence was deafening, the sounds of excited talk from the mill echoing into the room as they quietly worked.

In no time, the news of his failed engagement had spread throughout the mill – Myra had gleefully told the story to anyone who hear it.

Every so often, Larry would emerge, the sorrow in his eyes echoing as he looked at his friend in pain. He placed his hand on Jonah's shoulder and squeezed it tightly. 'Jonah,' he uttered.

'Don't, please,' Jonah responded weakly, a tear escaping his eye.

With a simple pat, Larry nodded and without a word the pair set to work once more, quickly moving the boxes out to the loading bay.

Both were panting for breath when Jonah stopped. He sat on an upturned box, drawing in deep, sharp breaths. Larry looked at his friend, seeing the pain that was crippling him.

As they wearily sat, Myra and her unfortunate shadow, Jimmy walked in, a sarcastic snigger escaping his lips.

'I see you two think you can have a day's relaxing because you've gone and gotten your heart broken,' he said maliciously.

'Come on, Jimmy' Larry said with a sigh, 'this is the first moment's rest we've had all day. Be kind for heaven's sake.'

Jimmy turned with a glare to Larry, a wicked smile contorting his face, before laughing hysterically.

Within seconds anger had consumed Jonah, a rage uncontrolled as he towered over Jimmy, his thick fist powering into his scrawny face.

Jimmy slammed to the ground, his nose crunching under the dirt as the blood pooled around him. Myra began screaming hysterically, bringing attention far and wide to the room in which they operated.

Immediately, Larry shot around the room, grabbing Jonah and pushing him towards the back entrance. 'Run, get out of here right now. Go, before they summon the police,' he said urgently.

Jonah, dazed, the blood staining his hand, faltered before reality hit.

'Thank you,' he panted breathlessly as he turned, running away from the quickly forming crowd.

Within no time he had surpassed the wrought-iron gates, his feet carrying him quickly down the main street, searching for sanctuary.

He'd given up calling the apothecary a home and Rose wouldn't have him decent, let alone wanted. Without thinking he sought out the friend he'd come to cherish, Baxter.

His feet dug deeply into the ground as he sprinted for the tailors, flinging the door open with a mighty crash.

Baxter looked at him startled 'Jonah, whatever brings you here at this time and in such a ghastly state?' he said as he strolled around the counter, shutting the door and locking it with a click.

He grabbed Jonah and dragged him into the back parlour room. It was filled with various garments draped on dressmaker dolls. There were a few pieces Jonah recognised as his own work, which made him smile just a little.

The room itself was big and had two comfortable armchairs, a large open fire and a soft white rug that Jonah often curled himself upon. An elaborate staircase at the back of the room led to Baxter's bedroom, a place he'd never stepped in, and to the left of the room was a stylish kitchenette, fitted with the finest tops and equipment.

Jonah took in the familiar space, feeling slightly relaxed as Baxter marched towards a small cabinet at the other end of the room which was elegantly detailed with flowers and cherubs. He unlatched the hook and opened it up, pulling out a bottle filled with clear liquid.

'Now tell me everything,' Baxter said, as he produced two glasses and poured large portions for both of them.

With his head in his hands, Jonah groaned and then began relaying his story, starting from last night right up until the moment he had punched his foreman in the face.

For the rest of the day, they hid behind their glasses, drinking deeply as they discussed the issues at hand and how Jonah could survive. He'd lost his job and was at risk of being imprisoned. His life was spiralling out of control.

Baxter listened intently, nodding ever so slightly in parts until Jonah finally finished telling his desperate tale of a love lost and a vengeance on the unsuspecting.

'Jonah,' he sighed. 'What a fine mess you seem to have gotten yourself into, but don't fret, we can solve this.'

'How?' Jonah interjected, hope rising within.

'Shush, listen,' Baxter commanded fiercely. 'I have a friend, a fellow tailor. He lives in Birmingham, he could continue teaching you, train you up in return for housing and food. I can pay for your escape, get you on the latest train to freedom tonight...' He paused, glancing at his friend as he formed the plan.

Nervously Jonah swished the contents of his glass, downing the stinging liquid before slamming his glass to the table.

Coughing, he breathed deeply, 'It's the best plan we have. I get a new life, one away from the mills.' He sighed.

'You're reluctant, why?' Baxter looked at him inquisitively.

Jonah paused. 'It's not much of a life I have, but it is my own and now I'm abandoning it. I know that this is the only way, but it's a life abandoned all the same.'

Baxter nodded. 'I understand friend, but this is the only way. We leave tonight and I'll arrange for a letter to arrive before you do.' He spoke firmly, before rising and leaving Jonah alone with his thoughts and the bottle.

As Baxter's footsteps fell silent, Jonah was left alone with his thoughts. He grasped his drink, gulping the liquid down as his mind span in disarray. By tomorrow his home would be no more. His friends gone, his mother left to wither away.

His thoughts were interrupted with the return of Baxter and before he knew it, Jonah was stood facing him.

'I need to say goodbye to my mother.' He spoke clearly, his eyes tired and sad.

Time froze momentarily, Baxter's face emotionless as he looked into Jonah's eyes before he swiftly nodded.

'Fine, but we should go soon, we need to be at the train station for eight p.m. sharp.' Baxter spoke slowly, his eyes boring into Jonah's who solemnly agreed to the fleeting goodbye.

Theresa

Theresa awoke to the docile tones of her horrid landlord, her head pounding and her vision blurry. She rolled out of her bed with a thud and crawled to the counter, pouring herself a hearty helping of gin. It hit the spot, and her mind cleared slightly as the liquid washed down her throat

A smile emerged on her face and she decided that she would pour another drink, only to find the bottle empty and with no money to buy more.

The urge was too much, and with that, she decided she would go and find her son — he would have the money she could use for gin.

She left immediately, the stench of alcohol and sweat oozing out of her, the rancid smell following her down the stairs as she entered the shop.

Mrs Welts smelt before she saw, and when her eyes fell on the drunken mess of her tenant, she began shaking with anger.

'You!' she screeched as Theresa looked at her in shock. 'I have had enough. You're a good for nothing drunk, and you will not darken my door again. Leave now and don't come back.'

Theresa looked at her, confused by the harsh words, but her mouth and brain weren't working, and before she knew it, Mrs Welts had marched her through the apothecary and out onto the streets, before she slammed the door in her face.

Distraught, Theresa drunkenly headed in the direction of the mill. She stumbled and staggered along as onlookers skirted around her, making choice comments. Theresa ignored the stares as she continued on her way, occasionally tripping over the hem of her dress.

Her patience was running thin as people got in the way of her swaying, so she left the safety of the sidewalk and into the street she trotted. She was haphazardly strutting in the street, making a spectacle of herself without a care in the world.

It was with that airy presence that she failed to hear the shouts of concern or see the unruly horse that had broken free from a carriage down the street. It charged towards her at great speed, but no one stopped her or tried to pull her out of the way.

The horse struck her with force, launching her off her feet. She was dead before her body hit the ground with a thud.

Cries began to burst from the crowd at the hideous sight, and within moments the police had arrived, covering her body, and murmurs in the crowd began spreading rumours about who the drunken woman was.

The crowd began to form and look on at the disarray as the police tried to keep the situation calm. They interviewed onlookers, who told the tale of the drunken lady, while a few told the police it was Theresa Heizium, last believed to be living above the apothecary.

Nodding towards the crowd, the police constable signalled for two policemen to go to the apothecary. As they entered, a small bell chimed, and Mrs Welts emerged through the curtain and smugly said, 'I knew you'd be back. I bet you've forgotten I threw your lazy backside out of here. Just give me one good reason why I should take you back. You're a drunk and a thief. You plead poverty and cling onto the fact that you're a poor widow. Fact, your husband died years ago, you've got a son who works hard, he provides for you and you drink the money away, even going as low as to steal the rent money.'

She was cut short by a loud cough, and when she turned, she saw the two policemen and her jaw dropped. In an attempt to compose herself, she came around the counter and was about to speak when the larger of the two men held his hand up and said in a deep, gruff voice, 'Theresa Heizium, you said she had a son. Where is he? This is important. I'm afraid his mother is dead— a horse broke free and killed her.'

Mrs Welts tried to hide her smile, before answering the constable's question. 'Well, sir that is a shame,' she said softly. 'I believe her son works at the mill over on Jackson Street.'

The men nodded and turned in the direction of the mill. They marched through the streets, quickly arriving at the thriving mill.

'You girl,' the larger policeman called to Myra who was dodging work in the yard.

'Sir,' she smiled sweetly, eyeing the men up and down.

'We're here to see a Jonah Heizium, can you tell us where he works,' the man gruffed.

'Not here, not any more, he punched a good friend of mine this morning and was dismissed,' her lips curled into a wicked smile.

'Fighting eh? Does the victim wish to press charges?'

Myra paused, cocking her head to the side before nodding sharply. The men nodded, and urged Myra to take them to Jimmy who eagerly shared the tale.

Not only was his mother dead, he was now a wanted man.

Other than the apothecary, nobody knew where Jonah could be, and so the police were forced to retreat and search the streets for the suspect at hand.

Jonah

It was almost time to leave when Jonah went towards the apothecary to pack what little he had and say a final farewell to his mother.

It had been such a long time since he'd seen and sat and talked to her, that he was almost sad to be leaving. He drew himself up tall, as he walked towards the place he'd laid his head for so many years. He slowly walked up the street, the pestle and mortar sign swinging in the wind. As he entered the shop he went to bypass Welts, but she stopped him in his tracks.

'She's not up there,' Welts said softly.

Jonah turned in confusion. For the first time in Jonah's life, she did something nice: she took him into the back, sat him down and made him a cup of tea.

He sat there, extremely confused, before she said the dreaded words he'd feared for so long. 'She died, Jonah, this morning. The police tried to find you, but, apparently, you weren't at the mill, and now you're in trouble.'

Jonah was in shock. His mother, his once loving mother, was dead. He put his hands on his head and wiped the tears that steadily fell from his cheeks. He was devastated. He was an orphan.

Mrs Welts patted his knee, before she said, 'I know it's sad, but let's face it, it was only a matter of time, Jonah; she was a lost cause. I ended up kicking her out this morning. Jonah's head whipped up, a dark look washing over him as he glared at her angrily.

'I had no choice,' she pleaded. 'Your mother was drunk and disorderly. She stumbled down the stairs, frightening my customers half to death.'

In a soothing attempt, Mrs Welts reached forward to place her hand on Jonah's knee. He jerked away as the pain slowly crept in, consuming his heart.

He gasped as Mrs Welts looked at him in despair; her reaction hit a nerve. She had never once shown kindness, and now it was her fault that Theresa had died. She had been upset at being kicked out and that's what led to her death.

He looked up with anger burning in his eyes. She was mocking him, he thought darkly, she wanted her dead. The rage burst through him, the gin coursing his body almost fuelling his anger. He lunged, grabbing at her neck, his thick fingers crushing into her windpipe. He pinned her against the wall, lifting her as he did so. She gasped, turning her head, her tongue sticking out as she coughed.

Her nails dug into his arms, drawing blood. The light in her eyes was fading when a hand yanked his arm away. It was Baxter. He'd arrived just in time to stop him from a despicable act. Baxter grabbed his arm, pulling him away. 'What are you doing? Stop, not here, not now,' he said, his eyes wide in shock.

He dragged Jonah through the shop as he began to sob. Mrs Welts was on the floor, heaving, as she drew in the lost air. Baxter returned, picked her up and pushed a wad of notes into her hands.

With a deadly stare, he whispered, 'Not a word is to be spoken about this, do you hear?'

She went to protest, when she caught a glimpse of his eyes: they were black, a terrifyingly harsh black. She shoved back in horror, grabbing the money and nodding as more tears streamed down her face.

Baxter turned on his heel, adjusted his collar and walked back into the front. Jonah was outside, sobbing with his hands in his head.

'What have I done, what have I done?' he cried.

'It's all right,' Baxter said, as he put his arm on his shoulder. 'Come on, we need to go.'

He steered Jonah towards his shop, half-carrying him as tears streamed down his face. People all around glanced as the pair stumbled along the cobbled streets.

The bell rang as the door to Baxter's shop opened. He pushed Jonah through into the darkened room and led him into the back. Just hours before, the pair were laughing, joking and knocking the drinks back. The gin sat there; the head still cracked open. It was a harrowing sight.

He sat Jonah down, poured him another drink and shoved it into his hands. He then set about lighting the fire. It had gone dark, and the chill was setting in.

Jonah continued to sob not so silently, as Baxter sat and watched, sipping his own drink. He slapped Jonah on the shoulder, and he looked up, his eyes red and nose snotty. He heaved a sigh.

'Sorry, it's just today has been quite the day. I've lost my job, my home and my mother. I am a homeless, jobless orphan. What am I going to do, Mr Baxter? What can I do?' he said, his voice shaking.

'I know. I know, but we've got our plan. A fresh start in a new city that will get you out of here, away from the police, from the sadness. Come now, we need to leave before anyone finds us. Dry your eyes, Jonah, for a new life awaits you.' Baxter spoke in a soft, authoritative voice as he grabbed Jonah's arm, dragging him to his feet and handing him a bag with a set of spare clothes, a few coins, a train ticket and some food for the journey.

They set out as the sky began turning a deep shade of blue. Keeping their heads low, they made a brisk march to the train station. If the police caught them, it could mean prison time, a horrendous feat that would leave a black mark against their names.

He either had to face the law or flee for another life, and that is what he did. They arrived in good time, both panting from the fast walk. The journey would not be an easy one. It would be long and tedious, with many changes and stops to endure.

Jonah boarded the train, shaking Baxter's hand firmly, before finding a seat and dropping into it with a sigh. It had been a long day, and too much had happened, and he was drained. He closed his eyes briefly and fell into a deep sleep as the train carried him away from his home, life and friends.

The Watcher

Alas, dear reader, the first Sin had come into play, devious as the nature of all sins are. They had started by turning his love away from the one that raised him and then ripped his true love from his grasp.

Jonah was a toy to them; it was fun to watch the pain, to feed off it and watch as the lives around crumbled as his pain echoed into the lives of others.

I say, dear reader, these events are just beginning. Jonah's life was going to get worse, and the events to come will surely disturb you, because the Sins are just preparing.

If I could stop it, I would, but it's strictly forbidden for me to cross over to the other side and interfere. The path has changed, and the forthcoming tales will only prove that.

I'll leave you now. I'll leave you to experience the next chapter of Jonah's life.

Jonah

Jonah got off the train in dismay, his heart heavy with regret: for his mother, for Rose, for his friends. No proper goodbye was said, no love was shared. It was an entirely new experience that whisked him away to a new life, a life he was detached from.

He'd slept most of the journey, exhausted at the thought of the events that prevailed. His heart was in his stomach the whole way as he anticipated being hoisted off by the police whilst also dealing with the grief and heartache of love. A terrible curse ever to lay upon a human being.

With hunched shoulders, Jonah began shuffling forward, making his way in the brand new city of Birmingham, with every footstep leading him away from his old life.

It was too much, and now he was in a city unknown to him. It was big and busy, and in the mass of people he was supposed to find a man named Mr Bentley on Rigley Street. He didn't have a clue where he was located or what he looked like.

Pulling his satchel closer, he started to push through the crowds of people who parted unwillingly, leaving a tiny gap for him to squeeze through.

As a big man, this sent many hurtling sideways, with some even hitting the ground. Yet nobody challenged him. Jonah suspected the huge bags under his eyes and a surly, almost vengeful, look on his face, combined with his large frame, deterred many.

Finally, he broke free and stepped out onto the street, revealing the big city of Birmingham. It was vast and wide, with cobbled streets leading in all manner of directions. The air was thick with smog. It was a good job his eyes were used to it — newcomers would be blind in this weather.

He began walking aimlessly, trying to avoid the crowds. The first pub he came to he ducked in. It was dimly lit and smelled strongly of ale.

A few people were scattered around the place, drunk, stained and delusional as they muttered to themselves.

He approached the bar, standing in front of a surly looking man, who was cleaning a glass with a grimy cloth.

Jonah cleared his throat loudly to get his attention, and he slowly raised his head, his eyes glaring.

'Yes?' he said gruffly.

With a furrowed frown, Jonah said, 'I'm looking for Rigley Street. I'm supposed to be meeting a Mr Bentley; he's a tailor.'

The barman nodded and placed his glass down, before saying, 'Down the street, take a left at the butcher's, a right at the bookstore and keep going down to the end; he's on the right.'

Jonah sighed in relief; he thought it was going to be much harder than that to get the information from him.

He turned towards the door and just as he was about to step away, the barman said, 'Funny, you'd be seeing him.'

Jonah cocked his head and raised his eyebrows. 'Why so funny?' he asked inquisitively.

'In all my years, I've never known that man to have any visitors. What makes you so special?' he replied.

Jonah paused. He didn't feel like telling a stranger his tale, nor was he willing to expose his criminal endeavours. The police, even in another city, would happily hunt him down.

He quickly said, 'Long lost uncle. I'm here to learn the trade, make something of myself.'

Before the barman could say anything else, he hurried out of the pub and into the murky streets. With determination, he set about following the directions, and, sure enough, he found the tailor shop in a speedy manner.

It was glorious. The shop looked freshly painted as the black frame remained unchipped, but the real beauty was the gold lettering and floral design. It stood out for miles and was a true beauty that stood boldly in Rigley Street.

The gleam of the windows meant he could see into the shop. It was packed with worker women who were grabbing material and sewing supplies, with each item looking fine and expensive.

Behind the counter was a young girl. She was small, with thick black hair that was neatly tied in a long swirling plait which rested on her delightful blue dress that was embroidered with flowers.

It fitted her perfectly, moulding to her body and moving in time with every step. Her face was slim, and her light brown eyes gleamed with every interaction, and her little button nose twitched at the dust raised from the garments. She was pretty enough, but she was no Rose.

As he stood watching, he could see the sweat dripping off her brow. She quickly batted it away, continuing to serve the mass of women that pushed and shoved their way to the front desk. Jonah scanned the entire place, but could not see Mr Bentley.

He moved towards the door, pulling it open, but before he could enter, a gaggle of women poured out, carrying boxes of all shapes and sizes.

They were talking loudly at the disappointment at missing the handsome owner and discussing the expensive items their ladies would be draped in.

He rolled his eyes at their inappropriate chatter, holding the door wide open as they trotted through and on to the street. Finally, he managed to squeeze into the shop. The crowd had thinned, but women still littered the place, handling the various items in the shop. He began gently pushing his way forward, being careful not to knock anyone over as he headed directly for the young assistant.

She stood there tidying up the disrupted items, and as Jonah's shadow loomed over her, she looked up and jumped, before quickly composing herself.

'Forgive me,' she said breathlessly. 'I'm not used to men coming into the shop; you made me jump. How can I help you today?' she asked inquisitively.

Jonah smiled sheepishly, before responding to the woman, 'I'm sorry, I didn't mean to scare you. I'm looking for a Mr Bentley. I've been sent here by Baxter Warren, he's a tailor up in Manchester.'

She nodded. 'Yes, yes, I remember Mr Bentley mentioning a new apprentice would be stopping by. I just didn't think it'd be you,' she said, looking him up and down, her finger tracing his height.

He pressed his lips tightly together and stuck his hands in his pockets. 'Yes, I'm never what people expect, yet here I am,' he said, lifting his eyebrows with a grimace on his face.

'Sorry,' she exclaimed, as the blood rushed to her face, 'sometimes I say things without realising. I didn't mean it, sorry. Wait here. I'll go fetch him.' She held her finger up and dashed through a door behind the counter, disappearing from view.

Jonah looked around the shop, taking in the array of clothes, threads, beads and buttons. He smiled at the enormity of it all.

As he turned around taking in all the elegant features, his eyes landed on Mr Bentley, who was a well-built, clean-shaven man. His dark black hair was sleekly parted to give a modern look. He wore the finest suit Jonah had ever seen. It was a mix of soft cotton with silk lining, and a gold chain that hung from his suit jacket and led into his top pocket and the tip of a gold pocket watch were visible. He was rich.

He surveyed Jonah, in his hand-me-down clothes that were dirty, tattered and on the brink of utter waste. He wasn't impressed.

Staring Jonah directly in the eyes, he spoke in a low, docile tone, 'Baxter sent you to me, asking for a favour. Asking me to teach you the trade; but the thing is, Baxter taught me — he's better than me, so why wouldn't he teach you?' he asked curiously.

Flustered, Jonah opened his mouth and then quickly closed it. He did this a few times, before muttering that he wanted a change of scenery.

Mr Bentley let out a sharp hum as he looked Jonah up and down. 'Very well, but let it be known I will make you work hard. Your look right now does not fit my beautiful establishment. Your clothes are tattered, you yourself are filthy; you remind me more of a vagabond than a tailor,' Mr Bentley said firmly.

Jonah's cheeks glowed red, and his eyes stung. He sighed, nodded and lowered his gaze to the floor, awaiting the next verbal battering from his future employer.

'First, you will wash and clean yourself up; then we'll get a suit fitted. You must look the part. Do you think Sarah here,' he said, pointing to his assistant, who was fiddling with some material, trying to look disinterested in the conversation, 'do you think she would be in such finery? No, she would not!' he answered, whilst Jonah nodded, still staring at his feet.

'This suit,' he continued, 'will be yours, and you will be paying for it. Each week I will take something from your wage, allowing you to pay it off in instalments. Half your wage will be used, but in return, you will have the nicest clothes you've ever earned.'

Shocked, Jonah looked up wide-eyed; that would leave him with very little, as apprentice jobs barely paid anything, but he was in a situation in which he could not argue or negotiate his way out. Again he nodded, taking a big gulp as he did so.

'Good lad,' Bentley said, clapping his hands together, before continuing, 'The rest of your wage will contribute to your board, food and training.'

Again, Jonah looked up, horrified. He wasn't happy about this — it wasn't what he was promised — but he was in an unknown city, and returning to Manchester wasn't an option.

He had no life up there; for all he knew, he was still being hunted for assault, and he didn't want to live in a place haunted by his mother's death.

Birmingham was a fresh start, one that would give him options and, once trained, a good wage. For now, he had the basics, a roof over his head and the promise of a job. He was learning a profession, something that would give him purpose, and if he tried hard enough, he'd be needed, and job security was the dream for many.

Gritting his teeth, he accepted the offer with a grimace, a dead look in his eyes as he thought about this situation and that of his home.

Mr Bentley smiled, but it wasn't friendly; it was a mocking smile that told Jonah that the man in front of him was cunning and deceiving, and he knew how to squeeze the last penny out of the poorest people. Money meant power, and he was willing to prove that statement wherever he ventured.

Jonah was in awe and jealous of his riches, and he realised as Mr Bentley was walking away, that one day he wanted to be that man.

He smirked, imagining what his life could be, his eyes glazing over as he contemplated it: the riches, the gold, the superiority.

Just as he was settling into his fantasy, a sharp snapping sound drew his attention — it was Sarah clicking her fingers at him.

'Did you hear me?' she asked, raising her eyebrows inquisitively at him.

Jonah looked at her, confused, before she rolled her eyes and spoke slowly, 'I said that I am to show you where you'll be sleeping, the rest of the shop and then teach you the ins and outs of this place.'

Jonah nodded. 'Yes, I heard,' he lied, waving his hand forward, motioning her to start the tour.

Sarah turned on her heel, marching her way into the back. It opened into a spacious room that was occupied by many fine items. The far-left wall, consisted of a large ornate fireplace and etched within the iron were needles and thumbs, all details associated with the profession.

Dainty yet elegant armchairs were dotted around the room, and next to each one was a small wooden table with a set of neatly stacked mats.

A rug filled the entire row, and as soon as Jonah stepped on it, his feet sank in gently, it was so soft and dreamy.

At the far end of the room a large brown cabinet gleamed; it had many drawers that had fancy brass handles, and each compartment contained items required for dressmaking. This was the parlour in which fittings took place.

To the left of him was a door that stood slightly ajar. He could see Mr Bentley crouched down, hemming a simple yet delicate black dress — that was where the items were stitched together.

Sarah led him through the room and down a small passageway into the kitchen. It had stone floors and wooden countertops which were built around the room, whilst a larger one dominated the centre. There was a massive fireplace with a stove, to boot, copper pans scattered around the room and a dead pheasant was hanging just above the stove. Jonah had never seen a kitchen so big.

Sarah explained that staff would come in in the morning and cook breakfast and make something simple for lunch, and in the evening, they would return to cook a divine meal for them to enjoy. The dining room was adjacent to the parlour and could be accessed by the kitchen. It had a grand oak table that could fit a host of guests. The room itself was another beauty, with soft carpet, vibrant red walls that were hung with multiple pieces of art. Flowers and plants were dotted in each corner and at the very end of the room lay two double doors which led out onto a beautiful garden that was blossoming with all colour of plants imaginable.

Sarah patted his arm, leading back into the kitchen, and as they entered, she made a sharp right turn up a set of creaking wooden stairs that Jonah hadn't noticed before.

The wood sank with his steps, causing him to lower his pace and lighten his step. He arrived at the top to see a less appealing corridor that had four doors.

Sarah looked at his perplexed face, before opening her mouth. 'This is where we sleep; you'll be in the end room on the right, I'm here' — she pointed at the first door — 'Louisa, the maid, is the next one up but you won't see much of her and this one here'— she nodded to the first door — 'is empty.'

Jonah nodded and pushed past Sarah, heading to his room. The door opened with a click, and he peered inside. It was small and dark, but he could see a bed, sink and chamber pot waiting for him; it was luxury like he had never seen before. He heard a distinctive clearing of Sarah's throat, and he glanced back, holding one finger up as he dumped his belongings on the bed and returned to her.

He followed her down the stairs and back into the main shop; it was busy once again, and people were growing tired of waiting.

'Ladies, please, calm yourself,' Sarah spoke over the crowd, raising her hands. 'This his Jonah; he will be starting today,' she smiled.

The women looked at him, admiring his beauty, whilst others glared at his dirty appearance. Mr Bentley appeared, clasping Jonah on the shoulder, and the women flustered as he flashed them a dazzling smile.

'Ladies, please excuse my new apprentice's look — he's come all the way from Manchester. But rest assured, he will be clean soon enough, and in a suit so fine, that royalty could wear it.' He spoke in a showman's voice, grasping their attention and wooing them over.

He pulled Jonah into the back, and his smile now became a vicious snarl. 'You embarrassed me there, boy,' he spat. 'Kitchen, now! Clean yourself up and put this on.' He handed Jonah a garment bag and a pair of shoes, before turning back to his room, in which a pale lavender dress now hung.

Jonah was ashamed, and once again he was fighting back tears as he hurried to the kitchen. Soap, a basin of warm water and a small towel were laid out on the centre table. He began furiously scrubbing his entire body, the dirt and dust muddying the water.

He cleaned himself meticulously, hoping never to be so berated in his life ever again. Once clean, he dried himself and unbuttoned the garment bag, which he had hooked on a metal pole above his head.

Inside was a black suit, freshly pressed and clean. It was soft to the touch, with the cotton running smoothly through his hands. He checked the passageway to make sure no one was coming, before quickly stripping off and working the suit on. He looked down at himself and smiled. He had never felt so rich in all his life.

Unsure what to do now, Jonah walked to the front of the shop to find Sarah. He'd been gone a while and hoped she was still there. She was, and as he approached, the women in the shop gasped, before muttering excitedly to one another.

Sarah beamed at him and gave him a small wink, before she began teaching him the layout of the shop, whilst stopping every so often to help customers, who eagerly eyed Jonah up.

That afternoon, Jonah learnt the basics of how Mr Bentley ran his shop, and he saw how Sarah could get even the most reluctant customers to buy accessories they didn't even want. He was taught where everything went, from the small beads, the assortment of threads and the extensive range of materials on hand. There was much to take in, and Jonah had barely touched the surface by the time it came to closing.

Once the closed sign was turned, he and Sarah dusted, swept the floors and wiped the windows, ensuring the shop was in pristine condition.

They made a good team and had the place looking spotless in no time. Sarah led Jonah to Mr Bentley's private room for his first session, before she darted off towards the kitchen.

Jonah watched her go as his stomach twisted as he raised his hand and knocked three times.

'Enter,' a sharp voice called.

Stumbling in the room, he smiled apprehensively. Mr Bentley simply pointed at a chair, beckoning him to sit. That night, Jonah watched his skilled hands craft a beautiful garment that would turn the heads of many. Mr Bentley's hands glided through the material, stitching with precision. It was so mesmerising to watch that Jonah was startled by Sarah, who stuck her head around the door to call them both for food.

While relieved at getting food, Jonah couldn't help but glance back at the magic of the exquisite dresses, embroidered with delicate designs. It was a welcome distraction, and one worth waiting on, as Mr Bentley led Jonah to the dining area, where Sarah sat, waiting patiently.

The table was half-filled with a chicken breast, carrots, potatoes and bread. Mr Bentley sat at the top and Jonah and Sarah at his side. He helped himself first and then Sarah, followed by Jonah.

They ate until they couldn't eat any more, the smacking of lips and sighs of delight masking the silence that held the room. It was the best meal Jonah had eaten to date, and he was slowly warming to the apprenticeship he'd agreed to.

Happy and tired, Jonah lowered his knife and fork and dabbed at his face with the cloth napkin, dreaming of his bed that lay just above his head.

It was a happy thought that was short-lived. Mr Bentley whipped him back to his room for the lessons to continue. It was a twice-daily task that prevailed until Jonah proved himself trustworthy of the needle and thread.

I

Months passed by, until Mr Bentley invited him to spend the afternoon in the parlour, assisting the women. His strong arms and large size often had the women customers in awe, whilst his charm convinced them to empty their purses for accessories they didn't need, just to please him.

Over time, he quickly realised this and used it to his full potential to seduce vulnerable women into spending what they couldn't afford.

His skills in the shop hadn't been the only success he'd seen: his work as a tailor had significantly improved. What little skills he'd learned from Baxter had been transformed, and his hands now glided through the material like Mr Bentley's. His fine stitching and unique designs were the talk of the town. Mr Bentley's shop was even more famous, thanks to the handsome northerner with the exceptional skills that brought to life the lavish garments that many women desired.

He'd become an asset to the place, but he hadn't reaped the rewards — he was still slumming it on his apprentice wage, much to his annoyance. He often found himself venting his grievances to Sarah, who had grown to be very good and confident, and they spent practically every day in each other's company.

He grew to like Sarah a lot, and she soon became the sibling he'd never had, sharing secrets and dreams, each supporting one another's successes and triumphs. Sarah quietly fought his corner, encouraging him to consistently stand up to Mr Bentley, to demand the wages he deserved.

Finally, after a week of very little sleep and the completion of one of the most extravagant pieces he'd ever done, he worked up the courage to confront Mr Bentley.

'Today is the day, I'm going to do it. I'm going to confront Mr Bentley at last,' he spoke determinedly, his eyes staring into the distance.

'Please do,' Sarah sighed, 'your constant moaning is giving me a headache.' She smirked at him, poking his side gently.

Jonah thought for a long time as he looked around the empty shop. It was the midday Tuesday lull, which often left him and Sarah a bit of time to tidy up and have a break. At the same time, Bentley housed himself away in his den, supposedly working, yet very little ever seemed to be produced now Jonah had started.

It was during those times that he and Sarah really bonded. They shared the deepest secrets and talked at length about all sorts of things. It wasn't surprising that neither had two pennies to rub together, which meant they spent night and day together, working as a team and learning about one another's past.

Sarah had been an orphan rescued at a young age by Mr Bentley, who took her in and gave her a job, decent food and a roof over her head. In exchange, she, too, had no wage — what she earned covered her clothes, food and rent, which left her in a similar position to Jonah. She also had no life outside of the shop, and hardly any human contact with anyone other than Mr Bentley until Jonah came. He was a friend that she could confide in, and she very much looked at him as an older brother.

Jonah smiled and looked at Sarah. She could be tough on him at times, but she had a realistic outlook.

'You may have a point, Sarah. If you don't ask, then you don't get; but you could say the same about yourself,' he said, raising his eyebrows and smiling at her.

'Don't be silly, Jonah. I have no right to ask for a rise. You, however, do; and besides, once you get that pay rise you can start taking me to nice places,' she said, returning his smile, grabbing at a pile of material and marching into the back.

He nodded, pursing his lips; he should have seen that coming. Ultimately, he knew that she was right — asking would be the only way he'd get an answer.

With that, he shrugged his shoulders and walked into the back, turning his head towards Mr Bentley's door. Jonah rocked backwards and forwards, his arms behind his back, nerves bubbling inside him as he envisioned the conversation he was about to have.

He stood there for a good few minutes, when a clicking sound caught his attention. He looked around and saw Sarah in the doorway of the kitchen; she was snapping her fingers and miming him towards Bentley's door, ushering him to complete the task at hand.

Throwing his head back and looking at the ceiling, he dropped his hands and marched towards the door. He lifted his hand to knock and froze. He just couldn't move, and Sarah was nowhere to be seen to physically push him into the room.

Like a statue, he stood until the door was flung open and Mr Bentley looked at him, confused.

'I thought someone was out here. What are you doing, boy?' Mr Bentley asked with a frown on his face.

'I'm... I'm here to talk to you,' Jonah said slowly.

'About what, boy? I'm a busy man, talk fast and talk straight. There's a lot to be done, and I need you to leave the shop early and work on the latest orders — we've had ten placed in the last two weeks, and only six have been started on,' Mr Bentley replied.

Jonah sighed. 'Can we talk in there?' He pointed into the dressmaking room.

Mr Bentley moved sideways, leaving a small gap for Jonah to forcefully push his way past into the room. The door shut sharply as Jonah turned to look the towering man directly in the eyes.

'Here's the thing, Mr Bentley, I was wondering or hoping that you've noticed how far I've come since starting here, the extra work I've taken on,' he said quickly, before he continued, 'With that, I want to ask when I'll be coming off my apprentice wage. I just want something that reflects how hard I work and I feel now is the time,' he said nervously, yet maintaining eye contact the entire time.

As he spoke, Mr Bentley's face or manner didn't alter, and there was no indication or even response to what had been said.

He nodded and placed a finger over his lip, tapping it gently as he stared up at the ceiling while Jonah stuttered his way through his well-practised speech.

'You make a good point, Jonah. Let me think about it. I'll get back to you,' he said thoughtfully, before he turned around and swung the door open, ushering Jonah through.

He left confused as the door shut behind him, and he slowly moved towards the kitchen, where he found Sarah grasping at a much-needed cup of tea.

She smiled as he came in, her brow rising in anticipation.

'He said, he'd get back to me. What does that mean?' Jonah asked nervously as he went to her, slumping against the worktop.

Sarah shrugged and pulled a face, before reassuring him it was a good answer, it wasn't a 'no'. It was an unsympathetic answer that had Jonah's stomach turning in knots.

That night he barely ate anything, swirling his fork around the plate as they sat in silence. Afterwards, he began work on another elegant garment for the odious Miss Hazel, a woman who thought too highly of herself for an unmarried lady in her thirties.

Jonah worked deep into the night, never faltering as he anticipated Mr Bentley's response; yet when morning dawned, no answer was given.

For days this went on, as Jonah worked himself tirelessly in an attempt to prove to Mr Bentley that he was dedicated and deserving of a full wage, despite his heart telling him he did.

The hours dragged by, each one painfully etching into his body, when finally, he was summoned into Mr Bentley's office.

He was overtired, drained, and nerves were stimulating his energy as he shuffled into his workroom.

Mr Bentley was sat with a cigar in his hand, the room filled with smoke, and he gestured for Jonah to take a seat, which he haphazardly did.

'I've thought about what you said, and I've realised that you're right; you've done good, and I'll pay what I owe. I'm a man of my word, and I'd hate to disappoint myself. A wage you will have; I feel you'll do well with it.

'Starting next week, you'll have a wage of £80 per year, more than the average man, and as you've proven a success, I will also give you ten percent commission on any dresses you sell. I trust that you have the skills to prove yourself worthy of this money. Now leave me, I've got lots to do.' He finished his speech with a puff of his cigar.

Jonah, stunned at the response, slowly backed out of the room without a word, utterly taken aback at how easy Mr Bentley had complied with his request. He heaved a heavy breath as he processed the unreal concept, especially as he half-expected to be turned out onto the street with an impending doom awaiting his fate.

Finally, he closed the door and simply stared at it, astonished at the prospect of a new life, one with riches and possibilities.

He was finally snapped out of his daze by Sarah, who demanded an answer as she dragged him into the front of the shop, away from the listening ear of Mr Bentley.

Jonah divulged everything in a secret whisper as customers browsed the various objects in the store. They excitedly exchanged words, giddy with the prospect of a new beginning and the start of a new life that meant chance and possibilities.

He had money, options and a life unforeseen, even unimaginable to him. He'd never had so much money, and on top of that, he was making a commission from each sale and dress. It was mounting up; he'd spent some here and there on fanciful items and even taking him and Sarah out to places, but he was meticulous with his money-making, sure to save enough for something big. He just wasn't sure what.

Each week he added to his pile of money that he squirrelled away in his room. At night he would sit and count it, mulling over his money.

Then every day he would wake, excited at the prospect of making more money. He would charm the ladies and present each of them finely stitched dresses that caressed the skin of each individual.

He was an in-demand tailor that fast became a novel attraction for the shop, one that many requested.

Mrs Cook was one such lady who had become a frequent customer who flittered into the shop weekly to buy garments, small and large. She made sure to talk at length with Jonah, detailing absolutely everything to the final stitch and excessively flirting as she did so.

Jonah happily obliged, as he knew the money he received from each sale, making extra time to lavish her with the most elegant dresses that sculpted around her body. He'd been working on a gorgeous lavender dress with a ruffled body that swooped around her and gracefully hovered above the ground.

Once fitted, Mrs Cook swooned and cooed at her new dress, one she was sure would make her the talk of the town.

'You know, Jonah,' she said with a pause, 'I've been thinking for some time that you should open your own shop, become a leading tailor and give Mr Bentley a run for his money,' she quipped with a gleeful smile as Jonah positioned a stylish hat on her head.

A little taken aback, Jonah replied, 'Me? Open my own shop? Can I do that?'

Mrs Cook laughed. 'Of course you can, silly, and I think you'd be great at it. I'll tell you what, you save up some money, get a decent amount behind you, and I'll be your sponsor. I'll help you find a place and fund some towards it, in exchange for a percentage of your earnings.'

Jonah's eyes widened as he heard the proposition before him, his jaw dropping as he dutifully thought about the offer that had been presented before him.

As he thought, Mrs Cook turned and placed her hand on his cheek. 'You'd be a fantastic investment that I'd be willing to put good money

161

into, and my husband is a businessman, he would help in that aspect, and we'd make an excellent and profitable team.'

He nodded vigorously, a smile emerging on his face as he practically screamed 'yes' in her face as the excitement bubbled inside him.

'Excellent,' she said, leaning in and pinching his cheeks. 'Come to my house tomorrow evening, it's on Marble Street, number 53. We'll iron out all the details, and we'll get a proper plan in place. We'll make this happen, Jonah, you mark my words.'

Jonah's mouth had run dry, and his mind was racing. Mrs Cook smiled as she gathered her things, changing back into her own dress and passing the new one to Sarah for wrapping up.

She left, reminding Jonah of tomorrow's meeting, which caught Sarah's attention.

'What was that about?' Sarah asked curiously.

'I can't say,' Jonah responded coyly. 'Not just yet anyway. Where is Mr Bentley?' he asked, changing the subject.

She pursed her lips in annoyance. 'He's out. He's been out all day. Why do you ask?'

Jonah nodded in relief. He was worried that someone had overheard their conversation, but apparently not. He smiled and walked towards the back room, patting Sarah on the shoulder as he did so. She simply looked at him, confused, and squinted her eyes at his strange behaviour.

The rest of the day passed by in a breeze. Jonah took it in his stride, taking charge where he could, managing the odd customers that came into the store, delicately taking orders and arranging the work accordingly.

By mid-afternoon, Jonah had left the shop in Sarah's capable hands as he retired to the back room to work on the ever-increasing orders for gowns.

He was motivated and energised, barely noticing Mr Bentley's absence, working hard to complete the work quickly and to a high standard as he thought about owning his very own shop.

These thoughts stayed with him right up until his head hit the pillow. He'd avoided Sarah and Mr Bentley by hiding away, insisting he had to get the work done. Sarah had left a plate of food for him to eat. Mr Bentley barely took any notice, having enjoyed a day out spending the hard-earned money made by Sarah and Jonah on lavish and unnecessary items.

New shoes, fancy pocket watches and rich dishes shared with classy businessmen and frivolous women, much to Jonah's annoyance.

II

The next morning woke early, the sun streaming dimly through the dusty window, the sky a light pink colour. But he was more awake than he'd ever been. For the first time in ages, he was excited and looking forward to the day ahead.

Today was a day of potential, one that could change his life forever, one that meant he would be the owner of his very own shop. He imagined it: the luxury, the life he'd be able to afford, one so far away from the dingy rooms he'd lived in, even dating back to when his father was alive, he had vague memories of small dusty rooms that were half-filled with donated items.

A shop of his own meant wealth; he wouldn't be the slave in the shadows, he'd be the king parading around, paying out for the most expensive meals, clothes, jewellery, and treating pretty women to the luxuries they desired.

It was these thoughts that filled his heart. The idea of a lavish life convinced him that he was becoming somebody, a name that people would remember, and he could truly build a life worth living. It was a refreshing feeling that lifted his spirits, one that lifted him from his bed despite the early hour.

He happily washed and changed into his suit; a suit that had made him so confident, he felt like he could conquer the world in it. The difference in appearance had always confused Jonah, but today he saw it as a blessing, one that may impress and lead to a future he'd never anticipated.

Once dressed, Jonah crept quietly to the back room, continuing to work on the ever-demanding requests for alterations and dress designs.

Those peaceful hours passed by quickly as he thoughtfully processed each stitch.

At midday, Sarah brought in a sandwich for him. He smiled happily at her as he willingly took the food, stretching his fingers as he did so. He'd been working non-stop, and they were cramping up.

'Thanks, Sarah, you're a good one,' he said, taking a bite.

She looked at him with a small smile. 'No problem, Jonah. I just thought you'd be hungry. I heard you get up early.'

Jonah swallowed a big chunk of his sandwich and coughed as it marginally stuck in his throat. 'Right, yes, I was, I couldn't sleep. Sorry if I woke you, and just to let you know, I'm not here this evening. I let the cook know this morning,' he said with a rasp.

Sarah furrowed her brow. 'What do you mean? Why won't you be joining us?' she asked inquisitively. Jonah never missed an evening meal, and this confused her and aroused many questions as to what he could be up to in the evening.

He smiled at her response, the excitement bubbling inside him. He desperately wanted to tell her, but he didn't want to share something so exciting when it wasn't definite.

'Sarah, please don't pry. I've got a meeting of sorts with a friend, but please don't make a huge thing of it. I've just got to be somewhere,' he said softly.

Sarah looked at him with a glare. 'Fine,' she retorted, before turning and slamming the door behind her as she walked back to the shop.

Jonah sighed, dropping his sandwich as he returned to his work, a heavy pit surging into his stomach.

The afternoon slowed dramatically as he anticipated the evening's events, whilst also feeling the icy chill from Sarah, who was thumping around outside. He knew she would be giving him the cold shoulder for days following their exchange.

He stayed quietly in the room working until his meeting. He decided he'd keep a low profile and try to sneak out when everything seemed quiet.

Creeping to the door, Jonah turned the handle, hearing the small click, and, drawing the door towards himself, he popped his head around the frame It was all clear, so he tiptoed quietly through the parlour room, through the kitchen passage and out of the kitchen door. He was lucky enough not to meet anyone as his shoes clapped against the cold hard flags that wound to a small back gate.

He hadn't spent much time in the garden. He regretted this, as it was a grand place filled with trees and flowerbeds, and even a couple of benches were placed around the yard for when the weather was nice. The gate was tall and made of thick iron that was painted black with touches of gold for unknown elegance.

Jonah turned the handle, and it creaked loudly. He paused, glancing around before heading out.

With great care, he shut the gate and turned down the road, quickening his pace as he walked towards the Cook residence. He was walking with a bounce and a big smile on his face as he twisted and turned down the winding streets of Birmingham.

Marble Street was a good walk away, but was known for the big, bolstering of houses and was where all the rich folks lived. Jonah was taken aback by the sheer size of the houses. It was a large row of estates that rose tall. Large pillars and long gardens complemented the houses, which were pristine clean.

Locating number 53 was easy enough, and just like the others, it was dauntingly tall and beautifully built. The garden was filled with vibrant coloured flowers that led up to the long black door that had a thick knocker engraved with swirling patterns.

Nervously, he reached up and grasped the metal, it was cold to the touch and heavy. He lifted it and knocked three times. It echoed loudly and rang throughout the house. Within a few seconds, the door was flung open by a short, bald man in a smart suit and white gloves.

He looked Jonah in the eye. 'Yes?' he asked inquiringly.

'I have a meeting with Mrs Cook. She is expecting me,' he replied with a smile.

The butler nodded and beckoned for Jonah to enter, sweeping his arm and directing him into the main hall.

It was magnificent. A large open room lay before him; chairs, tables, flowers and mirrors were placed all around the room. Underneath the expensive pieces was a thick wine-red rug that had golden thread woven throughout. In front of him were two oval staircases that led to the landing space and presumably an extensive array of rooms.

Jonah's jaw flopped open in awe as Mrs Cook came into view, laughing at his face.

He smiled, looking at her. 'Your home is outstanding, I can't compliment it enough,' he said breathlessly.

'Oh, you! So silly, but thank you. Now, come this way. We're going to have tea in the parlour room, and we'll discuss some more about you becoming an independent tailor, equipped with the most desirable shop in the entire city,' she said, beaming at him and pointing to a doorway just to the left of him.

He nodded and took a deep breath as he turned and walked towards the room, pushing the door open and entering. Mrs Cook followed him.

He entered with his head still turned to Mrs Cook, who was beaming at him, her eyes wide with excitement. He smiled nervously as he turned into the room, taking in all the grand features.

The room was unbelievable, and the ceiling was so high that he had to crane his neck to see that it was delicately painted with swirling flowers, in big, bright colours. The room itself was mesmerising; it was elegant and pretty, just as he had expected.

It was painted a dusty pink colour, with lavish paintings fitted with golden frames. The floor was covered with a thick carpet that his feet immediately sank into. In the centre of the room was a display of velvet sofas with arching backs, complemented by two large and comfortable-looking armchairs in a deep red colour.

A long, low oak table lay in the centre, fully loaded with a selection of cakes, plates and a silver tea set. It was enticing, and Jonah was looking at it with a mouth-watering gaze as his stomach rumbled. He hadn't had a morsel since the solitary bite of his discarded sandwich.

As he looked in awe, a swift movement caught his eye, and he looked up to see a fireplace that levelled his eye line. It was huge, with black grates covering the small flames of the fire. The fireplace was carved with dainty flowers.

A massive painting of Mrs Cook and a thin man with slick black hair and a big bushy moustache were glaring down at him. He was in a fine black suit like Mr Bentley's, and he was pulling at the lapel, his muscles bulging. Mrs Cook looked younger, thinner, but with the same cheeky smile and rosy red cheeks. In the painting, she had a white flowing dress with purple ribbon entwining throughout the gown.

He smiled at the painting and turned to see Mrs Cook, who returned his smile and sneakily poked her finger to the fireplace. He frowned, before turning his gaze. In awe of the room, he had failed to see a small man glaring at him; he was half-hidden behind a large drooping plant, and his short stature made him difficult to see.

It was the man from the painting, but he looked very different: he was shorter, less stocky and his hair was thinning and turning grey. His moustache was bristle, but still thick, and it was hiding his pursed mouth.

Jonah smiled and breathed deeply as he brushed his jacket, trying to iron out any creases. He nodded and reached his hand out. 'Good evening, sir, I apologise. I didn't quite see you there,' he said with a small smile.

'Why, because I'm short?' he aggressively said in a high-pitched voice.

Weirdly, the voice didn't match him, and that puzzled Jonah, who momentarily frowned and opened his mouth to speak. Before he could, Mrs Cook stepped in and said with a small laugh, 'Don't be silly, Charlie, he was merely admiring the room.'

'Yes, that's it, sir, I wasn't referring to your height. I simply meant the room... I've never seen anything so magnificent,' he nervously responded, adjusting his voice to sound a little classier.

Mr Cook snorted in dispute and continued to stare at Jonah with a fierce glare. Mrs Cook giggled. 'Come now, boys, let's sit and have some tea and cake, and then we'll talk business, shall we?' she said chipperly as she began ushering them both to sit down.

Jonah was forced to sit on the large sofa and was quickly followed by Mrs Cook, who sat very close by. Mr Cook decided to sit in one of the armchairs that fitted his posture, allowing him to sit tall and high above them, while Jonah sank deep into the sofa, perched forward with his elbows resting inelegantly on his knees.

Mrs Cook leaned forward, pouring the tea, as Jonah's eyes darted between awkwardly staring at Mr Cook's glare and around the room. The tea was poured quickly, and the fine china, was passed around, the cake cut, and each person had a plate resting on their knees. Mrs Cook tucked in, eagerly eating, whilst the men just let it sit there.

Between gulps, Mrs Cook kept looking and smiling at the pair of them, giddy at the meeting. Finally, she swallowed the last piece, smacked her lips loudly and drank deeply from her cup.

'You two haven't eaten or drunk a thing.' She looked at the pair of them.

Both men shrugged and mumbled about not being hungry, and she sighed and rolled her eyes at their behaviour.

'Well, suit yourselves. I guess we'll just get down to business, shall we?' She raised her eyebrows at her husband.

He matched her gaze and moved forward, angling his body towards Jonah.

Just as he was about to speak, his wife interjected, 'So, Jonah here is the most fabulous tailor in town. I've bought many finely stitched items from him, he's fully trained, and with the right backing he could be the owner of a thriving shop; but of course, he needs capital. Talent isn't always paid; you've witnessed that before now, Charlie.'

Unamused, Mr Cook responded, 'Yes, Margaret, I'm well aware of the many gowns this man has made you; they have been somewhat impressive, but what I want to know is why I should do this: why should I spend my hard-earned money on you?'

Jonah gulped. 'Well, sir, I'm a hard worker, always have been, and to be honest, sir, I just want my life to be more. I want something that I can be proud of and to feel successful at something.

'My father was a hard-working man, but he didn't have a career as he wanted, he didn't have the opportunity, and if there's a glimmer of hope for something, then, sir, I will do anything, absolutely anything to prove to you why I deserve this,' he said breathlessly.

Mr Cook raised his eyes in curiosity and hummed gently. 'An honest answer, I appreciate that. Can I ask what your parents did? I know a little about you: you're from Manchester, you trained as an apprentice, and you're very good at getting women to buy the clothes you make. Why is that?' he asked.

'Well, it's a long story, but here goes,' he said with a small smile at Mrs Cook. For the next hour, he talked happily about his mother and her sewing skills and then about his father, the strong work ethic and untimely death. He even went on to explain his ancestors, his German descent and his grandfather's choice to abandon a life of riches for love.

Over that time, Mrs Cook chipped in with giggles and gasps, touching his arm, as he spoke of his parents' deaths, and she continuously turned to her husband with sympathetic eyes. When Jonah had finished, he looked at them both with a soft smile.

'I must say, Jonah, you've got a unique story, a sad one also. You come from a land of riches without an ounce of gold, but your family has chosen love over riches many times. I can't decide whether that's good or bad; heart over head, can lead to unfortunate events, and your life is proof of that,' Mr Cook said, gently nodding.

As silence fell, Jonah bowed his head. Mrs Cook looked at her husband and went to speak, but Mr Cook waved his hand, silencing her.

'I need to think about this. While your heritage says one thing, your working life says another, and I'm conflicted about this. Give me time, and I shall give you an answer,' he continued thoughtfully, before standing up and returning his plate and cup to the table and then leaving the room.

The pair watched him leave, astonishment spread on both their faces. It wasn't a definite 'no', and there was still hope. As his face slowly faded away, Mrs Cook let out a squeak and clasped her hands together in excitement.

'He didn't say no,' she said excitedly. 'Oh, Jonah, he didn't say no! This is brilliant. I'm telling you, I can persuade him. You give me a few days, and you'll be the proud owner of your own store in no time!' she squeaked, grabbing at his arm and shaking him.

He chuckled deeply and let out a long breath. Mrs Cook smiled, leaning forward to pour a fresh cup of tea for both of them; then she took his still-full cup and returned it to the table, putting another piece of cake next to his uneaten one.

'Eat! You must be starving. I've had the cook make up some sandwiches which you can take with you when you leave, but for now, sit, relax and enjoy,' she said kindly.

Together they sat, giddy at the meeting, and ate the delicious cake and drank the sweet tea that Jonah was so desperately craving. As promised, Mrs Cook had a pile of sandwiches and a small flask made up for him to take.

It was a good job, too, as it was nearing ten o'clock when Jonah finally left, the sandwiches stowed away in his jacket and the flask he held as he briskly walked back to Mr Bentley's store.

He'd never been back so late, and no curfew had been given, so he was unsure whether he would be in trouble or not. He assumed Sarah wouldn't be best pleased, especially as he had no definitive answer as to whether he would have his own shop, so he felt obliged to keep it a secret.

Jonah smiled as he walked back through the dark streets; the wind tickled his face, and he pulled his collar up to shield himself from the chill. There was no one about, and it was an eerie setting, but the complete loneliness of it was peaceful. The few street lamps that had been lit danced in the night, paving the way to his borrowed home.

It felt like a much longer walk than before, but he persisted on. He knew the route now, and he could make it back easy enough. He walked with determination, mulling over the night's events, the unanswered questions, the hope that still lingered.

These thoughts absorbed him, and before he knew it, he was back at the wrought-iron gate that led to the back entrance of the tailors. He hadn't come across a single person on his journey, which was probably a good thing, considering Mr Bentley was a well-regarded man who was sure to be informed if his tailor was lurking around the streets at night.

Once again, he attempted to open the gate as silently as he could, very much aware that the night silence had fallen. Any noise would startle even the heaviest of sleepers, and shop owners were vigilant at night, as that's when thieves would strike.

With concentration, Jonah pushed the gate forward, shushing any creaking sounds as if that would end its noise. He made just enough room for him to squeeze through and left the gate partially open as he walked towards the back door. He clasped the handle firmly and pushed, but it wouldn't budge; it was locked. In all the excitement he'd failed to realise that the door would eventually be locked. He hadn't given a time when he would return, and they couldn't leave it open for fear of someone unwanted entering. He was stupid, and now stood outside in the cold, unsure what to do.

After a few moments of pondering and eyeing up one of the benches, a flicker of light caught his eye. It was coming from the kitchen and seemed to bob through the room before disappearing. Jonah was peering through the kitchen window in the hope of catching a glimpse of the bewildering light, when a small click sounded. Sarah opened the door gently and looked at Jonah with a stern expression as he smiled in relief. Stepping aside, Sarah beckoned him in with a nod of her head.

He was so grateful and was about to thank her when she raised her finger to her lip and pointed through the door. Mr Bentley must still be up. He nodded at her as she mouthed the word 'tomorrow' and pointed towards the stairs that led to the bedrooms.

At the top of the stairs, Sarah smiled and rubbed Jonah's arm, before returning to her room, while he tiptoed to his room. He entered, thankful that he wasn't to sleep on a cold, hard bench, but in his own bed that had moulded into his shape. Without a second thought, Jonah climbed into bed, placing the sandwiches and flask on his bedside cabinet.

Jonah was flummoxed. It had been one peculiar evening; he was nervous, excited and relieved. His eyes were drooping from exhaustion, and within moments he was sound asleep.

III

The morning glow of the rising sun streamed onto Jonah's face, waking him from a deep sleep. He was groggy and confused, half-remembering the previous night's events, which surfaced slowly, and he bolted upright.

He looked around the room and saw the sandwiches and flask given to him by Mrs Cook. Happiness absorbed him; his dreams were in sight, and he had every faith that Mrs Cook could persuade her husband to take a chance on him. A smile spread across his face as he reached for the sandwiches, and he bit into the stale bread with a crunch and chewed with glee on the rich ham filling.

In bed, he sat happily eating away and taking the occasional swig from the flask, which was filled with a sweet libation, one he had never tasted before, and he couldn't even describe it. Before he knew it, he'd drunk the entire thing and was sad that it had all gone so quickly, but he could still taste the nectar that filled him with joy.

It was a blissful moment, sitting in bed, a stomach filled with rich food and drink. Happiness coursed through him, but this feeling didn't last long as he heard a loud bang at his door.

'You up yet?' Sarah yelled through the wood.

He could hear the anticipation in her voice. She wanted to know where he had been and what he was doing. He sighed, knowing the storm that was to come.

'Yes, Sarah, I'm awake; give me one moment. I shall meet you in the kitchen,' he replied, deflated. The happiness washed away as he prepared himself for a trying day.

Clambering out of bed, he realised he had fallen asleep in his clothes and only had to put his shoes on, a simple task that meant he would be in the kitchen much sooner than he would have wished. With a shake of his body, he left his room and headed down the rickety staircase to where Sarah was leaning against the cupboards, her arms crossed and an inquisitive look on her face.

When she saw him, she stood up and rushed forward. Jonah held his hands up, ushering her backwards.

'Sarah, please, I know you want an explanation for last night, and I cannot thank you enough for your help, but I still cannot tell you anything, not right now, but soon I will, I promise,' he said pleadingly.

She sighed angrily. 'You cannot tell me? I'm supposed to be your friend, and yet you won't tell me?' With that, she turned on her heel and marched towards the shop.

Jonah dropped his head into his hands and groaned loudly; it was an impossible situation, and he was sure to feel her mood right up until he told her, and with no promise of when from Mrs Cook, he didn't know when he could confide in her.

A loud cough sounded and Jonah whipped his head around, his eyes landing on Mr Bentley. He had just finished up breakfast, a hearty one full of fatty foods by the look of the stains on his napkin.

He was staring at Jonah smiling widely, a twinkle in his eyes. 'Don't you worry about her, Jonah, she'll get over whatever you're arguing about. I presume it was about last night. You know there are better things to spend your money on,' he said, laughing.

Jonah looked at him, shocked, and tried to protest at what Mr Bentley was saying, but he merely waved the remarks away, continuing to laugh as he sauntered out of the back door. Jonah rolled his eyes. Mr Bentley thought he had been with a woman of the night! While a hideous thought, as the day moved on, he came to realise it was a blessing — at least he didn't suspect anything.

IV

The days that followed were tense ones, with Sarah giving him the cold shoulder and dead silence from Mrs Cook; she hadn't even been into the shop, which was strange for her.

Jonah was starting to get worried. His only friend was angry at him to the point of not speaking, which made the days and evenings exceptionally hard.

On top of that, he was hiding a secret that had no forthcoming answers, yet he dared not divulge anything in case Sarah, in spite, told Mr Bentley of the proposed plan. At best, he would be scrutinised and would lose trust from his employer; at worst, he would be turfed-out onto the street, destined to live a penniless and impoverished life.

The situation was stressful and agonising. The if's and but's, the lack of knowing was driving him insane. He'd wake up full of hope and by midday that would be destroyed, thinking it would never happen.

As a distraction, he threw himself into his work, locking himself away and completing orders faster than he ever did before.

By day five of complete silence and solitude, he was losing it. Had he come so close again for it to be ripped away so suddenly? He couldn't be sure.

When he awoke on the sixth day, hope had become a translucent feeling, and he was numb and exhausted as his brain anticipated the news while his body was drained from fractured sleep and hard work.

He set about the motions, getting ready and steadily making his way to his work. He'd taken to grabbing a dry roll for breakfast and reluctantly leaving. Mr Bentley had queried him on this, but he made a feeble excuse about the piling workload. Sarah, as usual, ignored his greetings, turning her head sharply whenever he dared speak to her.

The saddest part was that he knew he could fix the situation with a few simple words, but he feared that it would somehow jinx it, even now, when hope seemed to be at its weakest. With that, he retreated to the small room, setting about finishing a half-sewn dress.

It was a tricky one that he'd been putting off. The lady had demanded a style relatively new from France, and it required very unique stitching and styling, one he'd never seen the likes of before. By late afternoon he was on the verge of giving up and had slapped his face into his hands, grumbling away about his misfortune, when a sharp rap at the door made him jump.

He jerked his head in confusion as he watched the handle slowly move downwards, the door was drawn, and Sarah stood there, looking unimpressed.

'Mrs Cook is here to see you. She wants to talk to you about a new dress style she's seen,' she said icily.

Slightly dazed Jonah stood up and haphazardly walked towards the front of the shop. Mrs Cook was standing there, rosy-cheeked and gleaming in an emerald green dress.

Sarah had sauntered in behind him, watching their interaction closely.

Mrs Cook looked at him with a devilish smile and handed over a piece of parchment. 'I've seen this, and I want it,' she said gleefully. 'You'll be able to make it, won't you?'

Jonah unfolded the parchment, half-expecting to see an image of a new style, while wondering whether it had all been but a dream. Opening it gently, he saw writing: it was a note, inviting him to the Cooks' house, tomorrow evening. Nothing else was given, but Mrs Cook was brimming with excitement. Surely it was good news for her to react like that.

Dumbfounded, he looked around the shop, taking particular notice of Sarah, before responding thoughtfully, 'I think I can. I need time to figure this out, but I'm certain I can make it,' he said slyly.

With a squeal, Mrs Cook clapped her hands together and exclaimed, 'Good! I've wanted this for a while, and I'm glad to have such an eager tailor onboard. I shall be seeing you soon, and, hopefully, I'll get what I want through your talent.'

She winked at him as they spoke about mundane matters that meant so much more to one another.

Beaming, she turned and left the shop, leaving Jonah in the middle, clasping the note as the reality sank in. He still had a chance, despite the anxious days that had just passed — he still had a chance!

The rest of the day breezed by as Jonah fantasised about owning his very own tailor shop. He idly stitched away, bringing sheets of fabric together to create wonders that would grace the fine people of Birmingham.

He hummed as he did so, much to the annoyance of Sarah, who was furiously curious. That evening, Jonah stowed himself away in the back room, choosing to have a sandwich while he continued his work; it was practice for when he had his own place.

As usual, he worked deep into the night, before retiring to his room, where he slept peacefully, awaiting the next evening, when he would hear his fate.

V

The next morning, he woke up excited. Again, he let Sarah know he wouldn't be home that evening as he had errands to run. She simply shrugged, ignoring him. It affected him more than it should, but he still couldn't bring himself to tell her — there was too much at risk.

So, he decided to ignore her. She would be yet another woman on his list to distrust, and it was a heart-breaking notion, for he loved her dearly; she was both an adopted sister and friend, but her behaviour was destroying him.

Sadly, he sneaked away into his now-claimed office, for he was the only one using the room these days. Every order was being crafted by his own hand, and while the commission was good, he'd much rather have a space of his own and be running his place.

It was a glum day, despite the much-awaited meeting, and he worked in silence, venturing out to get a lump of stale bread that had been left behind. It reminded him of his days back at the mill, scraping by and hating what little he had.

By the time it came to meeting Mrs Cook, he was drained and left in silence. He'd worked himself up to misery and walked with heavy steps. The bounce that had presented itself in the first visit had all but disappeared, and he walked in silence, with the setting sun behind him.

His second arrival was as glamorous as the first. The house was big, the garden glorious, even in the night sky. Its presence excited him a little; while he may have lost a friend, he had the potential to live a new life. That, in his eyes, was enough: he would be rich, he would be powerful, he would be known, and as that slowly sank in, he realised that a friend was worthless in comparison.

He smiled as he concluded this: friends were pointless when an entirely new life lay ahead of him. He'd left before and started again. It was a new adventure in which he would grow and be better.

Walking up the path to the Cooks' residence, his smile and joy returned, the bounce in his step appeared, and he knocked with hope once again settled in his heart.

It rang throughout the house, and within seconds the butler was opening the door and beckoning him in, directing him towards the sitting room where he'd previously been.

He smiled as he entered, still looking around in awe, once again glancing at the exaggerated painting of Mr and Mrs Cook, before finally settling his gaze on Mr Cook. He was in the same position as the previous meeting, puffing away on a pipe and holding a nonchalant gaze.

He nodded towards Jonah, who nodded back, smiling, before awkwardly placing his hands on the back of the elongated couch, rocking backwards and forwards on his heels, awaiting the bubbly appearance of Mrs Cook.

The minutes ticked by, and Jonah painfully continued, before he broke the silence. 'So, Mrs Cook, when will she arrive?' His voice rose in pitch as he spoke.

Mr Cook smiled cunningly. 'She'll be here in a while, but first I would like to talk to you. I've reviewed my wife's proposal, and I'm interested, but I'm not fully convinced. I have a plan, one which requires a deposit of sorts.'

He stopped, with an eyebrow raised, looking at Jonah's response. He, too, was staring blankly, trying not to show weakness.

Again, Mr Cook smiled, before continuing, 'I want insurance. I want you dedicated and invested in this, and for me to achieve this, I need you to be forthcoming. I want at least £50, and let me tell you, I won't be putting a single penny down without a down payment. Do I make myself clear?' he said sharply.

Jonah thought and nodded apprehensively. 'That's fair. I can't expect you to fund my dream on your earnings. I'd say I have about £40 stored away. I save practically every penny and commission earned. I don't think it will take long before I get enough for fifty,' he said slowly.

Mr Cook looked at him curiously. 'You have that much already?' he asked, shocked.

Jonah chuckled and said, 'Mr Bentley pays a fair commission, and over the past few months I've been creating nearly every garment; that plus the small wage mounts up over time.'

'Commission must be high if you can afford that already, but I suppose tailors must earn a fair few bob, if most women are like my wife and are consumed with clothes; you'll be in demand. Of course, Mr Bentley's is the highest-regarded shop in town. People far and wide come for his unique clothes, even though I have had bits and pieces. Actually, I have a wonderful necktie that I frequently wear,' he said, thinking out loud.

Silence fell as both men thought. Jonah was contemplating giving up his entire savings; it was a lot to give, but he'd get so much more in return. Earning the remaining ten wouldn't be hard; he had a few jobs that would bring him the money he was missing. He presumed he'd be living above the shop he owned, which wouldn't be the same as holding his own like he was saving for, but it would be comfortable and practical.

After some time had elapsed, Jonah cleared his throat, and Mr Cook turned his head slightly as he was brought out of his haze.

They stared at each other momentarily, before Jonah spoke with confidence. 'How would this work, sir? Would you be taking a commission, would it be my place? When will this happen?' He was trying to air out the details, ensuring he was getting exactly what he wanted.

Mr Cook smiled. 'Thinking like a businessman,' he said. 'I like that!

'Well,' he continued, 'Margaret has had some input on this matter — she'd be better off ruling the courts, she has as much force around here,' he said with a small chuckle. 'She wants you to have full rein — owner, master, lead tailor — which is fine by me, but I want to handle the books. I have experience in that. Now, she wants me to teach you this. I will eventually, but the first few years I want you settled. With my wife's browbeating, I think we can make a profit in the first year. I'll be taking a sixty percent cut, which will cover the shop and purchases for running the place,' he said in a strong voice.

Jonah sat there thinking. It was a significant amount he would be taking, but a far superior amount to what he was currently on; plus, he would be free of a boss of sorts, and he could run the place how he deemed it.

Looking Mr Cook directly in the eyes, he said fiercely, 'I'm in.'

With a raised eyebrow, he smiled, leaned forward and grasped Jonah's hand firmly, shaking as he did so, confirming the deal.

'Good man,' he said. 'I'll get the papers drawn up, confirming our deal, and I have a holding of sorts a few streets down from yours on Maple Street. I've had it for some time — an aunt of mine left it to me. She, ironically, used to own a fabric store, just odd and ends that worker-women could turn into make-shift dresses. Anyway, she left that to me. I've rented it out on occasion, but nothing lasted longer than a year or so; but it'd be the perfect place for a tailor and it's close to the competition,' he said with a smug smile.

Jonah looked at him in shock. It wouldn't take long at all for him to be his own boss, and a huge smile spread across his face as he happily said to Mr Cook, 'Tomorrow I shall bring what money I have and return the forthcoming days with whatever I earn. I promise you that, and I shall continue to bring you what I earn each day,' Jonah said excitedly.

Mr Cook chuckled in response. 'I think that's wise. I won't commit unless I see something in return. I reckon once you have the money, you'll be in within a month or two. Now, I'm going to leave you. I have a feeling my wife is lurking on the other side of that door, wanting to know what's going on.'

He bowed his head as he marched to the door, swinging it open and coming face to face with his wife, who was beaming with excitement. Mr Cook rolled his eyes as he stood aside to let her in, before walking through and leaving his wife and Jonah together.

She rushed forward, grasping Jonah's hands and shaking them. 'So, is it good news, because you don't look sad?' she said happily.

Jonah smiled and nodded back. 'It is,' he said apprehensively. 'I just have to put down a payment of £50. Now, I have most of it, but I'm about ten short, so that will take some time to earn. I've been saving for months, for a house, I think. I didn't have a plan, just a sack of money,' he finished a little breathlessly.

'Is that it?' she said, shocked. 'Well, I'll give you that, don't you worry. Give it a couple of weeks and make up some excuses and pay him. This is going to work, trust me,' she said, smiling and still squeezing his hands.

His eyes widened in shock. His natural reaction was to flinch away at the offer, but he was tangibly close to a new life, that he didn't.

Instead, he pictured himself running the shop, welcoming the stream of customers and becoming the leading and most desirable tailor in the entire town. With that money he wouldn't have to work himself to the ground, scraping together every penny and handing it over. He could give what he had and earn commission on the side, allowing him to enter the deal with money in his pockets.

As he dreamt, he felt Mrs Cook's hands upon his, and he smiled. 'You would do that for me?' he said softly.

'Of course I would, deary. I'll fetch my purse and give it right now, and in a week or so you can bring the full amount by and then we'll get it all sorted. The shop will be kept a secret while it's refurbished, and you can continue to work, earning some keep until you're the true owner of your shop,' she squeaked, before raising her finger to her lips and dashing out of the room.

Confused, Jonah watched her leave only for her to return moments later, clutching it closely to her chest as she tip-toed across the room. She gently lowered herself next to him and opened her purse, pulling out a note which was stamped with a large twenty. Jonah gulped, taking it and stuffing it quickly into his jacket pocket. He didn't even question the extra amount, but gladly welcomed it.

Together they sat, each breathing quietly as they contemplated the future. They were happy, and Jonah let this feeling sink in. His face was aching from the amount of smiling, but he couldn't help it. In awe, he stared around the room. Finally, he noticed the clock; it was almost nine o'clock at night.

'Oh my, it's late,' he said, shocked. 'I need to go, otherwise I'll be locked out again.'

Mrs Cook looked at the clock, equally as surprised at the time. She stood up quickly. 'Of course you must,' she said breathlessly. 'Mr Cook will be thinking we're up to no good,' she said with a chuckle.

She grasped his arm, leading him towards the door. Before he left, Mrs Cook handed him a small package; inside was a stack of sandwiches. He smiled. She was a good woman, he thought, and in that second, he pledged to make it up to her, to make her proud of everything he did from that moment on.

Returning back to his lodgings was an easy feat, for he knew it wouldn't be forever. The air tickled him as he leisurely strolled back, eating the sandwiches, which were filled with fine slices of cured ham.

In no time he was at the back gate, tugging at it and strolling through, failing to notice Mr Bentley on the bench beside the door until it was too late.

He froze in horror as their eyes met. Mr Bentley had a glass of brown liquid in one hand and was swirling it around, curiously looking at his apprentice.

Jonah's mouth flapped up and down, before Mr Bentley waved it away and beckoned him to take a seat on the bench. Sluggishly, he walked towards him and sat. Beads of sweat ran down his face, and he pulled at his collar nervously staring straight on, not daring to glance at his boss.

A chuckle rang loud, and Jonah turned suddenly to see Mr Bentley holding his sides, laughing. Jonah, slightly stunned, began laughing, too, quietly and confused.

Between breaths of air, Mr Bentley managed to spit out, 'Don't look so shocked.' He paused, laughing. 'Your face!' He slapped his knee as a tear rolled down his face. Jonah didn't have a clue what to do, so he simply sat watching the uncontrollable laughter.

With a few deep breaths, Mr Bentley composed himself enough to hold a conversation. 'Don't be so ashamed. Men have needs, I understand it. I presume you're having fun with one of the rich bats that enter the shop, or is it a maid?' he asked out of curiosity.

Again, Jonah pulled at his collar, and Mr Bentley smiled, patting his knee. 'Don't worry, boy,' he said, slapping at Jonah's chest, "it'll be our secret. I've noticed Sarah getting a bit touchy over it; you might want to watch that. She's not had a lot of men in her life, if you know what I mean.'

Nodding, Jonah mumbled a response as Mr Bentley reached down, pulling a glass and a bottle from under the bench. He poured a hearty amount and handed it over to Jonah.

'Come now,' he said sharply, 'we'll have a quiet drink and get ourselves to bed; dawn will soon be rising.'

With that, they sat and drank. It was strong, nutty and sharp, and Jonah had never tasted something so unwelcoming, but he drank it all the same. After a few sips, it went down a little easier, but it wasn't something he'd take up in a hurry.

Together, they silently sat until each had drained their glass. Mr Bentley handed his over to Jonah, and he grabbed the bottle, heading to the back door. He let himself in, said his 'good nights' and left towards his more comfortable room.

His feet thudded up the stairs, his body exhausted from the excitement as he crept down the corridor and into the room. In the dark, he undressed, but first stowed away the money from Mrs Cook, before lying on his bed and closing his eyes, falling into a deep and welcomed sleep.

VI

Three weeks had passed since the meeting with Mr Cook, and Jonah was impatiently continuing on with his duties. Methodically he would wake, grab food and stow away in his den, stitching long into the night.

In those three long weeks, he had stitched a dozen dresses, earning more than the ten pounds that he had promised Mr Cook. It was finally time to finalise the deal but every second of every day ticked by slowly as he mindlessly worked, his hands gliding through the material.

It was torture, knowing that he had the money but keeping it a secret to protect the generous donation from Mrs Cook. Sarah was continuing to freeze him out and Mr Bentley was barely around; he couldn't recall the last time he'd seen him.

Anger bubbled inside as he stormed from his den where he had been hiding all morning and into the shop, almost colliding head first into Sarah who frowned.

'I was just coming to get you,' she huffed. 'Mrs Cook is here to see you.' She nodded to the beaming lady, draped in a beautiful plum dress he had created for her.

Relief washed over his face as he smiled before pushing past Sarah and pulling Mrs Cook to the side.

'Mrs Cook,' he smiled. 'I was just thinking about you, I have that package that you wanted. The full amount.' He winked with a gleeful smile as she beamed at him.

'Good,' she replied breathlessly. 'That was the reason I came.' She paused, looking around him, her eyes lingering on Sarah who ducked her head in shame and scurried into the parlour.

Lowering her voice, Mrs Cook said quickly, 'Come tonight, six o'clock sharp, Mr Cook will be waiting for you.' With that she left, the chime of the bell echoing loudly.

Before Jonah could process anything Sarah was by his side, her arms crossed as she pinned him with a curious stare.

'I can't,' he sighed, the sadness rising in him as he scurried away, ignoring her crestfallen face as he stole away into his den. He was overwhelmed as he returned to the tiny office, the excitement coursing through him, yet time seemed to slow. It felt like every second was scraping against the glass.

His hands shook as he attempted to work — he'd stitched and unstitched the same part of the dress for the last hour. It was infuriating, but eventually, the bolting sounds of Sarah locking the shop sounded. Hurriedly, he began haphazardly putting his needles, thread and material away before dusting himself down and brushing his suit to look presentable.

After sprucing himself up, he confidently marched towards his quarters, making sure to pick the money up, before bouncing down the stairs and out the back door, his gleeful goodbyes ignored.

He wasn't even trying to be quiet or coy — he was far too excited — and he made good time when he reached the Cooks' residence. The doorbell rang loudly, and he was welcomed into their home and into the parlour room.

Awaiting his arrival was Mr Cook, who firmly shook his hand and navigated him to the chair.

'It's good to see you, boy. I was losing faith in you, but Margaret kept insisting you were good for the money, and I'm glad you returned. You're the talk of the town, and I think our little venture is going to be a right money-maker,' he said, pouring himself and Jonah a drink and toasting it.

Jonah gladly took the glass and clinked it, before taking a sip. It was the same tasting liquid that Mr Bentley had given him.

With a slight cough, he said, 'Thank you, sir. This is unreal, I can't believe it's happening.' He smiled as he reached into his pocket. 'Your money, sir.' He removed a small envelope from his pocket and handed it to him.

Mr Cook smiled and opened the envelope and carefully counted the money. He raised his eyebrows, smiled and nodded his head towards Jonah. 'You did it, young man; well done,' he said, raising his glass for a second time and draining the remainder of his drink.

He stood up and walked to a small desk drawer, removed some papers and returned to the table, laying them in front of Jonah and leaving a quill and inkpot next to them. Jonah frowned and leaned forward, touching the papers his eyes scanning the scripted words.

Reading and writing wasn't his strongest talent; he remembered his father trying to teach him as a child, and then his mother when he had died. He knew enough to get by and could read for the most part, but complex words he stumbled on, and he knew this paper would be littered with them.

'It's a formality, a binding contract, if you like. It simply outlines what we're doing, and the money each will be given, what you're entitled to; you understand, of course?' Mr Cook spoke in a soothing tone as he explained it to him.

Jonah pursed his lips and nodded his head. 'Formalities, right. I get that, I understand. I take it I sign here?' he asked, pointing at the bottom of the paper.

'Yes, there is fine. Just one moment, though. It's best to have someone present in these situations; my lawyer is just outside, and he'll supervise.' As he was finishing his sentence, the door opened and a man entered.

He was a tall man, taller than Jonah, and with even broader shoulders, too. He had a long face with a strong jawline and chiselled cheekbones. His eyes sank into his skull and they were a dark brown, verging on black colour, similar to his slick black hair that was neatly parted in the middle. He held a strong gaze and walked with dominance as he headed to Mr Cook, grasping his hand firmly. He turned to Jonah, taking his hand, too, crushing it and shaking it with strength.

He sat on the adjoining chair and waved his hands, indicating for them to continue. Jonah glanced at Mr Cook, who mimicked the lawyer's notion. Gulping, Jonah picked up the inked quill, his hand shaking as he signed his name.

Mr Cook walked to his side, taking the quill and re-dipping it in the ink, and signed just below his name. They did this for a further three papers, and with each one Mr Cook picked them up and blotted the ink, before handing it to the lawyer, who studied each one, before stowing them away in his leather-bound briefcase.

Once they had all been signed and securely locked away, the lawyer stood up, shook their hands once more and left without a word.

Jonah was confused. It was so quick, so easy, that he sat there just gazing, with his mouth slightly open.

'Is… is that it?' he asked with a stutter.

'That's it, Jonah, we're in business. Work starts tomorrow on the shop; we'll be up and running within three weeks, and you'll be at the helm. For now, we keep it a secret. We'll keep you informed, of course, but for now, you will stay where you are and then it all changes,' he said, breezing through the details.

A little stunned, Jonah stood up, and Mr Cook walked him towards the door opening and led him to the hall, where he handed Jonah some sandwiches and a flask, shook his hand once more and showed him out onto the street.

He breezed back to his lodgings, the night's events slowly setting in, and with each step it seemed to get even more real. He skipped, shouted out with glee and hopped through the streets as he happily made it home. Swinging the gate open, he walked to the door. Sarah opened it before he could turn the handle.

Her eye was twitching in anger, and she looked furious as she turned and marched up the stairs, utterly refusing to acknowledge his outlandish behaviour.

Giggling like a child, Jonah crept through the kitchen, up the stairs and down to his room, barely containing his glee.

VII

Waking up, knowing what he knew, was unbearable; he was excited but had no one to confide in. He was bursting with emotion, but containing it all. It carried him through the days, his smile constantly plastered upon his face, despite the long hours and lack of interaction from Sarah.

The days breezed by as he imagined his future, the riches it would bring him. He was desperate to tell his closest friend, to end the iciness, but was still so reluctant; her behaviour had left a horrible taste behind, and he wasn't sure he was ready to expose himself or even let her into his new life.

He'd been mulling over it, and a week or so had passed since the finalisation of the contract had been signed, when she threw the door open to his hidden workspace. He'd been stitching at the time and, in shock, stabbed the needle into his index finger, crying in pain as he did so.

She looked at him in surprise, before shutting the door and crouching down on the footstool by the unfinished dress.

'Have you heard the news?' she asked as Jonah sucked on his bleeding finger.

He looked at her unamused, his nostrils flaring, and he spoke through gritted teeth, 'Surprisingly not; there aren't a lot of people who talk to me — even the maids that come to the shop turn their noses up at me,' he replied coldly.

Sarah looked down shamefully, twiddling her thumbs, before quietly saying, 'Look, I know I've not been the best recently, but I was hurt, really hurt; but there's something that's happened that I need to tell you.'

Jonah didn't flinch; instead, he simply looked at her as he folded his arms, unamused.

With a downcast face, she looked at him. 'There's a new tailor shop opening a few streets down, not far from here. It's not known who owns it — the sign's covered with a sheet — but it looks fancy, fancier than here. Mr Bentley isn't happy; he looks worried,' she said, the excitement barely hidden in her tone.

Jonah's stomach dropped, and a bead of sweat ran down his face. He batted it away quickly, before composing himself. With confidence, he brushed her off. 'There's no proof it's a new tailor shop. Leave it for now. Let's not spread gossip; simply let it be and see what happens,' he said reassuringly.

Sarah nodded, before she responded gravely, 'That's true, and I do agree, but Mr Bentley wants to see both of us tonight. No excuses, we need to be there,' she said fiercely, before giving him a sweet smile and a pat on his shoulder before leaving.

Jonah spent the rest of the day on edge; he was scared and shaking, and he knew the outcome wouldn't be good, he knew something bad was to come, especially when Mr Bentley found out he would be the new owner, the new competition. It was an uneasy day, and he got barely any work done as he heard the restless Mr Bentley march throughout the house, random words echoing throughout the shop.

Time was passing fast, and Jonah was becoming increasingly nervous as he awaited his meeting with Mr Bentley.

It felt like moments had passed when Sarah gently knocked on his door. Poking her head around, she said timidly, 'It's time. Come now, he wants us in the dining room.'

Silently, they both walked to the dining room, their shoulders slumped. When they entered, Mr Bentley stood there glaring at the pair of them. He motioned for each of them to sit down so that they faced him.

'So, a new tailor is coming to town,' he said without expression. 'Competition has come.'

He spoke softly as he paced up and down, glancing at his employees, who followed his movements, listening to him talk.

Without warning, Mr Bentley threw a glass at the wall, startling the pair, who jumped.

'This is a disgrace!' he shouted. 'Somebody is sneaking in, stealing my money, and they don't have the good manners to come forward and claim it as their own. What do you two know?' He slammed his fists down on the table, which shook under his weight, as he glared at them.

Sarah shrieked and said nothing. Jonah opened his mouth, but no words came; he didn't dare to speak up and face Mr Bentley's anger. Furiously, Mr Bentley launched another glass at the wall, before turning and marching off, screaming insults as he did so.

Both Sarah and Jonah let out deep sighs, each one shaking slightly. They sat for a few moments, breathing heavily, before Sarah stood up, wiping tears from her eyes, and headed to her room without a word.

Jonah sat there, quietly contemplating his next move. He stayed there all night, trying to think of how he could break the news to Mr Bentley without receiving a hiding or being booted out of his quarters before his place was ready.

The days that followed continued in the same manner, with aggression and hostility in the air.

He was awaiting his time, thinking of when to tell Mr Bentley, but that day never came. The happiness of reuniting with Sarah had been the shining light on such a hateful and angry atmosphere.

Everything was happening so fast, and the move was less than a few days away. He was sitting down for his evening meal with Sarah; their rekindled friendship had gone unnoticed by Mr Bentley, who was spending even less time at the shop, constantly out, digging for information on the new tailor shop and the new owner.

That night they went to bed early, both nervous for the return of the unpredictable Mr Bentley. It was late when Jonah was woken up by a loud crash followed by thunderous steps heading towards his room.

He was groggy and confused when the door swung open, revealing a rabid Mr Bentley, who grabbed him by the scruff of his neck and hurled him down the hallway. Sarah appeared at her door, pulling her dressing coat on, when Jonah landed at her feet. She gasped and bent down to help him up, when a large leather shoe hit him in the stomach.

She squealed and jumped back as Mr Bentley grabbed hold of his hair and lifted him upwards.

'You!' he spat venomously. 'After everything I've done for you! I've taught you, fed you, housed you — and this is how you repay me?' The vein in his head was throbbing as he pinned his face against Jonah's, who was panting in horror.

Sarah grabbed on to Mr Bentley's arm and tried to prise it away. He sniggered at her feeble attempts, before striking her hard. She slammed into the door and sank to the ground.

He hit Jonah's head on the wall. 'Get out, the pair of you!' he said through gritted teeth. He released Jonah and stomped down the stairs.

Terrified, Jonah helped Sarah up. 'We have to go now,' he said urgently. 'Grab whatever possessions you can, but be quick.' He looked towards the stairs, before creeping back to his room, grabbing his stash of money and hastily changing into his suit.

He glanced at his pitiful room, before heading toward Sarah's room. She stood numb as she realised the unexpected loss. Without hesitation, Jonah entered her small room. Her dress was hanging perfectly, and just below was a small bag. He grabbed it and shoved everything he could see in the room into it, before he dragged her down the stairs in her slippers and out the back door.

Thankfully, Mr Bentley was nowhere to be seen as Jonah half-carried Sarah out onto the chilly streets of Birmingham. He was tired and scared, but he knew where he was going. Mrs Cook would take them in for the time being, and with that, he made his way there, Sarah in tow as she staggered along.

The Watcher

Well, dear reader, there you have it. Greed had come, offering with it riches, gold and a frivolous lifestyle that Jonah had only ever heard about.

He'd seen and watched how Mr Bentley had lived; he absorbed his greedy lifestyle and betrayed the man that had given him everything.

For now, dear reader, it looks like Jonah is winning: he has his own business, a new home and a new life waiting; but everyone knows, greed is the destroyer.

Sadly, dear reader, this is just the beginning of more pain and heartache. Despite his beliefs, needs and wants, Jonah isn't ready or prepared, but I shan't say any more. This is his story, and the good parts or bad — however you view it — are only just beginning.

Pride

The night at the Cooks' was a turbulent one. It had started with Jonah waking the entire household. Mr Cook had been less than pleased, whilst Mrs Cook had gone into a frenzy, running after them both, having a bed made and a fire lit to warm them up.

Sarah had yet to speak a word as she timidly sat by the fire, her palms raised as if to keep the cold at bay. Jonah had retold the tale, showing off bruises and scratches that Mr Bentley had bestowed on him.

He was relieved when Mrs Cook said she would house the pair of them until the shop was entirely refurbished. Even Mr Cook agreed; the white face of Sarah, painstakingly stunned by the night's events, opened his eyes to the harsh lives the poor endured.

After sitting for a while, the pair were led through a narrow corridor and into the servants' quarters. Two rooms had been set aside, made up and had gentle fires warming the rooms. Together, they got Sarah to bed, and she immediately lay there, weeping into her pillow. The frail, dainty nature of her hurt Jonah and anger bubbled up inside him.

Now it was his time to destroy Mr Bentley, to beat him and then break him by becoming the most desirable tailor in town. When he finally lay down in his bed, he was fuming, and the anger seared through his body.

He had a restless night, tossing and turning until first light dawned, which is when he gave up. Angrily he whipped the cover off his body and quickly pulled his wrinkled clothes on,before stepping out into the cold hallway. It was clean, and the floors didn't creak. The hall was lined with doors one after another on either side, which ended at a door directly to his left, which separated the men from the women. This was a luxurious home, filled with multiple servants who were dedicated to individual tasks.

To the left of the door was another hallway that led through to the kitchen and on into the main house. He was tired, groggy and confused on where to go or what to do. The corridor in which he stood was empty and silent.

He stood, half-turned to the room he had left, and half-turned towards the stairway to the kitchen. Rubbing his face, he cleared the sleep from his eyes and slowly staggered forward, his bones aching from the aftermath of Mr Bentley's beating.

With a slight limp, he made it to the bustling kitchen that was filled with smartly dressed maids, and he spotted the butler who had welcomed him into the Cooks' house so many times. Everyone was in such a hurry that nobody took any notice of him. He slowly shuffled forward and was graciously welcomed by a bright-faced, plump woman in a long apron. She had thick curly brown hair that was untidily stuffed under a tight cap.

'There you are,' she said with a warm smile. She had a few teeth missing, and her face was bright red from the heat, while her blue eyes sparkled with her smile. 'We've been wondering what's been keeping you. Take a seat and I'll get you some breakfast,' she said cheerily, pointing towards a long wooden table at the far end of the room.

He moved through the people, taking in the vast size of the kitchen. It was a fine place, with delicious smells from the gleaming pots that were overflowing with food.

A large work station was in the middle of the room, where many young girls were working large dough balls for bread, mixing various concoctions and chopping up ingredients. He walked past them, giving them a slight smile, which caused them to blush and giggle.

Finally he reached the table, it was basic, but long and wide enough to seat all the servants. To his surprise, he found Sarah sitting there, holding a small cup in her hand, the look of shock now entwined with lack of sleep still present on her face.

'Sarah,' he said breathlessly, 'how are you?'

She looked up at him and shrugged her shoulders, her feeble frame showing a ghost of her true emotions. Jonah sat opposite her and took her hand, squeezing it gently, as a serving girl placed a plate of meat and eggs in front of him.

He looked down, his stomach grumbling in pain as he saw the fresh meal in front of him. He immediately dropped Sarah's hand and ravenously began eating, overloading his spoon and shovelling the food into his mouth. Spoon after spoon he ate, barely chewing his food, when Mrs Cook walked into the kitchen. Everyone froze and began addressing the lady of the house with proper callings.

Jonah, still chewing his food, stood up abruptly and smiled, waiting for her to speak.

'Hello, hello, everyone, I hope you are all well. I'm just stopping by to see how my guests are doing,' she said sweetly.

'We're fine,' Jonah smiled, his eyes casting over Sarah worriedly.

Mrs Cook laughed nervously, 'Of course you are dears, she paused. 'I've actually got a bit of good news, come meet me at the front.'

She smiled and retreated back into the house, giving a fleeting smile to Jonah and her employees.

Jonah swiftly moved around the table, grabbing Sarah by her elbow and lifting her up and shaking her. She looked at him in shock, her eyes meeting his, and reading the sadness within them.

Although confused, Sarah trusted Jonah and walked with him to the front door, where she stood and stared at his face while they waited for Mrs Cook, who took her time in putting the finishing touches to her outfit, which included a large feathered hat and a long draping coat with a fur lining.

She tottered along, looking at the both of them with a smile as she pulled white silk gloves onto her hands. She never said anything, but simply walked with both in tow. It was only when Jonah realised that they were heading towards Mr Bentley's shop that Jonah got nervous and quietly skipped to Mrs Cook's side, leaving Sarah tottering behind.

'Mrs Cook,' Jonah said nervously, 'where is it we're going?'

She looked at him and patted him gently, before leaning in and smiling. 'Taking you to your new place, silly,' she whispered.

Jonah smiled, his grin extending to his ears as he dropped his pace to that of Sarah's as he stepped in line with her. He walked with a bounce, placing his hand on her back and pushing her slightly forward.

They walked for a short while, before Jonah stopped and turned towards a small shop.

'What's this?' Sarah said, as she wiped her snotty nose on her sleeve. She had been gently crying as they walked down the familiar route, barely taking notice of what was happening. She stood, dumfounded, looking at Jonah's gleeful face.

'My shop,' he exclaimed excitedly.

Before she could open her mouth, Jonah continued in a rush, 'Don't worry, you're more than welcome to work here with a roof above your head and decent pay.'

Sarah's mouth dropped open as she daintily moved to the front of the shop, placing her hand on the wooden door frame as she gazed up towards the half-covered sign, on which she could just about read the end of Jonah's last name.

Suddenly, an awestruck smile spread across her face as she gasped and began to laugh hysterically.

Jonah returned her smile and said, 'Stick with me, Sarah, and we'll become the best tailors in Birmingham, and Mr Bentley will be a distant memory to those who relied on him.'

Mrs Cook marched past them both, pushing the door open and stepping aside, motioning Jonah to take the lead, which he happily did. He marched forward, pulling Sarah with him.

Mrs Cook followed, and began showing the place off, detailing what each area would be. The door through which they entered would be the front of the shop that would house the fabric and sewing essentials and would ultimately be Sarah's domain. It was painted a bright white colour that made the front store look twice the size.

Behind the fittings of the wooden countertops was a wide opening which could fit Sarah, Jonah and Mrs Cook with ease. It led to the back end of the shop.

Mobile partitions were laid against the soft lilac walls, ready to be placed around the back room for fittings. At the far end of the wall was a measuring table and three life-size dolls that were neatly lined up in front of the unlit fireplace, whilst a soft velvet couch lay in the middle of the room, encouraging customers to sit, talk and buy.

It was vast and far more sophisticated than either of them had ever seen. They stayed and admired in awe all the small details that finished the room.

Eventually, Mrs Cook broke the silence with a small cough, drawing their eyes from the room and to a small corridor that led into the kitchen, similar to Mr Bentley's back room. It was much smaller and was fitted with only the essentials, which included a sink, cooking station and a fireplace and oven combination. There was no dining area, just a simple table with a couple of chairs.

Jonah nodded as he looked around. It wasn't grand, but it was enough, he thought, as he turned on his heels. On his second turn, he noticed a sturdy sycamore staircase that led to a small landing. He glanced at Mrs Cook and pointed to the stairs, and her eyes gleamed as she nodded towards them. Jonah took the hint and quickly walked forward, taking two steps at a time in his haste. He reached the landing to find a narrow corridor with a single door on either side of the wall.

He turned to call Sarah and was surprised to see her at his elbow. 'There you are,' he said with a smile, 'these are our rooms.' He pointed to the room on the left, the same side she had at Mr Bentley's.

'My room,' she said, taking a few steps forward and gently grasping at the cold metal handle. She pushed on it, and the door opened. Her jaw dropped: the room itself was massive and spread across the entire corridor. She had a large bed, a wardrobe and a small dressing table, and in the centre was a medium-sized fireplace. It was all second- or even third-hand items that had worn down over time, but it was more than she had ever had, and it was personal to her.

Tears filled her eyes, this time in happiness, as she looked at Jonah with a quivering smile. He returned her smile and turned to inspect his own room. He crept gently across the hallway, careful not to disturb Sarah's tranquillity, as he inspected his own living space. He nervously grasped the handle and pressed down, swinging it forward to reveal an envious room that was vast in space. It had a padded bed, thicker than he had ever seen, the kind only left by the rich on their death.

A large wardrobe took up a large proportion of the room, a suspected ploy to buy and carefully maintain expensive suits, something which Jonah was sure Mr Cook was behind. To the left of the room was a medium-sized fireplace with a small basket of coal that sat on a dusty dark rug.

He nodded; he appreciated it, but knew as the owner he was entitled to this — after all, everything presented to him was his own.

I

The next few days were a bit of a blur as the pair began settling into their new lives. It was hectic, especially as the shop needed to be readied for the big opening. It was to be a fabulous event, with Mrs Cook asking her circle of friends to make special appearances at the shop.

Until that day, Jonah and Sarah were tasked with presenting the shop. Everything needed to be in place, and each day a new box would arrive with buttons, thread, material, ribbon and anything that a tailor shop required.

Sarah took charge of the front of the shop, placing everything in the necessary places in clear view, while Jonah worked in the back ensuring they had the right materials for opening day. Mrs Cook donated two elegant dresses to be displayed in the window until Jonah had time to create his own.

Taking inspiration from Mr Bentley, Jonah also asked Mrs Cook to donate some of her finer hats and shoes to present around the shop, as potential extra sales for the store, which she happily did.

Dusk till dawn, the pair worked tirelessly to get everything finished, barely breaking for sleep or food. It was the endless challenge that they each committed to, and after a gruelling six days, the shop was ready for the public.

Mrs Cook had viewed the final arrangement and gave it her seal of approval, ready for the opening on Monday It caused quite a stir in the city, having been the gossip of the week among the women as the scandal slowly emerged, that Jonah and Sarah had abandoned Mr Bentley and left him in the lurch.

The news had spread fast, and the excitement for the shop opening had the city in a frenzy. By opening day, both Sarah and Jonah were nervous. They had gotten up extra early to prepare for the long day ahead.

Both Mr and Mrs Cook had made an appearance to cut the ribbon as a gaggle of women stood outside, talking in quiet whispers. Mr Cook had made a small speech introducing Jonah and emphasising his own role in the business, much to Jonah's annoyance. It was his shop, not theirs.

As soon as the door opened, the women pushed their way through, entering as they pleased. Talking loudly about how the shop looked, to Jonah's relief everyone seemed happy. Jonah was rushed off his feet as he took orders for dresses, with each one coming with precise specifications, design and detail.

Sweat was dripping down his face by the time it came to closing; he hadn't had a break, and neither had Sarah. Mr Cook departed for work moments after cutting the ribbon, while Mrs Cook had stayed for an hour or so, talking with her friends before leaving, but she'd promised to return that evening, which she did.

She strode into the shop with elegance, her cream dress with a ruffled skirt swaying in the breeze.

'Hello, hello,' she said happily, looking at Jonah and Sarah. 'How has it been? Have we had much custom?' she asked inquisitively.

A little put out, Jonah replied, 'Indeed I have, Mrs Cook; there have been plenty of fine women who have placed orders today.' He emphasised the 'I', making it clear he was the one in charge.

Mrs Cook smiled shortly and narrowed her eyes as she opened her mouth to snarkily reply, when Sarah quickly jumped in. 'Likewise, ma'am. I, too, have sold plenty of fine assortments to the ladies of the town. They were very eager; alas, many wanted to know the tale, but I kept it brief,' she said in a cheery voice.

Turning her gaze away from Jonah, Mrs Cook looked at Sarah and gave her a dazzling smile, before she sweetly replied, 'That's good, my dear; let's hope the pair of you keep up the good work, otherwise the shop will be a distant memory.' With that, she turned on her heel, shutting the door noisily.

Sarah turned quickly to Jonah. 'Was that necessary?' she asked angrily.

Rolling his eyes, he spoke, 'Yes, it was. This is mine, my place, and they need to realise that. I didn't leave one tyrant to be put under another.' He spoke softly but defiantly, before returning to the back room, squatting behind his machine as he began making his way through the orders with haste.

He was tense as he began to create the endless list of garments, the conversation with Mrs Cook whirling around his head, when a slender shadow fell upon him.

Startled, he looked up and found himself looking up at an angry Sarah. With a stern voice, she spoke, 'It's the beginning of a new life, and we're going to eat together.'

Without another word, Sarah marched back into the kitchen, with Jonah slowly following behind her.

A delicious smell was wafting through the air, and he came to find Sarah had made a thick stew. A little shocked, he sat down facing her, before Sarah smiled as she dished the food out.

They didn't speak much, just ate silently as the tiredness hit them. It had been a long, hard day that had followed hectic and draining days before. They barely made it through their meal without falling asleep, and agreed to leave the dishes and just go straight to bed and start the next day of their new adventure.

II

The rising sun and distant caw of the birds echoed throughout the city. Jonah woke up tired and aching. It had been a few weeks since the opening of the shop, and days seemed to blend together as Jonah fell into a new routine with Sarah.

They would open up, work non-stop throughout the day, eat quickly and sleep, only to repeat it all within a few hours.

During that time, Mr Cook had become a frequent visitor to the shop, much to Jonah's annoyance. He expected it at first, but as the weeks went by, Jonah realised it was to be a permanent visitation in which he would drop by unexpectedly, often bringing a clerk who would scrutinise every payment taken and penny spent.

Without consulting Jonah, Mr Cook had decided neither had the skills to manage the books, so instead hired a man who would. He was a snobbish man, small in size, with a shiny bald head and a long pointy nose that was always angled towards the ceiling. His black beady eyes would dart quickly around the room, and he teetered around the shop like a small mouse. It infuriated Jonah, who would stand at the bridge between shop and fitting parlour, leaning against the wooden frame, with his arms firmly crossed.

Mr Cook had explained it was a business decision, but Jonah felt it to be disrespectful; it was his shop, and he intended to run it as he saw fit.

Despite the animosity, Jonah continued to work through the orders. He was becoming inundated with requests, with the first week sinking him under. He'd never had so many orders at once and was overwhelmed with the workload, especially as the shop continued to take on more orders at the request of his eager customers.

He would sit furiously stitching and had Sarah take measurements and cut the fabric to the correct pattern. The first batch of orders was well received, but he had taken his time, and now people were getting impatient and would visit the shop daily, hoping to get the clothes they had ordered.

The pressure was getting to him, but he refused to ask for help from Mr Cook; he didn't want him to see the cracks appearing.

'I can help,' Sarah spoke softly, her voice pleading as her fingers stroked the material.

'No, thank you,' Jonah sighed. He didn't have time to correct her mistakes as he dismissed her offer.

This left him with a pile of colourful fabric, with each one destined to go from a flat sheet into a dress that would blend into the skin, tracing every element and showing their elegant figures draped in delicate fabric.

It was with that he cut corners, making dresses that weren't carefully drawn at the seams or with stitches no longer straight and strong. The loose gathering looked untidy and was destined to rip, but Jonah chose to ignore this, as he was determined to get the orders done.

Sarah watched as he worked endlessly, seeing his skin break and bleed, his bones ache from sitting for so long and the bags that rested under his eyes. He was constantly on edge and nervous of any sudden visitations from the Cooks.

When they came, Jonah would jump up in a mad frenzy and rush to clean the place up, as Sarah stalled them at the front desk. The last thing he wanted was for Mr Cook to see the number of incomplete orders.

The stress of these orders had been building, and Sarah had cleverly come up with the idea of hiding them and the money from the books until complete, to make the orders seem frequent but not too overbearing.

'Jonah, you can't seem weak,' she whispered, as they devised the plan. 'You need to show them that you can hold your own. I will help where I can, but for now we need them thinking you've got this under control.'

It had been a convincing speech that Jonah readily heard, consumed and ultimately devised the plan, stowing the orders and money under a loose floorboard in his room. Mr Cook was prone to checking the kitchen to make sure they weren't living like royalty on the profits of the shop.

He was in a vulnerable position that left him open to criticism from groups of fickle women drooling for new and expensive items that they could flaunt in front of their friends and maids, proving their status in society.

They were influential people, but Jonah's new tactic was paying off; he was getting more dresses made, which was boosting his confidence. He was ignorant of the low quality and hiding that he had been fervently taught to avoid at all costs.

Sarah, too, was feeling the pressure and didn't question Jonah's dressmaking; she simply handed them over.

They had some complaints, but Jonah had brushed these away, placing the blame on the women. His tall stature and rough accent scared them and after a few stumbling words, they would leave without demanding a replacement or refund.

To Jonah, he saw this as a triumph, as he thought they'd seen sense and realised they were wrong, never doubting his skills or talent.

Word hadn't got out about the half-standard tailor; it was still early days, but the whispers were slowly circling the town. Many of Jonah's regulars from Mr Bentley's shop had stopped going to his shop, returning their custom to his old employer.

III

Although he was blind to this, Mrs Cook wasn't. She was a leading lady in society and heard a lot of gossip. The recent tales mainly focused on the new tailor, and what she was hearing didn't please her.

The women in her circle had high expectations, and she knew Jonah had potential, but was now doubting whether he was ready for such responsibility. She was reluctant to tell her husband this, for she knew he would criticise her. After all, she had pushed for this to happen, and even sneakily paid towards it.

Unwilling to be blamed for this, she began rectifying the situation by calling on the most prolific women in society. If they showed their support, no one would question the tailor ever again — they would happily spend their money whether the items were good or not.

With her reputation on the line, she decided that she had to get the most notable woman in town to visit the tailors and buy a dress so lavish that all the women would rush to know where she got it from. There was only one person that Mrs Cook could think of, and that was Mrs Harrison. She was an influential woman who was adored in society: whatever she did, people followed suit. Whatever she wore, people would complement and copy. She was the leading woman that would turn the shop into a desirable attraction.

Mrs Cook was a well-bred woman who had strong connections, which made it easy to arrange a luncheon with Mrs Harrison. It took less than two days to get the meeting arranged at the Pearl Hotel. It was a renowned place that served the fanciest afternoon teas, and it had been months since Mrs Cook last visited, and she was both excited and apprehensive of the meeting.

The morning of the event, Mrs Cook pulled out her favourite white dress that had delightful ruffles in the skirt and silk ribbon that threaded through the rim of the dress. It was delicate, elegant and gave her confidence. To top it off, she had a deep purple hat with a big fluffy feather. It was her statement piece that always turned heads, and she felt so empowered when dressed with such elegance.

Looking at herself in the mirror, she smiled as she confidently turned and glided down the staircase, calling out her goodbyes and issuing commands to her staff, before the butler opened the door and waved her off to her horse and carriage that she had called for.

Inside, she sat prim and proper as she watched the world go by, the horse trotting along over the cobbles, towards the Pearl Hotel. It wasn't a lengthy journey, which she was pleased about; the bumps over the cobbles hurt her bottom, and she rarely made long trips because of this.

She was thankful when the carriage began to slow down and pull up to a stop outside the hotel as a concierge pulled the door open and the footstool down and helped her to the ground. She looked up at the grand building that had two large doors that stood wide open and welcoming.

Walking through, Mrs Cook was welcomed in the hotel by all staff as her feet clattered over the black and white marble floor. The hotel was beautifully decorated with plants, paintings, mirrors and sculptures. There was a grand oval staircase that led to the rooms, and directly below was the main desk that was occupied by a smartly dressed man with a thin pencil moustache. He smiled widely at Mrs Cook as he stepped from behind the counter and greeted her.

'Mrs Cook,' he said in a deep voice, 'it's lovely to see you again. I think we can both agree that it's been far too long.'

She laughed and replied, 'Indeed it has, Mr Jones. I've been so busy these past few months, but I can tell you I'm very much looking forward to having one of your scrumptious afternoon teas.'

Taking her arm, he led her through a set of doors to the left of the room and into a huge open dining room. The ceiling stood tall, and a glorious chandelier hung down, with its glittering glass teardrops dangling.

Tables spaciously filled the dining room, and Mr Jones walked her to the window seat that looked out onto the bustling Birmingham streets. She smiled as she took her place and informed him of her soon-to-be-arriving guest.

She sat for a while, watching the lives of others through the window, patiently awaiting her guest. Mrs Harrison arrived promptly on time and marched towards Mrs Cook, who stood up and shook her slim and bony hand that was draped in a lace glove.

'Hello, my dear, thank you for inviting me today. I haven't been here in quite some time; let's hope they still offer their signature afternoon tea.' Mrs Harrison spoke in a soft voice as she clicked her fingers, summoning the waiter, who swiftly arrived, pulling out her chair and taking their orders.

'Mrs Harrison,' Mrs Cook said sweetly.

'Call me Helen, please; there's no need to be so formal, Margaret,' she said with a twinkle in her eyes.

She smiled. 'Thank you, Helen, for meeting me today. Now, I have a reason as to why I want to meet you: I've recently invested in a young tailor who has serious potential.

'My only issue is that the shop isn't getting as much attention as it should be doing. He's young and not as established as others, and I was hoping you would be a customer and potentially tell your friends about the shop,' she asked timidly as she tried to phrase it diplomatically.

Helen listened carefully but didn't say anything; she had an excellent poker face, nodding at each statement.

'I see. Well, I appreciate your honesty and I think this is one of the funniest ways a person has used me for my status, but I suppose I do need a new dress. Leave me the address and I'll pop down and get something special for myself,' she said, openly calling Margaret out on her motives.

Blushing, she tried to protest her actions, but Helen waved them away. 'Don't be shy; we don't get to these positions without help from others,' she said with a smile.

With a red face, Margaret nodded as the waiter appeared at their table, setting up the tea and placing a tower of cakes and sandwiches in front of them.

'Delicious,' Helen said excitedly as she pulled her napkin over her lap and placed a hot cross bun on her plate, then eagerly tucked in. Margaret followed suit, and for the rest of the afternoon they sat eating and drinking tea, laughing merrily as they discussed some of the more recent social tragedies. It mainly consisted of pointing fun at terrible outfits and scandals that had emerged.

When the luncheon finally ended, Margaret left in high spirits and gladly climbed into her carriage, waving her goodbyes to Helen, who had promised to visit Jonah's tailor shop in the morning.

Nervously, Margaret went home and wandered through the house aimlessly, rearranging the smallest items and waiting for the morning to come. She decided not to tell Jonah about the planned visit and use it as a test of his abilities. This was to be the ultimate test that would either make or break the tailor shop; for his and her sake she hoped it paid off, otherwise Mr Cook would have hell to pay.

JONAH

Dawn was approaching on what seemed like a typical day. It was the time of year when the clouds hung murky in the sky, when the shadow of the sun was dimmed and dismantled by the fog. Jonah was already awake. His natural body clock had stirred him at the same ungodly hour it did every day. He ached all over; the days and nights hadn't been kind to him, and he rose with the weight of success riding on him.

Sitting on the edge of the bed, he rubbed his face, groaning, before reluctantly standing up and pulling his clothes on. His eyelids felt heavy as he walked down into the kitchen. It was empty, the muffled footsteps of Sarah echoing above. He went to the back door, unlocking it with a sharp click; he pushed it open and a cool morning breeze ruffled at his skin. Reaching down, he picked up a bag that had been left by the Cook residence.

In a bid to keep costs down, a satchel of fresh food was delivered each day. It consisted of the bare minimum: a chunk of bread, the odd egg and sometimes slices of meat. It often left them hungry, and Jonah knew it was Mr Cook who was the mastermind behind the food parcels. Mrs Cook would lavish them with huge helpings if she was allowed. On occasion, she would stop by with a big pot of stew with thick chunks of beef soaked in thick gravy and filled with soft carrots and potatoes. Even thinking about it, Jonah's stomach was rumbling.

He gulped in the open air before turning back inside, kicking the door shut with his foot as he went to the table and dropped the bag down. He opened it up to find a large chunk of bread, four eggs, a bottle of milk and two large slices of cake wrapped up in a soft handkerchief. He smiled. Mrs Cook had added to this package and left treats and more food for both of them.

Without a thought, he picked up the cake and ate it ravenously, and within moments it was gone, the sweet delectable taste still lingering. Before he knew it, he reached for Sarah's slice and ate that just as quickly, whilst glancing up at the stairs as cake crumbs fluttered all over the place. Slightly choking, he reached in and grabbed the milk, chugging the delightfully fresh liquid that was still chilled from being sat out in the cool morning air.

He was halfway through the bottle when he managed to prise the delicious nectar from his lips and hastily put it on the table. He grabbed the handkerchief and wiped his mouth, before stowing it away in his pocket as Sarah wearily descended the stairs.

She looked at him with sleepy eyes. 'The food parcel has arrived then. Anything good in there?' she asked in a soft voice.

Gulping, he looked at Sarah and then at the bag with wide eyes as he realised what he'd done, before replying in a small voice, 'Yes, yes, the food has arrived. Good helping today: four eggs, a large slice of bread and some milk, bit more than usual, but not anything delicious,' he lied, as he tucked his hands into his pockets and shrugged sheepishly.

She smiled and excitedly said, 'Four eggs and bread? That's enough for the entire day. I don't have to scramble or take money from our hidden orders to buy food,' she happily cried.

Jonah nervously laughed. 'Yes, indeed, but this is my shop and my money, so why is that an issue?' he asked, the pitch in his voice rising in frustration.

Sarah's eyes widened, and her cheeks blushed. 'Of course it is your shop. I just meant we weren't taking from the profits when they should be paying for our food,' she said, emphasising on the 'they' in fake anger.

Jonah nodded in agreement and pointed at her. 'You get this, thank you,' he said, pointing at her with a happy smile, before turning and heading into his domain. For the first time in what seemed like ages, he sat down behind his machine and began arranging the orders, stitching with glee without a care in the world.

He was still cutting corners to get the orders done quickly, and he did it without shame. At first, it had pained him, but as the pressure had grown, he gave in to demand and quantity overrode quality.

From the moment he sat down, he happily worked and watched as Sarah dispensed the ready-made orders and pottered around the front end, making everything look presentable.

A few hours had gone by, and Jonah was still riding on a high when the bell rung. At first, he ignored it until he heard Sarah's voice change.

'Mrs Harrison,' she said breathlessly. 'What, no, how do you find yourself today?' she asked, unstructured and confused.

A light and amused laugh filled the room.

'Well, my dear child,' replied a graceful voice, 'the aim is to buy a dress, a dress that is envious of all that I know. I want something brilliant, and my usual tailoring isn't doing the job, so to say,' she said in a saddened tone.

'Of course,' Sarah laughed. 'How silly of me, how can I help?' she asked in a desperate voice.

Mrs Harrison requested a meeting with the tailor, at which Sarah willingly obliged, much to Jonah's dismay. He was rolling his eyes as Sarah entered. His mouth was open as he pointed at his machine and then drew a line across his neck, signalling that he wasn't available.

Sarah shook her head feverishly. 'Jonah, Mr Heizium,' she corrected herself quickly, 'Mrs Harrison is here to place an order,' she said, as she pointed at the woman with excitement.

Jonah, slightly confused, looked at her, eyebrows raised. Rolling her eyes and sighing, she rushed forwards and quietly whispered, 'She is the most famous woman in town; you get her, and you'll have everyone flocking to this place.'

Her nails dug into his arm as she spoke and gently lifted him from his seat, dragging him towards the front of the shop.

Half-walking, half being pulled, Jonah entered to see a beautiful, long-haired lady who was brimming with elegance and poise. Her small frame was dressed in a decadent white dress that covered her bust and tied in at her waist. The skirt was the main attraction of the piece; it was long and ruffled, which reached down to her ankles, and the rim of the dress had a contrasting ruffle that was entwined with light pink silk lace.

It was a delightful piece that complimented her. She was a beautiful woman with high cheekbones that highlighted her aqua blue eyes that shimmered and danced in the sunlight. She had a sharply pointed nose that hung just above her plump red lips that stretched far with every smile. Big bountiful curls of red hair hung past her shoulders, making her a stand-out treasure anywhere she went.

One look at her had Jonah's mood changed from annoyance to shy excitement as her beauty astounded him.

Taking a deep breath, he softly spoke, 'My dear Mrs Harrison, how may we help you today?'

A dazzling smile spread across her face as she turned from playing with the hem of Mrs Cook's dress in the window. It was a fine piece made of silk, woven with gold glitter thread. This dress was a head turner and a prize possession of Mrs Cook who had insisted on using her signature dresses in the window, even if Jonah hadn't made them.

'Well...' She paused as she looked at Jonah and raised her eyes at his beastly nature, strong arms and flowing blond hair. 'I want a dress, a dress so marvellous that every head in the room turns to me, a dress so different that nobody in the entirety of Birmingham would possess. I want a masterpiece,' she ended with a gasp, her hands clasped together with a smile.

Jonah nodded and held his finger up as he rushed into the back, reappearing with a pencil and a piece of paper.

'Tell me more,' he said excitedly as he placed the paper on the countertop and raised his hand with the pencil, awaiting further instruction.

'I want a layered dress with royal blue material that daintily overlaps with material that wraps around my body, with each layer having a small lining of lace. I want the shoulders to have a thick strap with lace that graces my arms,' she said, stroking her arms as she described the dress.

Jonah was feverishly drawing and making notes on the side as the complexity of the dress was spoken to him.

Flicking her fan open, Mrs Harrison began wafting it towards her face as she watched Jonah work. After a few minutes, she snapped the fan shut, placed her hands on her hips and began tapping her foot.

With a nervous chuckle, he looked up, a bead of sweat running down his face as he presented her with a rushed sketch of the dress.

She took it and stared at the design intently. Jonah, with a worried frown, looked to Sarah, who shrugged her shoulders and shook her head.

Mrs Harrison looked at the drawing and scribbles before she turned to Jonah with a devilish smile and said, narrowing her eyes, 'It's perfect! But the question is, are you capable of such advanced dressmaking?'

Standing up straight, he looked proudly and spoke with confidence. 'Of course I can, ma'am. I am a talented man, trained by two skilled tailors who taught me everything I know,' he said.

With a worried frown, Sarah looked at Jonah; not only was that an extremely complicated dress that he had never attempted before, but he had a backlog of dresses for seventeen women that he had to complete by the end of today.

Mrs Harrison let out a joyous laugh. 'Excellent! I shall pick it up Friday, just in time for the ball.' She smiled as she wrote her measurements down on the piece of paper, before turning and marching through the door and onto the street.

Jonah stood there, his mouth wide open as he watched Mrs Harrison enter her carriage and leave. He was resting on the counter, the sleeves of his shirt rolled up as he peered down onto the sheet.

'What have you done?' Sarah shouted. 'Jonah, Friday is less than two days away. You have seventeen dresses due today, and now you're going to create the most extravagant dress you've ever undertaken in just two days?' She was practically screaming at him as she tugged at his shirt.

Positively terrified, Jonah peered at her. 'We can do this. I've done fifteen of the dresses already; just a few more to go and you, you could do them,' he said, pointing at her with a smile.

'Me?' she said in shock. 'But you always said I didn't have the skills for that.' She pointed at him, her face turning red in anger.

Jonah placed both of his hands up, his index fingers raised as he slowly began stepping backwards.

'Yes, I did say that, but that was before; this is now, and you told me you had the skills for this, and now I'm going to put trust in them. Come on, quick as you can.' He smiled as he pushed her towards the back end as he rushed forward, turning the opening sign to 'closed' and hurrying back to Sarah.

She had placed herself at his machine and was stitching with haste as he began grabbing at the royal blue material. It was one of the more beautiful rolls he had in his possession, and he knew it was time to put it to good use.

Grasping the sheet, he began planning the creation of the dress. First was to measure out the material; he would need one long piece that would drape her entire body and three shorter pieces that would layer upon the dress. Quickly he began marking out her small measurements and laying the material on the large worktop as he began marking down her size.

For the rest of the afternoon, he measured every single piece of material and cut it with precision to match.

At the same time, Sarah continued to stitch; she had managed to piece together three dresses. The street at the front of the shop started to get crowded as women gathered to collect what they were owed.

They could hear the rumblings of the crowd and then came the tapping on the window. He looked at Sarah; so far, he'd just laid the finished dresses on boxes and stacked them one after another behind Sarah. He ran forward as the noise of the crowd increased.

'I'll let them in, you start boxing up the dresses as quick as you can,' he said, urgently waving his arms towards her.

She had just placed the sixteenth dress on the sewing machine. Abandoning it, she jumped up and began pulling each box and dress down. Thankfully, she'd already lined them with paper, and the dresses just needed to be folded and wrapped up. In haste, she rapidly folded, wrapped them up and placed the lid on each box.

In the meantime, Jonah went to the front of the shop, pulling the door open and beckoning the women in with a gracious smile.

'My dear ladies, welcome, welcome,' he said with a forced smile.

The glaring faces took one look at Jonah and softened at his masculine presence as he walked to the back of the counter.

Addressing the women, he smiled nervously. 'If you would just hold on one moment, my assistant Sarah will be with you and bring out all the dresses.'

Leaving the angry crowd, Jonah dashed back to see that Sarah had messily boxed up most of the dresses.

He smiled, looking at her. 'Keep going; you've got this, and I'll continue with the remainder of the dresses,' he said breathlessly.

Sitting down, he began to stitch, making the material come together as Sarah rushed behind him. Within ten minutes and a lot of angry voices, Sarah started to bring the boxes out, one by one, calling each lady as she did so. She collected the remainder of the money, noting it down, which bought him some time.

By her third delivery, the crowd had settled and began talking among themselves as Sarah's chipper nature calmed them down. Jonah had finished the sixteenth dress, and it was barely presentable but finished.

He laid that on its box and pulled the material for the final dress and set about ending this headache of an order. Together, they managed to get each order out, with women paying their dues and leaving quickly to avoid the crowd, failing to check whether it was worthy of wearing.

The last dress was finally done; it took no time, but then again no effort was put into it. It was simply stitched to be over with, and Jonah was brimming with sweat as he kept glancing at the royal blue material to his left. Finally, he placed the last stitch and held the dress up to him. The ruffles were a bit misshapen, and the shoulders not quite even, but he didn't care. These women had ordered the basic dresses at the basic rate, so this is what they got as he handed it to Sarah to box up.

The last customer left, and together he and Sarah locked up, releasing a deep breath as they did so.

Sarah looked at him, her eyes popping. 'Never do that to me again,' she growled.

He watched as she marched into the back and slumped to the floor. He sat and breathed as he felt the day's events wash over him. It had been manic, and now he had even less time to finish Mrs Harrison's dress, but at least now he could focus on that. With the adrenaline still pumping through his body, he returned to the back: it looked like a bomb had hit it. He internally groaned as he shifted items out of the way and slowly made his way over to the royal blue material.

The material sifted through his hands gently. He'd somehow managed to get most of it cut, and he had enough to start on the bodice, leaving him almost two days to finish the intricate designs.

Pulling the material across the room, he sat behind the machine and carefully laid the separate material on top of one another and gently slid it under the needle. He replaced the thread with a pure white one to make it stand out further, and then he began turning the wheel and started the process.

He worked quietly with precision, while Sarah stayed away in the kitchen for some time before she emerged. She was still angry and began clearing up aggressively around him.

Jonah continued to work, trying to ignore her, and after she'd finished, she looked at him, her hands on her hips. He slowed down his stitching as he slowly looked up sheepishly.

She glared, her face unamused. 'Food is on the table, get it when you're ready. I'm going to bed and hopefully tomorrow will be better,' she said, the anger fading out of her voice with every word.

His muscles tensed up as he returned to work. He'd pushed her too far today, and he knew he'd have to make it up to her somehow, but that would have to wait; this dress was his ticket to establishing himself as a better tailor than Mr Bentley.

Remaining in his seat, he finished the first layer before grabbing one of the mannequins and placing the basic dress on the frame. The stitching looked perfect, but it was still a blank canvas. He returned to the rest of the material, draping it over his left arm and grabbing a pile of pins.

From there, he began pinning the various elements to create the envisioned dress by Mrs Harrison. First, he pinned the longer layer and ruffled the bottom with more pins; he did this a further two times, creating a skirt that bunched out in ruffles, leaving a thin middle that was completely untouched. It looked wonderfully unique, and he was surprised that he'd managed to create something this beautiful.

It was coming together, but he still needed to work on the top half of the dress. Returning to the front end of the shop, he began sifting through the rolls of material. Nothing seemed perfect, until his eyes landed on the far-left window on Mrs Cook's dress. It was an elegant dark blue dress with slim lace sleeves, just as Mrs Harrison had described. He smiled. It wasn't a perfect match, but it would complement the dress and match that beautiful woman's dress.

Without hesitation, he grabbed it from the window and returned to the parlour, cutting into it without a second thought, removing the lace top and discarding the floaty skirt. He placed it over the mannequin and onto the dress. It needed taking in, but Jonah saw the dress come to life, and he knew he had it. It was divine, and he sighed happily. Placing his head in his hands, he laughed and then quickly covered his mouth to not wake Sarah.

Still chuckling, he walked into the kitchen, grabbing at the hunk of bread Sarah had measly left him, and he tucked into it as he walked up the stairs and finally into bed, where he collapsed and fell into a deep sleep.

I

That night he dreamed of himself, of how the dress graced Mrs Harrison as she strode through the doors at the ball, how every head turned, the men swooned, and the women cooed at her outfit. The entire ball was about the dress, as women fawned to know who her tailor was. He dreamed of hawking his prices and watching how the elite socialites flocked to his store the following day, and the orders came in, but this time he dictated the timescale; the women waited for him.

He saw the money roll in and riches before him, and he saw himself hiring more people to do his work while he went on to dress royalty, his little shop growing into an empire.

Smiling to himself, he rolled over, only to be rudely woken by a loud banging on his door, and he groaned as the dream slipped away and reality sank in.

'Time to get up, there's a lot on today,' the muffled voice of Sarah came through the door, and she still sounded angry.

Wearily sighing, he rose and began pulling his clothes from the floor. He methodically put them on and sat on the bed to tie his worn shoes before heading downstairs.

Sarah had retrieved the bag from the back and was pulling out the food supplies.

'It seems Mrs Cook has packed this one, there's cake in here.' She smiled at him, happy at the treat, as she waved a loose napkin with cake enclosed.

He smiled and nodded, stuffing yesterday's napkin further into his pocket nervously.

'So, I take it you're not still angry at me?' he asked apprehensively.

Looking at him, she smiled. 'Yes, I'm still angry, but we got the backlog done, we've got cake, and I see you've made an excellent start on Mrs Harrison's dress, so I guess I'm on my way to forgiveness; but you do that to me again, and I swear...,' she said, playfully pointing at him.

He laughed, grabbing a slice of cake from her and biting into it happily.

They ate it slowly as they savoured the light buttery cake with fresh whipped cream. It slithered down their throat with delight. It was an excellent way to start the day, and Jonah almost felt bad for taking the slice after eating two the day before.

After demolishing the cake, he wandered through to the tailor room, dusting his hands as he went. Once all the crumbs had fallen, he looked at the dress and began planning how he was to finish it. He would need to strip it back to the first layer, stitch and then slowly add the remaining pieces.

It didn't take long to deconstruct, but he soon realised he'd have to hand sew most of this, which would take time, but this one he wanted perfect, and by three p.m. tomorrow he would have it finished.

Taking the dress, he sat in one of the comfier chairs and pulled out a needle and thread and began stitching. It had been a while since he'd done it this way, but was confident in his steady hand. He'd barely begun stitching when Sarah walked into the front of the shop and let out a blood-curdling scream.

Stabbing himself in the finger, he, too, let out a shout as he dropped the dress and ran to Sarah.

She was pointing at the empty doll in the window. 'It's gone, it's gone,' she said frantically. 'One of Mrs Cook's dresses has gone; it's one of her prized possessions,' she screeched, waving her hand at the empty window and looking at Jonah in sheer panic.

Running his hands over his face, Jonah looked at her and cocked his head to the side. 'Sarah, don't panic, but I may have borrowed it,' he said, a little high-pitched.

Her eyes narrowed as she looked at him. 'What do you mean?' she said, weirdly calm as she moved forward, her arms raised, her thin frame suddenly changing to a scary one.

He gulped. 'We didn't have the exact material to make the bust of the dress for Mrs Harrison, but that dress matched perfectly, so I took it and used it,' he said, his voice trailing off as he spoke.

Sarah widened her eyes in horror as she realised what he had done. Gasping and raising her hand to her heart, she whispered, 'Why would you do that?'

Jonah looked at her with blatant disregard. 'It was the only way to get it done. She will understand,' he said nonchalantly.

Before she could even speak, he walked away, leaving Sarah stood in horror and disbelief as Jonah ignored her.

The day was a strange one. Sarah methodically worked, still consumed by his actions, while he continued his work in silence, adding piece by piece with his hand. They'd had a few sparse customers throughout the day, mainly those buying supplies, and no order had been placed, much to his relief.

When closing time struck, he had just about got the three layers on the skirt. He'd been stitching swiftly, so the result wasn't as precise as he would like, but once on it would be unnoticeable. It was a quick stitch that would work, but he only had until three p.m. tomorrow to get it done, and he had to resize the lace top and attach it, which would take the entirety of the morning.

That night, he settled in nicely and woke happily, bouncing down before Sarah, ignoring the food parcel to continue his work. He quickly cut into the seams of the lace top, bringing them in and finally attaching them to the skirt; they fitted seamlessly.

It was a rush job, and Jonah was just finishing when Mrs Harrison came through the door, the bell ringing with a chime behind her.

She flitted through the shop and into the back, much to Sarah's shock. She didn't even announce herself, just presented herself as Jonah was finishing the last stitch.

He smiled and awkwardly waved at her, before dropping his hand in embarrassment. He pointed at the dress and said sheepishly, 'It's ready.'

Mrs Harrison held her hand up, waiting for the dress to be laid into it, which Jonah willingly obliged as she headed to the dresser behind the curtain, beckoning Sarah with a click of her fingers.

After a few minutes, Mrs Harrison cried out, 'You imbecile, this dress doesn't fit.'

Jonah, in horror, spoke quickly, 'What do you mean? I took your measurements correctly, and each material was cut to that,' he said, his arms raised.

'Oh, please tell me you made the extra layers larger,' she said, exasperated, lifting her hand to her forehead.

Jonah widened his eyes in shock; he hadn't, and realisation struck him. Mrs Harrison looked at him in disbelief. 'You imbecile!' she repeated. 'The ball is tonight; how will you fix this?' she said aggressively.

He floundered, his mouth flopping open as he realised his mistake. 'I'm sorry, I don't know. What can I do?' he asked sadly as he racked his brain on how he could possibly fix it.

Mrs Harrison looked at him with pure hatred as she thought, her nostrils flaring.

Taking a deep breath and closing her eyes, thinking, she suddenly clocked her head towards the front of the shop and opened her eyes with a mischievous smile.

'Well,' she said, her eyebrows raised, 'it'd be hard to do much now for this dress, but you could resize the one in the window to my measurements, with ease, I'm sure.' Her smile widened with an evil glare.

Jonah, wide-eyed, looked at her and then to the front of the shop. He stuttered as he spoke. 'That's... that's Mrs Cook's. I can't,' he said nervously.

'Oh, but you did before,' she said with softness and doe eyes as she stroked the blue lace on the dress Jonah had presented to her.

He stumbled for a second, his mouth flapping. He could feel Sarah's eyes burning into the back of him as he thought.

Mrs Harrison began tapping her foot impatiently, and before he knew it, he agreed, with the mentality that Mrs Cook would understand.

He reluctantly walked to the front of the shop, unhooking the dress and bringing it to her, all the while ignoring Sarah's glaring eyes.

Mrs Harrison went behind the curtain, and Sarah followed, helping her into the dress. Together they pinned the material to her measurements, before handing it to Jonah to resize right there and then.

He drew it in tightly and used the machine to fix it quickly to the size Mrs Harrison demanded. She waited on the chair, consumed by his talent until it was done. Sweat was dripping from him when he handed it to her shakily.

She laughed, before returning to the curtain as Sarah followed to help. It looked beautiful and fitted perfectly.

'I simply love it,' she said happily, looking down at her small frame. 'I'll take it gladly, and I'll be happy to show it off,' she said smugly, knowing how much it would annoy Mrs Cook.

Jonah was internally groaning as Sarah angrily boxed up the dress while Mrs Harrison got changed. They didn't even take payment for any of the dresses either, as she insisted it was their mistake and it should be on the house.

They gladly watched her leave as they both collapsed in the back. For now, they had to let the events unfold.

Mrs Cook

On the other side of town, Mrs Cook was dancing around her powder room, excitedly getting ready for the upcoming ball. It was a major social event that saw the elite members of society get together and have fun.

She was looking forward to dancing with all the strapping young men, being held firmly and spun around delicately in a large open room with marble flooring that gleamed underneath them.

Plus, Mrs Harrison would be there showing off her latest dress designed by her young entrepreneur. It had been an event she had been looking forward to and was at the door before Charlie, much to his surprise.

Before he could even speak, she had whisked him outside not even hesitating about the carriage ride, but jumping in with glee. Her husband looked at the driver, shaking his head as he followed suit.

They were heading to the Peaslys, who were the wealthiest family in town and had a grand manor on the outskirts of town. It was a fair ride away, but a yearly event the Cooks never missed.

The ride was a bumpy one, but Mrs Cook maintained her chipper mood, and when the carriage finally stopped, she hopped out, greeting the waiting servants who welcomed them into the stately manor.

It was the grandest place she had ever been to. It was so magical and one on which she had tried to model her own minuscule home.

The home stood grand and tall like a castle; over fifty windows peered out at them, dancing lights from the candles shimmering out of all of them. Two large pillars guarded the front door, which stood at least two-people high.

A red carpet led through into the home, which Margaret elegantly strolled through, showing off her latest dress from Jonah, silver thread woven through the deep purple gown that fitted around her body perfectly. She had hoped to wear her statement pieces, but sadly had lent them to Jonah, and in her haste forgot to have them collected, much to her disappointment.

Nevertheless, she entered the grand hallway, with ceilings that reached to the sky. Everything was perfect; all the furniture had been cleared, and other surfaces were consumed with bouquets of fresh flowers, many of which she didn't recognise.

Following the red carpet, she entered the grand hall that was filled with many people who greeted her gladly.

Just as she remembered, the marble gleamed beneath her feet; it was her favourite room in the house. It reached far and wide, and great pillars surrounded the room in a large oval, each one a golden-brown marble that contrasted beautifully with the white flooring. The walls were a deep red colour, with large paintings lining up one by one, with painted golden flowers entwined around the frames.

A grand piano was placed at the far end that played the most enchanting music she had ever heard. Directly behind the piano were two large glass doors that led into the garden. It was the best garden she had ever seen: large bushes, wildflowers and big statues decorated the first acre of land. For tonight's event, they had it all lit up with candles and servants to show the brilliant masterpiece that it was.

Servers handed out drinks continuously, and Margaret gladly took each one, drinking heavily as she peered through the crowd, hoping to see Mrs Harrison, but she had no such luck. Charlie had wandered off, talking with associates, and she was left in the company of Lady Eugine, a funny woman who Margaret enjoyed sharing her company with.

She was a tall and large lady, draped in a fabulous red dress that highlighted her dark brown hair and deep brown eyes. Her face was round and her cheeks red, just like a tomato. Margaret clasped her hand as they looked at each other in excitement.

'Lady Eugine, how happy I am to see you and be in your company once again,' she said with a wide smile.

She laughed and patted Margaret on the hand, 'So, tell me about you; rumour has it that you've opened a tailor shop in town?' she asked inquisitively.

Without haste, Margaret spoke about Jonah, the shop, the promise from Mrs Harrison and the potential that was before them.

Eugine listened intently as she finally pulled Margaret in front of a giggling bunch of women, who immediately stopped laughing when their eyes fell on Margaret.

'What are we laughing at, my dears?' Margaret smiled intently at the crowd.

The women looked at each other awkwardly, before an elegant voice echoed through the crowd.

'At you, of course,' a thrilling voice sounded as the women parted, allowing a shocked Margaret to view the speaker. It was Mrs Harrison, and she was draped in a familiar dress.

Confused, Margaret went to open her mouth, before being cut short.

'We're laughing at your shambles of a business,' Mrs Harrison said loudly. 'Half the women in here were supposed to be dressed by your fabulous tailor, except the dresses don't fit; they're badly sewn and a complete mess. A child could have done better!

'I presume you came begging to me and asking for me to accept a dress from such a hideous tailor. He tried, bless him, but he failed, and in the process ruined your best dress, and resized this one to fit me. I've always admired this dress,' she said gleefully.

Margaret looked at her dress in horror, her mouth hanging open, and the hurt surged through her body as the many onlookers looked on at the drama. Tears began rolling down her cheeks as the women laughed at her. She rushed through the room, knocking people out of the way, until she reached Charlie, bawling at the need to leave.

With shame and sadness, Charlie left as the entire room fell to silence, watching the respectable couple hurriedly leave in distress.

Outside, Margaret was clasping at the concrete pillar, taking deep breaths through pained sobs. Charlie came to her side, beckoning for his carriage to be drawn and trying to shield his wife from the new arrivals.

With haste they left, watching as the party gathered at the windows to watch them the pointing and laughing following them.

In the carriage, Margaret sobbed onto her husband's shoulder, slowly making her way through the story as she cried.

The anger surged through his body, as a red mist descended over his eyes. He began calling Jonah every name under the sun, cursing him to hell as he watched his broken wife curled into him. The carriage sped hastily towards the Cooks' home, and the pair got out. Margaret's face was bright red and ugly from crying, her perfect hair strewn across her face. Charlie's suit was dishevelled and damp from the many tears.

As he put his wife to bed, he began to think of how he could seek revenge and destroy that smug boy. All night he was up, pacing in the living room, when it finally hit him.

Jonah

Nerves had kept Jonah up for most of the night as he thought about the promised dress he had ruthlessly cut into. He'd barely slept when he stumbled downstairs, automatically going for the sack of food, only to find the doorstep empty.

Confused, he closed the door, they must be preoccupied after the party, he thought as he wandered into the parlour.

They opened as usual, but nobody had yet to stop by. It was approaching mid-morning when Sarah demanded money to buy food as the pair were starving. He handed over a few coins which she happily took and left quickly, clutching a small shopping list for the daily food.

Jonah was left manning the shop with nothing to do. He was bored to the point of cleaning as he tidied up the back room. Once that was done, he perched on the fancy chair, sighing and wondering where Sarah was.

After an hour had gone by, he began to get worried and started to pace in front of the shop door, occasionally popping his head out to check up and down the street. He was readying himself to go to the police when Sarah ran through the door, hitting Jonah.

He grabbed her, keeping her afloat. 'Sarah, where have you been?' he demanded.

Gasping, she grasped at his hand. She was panting, and her face was red as she took deep breaths, trying to steady herself. Her hair was a mess, and the bottom of her dress was splattered in mud.

After a few moments, her breathing steadied, and she looked at him with fear. 'She knows,' she said cryptically.

Jonah shrugged his shoulders and looked at her blankly. Sarah rolled her eyes in frustration, before shaking herself free. She locked the door and turned the sign, grabbing Jonah by the hand and dragging him into the back.

She looked at him and twisted her hands as she paced in front of him. Finally taking a deep breath, she met Jonah's gaze with worried eyes.

'The ball yesterday...' She paused, then continued in a timid voice, 'It went horribly. Mrs Cook is the talk of the town, and not for the right reasons; she was publicly humiliated by Mrs Harrison, who has also made it known how terrible a tailor you are.' Her voice trailed off as she finished.

Jonah paused, his mind spinning as he drank her words. 'I am a bad tailor?' he asked, the anger rising in his voice as he stared at Sarah fiercely.

'No, no, I think you're a brilliant tailor; it's just you've been cutting corners recently, and the dresses haven't been up to your standard, and the women haven't been happy. All of them have been the upper ladies of society, and then, of course, there was Mrs Harrison.' She spoke quietly as she listed off the many reasons.

He let out a long breath as he rubbed his chin in thought, pausing slightly, before opening his mouth and closing it again.

After a moment's pause, he stumbled. 'It's not that bad; she'll get over it,' he said.

Sarah's jaw dropped in horror. 'You don't understand; everyone is talking about her — it's a shambles; you're in trouble and Mr Cook is angry.' She spoke forcefully, emphasising each word in an attempt to get through to him.

He looked at her as each word fell into place and he slowly realised what this meant. He was about to speak when the front door crashed open. They both jumped as Mr Cook marched into the back, looking at the dishevelled pair.

'You,' he shouted, 'do you realise what you have done?'

Before Jonah could open his mouth to protest, Mr Cook began ranting. 'You destroyed my wife and ruined our reputation, and God knows what that will do to our social and business prospects,' he said, the afterthought suddenly hitting him, which fuelled his anger more.

With a deep inhale, he calmed himself slightly and looked Jonah in the eye. 'You've ruined this,' he said. 'You've been lying to me; from what I could tell at the party, multiple women had bought from you, which means you've been lying about the number of orders and the amount of money that has been handed over to you.'

Every word rang around Jonah's head, and he saw the puzzle form in his mind: it looked as if he had stolen the money.

He paused momentarily, before saying, 'Yes, Mr Cook, I have been hiding orders. I didn't want you to think I was overwhelmed and unable to do the job,' he said sincerely.

He continued quickly, to cut Mr Cook off, 'Sir, this will all blow over; the women will be back soon, and your reputation will be fine.'

Mr Cook's eyes narrowed, and he smirked. 'You're a child, you don't understand the gravity of this situation. This experiment is over, and you are done,' he spoke clearly and calmly.

Frowning, Jonah remarked, 'This is my shop. You can't do this!'

This time, Mr Cook laughed out loud. 'Please,' he hollered, 'I funded this place, this is my shop, and as per the agreement you signed, you have no power. Do you think I was stupid enough to actually make you the sole owner of this place?' he snorted.

Jonah's eyes popped as he looked on in horror as he stood frozen. Suddenly, the chime of the door rang loudly and heavy footsteps sounded. came into sight, their uniforms freshly polished. They tipped their hats to Mr Cook, before they turned to Jonah.

'Hands behind your back,' the first policeman said gruffly, while the second one approached him and grabbed him by the arm. He tried to protest, but as soon as he moved the first policeman pinned him to the ground and placed handcuffs on him.

They dug deep into his wrists as he lay face down on the floor, inhaling the musty smell of the carpet.

He lay there for an eternity as he watched the policemen strip the place apart, before his heart was truly ripped from his chest when Sarah betrayed him.

'It's upstairs, under the floorboard beside his bed.' Sarah spoke clearly to the policemen, no sorrow or sadness in her voice. 'He said it was to be our secret, to use the money as we pleased because it was his shop.'

'I knew it,' Mr Cook shouted triumphantly.

A muffled protest escaped Jonah's lips as he squirmed under the policeman's weight. It was like a knife had been plunged into his heart at the betrayal from his best friend, his adoptive sister.

The thudding steps echoed as the first policeman returned with a wad of notes clutched in his hand.

'Found it, just like the young girl said.' He nodded to his colleague who dragged Jonah to his feet, using his hair to grip him tightly.

Jonah groaned, his face twisted in pain as he begged and pleaded.

The final parting words came from Sarah, who looked him in the eye with fierce eyes. 'Your pride is your downfall; you should have taken my help when I offered it.'

It was a cold statement that shook him to his core. He hung his head, blinking rapidly to stop the tears that welled from escaping.

'No,' he mumbled, the pain searing through him. It suddenly dawned on him how much trouble he was in. Theft from the rich was prison punishable crime and Sarah had sealed his fate with her tactful lies.

Before he could say anything else, the policemen hauled him out, each one firmly grasping his arms as they dragged him out into the street. A crowd of people had gathered, their heads bowed together as they whispered and pointed at Jonah, who was thrown into the back of a carriage.

I

Jonah spent a long night in the cells, barely recalling his surroundings but wallowing in his sorrow, having lost everything, including his best friend, in one night.

By morning light, the rumblings outside began to grow louder, and his cell was eventually opened. He was hoisted out and carted off to the courthouse. It was a large stone-walled building that Jonah had never laid his eyes on before.

He was tired, and his legs ached as he was dragged up the stairs and into a room that was filled with benches full of men and women. He kept his head bowed as he was placed on a wooden box in front of a chubby, red-faced man in a silly white wig. His glasses were perched on his long, wrinkled nose and he was peering down at a sheet of paper before he looked up at Jonah.

'Jonah Heizium,' he declared loudly and boldly, 'you are here facing charges of theft from one said Mr Cook. The court today finds you guilty following evidence unearthed by our fine policemen and statements from one Charles Cook, Michael Bentley and his wife, Sarah Bentley,' he said without emotion.

Jonah looked up quickly and then at the judge and then at the crowd of people, where his eyes landed on Sarah, who was wearing a pretty blue dress, her arm interlinked with Mr Bentley's. Both wore smug grins, Jonah looked on in horror and disappointment. It was in that moment that he realised he had never even asked Sarah her last name, presuming her to be a nameless orphan.

Sickness rose in him as the betrayal washed over him again. The pair had clearly planned his demise and Jonah had given them the opportunity on a plate when he accepted Mrs Cook's offer, he thought numbly.

Given the stature of the witnesses, no evidence was presented in his defence — their statuses overrode that of a penniless orphan.

The judge looked at Jonah and without flinching said clearly, 'Jonah Heizium, I hereby sentence you to seven years in prison.' He hit his mallet hard on the wooden tabletop, validating the decision.

Jonah couldn't move; he was in shock and pain as he was pulled from the box and taken to the closest prison, which was to be his confined home. He was emotionless as he was stripped of his fine clothes and placed in old rags, before being placed in a damp cell with thick metal bars on the door.

His bed was a slim mattress and thin blanket. In the corner was a bucket that stank of stale piss. He turned to the guard, who promptly shut the door with a loud clatter and spat in his face, laughing as he walked away.

The Watcher

Dear reader, I'm so sorry, I'm so very sorry. This isn't a proud day for me, and I'm ashamed at the life that Jonah is living; it was one that could have been prevented.

Jonah's life once had a purpose, one that wasn't supposed to cause destruction. You see, he was supposed to be a contributor to the world you live in.

Alas, this is what it is. It is life, things happen, as you would say. I feel sad about what happened. Jonah was supposed to have a happy life, he was supposed to be loved and cherished, to be built upon, to be infused with the nostalgia of true love; but that wasn't to be, he was to be a tortured soul.

The Sins, those devilish fiends, were poison; they had a reason, a purpose, and I wish, I honestly wish that I had the power to change him, to affect him as the Sins had.

He was a poor soul; he was one manipulated, one hurt and devastated.

I'm the Watcher. I watch, I look, I listen and then I guide. I didn't think I mattered. I just knew my goal. To get one person to another place, not to be an influencer in the affairs of humans.

It's with a heavy heart that I report this tale and I fear for the outcome. Jonah had the potential to be a good man, even a great one; if he had half a chance, he may have succeeded.

The Sins are a manipulative and hateful race that had stalked the Hollow for centuries. They're a gruesome collection that has one goal, just one, which is to destroy. They blend into your world infecting every element, attempting to crawl into the lives of as many people as they can.

They're a strong strain; even without physical form, the Sins have the ability to reach the human race. Every essence is portrayed in the lives, everyone is experienced, and there are very few humans that truly live without being possessed by them. Very few indeed that don't over-indulge, don't fight, don't let themselves be ruled or let themselves become living monsters on their behalf.

Now they're loose, they're having fun, and I cannot imagine the extent that they would go to destroy; but time is ticking, and the life of Jonah is coming to a close. To be honest, I don't know what will happen next, how they will react, how the Hollow will be rippling with excitement.

This is a turbulent time, and I'm still guiding, still trying and still attempting to keep one eye on the Sins. The reality is, I'm losing; this fight is being led and turned by those hideous creatures.

I pray for Death, for he will know what to do, but he's a busy being, a fearsome being, an entity who I hate to disrupt.

For now, dear reader, I'm going to stick my head in the ground, like the silly animals you so love to dissect. I will be here, watching, waiting, biding my time and documenting this sad state of affairs. For now, I will leave you with Jonah once again. He's facing two evils, two disasters that will surely berate and beat Jonah down once again.

A Pair of Two Evils

Seven years was a long time, and Jonah felt like he'd experienced every excruciating second three times over. His life before was a distant memory, even that of the dark days back in Manchester under the tyrant Mrs Welts and his drunken mother. He longed to have the days back when his heart ached for lost love, his soul broken under pressure and his mind worried in fear for his departed mother.

His imprisonment was a draining experience, and he made very few friends there. His large size often meant he was a target, despite his efforts to keep his head low. To avoid the constant battles, he took on more work, labouring the days away. It was also a way to get beyond the stone walls as the prisoners were led out in chains to work the worst jobs on the streets. They were heavily guarded, and many people avoided wherever they worked for fear of the ghastly criminals.

Other than the few days of terror when he first arrived, Jonah had lived in solitary, all the while still firmly believing he was innocent, and just like many on the outside, he wanted nothing to do with the despicable inmates that surrounded him.

It was with that, that seven years became an eternity and the sheer thought of release seemed a forlorn promise. When the final days approached, he began to get hopeful, and the feeling had shocked his system. He hadn't felt it for years.

The feeling lightened his soul, and a small bounce returned in his step. He could taste freedom on the tip of his tongue, and he relished the thought of fresh air hitting his free face. Every second slowly ticked by as Jonah waited for his release.

He was becoming restless and was doing everything in his power to keep his head down, praying that he could make it out alive and without a mark on his card.

Finally, the last night arrived. Jonah had spent the day mainly in his cell, memorising every inch of the place he had laid his head for so many years. He was tense and nervous, expecting some heated argument to arise; but, much to his relief, he was left alone for the entire day. Lights out were called, and Jonah lay down in anticipation.

A dim candle light was flickering over his face when suddenly a shadow swept over him. He moved, his eyes darting but not seeing anything until a hand reached down and dragged him up by his throat. Gasping and spluttering, Jonah desperately clawed at the rough arms that firmly held him in place.

Breathing was becoming impossible, and the lack of air was causing him to go dizzy; he was blacking out when the adrenaline kicked in, and he punched at the arms repeatedly until the man dropped him and quickly left.

Choking on the air, he looked to see thick black boots in front of his face. As he was about to look up at the man's face, the boot struck his chin hard, knocking him unconscious. He awoke on the cell floor, his jaw aching and bruised. The rusty taste of blood lingered in his mouth as he spat dried clumps onto the floor.

He pushed himself onto his knees just as the door opened to reveal a tall man with a thick black moustache and black beady eyes that were wrinkled from squinting. He was a wide-chested man whose uniform stretched over his bulging muscles, his belt slightly strained, but his baton was firmly in place.

Bending down, he grasped Jonah under his arms and lifted him to his feet, swatting the dust from his clothes.

'You look like you've had an entertaining night,' he said gruffly.

Jonah groaned as he opened his mouth and muttered, 'Indeed, someone with similar shoes to you attacked me in my sleep.' He stared deep into the man's eyes.

Shaking his head, he said, 'On your last night, how unfortunate; it's a pity what happens to the inmates in here.

'I'd say I would help, but you are leaving today. I'm here to collect you and present you with your freedom.' He fluttered his hands in front of Jonah's face as he finished.

Snorting, Jonah broke character and winced as he patted him on his shoulder. 'You know, Alex, I think I'm going to miss your sense of humour, but I must say I can't wait for my freedom,' he said, mimicking his actions.

The guard smiled and Jonah rolled his eyes before grasping at his face in pain. During his confinement, Alex had become the closest thing to a friend; he was a good man, and unlike many other guards, he spoke to the inmates like people. Jonah hadn't had an easy journey in prison, and Alex pitied him for it. He often found he would go out of his way to speak to him, and over time, a mutual respect had developed. It only seemed right that he was the one saying the final farewell.

Alex led him through the prison and to the release office, where Jonah was given his possessions, which consisted of his suit and a few coins. The suit was loose on him. He'd lost a fair bit of weight on the inside and it was dusty from being stored away for so long.

It was strange to be in something other than his prison uniform, but it also felt good, really good; he was there, he had made it.

'I can taste it, Alex,' he said as he looked down at his more presentable self.

'What? Freedom or blood?' Alex replied with a small smile, which Jonah returned, shaking his head at the cheeky joke.

After chuckling for a few minutes, he grabbed Jonah by the shoulder. 'Let's go. We can't keep your guest waiting,' he said with a twinkle in his eye.

Jonah went to open his mouth, but Alex cut him off with a whistle as they marched side by side to the main gates. He was confused as to who would be meeting him; he hadn't had a single visitor during his entire imprisonment, and it seemed unlikely that anyone in Birmingham would wish to see him again. He didn't have a friend in the world, so how did he have one now?

With a thoughtful face, he walked across the gravel floor, the stones crunching underneath him. In the distance he could see that a figure was hiding in the shadows, but he couldn't quite see who it was until it stepped into the morning light.

Gasping out loud, Jonah stopped as Alex continued to walk. To his great surprise, he saw Baxter, his old friend. A man he assumed was lost in his past. With his mouth hanging open, he stumbled forward towards Baxter, who embraced him heartily.

'Jonah, my old friend,' he said in a sad voice. 'How sorry I was to hear of your plight.' His eyes were full of sadness as he spoke gently.

'We have much to talk about, me and you, but for now you will come with me. I'm going to get you back on your feet,' he said, jabbing at Jonah's chest and wrapping his arms around his shoulders as he dragged him through the gates and into the fresh air of the morning light. Jonah turned and gave a small wave to Alex as he was led away, still in shock.

I

Baxter slowly led him down the winding streets, taking back alleys to avoid the bustling crowds that were emerging in the morning light.

They artfully made their way across the city, finally arriving at the train station which was to take the pair of them back to Manchester. Baxter paid for the tickets while Jonah lingered behind.

The station didn't look any different than his first and only visit when he arrived in Birmingham. There were people all around in the morning rush, and he was feeling nervous. He pulled at his shirt, moving it away from his sweaty neck as his eyes darted around the station taking in the many faces, wondering whether any of them knew him to be a criminal. Most stared at his bruised face and circled past him, and those who caught his eye quickly turned away.

Swallowing deeply, he looked to find Baxter, who was making his way through the crowd awkwardly, finally reaching him. Again, he grasped Jonah's arm and led him to the correct platform. Their train was waiting, and they boarded quickly, finding a secluded seat to rest.

Before long they were passing through the country. Neither had said much as Jonah stared out of the window, watching the blurred countryside fly by. Baxter focused on him, staring intently at his old friend. How different he had become. Prison had aged him considerably: he looked ten years older than what he did, and he was skinnier as well, his muscles less prominent than before and his hair thin and scraggly. He looked at his bruises and frowned; they were purple, and blood was still crusted around the wound. Baxter rolled his eyes. He wanted a strong and civilised man, yet in front of him sat a weak criminal with the injuries to boot.

For the entire journey, they stayed in silence, Jonah glancing every so often at his former boss as if checking that he hadn't left. By midday they arrived in Manchester; they both stood, stretching from the long journey and made their way onto the platform.

It was hectic, and they both had to fight to get out. The sun danced on Jonah's face as he took in the vast city that was dense with fog. He was home; it seemed bigger than before and was filled with men, women and children of all classes. Most were working, but a select few of the socialites were out spending money frivolously on pointless items and rich food.

Jonah shook his head as he saw the mixture of lives walking the same roads but having entirely different destinations.

Baxter slapped his back harshly, startling him. 'Come,' he said, 'let's go have a bite to eat at the Hogs Head. I don't know about you, but I'm starving.' He smiled as he walked down the stone steps with Jonah following behind.

The old cobbles echoed on Jonah's feet as he gormlessly walked the familiar streets, inhaling the same stench still lingering in the air. It was strangely familiar to him, and he enjoyed the slow breeze that was tickling his face, the freedom still washing over him. It was a pleasant walk to the pub and Jonah was truly getting into the spirit of things; he had a smile on his face as they approached the Hogs Head.

It was a small pub that sat squarely in the middle of Lightman's Road. It was a thin and rickety lane that was filled with houses and small shops that sat closely together. The pub had been a long-standing feature of the road, and it showed. The whitewash was dirty and peeling, while the thick stained-glass windows were covered in grime and mould. The wood was rotting, and the hogshead sign swung, creaking in the wind.

Welcoming light was flickering inside as Baxter and Jonah entered. A few people were milling around, but for the most part it was quiet, as many were still at work.

The inside was dated, with fragile-looking tables and chairs, and old peeled paintings hung on the wall, giving a worn and shabby feel to the place. The bar was a thick oak bench and behind it stood a large, tall man with a bald head and thick brown moustache. He wore an apron that covered a dirty shirt and protruding under his thick neck was a black bowtie.

He greeted them with a small smile. 'Gentlemen, how may I help you?' He eyed Jonah consciously, looking at his bruised face.

Baxter cleared his throat. 'Just two beers and a plate of food; anything will do.' He tipped his head and placed a few coins on the bar.

The barman scooped them up and began pulling some glasses down while the pair took to a small corner, sitting at one of the sturdier tables.

They waited in silence until the food and drinks arrived. Jonah drank heartily and pausing to shovel food into his mouth as Baxter watched his every movement.

After a few moments, Baxter cleared his throat loudly, halting Jonah mid-bite as he looked at his old friend like a rabid beast. He smiled, chewing and swallowing the food with a big gulp.

'There's a reason I collected you, Jonah. I want you back at my shop again, working, of course, to earn your keep. From what I heard, you were quite the tailor before the unfortunate circumstances.'

He paused to take a drink. 'I have two women working with me now; they know what happened, I couldn't lie to them.' He tapped his fingers on the table, before continuing, 'As per the agreement, you'll have to be a silent worker that doesn't leave the shop; for now, that is anyways.'

Jonah looked at him, shocked. 'So I'm trading one prison for another?' he asked, placing his fork down harshly.

Baxter sighed. 'For now, yes,' he said fiercely, before lowering his voice. 'Not every convict gets this opportunity,' he spat. 'You should consider yourself grateful that I took pity on you like this.'

He snarled, his face contorting in anger as Jonah looked at him startled and ashamed. 'I'm sorry,' he said, 'I didn't mean it. It's just that I thought I was free, fully free — but you're right, I should be kissing your feet for your charity.'

He lowered his gaze, and Baxter chuckled. He looked up nervously and smiled. 'Shall we talk of something else?' he asked. 'Maybe you could tell me about our former neighbours and friends?' He raised his eyebrows in curiosity at Baxter, who looked at him with a small frown.

'Friends?' he asked awkwardly.

'Yes, you know, Larry at the mill, even Mrs Welts, and I...I suppose it'd be nice to hear about Rose, even if we ended on bad terms,' he smiled.

Baxter rubbed his face and groaned. 'Oh, Jonah, I wish you hadn't asked that; it's not a pleasant tale.'

Jonah looked at him, and his face fell as he encouraged Baxter to continue, much to his regret. With little tact, Baxter began to tell the gruesome story, and it would seem his departure hadn't removed the infected areas that he had touched.

'Very well,' Baxter sighed. 'Your friend, Larry, from what I heard he ended up in prison. He beat a girl to almost death at the mill. Myra, something, I'm not too sure on the details but he claimed she had been taunting him.'

Jonah hissed. 'Of course it was Myra, that slut,' he spat.

'Quiet with that language,' Baxter hushed him quickly before carrying on with his tale. 'Prison wasn't kind to Larry, he was an easy target and it was rumoured that he was killed in the very bed he slept.'

Jonah swallowed, frozen and devastated. Larry had died defending his name, and he never even knew. He was numb, not even a morsel of his being had been aware of Larry's plight.

Dabbing at his tears, he said weakly, 'Dare I ask about the others?'

Baxter sighed again. 'Isn't it better if you heard it from me?'

Closing his eyes and removing the remainder of his tears, he nodded, sniffing loudly as he looked at his friend with blurred vision.

'Let me see, Mrs Welts.' He paused. 'It seemed after you left that she became nicer, more generous both with money and medicine. She built many friendships during this time, including that of a young gentleman who she ended up marrying.'

Jonah smiled; even though she had given him hell, he was glad that she had turned her life around and managed to find new love.

Baxter paused. 'I know you smile, but alas, it wasn't a fairy tale romance. She had been tricked, just as she had tricked Mr Welts. It was a painful marriage, everyone could see how badly he would treat her. 'We all pitied her and it wasn't long before her health declined. Mrs Welts lived her remaining days trapped in a loveless marriage.' Baxter shrugged as he ended the tale, his fingers tapping on the wooden table.

'How sad.' Jonah sat thinking, a frown on his face before he finally spoke. 'I'm surprised and I must admit that I do feel sorry for her.' Despite everything, sorrow did touch him but he couldn't help but wonder whether karma had come to play its part. That she had been treated how she had treated others when weak and kind.

Jonah thought for some time, pondering on the trails of life, how time could be cruel even in the shortest of seconds that pass.

Glumly, he raised his head, meeting the solemn gaze of his friend, and gently he said, 'Do I want to know about Rose? Pray tell me her tale has a happier ending?' He was almost pleading with Baxter, hoping that somewhere in the city there was a bit of good news.

With a huge exhale of air, Baxter shook his head. 'Sadly not, my dear friend; your former betrothed has since passed on.' He spoke gently, reaching out to pat Jonah on the arm.

He choked back a tear, coughing slightly, the vision of Rose's sweet face swimming into his mind, her beautiful doe eyes and darling smile.

With free flowing tears, Jonah managed to gasp, 'How?'

Baxter averted his gaze and reached into his pocket, withdrawing a small handkerchief with his initials neatly sewn in the corner. Jonah dabbed his face, hiding it from the patrons of the pub who had begun to look at the strange couple in the secluded corner.

Lowering his voice, Baxter began to whisper, 'Rose had become somewhat of a hermit. She shied away from view following the public dismantling of your engagement. She lived in solitude, her charm dispensing day by day. Yet the Bakery Bank was popular as ever and after a year or two, Rose emerged, slowly reaching out into society. From what I understand, she didn't want to die a spinster and it wasn't long until she was married.'

Jonah nodded, his heart aching at the love he lost. 'Was he a good man?' he asked timidly.

'Yes, he was of good breed, as they say. New to the town but he fell for her at first sight and Rose accepted his proposal. On the outside life looked good, the husband took over running the business and it wasn't long until they announced a new baby.'

'She always wanted to be a mother, she was perfect for it,' Jonah chimed in quietly.

'Yes, but it was a complicated pregnancy and they had chosen to live outside of town. The doctor was too far away and when the baby came early, he couldn't get there in time.' Baxter paused, eyeing his friend before finishing his tale.

'There was too much blood and no one to help. That night, both Rose and her child passed. It rocked the city to know that one of the sweetest souls had died. As you know, the bakery had been a popular one, and Rose had been a memorable character from the day she took her first. It was a shame,' he nodded, the faintest flicker of sadness flashing through his eyes. 'The husband is rarely seen. If only they had lived closer, if she had gotten pregnant sooner, then it wouldn't have been so complicated.'

A dark pit formed in Jonah's stomach as he openly sobbed. He felt as if his heart was breaking all over again. If they had gotten married when they planned, she would be alive today. She was a soul taken far too soon when great joy should have been experienced.

He spluttered, 'My dear Rose, how sad it is, how foolish I was.'

Baxter nodded. 'I'm sorry, Jonah, I knew she meant a lot to you. I would have written, but I didn't know where you were, not until a mere few weeks ago,' he explained sadly.

The uncontrollable cries from Jonah were causing much attraction from the neighbouring tables, and Baxter was fearful of people asking too many questions, and the story of an ex-convict in the city, working in his shop.

Glancing around, he leaned forward and whispered to Jonah, 'Come, we should leave; we've got lots to do, and I think we're overstaying our welcome.' He nodded to the barman, who was staring over intently.

Ashamed, Jonah hid his face, wiping at his tears furiously as he stood up quickly, knocking the table, causing the glasses to fall and smash on the ground. He cursed loudly as Baxter rushed to the bar, dropping a few more coins, before gesturing to Jonah to leave quickly.

Once again Baxter led the pair down side streets and back alleys to avoid the crowds. Jonah was barely paying attention to his surroundings, just aimlessly following his old friend, the fresh wind drying his tears as they walked with speed.

The journey had been a blur. They'd walked hard and fast, finally emerging through a gate and into an overgrown garden with a beaten path that led to a perfectly polished oak door. Baxter unearthed a key from inside his jacket and smoothly slotted it into the keyhole, turning the lock with a small click.

He entered, motioning Jonah in behind him. They stood in the pantry, food stacked high on either side of them. The kitchen was looming in front, and a body was pottering around. She was a large woman with a big behind, and her grey hair stuck out under a small white cap. They walked in and Baxter coughed, announcing their arrival.

The woman was bent over a large stove, slowly stirring a pot of bubbling beef stew, and she jumped at hearing the noise and turned quickly. As Jonah imagined, she was a bubbly character with bright red cheeks and bright green eyes shimmering under her bushy grey eyebrows. Her lips spread wide in a smile, before faltering after her eyes landed on Jonah and, more importantly, the growing purple bruise on his mouth.

Her smile flashed as she put down the spoon in her hand and began wiping her hands on her apron, before waving gently at him.

'Oh, hello, dear, you must be Jonah. I'm Miss Sandra, I'm the cook,' she said nervously, looking at Baxter, who nodded in encouragement. She swallowed, looking back at Jonah. 'This is my kitchen.' She pointed all around.

Jonah looked around. It was bigger than before, with a central thick wooden tabletop. The outskirts of the room had a long line of cupboards and directly behind Miss Sandra was a large open fireplace with an iron grate in front. Flowers, vegetables and food were hanging all around, giving it a homely touch.

Similar to Mr Bentley's place, there was a long staircase that presumably led to rooms, one which he hoped would be his.

Jonah's mouth hung slightly open as he twirled, his feet echoing on the stone flooring.

Miss Sandra smiled. 'Baxter here has let me make this my own.' She looked around happily. Baxter smiled back and placed his hand on Jonah's back, pushing him gently towards the door to their right.

As they left, Miss Sandra shouted after them that dinner would be ready at six p.m. promptly, and they were to be scrubbed and cleaned in time.

Chuckling, they persisted forward into the parlour room, and it was as Jonah remembered: the chairs, the rug, the layout of his craft and materials set up in the far-right corner. For the first time in forever, he felt at home, at peace.

He stroked his fingers across the fraying material of the old chairs as he strolled behind Baxter, who raised his arm suddenly, stopping him. He looked at him curiously, but he simply beckoned him into one of the chairs.

As he lowered himself down, Baxter walked to the front of the shop, and Jonah could hear him exchanging words in whispers with a woman. He couldn't hear what they were saying, but he could see the frustration and waving of arms as they spoke in hushed tones.

He sat waiting as the worry ebbed, the fear of the unknown outcome settling on his stomach. After some time, Baxter walked into the parlour, fiercely dragging the curtain behind him as he marched towards Jonah and threw himself into the chair facing him, sulking.

As his fury emitted, Jonah sat, until a dainty woman with a slim figure, chiselled cheeks and pursed lips walked through. Her eyes were wide, the black of her pupils shimmering through as she stared at Jonah. She wore a black lace dress that was finely fitted to her body, the lace cuffs caressing the backs of her hands.

'So you're the criminal?' she demanded. 'You're the person I am to serve and advise?' She sat angrily.

Baxter sighed. 'Are you to be this cruel, this arrogant?' he said venomously.

Jonah was shocked at the bluntness of the lady and attempted to stand up, but thought better of it, leaving himself in a seated position, his bottom hovering over the seat.

He met her gaze and gently spoke, controlling his voice to sound calm and collected. 'I served my time for a crime that I was framed for. I was tricked and misled, which ended up in me serving time.'

The girl stared at him intently, folding her arms across her chest. 'I suppose all criminals would say that, and I bet the bruise to your face was an attack and not a fight?' she snorted.

Jonah's eyes narrowed, and his nostrils flared. 'As a matter of fact, that's exactly what happened,' he said as he stood up, towering over her.

She took a few steps back as Jonah raised himself up and said politely, 'Look, if you don't give me a chance, then I can't prove to you that I was wronged. I had everything in my grasp, and it was brutally ripped from me. I served seven years in a rotting cell, and then I've come back here to find everyone I care about is gone, so please, just please give me a chance,' he finished, exasperated as he pleaded with her.

Shaking her head, she breathed out. 'I will tolerate this because I have to, but I will not change my opinion, and you'd better keep yourself hidden. I don't want people knowing that I'm working with a criminal,' she angrily said, before turning and heading back into the shop front, making sure the curtain was fully closed.

Disheartened, Jonah cast his gaze to the ground as Baxter rubbed his face in his hands. He, too, stood up and put both hands on Jonah's shoulders.

'Don't worry, Cissy will come around eventually, and Miss Sandra will more than likely talk some sense into her. It's a damn shame, but let's face it, this is your life now; criminal or not, you've got a black mark against your name.'

He squeezed Jonah's shoulders, before slapping his back firmly. Glumly, Jonah stared at Baxter as the harsh truth sank in: he was hurt and felt like all hope had been sucked out of him.

'I'll show you where you'll be staying; originally you were to be up in the servants' quarters with Miss Sandra and Cissy, but alas they weren't having any of that,' he said awkwardly.

He pointed to the door half-hidden in the corner, just left of the curtain. He walked forward, past the curtain and around large rolls of material that were haphazardly stacked around the door.

'We've been meaning to clean this up, but we've been very busy as of late, which is why I'm glad you're here, cutting material, fixing up simple bits while I work on the main pieces,' he said, breathing out slowly as he moved a particularly big black roll of material.

Jonah was squeezing past and just behind him as he bent forward and unlocked the dusty door. It creaked open to reveal a dark and tiny room. It had been neglected for what looked like years.

The wall was festering in mould and was peeling off in places; the floor was old wood that had a thick layer of dust and creaked with every step. In the centre of the room was a rusted bed with a thin mattress that was dotted with yellow stains.

Baxter coughed as he looked around the room. He raised his eyebrows and pushed out his cheeks. 'Well, I guess we didn't get round to doing it, after all,' he said with a nervous laugh.

The fury pumped through Jonah as he exhaled fiercely. 'Well, that's obvious,' he said through gritted teeth.

Taking a step back, Baxter laughed at Jonah's anger. 'Don't worry, we can fix this. I'll get you everything you need to clean this up nicely. There's a spare bed upstairs which you can have.'

Jonah rolled his eyes as he agreed, annoyed at having to take on such a huge renovation. His friend left him as he poked around the room, pulling at bits off the wall and rubbing it between his fingers.

Within moments Miss Sandra appeared at his shoulder, carrying a bucket, mop and scrubbers.

'Here you go, deary,' she said, placing them at his feet. 'Now you can get water from the kitchen and some soap; there's a bit of paint in the pantry if you want that, and in the far room upstairs is a bed you can help yourself to,' she said cheerily as she patted him on the back and left him to it.

He circled the room before deciding on taking the old bed apart and moving it into the backyard. He grunted as he moved the rusted hatches, the grooves of the bolts etching into his skin. He was at it over an hour before the entire thing disassembled. It was a victory, the first he had had in seven years, and he took it gleefully.

The sheer happiness spurred him on, and he began to work harder, cleaning up bit by bit, before Miss Sandra called him to get clean for the evening meal. She had placed a bowl outside with a cloth and soap. He was to wash like an animal, dabbing at his skin, crouched on the floor. After removing the dirt he beat the dust from his clothes and walked into the kitchen, almost presentable. A table had been set out, and Baxter was sitting with a bowl in front of him while Cissy and Miss Sandra lifted a large pot of stew onto the table.

Miss Sandra spooned stew into Baxter's bowl, making sure to give a hearty amount, while Cissy placed a large chunk of bread on the plate next to him. Jonah was drooling as he watched the large ladle fill the bowl, his stomach rumbling in anticipation as Miss Sandra reached for his bowl, filling it to the brim. His bread hit his chest as Cissy threw it at him, and he managed to catch it before it hit the floor. Baxter snarled as Cissy retreated to her seat, awaiting her food with a satisfied smile.

Miss Sandra finished with her own bowl, leaving plenty still in the pot, and together they said a small prayer, before gladly tucking into the meal. Jonah was ravenous and practically inhaled the succulent meat entwined with thick gravy, carrots and onions. He dunked his bread happily, and before he knew it, the entire bowl was empty, but he was nowhere near full. Just as he was placing his spoon down, Miss Sandra refilled the bowl with another huge helping, ensuring to pull out the largest pieces of meat, and complemented it with another large slice of bread.

He thanked her graciously as he once again began shovelling the delicious stew into his mouth as the others watched.

Chuckling, Miss Sandra said between a mouthful of stew, 'It's always nice to find someone who likes my cooking.' She smiled with a twinkle in her eyes.

Baxter laughed. 'Well, you do make a delightful stew, and I bet this is such a luxury for our dear guest, who has been hard at work all day. How is the room coming along?' he asked.

Swallowing a large piece of bread, Jonah cleared his throat. 'Good,' he said, wiping the back of his hand across his mouth. 'It's cleared up a bit, just needs the bed now. I've broken the old one down, it's in the back.' He pointed to the door with the bread still in his hand.

'Oh, good, a new feature for the garden,' Cissy piped in sarcastically as she lifted her spoon through the mixture.

'Enough, Cissy,' Baxter said firmly. 'You've shown your feelings, now let it go. Once Jonah has finished his room, he will be working with you, and you've got to understand that.' He glared at her as he pronounced each word.

Cissy rolled her eyes and sighed. 'Fine,' she said defeatedly. 'I'm going to bed, I'm tired; don't wake me dragging the bed down the stairs.' She narrowed her eyes at Jonah as she threw her food back in the bowl and scuttled upstairs, leaving Miss Sandra to clean the kitchen.

'She'll come round, deary just you see,' Miss Sandra said gently, squeezing his hand. She ladled the rest of the food into his bowl as Baxter excused himself.

Jonah sat happily eating as she worked around him, whistling gently as she cleaned. He lapped up the third bowl as if it was his first, and he sat as the food gently rested in his stomach.

Before long Jonah's head began to droop, and his eyes fluttered shut as he drifted off to sleep.

II

The caw of the birds echoed through the morning light, startling Jonah, who jerked forward, wincing at the ache in his neck and the bruise on his face.

He momentarily paused, the day's events washing over him as he stretched his body, his bones cracking with every movement.

'Good sleep, eh?' a warming voice said from behind him.

He jumped, turning quickly, pulling his neck and sending his back into a slight spasm. Jonah called out in pain as his eyes landed on Miss Sandra, who was dusted in flour.

Her eyes widened as she rushed towards him, placing her hand on his shoulder and firmly pushing him back down.

'I'm fine,' Jonah reassured her as he moved her hand away and pulled himself up, his eyes watered as the stabbing pain shot up his back.

After a few moments he attempted to stand, his feet shuffling forward until he slumped against the countertop in pain.

Miss Sandra stood tentatively at his side, biting her lip. After a few moments, she began pottering around him as he stood, panting.

He waited, biding his time, before he spoke through gritted teeth, 'I'm going to get that bed down before the morning commotion. I trust there will be breakfast?' he asked.

Miss Sandra simply nodded as Jonah made small steps towards the back staircase. He pulled himself up the steps with the help of the banister. Finally making it to the top, he hobbled to the last room, pushing the door open to see a small bed. It was slightly rusted, but entirely usable.

The room was clean and large, and it would have made a comfortable home had it not been for Cissy, he thought bitterly as he hobbled forward. There was very little light as Jonah bent down, grasping the frame while holding the lower part of his back. He began to drag the bed, grunting with every movement.

The pain in was becoming unbearable until a sharp tug of the bed caused his back to crack loudly, easing the pain.

He let out a joyous cry as he lifted the bed from the ground before haphazardly pulling it from the room.

He had got it halfway out of the room, the bedpost grinding on the door frame, when the door behind him was flung open with a loud bang.

He turned, his back cracking loudly, once again relieving the pain. Directly facing him was an angry Cissy, wrapped in a thin dressing gown.

'What are you doing?' she hissed.

Jonah pointed at his bed, his mouth slightly ajar, and she huffed loudly, before turning and slamming the door with force.

Closing his eyes and resting his head on the bed, he let out a muffled groan, before he began to carefully draw out the bed, dragging it gently across the floor and to the top of the stairs. He went first, using the slant to bring the bed down slowly.

Miss Sandra was still strutting around, the smell of fresh pastries wafting through the air, and she smiled as she saw him.

'You look better; those back cracks must have done the trick,' she said with a twinkle. 'Get that in your room and come back here for breakfast,' she commanded, as she walked to the pantry.

With extreme care, he dragged the bed to his room, the metal poles screeching as they went across the concrete floor. By the time he reached the room, he was dripping with sweat, and the ache in his back was returning.

He flung it into position, before sitting down on the thin mattress, taking deep breaths. Looking around the room, he smiled; it was cleaner and now, with a bed, more homely. There was a lot of work to be done, but it looked ten times better than the previous day.

A smile cracked on his face as he stood up and staggered to the kitchen. Cissy was sat quietly eating, and she turned her back when he entered the room, ignoring him. Rolling his eyes, he sat in the same seat as the previous night, just as Miss Sandra came through the pantry carrying a basket full of food. She quickly set it aside as she saw Jonah and began placing food in front of him and fixing him a drink.

Just like the previous night, he wolfed it down, with Miss Sandra continuing to place the crisp bread rolls on his plate. A large dish of butter and a jar of fresh strawberry jam sat in front of him, and with each roll he graciously spread the two, taking huge bites. The bread was still warm, and the butter melted gently into the bread, while the jam sweetened the mixture. It was divine, and he couldn't resist helping after helping. Miss Sandra simply watched with glee as he shovelled the food down.

'Baxter is out today; he has many errands to run, but he told me to tell you that you are to finish the room. He's left supplies and cleaning equipment in the yard,' she said with a smile as she lifted a tray of meat onto the table, once again filling his plate.

He nodded and greedily ate, as Cissy excused herself in disgust, but he didn't care; he was happy, and the tender meat was gracing his taste buds. He ate enough to feed at least three people, again needing another rest as his stomach bulged. He couldn't resist overeating, especially as Miss Sandra repeatedly filled his plate up as it neared empty.

For most of the morning, he sat, his gut hurting with how full it was, as Miss Sandra moved around him. Every so often, Cissy would appear and glare at him through the door as she picked up orders for customers.

Jonah sat contemplating, before summoning all his energy to move, dragging himself into the yard and slowly collecting all the items he needed to restore his room. He pulled the buckets, paint cans and brushes into his room and gently closed the door behind him. He was shattered; that bit of exercise had exhausted him. He perched on the bed and lay down slowly, closing his eyes for just one moment.

A loud knock at the door stirred him from his sleep, and he pushed himself up, wiping the drool from his face as he did so. Scrambling forward, Jonah moved to the door, crashing into the bucket and cans on the way. He cracked the door open, peeping his head around to see Miss Sandra.

'Hello, dear, it's been awfully quiet in here. Are you all right?' she asked softly.

With a small smile, he said with a yawn, 'Oh, yes, I'm very well. I've just been arranging things, trying to keep the noise down for Cissy.' He wiped the sleep from his eyes as he lied with confidence.

She nodded and turned around, before sneakily handing him a brown bag. Curious, he took it and opened it, to see a large sandwich with a large slice of cake underneath. He smiled as she passed him a flask of ale with a wink before she turned and left.

Smiling, he returned to his bed, taking care to step over odds and ends on the floor, before diving onto the bed and tucking into the giant sandwich. The soft bread had a thick layer of juicy beef which was drizzled in thick gravy. He messily ate the sandwich, with the juices dripping down his arms and onto his shirt. It was another long break that distracted him from his work, and it was well into mid-afternoon before he began to move and fix up the room as Baxter had requested.

Moving slowly, he began to sweep the floor, removing the debris and emptying the remains in the bucket. His next task was to clean the walls, and even looking at the job at hand made him weary. He groaned internally as he rested his head on the wall and looked at the ceiling, following the dots of mould as he contemplated his former life and that of his future. He had nothing, nothing but a bare room hidden away and festering with mould. He had grown used to the solitary life in a cell, and despite the shackles being removed, he found himself back there.

The moments ticked by, his breathing heavy as the sad realisation hit him; he would never truly be a free man.

Time passed steadily, and he was only drawn from his daze when a sharp knock rapped at the door. Jonah jumped as he turned as Baxter walked in, he was drawing a pair of fine leather gloves from his hands, his long coat billowing behind him.

His thick head of black hair was windswept from being outside, and he brushed it with his hands as he glanced around the room. The wrinkles around his eyes stretched as he noticed the lack of work that had been done.

Baxter cocked his head towards Jonah, his strong jaw angling in the air as he rubbed the bristles of his beard in annoyance.

Stuttering, Jonah opened his mouth. 'I... I've made a start on the room, as you can see. I'm just... I pulled my back earlier on, and this is the comfiest position I've found myself in,' he lied.

Nodding, Baxter looked at him. 'I see,' he said with a sigh. 'Maybe you should rest for a while, and I'll have Miss Sandra bring your meals in until your back is better. Would you like me to fetch the doctor?' he asked wearily

'Oh, I don't think a doctor is necessary,' Jonah said awkwardly as he waved him away. 'Rest would be appreciated, and then, of course, I'll get right back to cleaning up the room.'

'Very well then,' Baxter said with a small smile, before he turned and left.

Jonah smiled as he rested his head on the wall; genuine rest, he thought gladly, as he folded his arms and crossed his legs and leaned gratefully on the solid wall behind him.

Rest, he thought happily, a quiet laugh escaping his lips as he revelled in his glee until another knock came, this time with the friendly face of Miss Sandra. She brought with her a tray that was filled with a big bowl of soup, two large sandwiches filled with beef and three large scones with slabs of butter and jam on the side. Tucked under the crook of her arm was a large jug of ale.

She placed it on the bed and patted him on the arm. Leaning in, she whispered, 'Baxter is going to be out again tomorrow. I think we should get a desk in here so you can eat a bit more carefully. I'll help if your back is still hurting, deary.' She smiled as she left.

He waited a few moments before quickly walking to the bed. He crouched down and began eating the delicious food; there was so much, and it was all so rich and creamy. The sandwich and soup went down a treat, and it was time to turn his attention to the scones. They were crunchy on the outside and delightfully soft on the inside, and he greedily applied the butter and jam, taking bites of the divine sweet treats.

At that moment he was the happiest he'd been; he was in his own company, with no harsh looks or fear of being hurt. He didn't even realise he was crying until Miss Sandra came in. She'd tapped gently on the door before entering with another large jug of ale and even more scones.

Wiping a stray tear away, she smiled at him again, before leaving and returning with a wooden chair, and she kindly placed a pillow on the back. He crawled onto it and was trying to thank her between a mouthful of food as she left, closing the door behind her.

He chewed feverishly, inhaling the food, and he didn't stop until all but a few crumbs remained. After finally finishing the last of the food, he rested back on the chair and lifted his feet to the bed like a slob. His stomach was so full, but he was thirsty, so he slowly reached down and grabbed one of the jugs, drinking heartily.

It took him a while to finish, but once he had, he reached for the second and began to drain that steadily. By the time he was finished, he was merrily drunk and simply laid there full and happy. Once again, he drifted off to sleep, his head lolling down as he drunkenly slept into the night.

The clattering of the jug hitting the floor as it slipped from his sleeping hands made him wake suddenly, jerking his body forward, and he slowly opened his eyes, his head aching in pain. He grasped it, groaning loudly when the door was flung open causing him to yell.

Miss Sandra slowly came into view; her figure was blurry, and he was blinking furiously, trying to get his eyes to focus.

'No wonder your back is hurting,' she said loudly. 'Sleeping in that chair! You should be in bed.'

Her voice rang high and loud as he swayed and lifted his hand over his face, shielding himself from her looming body. She scuttled around him, picking up the empty jugs and plates from the floor. She swatted the crumbs away, before nudging him to get into bed, and he willingly obliged; as she left, he leant forward and crawled in between the sheets.

There he snuggled his head into the pillow and wrapped himself under the cold sheets as he prepared to go back to sleep, only for Miss Sandra to walk back in again. Eagerly he lifted his head, watching as Miss Sandra brought in a plate of eggs, sausages, potatoes and bread, followed by another large jug of ale.

He smiled as the smell wafted through the air, his stomach grumbling in anticipation. Happily, he reached forward and wolfed the food down, the juices of the sausage and bacon engulfing his taste buds. He mopped up the fat with the bread and finished the large plate off in moments, before lowering his head and sleeping the morning away, happy and full.

When he awoke, Miss Sandra was back in his room, removing the plate and leaving another plate of freshly baked bread seeped in butter and yet another jug of ale. This time he sat himself up, taking gentle bites and savouring the food. Like a hospital patient in bed, he sat there leisurely eating, before turning his attention to the ale. For the remainder of the afternoon, he sat and drank from them, the alcohol infecting his body as he joyfully lay, hearing the murmurs of Cissy and Baxter beyond the door. They were busy: gaggles of people were entering the shop and back room for fittings and measurements. He was glad to just sit and rest, for their efforts were making him tired enough.

He had just drained the last of the ale, when in came Miss Sandra again with a plate of fruit and another jug tucked under her arm. She collected his empties and left, promising him two large pies and potatoes for tea, which was to be delivered soon. Again, he tucked in, waiting for his meal, which finally arrived, smelling of delicious baked pastry entwined in a beef broth; the crust was buttery and once more the juices flowed.

The pies were the size of his hands, and he had big strong hands. He ate with both of them, deliciously absorbing the food into his filled belly. It was delightful to be treated so lovingly. After the meal, he drank heartily as Miss Sandra bought him more ale and the occasional gin to soothe the pains in his back.

By the time he was ready to sleep again, he was well and truly drunk, and he drifted into a deep sleep still perched upwards.

III

For the next week, the same events followed: he would awake uncomfortably and be presented food without so much as a word. He would sit in his bed all day, eating and drinking to his heart's content.

Miss Sandra would do all the work, bringing food and taking the plates, even removing his chamber pot and emptying it.

During this time, his stomach expanded and his chin filled as he enjoyed the solitary life of rich food and alcohol with the help of a willing slave. All day, he would listen to the ongoings of the shop, the woes and constant footfall of the customers echoing around as the work continued to pile up.

Prison seemed years ago as he settled into his new life, one free of pain and one he deluded himself into earning. He enjoyed having zero responsibilities, but always being a part of his surroundings. He liked to eavesdrop on Cissy and Baxter, only to hear their woes, and thank heaven that he wasn't in the heart of the hardships.

For the most part, they grumbled about the rude and obnoxious ladies and the ever-growing demands made daily. The socialite balls were commencing, and they were inundated; they were tired and grumbling when Jonah heard Cissy and Baxter start to hiss at one another heatedly. It was his usual sleep time, but his ears perked up at the thought of the entertainment.

'We can't keep going on like this,' Cissy spoke harshly. 'We need help, and your little inmate isn't pulling his weight — he's just eating it.'

Baxter sighed. 'I know that. I'm just as angry, and I know I keep saying it, but I will kick him out if he doesn't start working. Next week, I promise, I'll talk with him.' He spoke in a low and angry voice.

Cissy laughed. 'You keep saying this, but it never happens. He needs to leave!'

There was silence for a moment, and Jonah nervously awaited Baxter's response. Drawing the covers close to his face, straining to hear his fate, and his heart was racing when Baxter uttered firmly, 'He has one week.'

Beads of sweat formed on his face as he heard the clatter of Cissy's shoes over the hard floor. He gulped as loud footsteps approached his door. Without hesitation, he jumped up, his bare feet hitting the floor for the first time in days, and it felt strange and alien to him. He looked down to wiggle his toes and was surprised to find a large belly hiding them. He jiggled it with his hands and marvelled at how big he'd gotten. The door opened, and he moved quickly to make the bed and move the chair as Baxter walked in.

He looked fierce, his forehead wrinkling as he marched in, shutting the door behind him, and momentarily his eyes fluttered as he saw Jonah standing.

The shock caused him to pause, in which time Jonah managed to speak, quickly saying, 'Baxter, I'm just about to start working again. My back just clicked back into place, although it aches.' He grasped his back in fake pain as he lowered himself down to the ground, picking up a sponge.

Curiosity breezed over Baxter's face as he cocked his head and frowned. 'A surprising turnaround,' he said, choosing his words carefully. 'I'm pleased to see you awake and willing to work once again, earning your keep, as it were.' With a fleeting smile, he left, leaving Jonah standing there with a dry sponge in his hand.

He stared around the room, gulping loudly, before he reached for the bucket and walked to the door, which he peered his head around to make sure there were no customers. Thankfully, the room was empty, but he could hear Baxter and Cissy muttering in the front of the shop. He paused to listen, but they were talking too quietly.

He tried to move closer to the door, but the wood creaked under his weight, which caused them to stop speaking abruptly. Baxter lifted the curtain that divided the rooms and stared at Jonah, who sheepishly waved the bucket at him. Baxter nodded, before drawing the curtain closed, and Jonah walked away from them and into the kitchen.

Miss Sandra was nowhere to be seen, much to his relief, and he marched confidently into the kitchen and helped himself to water, before carrying the full bucket to his room. He was gasping hard at the weight, before gladly lowering it to the floor. It had been a long time since he'd carried something so heavy, and he was feeling it.

He grunted under the weight, and he was heaving heavily as he sat on the bed, looking at the room before him. It was a mess, and it was only then that realised he had to live in the shite he had. He felt the pain, he felt the hatred, and he let it fuel him as he grabbed the sponge and scrubbed the walls, removing the mould with force.

For two days he worked hard, sleeping for a few hours to get it done, and he hated what he had become. The work drained his life source and broke him down. It destroyed his body to have done so much. He was a weak and overweight man, making futile attempts to stay above water.

That aggressive work completely wrecked him, but at last the room was finally finished, the mould removed, the floors cleaned, and it looked brighter, nicer and less like a cell. It did make him proud, but his chest was tight and his bones were weary. For the first time in two days he crawled into bed at a reasonable time, pulling the covers over him, his eyes immediately closing when his head hit the pillow.

IV

A loud clatter sounded, startling Jonah who immediately sat up, looking to see his intruder. He'd been having a nightmare: he was back in his cell and the morning had dawned. He had a vision of a thug in uniform approaching his room; he was panicking, his breath had become short, and he was sweating profusely.

As his vision cleared, Jonah saw Baxter approaching him, and with great effort he heaved a deep sigh as he lifted himself up on one arm.

'I see you're back in bed,' Baxter said wearily.

'Yes, sorry, I have finished the room,' he said groggily, pointing around the room. 'I was just so tired; the work really took it out of me.' He grimaced at his weak excuse.

'Right, of course it did. I think we need to talk.' Baxter spoke softly as he pulled the chair to the bed.

'We had a deal. I liberated you from a life of misery and in exchange you work for me. We're drowning in work out there, and you need to get up and get working,' he said defiantly.

A few moments passed as Jonah sat groggily absorbing Baxter's words.

Finally he nodded, 'Of course.' He paused, the guilt washing over him. 'I'm sorry. I know I've disappointed you, but I'll be in the shop first thing tomorrow.'

Baxter stood up without warning. 'Not the shop! You'll work here, and Cissy will bring you work to do; likewise, Miss Sandra will be providing meals. I need you to be a secret for a little while longer,' he said, as he walked back through the door, closing it with a loud snap.

Jonah wiped his hands over his face and flung his body back, groaning loudly. The bed shuddered and wheezed under his weight.

Tomorrow he was back at work, tomorrow everything was to change and the motivation to be the person he once was had long gone.

A sudden feeling of dread hit him hard. His mind was whirling as he tried to recall how to stitch and sew, how to take rags and make them into riches that graced the fine men and women of Manchester.

A gentle knock pulled him from his self-pity, and he shouted for whoever it was to enter. Miss Sandra waddled in, a large tray in hand with a plate of meat and two bowls on either side, one overflowing with crisp potatoes and the other filled with green beans and carrots. His mouth was watering as he quickly sat up, readily receiving the tray. She smiled at his delight, before walking out and promptly returning with two giant jugs of beer.

By which time, Jonah had begun eating the enormous amount of food. It looked like he had half of a large meat joint, and it was dripping in thick gravy. The potatoes and vegetables were smothered in butter and delightfully slid down his throat. He was so distracted by the food that he didn't even notice that Miss Sandra had been and left twice, first with the drink and back again with a plate full of scones and jam.

Jonah sat and ate like a pig, shovelling the food in, and by the time he was finished, he was so full that his stomach ached. He loosened his trousers and breathed deeply as he reached for the first jug. There he sat and drank heartily, glugging the first one, his head feeling light and his vision funny, before grasping the second one.

Once more he drank deep into the night, before he dropped into a deep sleep, the jug resting on his chest, snoring contentedly.

V

Morning dawned and Jonah was startled awake by the sounds of Miss Sandra clattering into his room. Throwing his head back against the metal frame, he grumbled as she cleared up the mess and removed the cleaning supplies, before returning with a large bowl of porridge. He was groggy, and his head was thumping as she forced the hot bowl into his hands.

'Wake up, deary,' Miss Sandra whispered. 'You're back at work today; you need to be up and raring to go soon.' She patted his shoulder as she left.

Jonah sat, his stomach queasy as he slowly ate the food. He was taking his time, the pain of his head clouding his vision and slowing his pace.

Suddenly, a rap at the door sounded, he jumped and quickly stared at the old wooden door. 'You'd better be awake and ready to start working,' Cissy's voice came through loud and angry.

Scrambling, he moved quickly, throwing the half-eaten food down on the chair and attempting to fasten his trousers and get his shirt and shoes on to look presentable. He draped the sheet over the bed to look as if he had made it and slowly walked to the door, pulling it open.

Cissy took one look and rolled her eyes. 'With me,' she said, turning on her heels and marching into the back room.

'You are under my command now,' she said with an evil smile. 'You'll be working from your room, doing whatever task I deem important.'

'This,' she said, pointing at half a dozen cuts for dresses, 'needs to be done today; they need stitching neatly and hemming tidily. We have standards here, and I will be checking.' She pointed her bony finger at him.

The sweat started to form on his head. 'I will do my best,' he said, faintly looking at the dresses.

She huffed, judging his capabilities.

He sighed as he reached for the dresses, retreating to his room and laying them on the bed.

Unbeknown to him, Cissy had followed him to the room and startled him when she spoke in his ear. 'You'll need to set the room up first; this should have been done days ago, but, of course, you spent it eating and drinking merrily while we slaved away.'

Jonah gulped as he eyed her; she was leaning into his ear, whispering angrily, calling him out of his laziness.

Nervously, he walked back and forth, collecting needles, an assortment of threads and a set of sharp scissors that Baxter had set aside for him. He cleared the dust on the sewing desk, before laying out the tools and setting the chair in front, readying himself for the day's work. Ignoring his rumbling stomach, he discarded the bowl on the floor and pulled up the first dress.

It took him a few attempts to get the cotton through the eye of the needle, and then he sat, slowly working, his head throbbing.

Moments later, the door opened and Jonah let out an angry sigh, half-expecting another telling off, until he realised it was Miss Sandra, back with yet another plate of food. To his surprise, midday had arrived and he had barely got anything done, but he didn't let that stop him from enjoying the hearty meal that came with a layer of meat, cheese and bread, all of which he washed down with half a jug of beer.

Merrily he returned to his work, finishing up three of the dresses, when Cissy came in to announce the closure of the shop. He simply handed her the dresses he'd finished and placed the remainder on the desk in preparation for tomorrow.

'You're not going to finish those tonight?' she asked snidely.

Jonah looked at them, hoping he'd be done for the night, and his hands wandered over the soft material before he said, 'I will finish them later. I'll just have my food, and they'll be ready for the morning.' He smiled tiredly at her.

Once again, she huffed, before turning around and marching out of the room, loudly slamming the door behind her.

It had barely closed when Miss Sandra knocked, and Jonah opened the door, to be faced with another large tray of food and another jug of beer.

Not wanting to lay the tray on the desk, he sat on his bed and placed the tray on his lap as he tucked into the two large bowls of stew with three large chunks of bread that he eagerly dipped into the thick juices. Then he drank, the effects of the alcohol seeping into his mind and once more lulling him into a deep sleep.

VI

In the early hours, Miss Sandra bobbed in, waking him from his slumber and readying him once more for the day, breakfast in her hand, enticing him from his sleep.

He gladly ate his overly large bowl of porridge, shovelling the wholesome hot meal down his throat as he sat in bed. It was a wondrous feeling that was short-lived by an angry Cissy marching into his room without notice. He jumped and looked around wide-eyed as she went to his sewing desk, where yesterday's work sat, unfinished.

Her nostrils flared as she glared at him, 'I see you haven't got the work done as I asked,' she spoke through gritted teeth.

'Ah,' he said, raising his finger at her, while he sat in bed, 'I was going to do it, but I fell asleep. I think strenuous work at the moment isn't good for me. I need to work myself up, if that makes sense.'

Her eyes narrowed, her face contorted in anger as she towered over him.

'Oh, is that right?' she asked. 'Well, I guess I'd better reduce your workload — I'd hate for you to tire yourself out doing an actual job,' she sneered sarcastically, before stomping out of the room.

Jonah watched her leave. His heart was racing as he wiped the clammy sweat off his forehead as he stood up, looking at the work in front of him.

Once more, the door was flung open, and he turned to see Baxter, who smiled at Jonah, looking at his scruffy appearance.

His hair was a mess, his trousers and shirt crinkled and tight, his stomach was hanging over the button of his trousers, straining against the weight.

'Jonah, we need to get you some new clothes. I'll arrange for Miss Sandra to bring some in. I'd have Cissy do it, but she isn't talking to you at the moment.' He sighed, rubbing his eyes.

Jonah nodded. 'That's very kind of you, sir. I know Cissy hates me, she's made it perfectly clear; but, Baxter, look at the workload. I'm in the process of reteaching myself here,' he sighed wearily, holding his hands up as he tried to excuse his actions confidently.

Hands on his hips, Baxter looked up at the ceiling, biting his lip in annoyance. Breathing deeply, he met Jonah's worried look.

'Fine,' he said, 'we'll go at your pace, I guess. Your suit will be coming soon; get changed and get to work for me.' Baxter nodded again, before leaving him alone in the room.

Jonah smiled and clasped his hands together. It was going to be an easy life from now on, he thought. He waited until Miss Sandra came back; she had his suit and a plate of buttered bread in her hands.

He thanked her gladly as he got into his suit and once again ate the food willingly. He returned to his work, his hands moving slowly over the material.

It was approaching midday when a gentle knock sounded and Jonah smiled, patting his stomach as he called for Miss Sandra.

To his surprise, Cissy walked in, her head slightly bowed. 'I need to speak with you,' she said softly. 'Baxter has informed me about your need to relearn your skill; he's also told me not to be so harsh on you. I admit I've been tough, but Baxter is a good man.' She paused as she looked at him.

He was just sitting at the desk, fiddling with the same dress he'd been working on earlier that morning.

'I'm going to lessen the work, make it easier for you. I might just give you simple tasks that you can even do in your bed.' She patted his hand and smiled.

Jonah's eyes widened in happiness. 'This is going to really help me. I can't believe you're being so kind, but I will take it.' He smiled widely at her as she lifted his hand and dropped it in his lap.

She gathered the clothes and left without another word, leaving Jonah still in the chair and with only one dress to finish for the day.

For the remainder of the day, he worked slowly and awaited the quiet taps on the door from Miss Sandra, who would walk in with food and jugs of ale for him to indulge in. All is right with the world, he smiled happily to himself. For the first time in his life he wasn't starving thanks to the lovely Miss Sandra and now, Cissy is even being nice. His smile broadened as he rested in his chair.

It was bliss, and he finally had everything he wanted: a comfortable life with everything he needed to sustain him. He decided to take it in his stride; this, after all, was what he was owed after he'd been robbed, broken down and lived in unimaginable states — now it was time for him to have it easy. To live as a king like he would have done if his grandfather hadn't run off with a poor wench.

As the following weeks passed, Jonah was finding the new routine was working for him. The animosity seemed to have settled, not that Jonah barely ventured outside of his room; Miss Sandra would clear out his chamber pot and bring him food, while Cissy would drop his work off and collect it when finished.

Sometimes she even stopped in his room throughout the day doing the work for him as he lounged on the bed.

The first time this happened, Jonah had just polished off a huge roast dinner with a large slab of meat and potatoes. He took to the bed so that he wouldn't drop any food on the shirt he was hemming. Cissy barged in, carrying a box of buttons. Jonah had lunged forward and with a mouth full of food he tried to give an explanation, but Cissy didn't flinch; she stood, her hands dropped, and she heaved a big sigh.

'Jonah,' she groaned, 'this needs to be done today. Mr Hanson paid extra to get it finished. I thought you'd be done by now.'

Instead of chastising him like he thought she would, she sat down at the desk and began doing the work for him, much to his surprise. He tried to protest, but she waved him away, telling him to finish his lunch. He awkwardly stood, hovering around her, before reluctantly sitting on the bed and eating

She worked with grace, finishing the shirt off within a matter of minutes, making it look easy while he had been struggling all day to keep the stitching straight.

Over the following days, Cissy became a frequent visitor, stopping by shortly after Miss Sandra brought him his lunch. Every day she would pick up where he left off while he sat on the bed, awkwardly watching her work.

'Cissy.' Jonah paused as she looked at him. 'Why are you being so kind?'

She smiled and bowed her head. 'Baxter, he, well he threatened me with my job, told me to go easier on you. He, well he told me a bit about you. About Rose, your mother and that you had been betrayed in Birmingham.' She bit her lip, waiting for his response.

Jonah poked the crumbs on his plate and shrugged his shoulders. 'Yes, it was awful, although I did tell you this when we first met.' He raised his eyebrows, playfully smiling at her.

Cissy rolled her eyes. 'Yes, well, most criminals would say the same.' She turned in the chair and leaned forward, her eyes meeting his. 'I am sorry for how I treated you. It seems you've been subjected to a harsh life.'

'I understand, working with a criminal isn't ideal but thank you, for everything.' He patted her hand, relief washing over him.

That conversation changed everything. The days became less tiresome as Cissy took it upon herself to do his afternoon tasks. Jonah had grown accustomed to this, he'd earned it, he thought righteously. I have lived a terrible life, now it's time to live in comfort. From then on, he would rest on the bed, using only the muscles in his arms to reach for food and ale. He knew the work, no matter how tedious, would get done by her.

Often, he would find himself smiling at the two women whose lives he had bundled into. He relied on the pair to keep him fed and housed. Life was good, he contemplated, it was exactly how it should be.

The Watcher

Dear reader, dear, dear, reader, I am forever sorry for the story of Jonah, the story that you have persisted with.

He lived a life of turmoil, and now he had been tricked into one that was redundant and false; he was so happy to have a free life out of prison, but failed to see he had swapped one prison for another.

Without his permission, he'd been sweetened by Sloth and Greed, who had portrayed their parts beautifully. They presented themselves brilliantly, gaining his trust, winning his heart and soul, while taking what little he had

Sloth and Greed are disastrous in their own right; they wonderfully seep into lives, often undisguised, until it's too late, too hard to abandon.

Laziness is barely beaten, it is too easy to fall back into old habits, to give up and sit back, especially if everything is handed to a person — there's no need to be active if someone is so willing to be the provider.

It's a disheartening thing to witness, to see a man who would have worked day and night to achieve his dreams, to becoming one so reliant on others and redundant to his peers.

Dear reader, our story is coming to a close. I fear there are few Sins left that have to entwine into Jonah's life. The end is nigh, and my woes for the future of Jonah are ever-increasing; what they have planned will surely be horrid.

They are creatures of evil; they seek to destroy in ways that don't always seem effective, but one act, one notion changes the entire future. Remember what I said when I first met you all those years ago: the paths are set in stone, some walkways branch off, ones that suddenly change the course of direction.

Jonah had been coerced down so many, some that he wasn't even to have glanced down, some that shouldn't have even been built for his life; but alas here we stand, here we see the terrible turmoil that shook and rocked his life.

Constantly building and breaking the man, deconstructing his soul, one that should have been happy and strong. Let's not forget he was created from the love of a soulmate; those kinds of connections are bursting with energy, strong as an ox, indestructible, like the rivers of lava that flow deep below the Earth.

I have mixed feelings. I fear for Jonah's future, but cannot wait for the Sins to return to the Hollow, to feel their ghastly presence once more and not scheming in the world, destroying the simple souls, changing their lives with that of Jonah's.

Now, dear reader, I sadly must leave you. I don't want to, I don't want you to hear these events, but this is it, this is the climax. It will be deafening, and I hope that you finally hear my deepest sorrows and know that I, too, felt the pain of these hideous events.

Envy

Baxter had been pacing around the shop floor, methodically glancing at the clock and then at the curtain that led into the sewing parlour.

Cissy had been leaving the front end unattended freely for the past few weeks, not long after he'd given her the biggest berating of her life to ensure Jonah continued to work. He didn't know if it was in defiance or if she was listening to him and helping Jonah to become the tailor he required.

Either way, his shop being unattended was a risk to his business — seven customers had freely walked into the back, noting that nobody was there to welcome them. It always seemed to be the prolific customers that marched their way in, the ones that had the power to destroy a reputation with a single word.

He was pacing back and forth, hearing the muffled voices of Jonah and Cissy as the shop remained abandoned. The hand on the clock had strolled past the hour as his patience began to wear thin, when the door suddenly opened.

Cissy came strolling into the room, carrying a vibrant green silk dress with a happy smile upon her face.

She jumped at the sight of Baxter, who was staring at her, his finger lifted to his chin, gently stroking it.

'Baxter, you made me jump. I have Miss Louise's dress here; she should be here any minute to pick it up,' she said with a smile.

He nodded at her. 'We need to talk,' he said calmly. 'You've been spending an awful lot of time doing his work for him, and you've been neglecting your duties here.'

He paused, before continuing, 'I can't have this any more. You've done what I asked, but a price has come with it. I can't have you removed from the shop, but I need the work done by Jonah, who clearly isn't capable at this moment. We need to get him confident, we need someone to help him.'

Baxter was pacing back and forth as he spoke. 'I'm going to take on an apprentice. I'll train him up in the evenings, and he can run the shop and help Jonah. We're so busy that an extra pair of hands is easily affordable; apprentices are cheap, and we do need the help.'

With confidence, Baxter looked to Cissy, who held the dress close, her head bowed as she frowned, thinking.

'I suppose that would work, Jonah. He's not too bad once you talk to him; a lot of hate towards the world, bathes quiet and let's you get on with your work.' She smiled as she spoke, before raising her gaze.

'An apprentice sounds like the perfect action?' he asked.

Cissy nodded furiously as he spoke; he'd clearly asked her a question that she had neglected and was wanting an answer that he already had.

Smiling, Baxter looked at her. 'Good. Now place this ad in the window for men only — after all, Jonah is a man, they'll be working together, and he is a criminal,' he said, pulling a small card from his jacket and handing it over to her, before heading into the back with a smile.

Cissy placed the advertisement in the window and was sure to mention it to every customer that came in. The tailor hadn't hired in a while, and good work or the potential of a career was slim.

Over the forthcoming days, many young men approached but Baxter was insistent on hiring a person of strong will that could confidently work in the back room with Jonah. Those that had enquired were poorly skilled. They were built for labouring, not for the art of dress making.

What he wanted was a young Jonah, a man who had a rough idea of stitching, one who would learn quickly and one that was eager to have a better life than the one they were destined for.

It was well over a week before a decent candidate walked in. Baxter was at breaking point when the surprise arrival of Jimmy Flack came. He was a strapping lad, way over six foot, and he had to stoop to get through the door.

He had thick black curls, deep silver-grey eyes, a sharply pointed nose and chiselled cheeks. Freckles dotted around his face, giving him a boyish yet handsome presentation. He wore a suit, worn and thin in patches, but smart enough for the area.

He Strolled to the counter confidently and smiled softly to Cissy. 'Hello,' he said charmingly, 'I'm here about the job.' He pulled the card out of the window and pocketed it.

Cissy raised her eyebrows in a combined shock and awed notion. 'You are, are you?' she asked.

He nodded, pulling at the collar of his jacket as he looked around the shop.

Cissy narrowed her eyes as she watched him walk around the shop. 'And what makes you think you can do this job?' she asked.

'Well,' he said confidently, 'I have a bit of experience. My mum is a seamstress, a good one, too, worked all her life altering the rich ladies' clothes. She taught me a fair bit; my mum always said that a man needs a skill.'

He walked to the front of the desk, resting both hands and peering into Cissy's eyes. She looked at him and smiled sweetly, before turning and heading into the back without a word.

'Baxter,' she called as she entered the back.

He wandered in from the kitchen, chewing on a muffin, while Miss Sandra rushed by with a massive plate of food and a jug towards Jonah's room.

'Cissy, my girl, how can I help you?' he said, rolling his eyes at Miss Sandra as he caressed his muffin.

'Well, I think we've found our apprentice. He's in the shop — he's got experience, he's big, and he's confident,' she said methodically.

A smile spread across his face. 'Excellent news! I thought we weren't going to find anyone,' he said, placing the muffin on the table as he walked towards the shop floor.

He strolled into the shop, his eyes resting on Jimmy's large frame as he stood tall in the shop, looking out of the window and onto the street outside.

Baxter cleared his throat loudly. Jimmy jumped and spun around, facing him, a look of surprise on his face.

'Hello, sir,' he said, swallowing. 'My name is Jimmy Flack, and I would like to be put forward for the apprenticeship.' He smiled weakly as he kept eye contact with Baxter.

'Yes, Cissy said so; she also said you had experience, so let's head into the back room and talk about this some more,' he said, smiling as he lifted the countertop for Jimmy to enter the back.

Wonder washed over his face as he followed Baxter, who sat on the armchair, gesturing for Jimmy to sit on the sofa next to him. He called for Miss Sandra to bring tea and cake for them to enjoy while they talked.

Jimmy spoke eagerly, detailing his experience and excitement to be training under Baxter. For over an hour they talked, drank tea and ate together, even sharing the odd joke.

Baxter had him help with some hemming and was surprised at his skill. 'You are going to be a good asset to my shop. Now let me show you around, and you can start settling in. Tomorrow we begin work,' he said, watching the glee emerge on Jimmy's face.

'Thank you, thank you so much, sir. I cannot tell you how happy I am,' he said, shaking Baxter's hand furiously.

Baxter smiled, clapping Jimmy on the shoulder as he led him through the building, showing him the place, introducing him to Miss Sandra and Cissy formally. He was designated a room next to Baxter's: it was small, more a cupboard than a room, but it had all the essentials for a comfortable night's sleep.

'Well, I'm happy with all of this,' Jimmy exclaimed in the kitchen as he excitedly looked around as Miss Sandra brought him a muffin to eat.

'Is there anything else that I need to know?' he asked, taking a bite of the warm muffin, a huge smile on his face.

Miss Sandra and Baxter exchanged looks as he nervously flicked at the crumbs on the tabletop. 'Well, there is one thing. You see, throughout the day I will be busy with orders, and I'll need you to do odd jobs with my other apprentice, Jonah Heizium; he has his own room that you'll be working in.'

He looked up and met Jimmy's eyes, who was looking confused. 'Jonah has an unusual background: he was imprisoned for theft in Birmingham, he's a good tailor but has lost his way and needs guidance. Are you still willing to take the job?' he asked as he explained the situation.

Rubbing his face with his hands, Jimmy looked at Baxter and then to Miss Sandra, who smiled warmly. 'He's a lovely man, Jimmy, and you'll be fine in there with him,' she said as she patted his hand.

Jimmy nodded. 'Right, well, I wasn't expecting that. Will everyone have to know that I work with a criminal?' He spoke methodically as he asked the question.

'No, we keep Jonah in his own room and out of sight of the customers. Alas, his work ethic has dwindled since leaving prison, which is why I need you,' Baxter said quickly.

Jimmy took a deep breath. 'I accept your offer.' He paused. 'It's a better life than one in the mills.'

Baxter smiled in relief. 'Excellent news my boy!' he cried out in joy. 'Don't worry too much about Jonah, and to make up for him I'll give you an additional two shillings.'

A gasp left Jimmy as he eyed his new boss. 'That's very generous, sir. I can't wait to tell my mother, she'll be so proud.'

'Of course. Go now and collect your things to be placed in your new room,' Baxter ordered him and without hesitation, Jimmy waved goodbye.

By mid-afternoon, Jimmy had returned, a small satchel bouncing on his back as he walked into the parlour. Miss Sandra took him upstairs where he unpacked before wandering back down into the kitchen.

Baxter was waiting for him. 'Come, I'll run through the basics.' He marched into the parlour with Jimmy swiftly following.

They sat at the far table, Baxter pulling a half-sewn dress and showing Jimmy how he stitched the seams, how the dress went from a sheet of material to a delightful dress. During this time, Miss Sandra was constantly marching back and forth to the room just before the shop; to the criminal. It seemed she was either bringing or removing jugs and plates, always leaving with empty pots left by the disgrace.

It seemed that the former criminal just ate and drank his days away while being waited on by a sweet old lady, Jimmy thought disgustedly. Although the trips were frequent, he didn't get a glimpse of Jonah and before long, the day's end had come.

That evening, they all sat and ate, and Jimmy broached the subject of Jonah, asking where he was.

'Jonah stays in his room, and it became an unspoken agreement following an injury. Miss Sandra takes care of his needs, ensuring he is fed,' Baxter said as he put his wine glass to his mouth and readily drank the sweet red nectar.

Miss Sandra laughed and said cheerily, 'Jonah likes to eat. He has a big appetite, and I like to cook, so it goes hand in hand.'

'Yes, and because of that, he never gets any work done, so I usually do it for him,' Cissy said, rolling her eyes.

Jimmy frowned. 'Doesn't that annoy you all?' he asked.

'Of course it does, but I pity him; he was close to being his own tailor with a shop, but he lost it all,' Baxter said thoughtfully.

Jimmy played with his food, thinking it over. It seemed to him that Jonah was a freeloader and living a good life at the expense of others. Unlike his employer, he did not have the same attitude; he had been brought up to take pride in his work and to work hard for a living.

He came to the conclusion that Jonah was of no good and he was not to be taken advantage of by a lay-about.

They sat in silence for a few moments, before Miss Sandra insisted that Jimmy tell them more about himself. He gladly obliged, talking about his family, especially his mother, who he was very close to. Together they sat and talked deep into the night, getting to know one another, as Miss Sandra wandered around, cleaning up the food, bringing out more and readily topping up everyone's drinks.

Baxter eventually called for them to head to bed, as the sky grew darker. They gladly followed suit, each one full and sleepy.

I

The morning dawned, and Jimmy was drawn out of his sleep by loud thuds on his door and the unmistakable call from Cissy as she aroused everyone.

Sleepily, he got up and began pulling his clothes on. He quickly ran a comb through his hair and headed down to the kitchen.

Cissy was sitting at the table, looking pristine as she sipped a warm cup of tea and flicked through the morning paper.

'It's a help-yourself system in the mornings,' she said, not looking up.

He pressed his lips together and reached for a slice of bread and a cup, pouring himself some tea. There he sat, quietly chewing the food that he had buttered and ladled with ripe strawberry jam.

Baxter walked in just as he took the last bite. He smiled, taking the head seat.

'Good morning, all,' he said cheerily. 'I hope you each had a good night's sleep.'

'Indeed, I did,' Cissy chimed. 'Now to the daily grind.' She smiled as she threw the paper down, drained the dregs from her cup and glided out of the kitchen.

'That time again, eh?' he said to Jimmy, smiling. 'If you go to the front with Cissy and grab the work she wants doing, I'm going to let Jonah know you're here.'

Jimmy nodded and left, his eyes darting back as he watched Baxter enter the convict's room. Baxter crept in, making sure to hide Jonah who was inhaling his large breakfast that Miss Sandra had delivered.

Jonah quickly stopped eating at the surprise intrusion. He threw the food down, looking at Baxter in shock as he smiled upon his entrance.

He confidently walked in, taking the seat and placing it in front of him as he brushed the food away.

'Jonah,' he sighed, 'I've hired an apprentice and I've made the decision for him to start working with you, we need the extra help,' he spoke clearly, the disappointment ringing in his tone.

Wide-eyed, Jonah pulled the covers off him, revealing his massive stomach straining under his shabby pants. He kicked his feet out and tried to pull himself upwards.

'A new apprentice starting today? Will he be working in here?' he asked.

'Yes, it will be crammed, but we can easily fit another chair in here, or you could perch on the bed,' Baxter replied, as he stood up, replaced the chair and walked towards the door.

Jonah jumped up, scrambling to make the bed and straighten the place up. He ran his hands through his hair, trying to flatten it, then began brushing his clothes, batting at the dust and stains. He huffed, fully aware that he looked awful, his skin pale and clammy, his suit wrinkled and misshapen.

The door was flung open and in came Baxter and the new apprentice. Jonah noticed his large stature, good looks and slim body.

'Jimmy, meet Jonah,' Baxter said, gesturing at Jonah. 'Jimmy here has today's work, so I'll leave you to it.' He smiled as he left.

The new apprentice walked in holding three garments in his hands. 'Jimmy is the name,' he said bluntly. 'I'm a non-criminal man, destined to live a life with a future,' he said firmly.

Jonah frowned, looking at him. 'You know about my past?' he asked.

'Of course I do, you lay-about,' he said venomously. 'It's why I don't pity or care for you. I don't like you, you lay-about,' he emphasised. 'I got hired to replace you, and I'm going to work to destroy you,' he laughed.

Jonah was taken aback by his animosity. 'I was betrayed and set up,' Jonah hit back fiercely.

Jimmy waved his hand and rolled his eyes, 'Even if that was true, you've come here and acting like a fat, lazy sloth who does nothing but eat and drink all day,' he spat.

'That's not…' before Jonah could finish, Jimmy interjected.

'I'm going to enjoy berating you day and night, but for now I'm going to sit and work, while you just look on. I have a work ethic, and I'm going to get the life that you have always wanted; that is, until your criminal ass ruined it,' he said mockingly as he sat at the desk, working on the garments.

Jonah sat back on the bed, shamefully watching the man's back, saddened by the hurtful words. He was trapped in the room with him, unable to leave his second prison, in fear of running into a customer and shaming Baxter's business.

The entire day was filled with ridicule as Jimmy did the work, calling him out, tutting at the lack of response, while he worked hard throughout the day.

When the shop closed, Jimmy retreated, taking his work with him to the front end, chastising Jonah as he left.

Defeatedly, Jonah sat there, embarrassed at the harsh words. A tear streamed down his face, and he quickly batted it away. He was angry at his shame, and that he'd let a man so young hurt him, and he realised his downfalls. The hate filled him, as he couldn't help but feel cheated out of a life that Jimmy was destined to have.

He hid his woes well, putting on a brave face for Miss Sandra, who willingly brought him his evening meal, but he crumbled upon Baxter's visit. His sadness echoed out, and, eventually, he told Baxter the day's events, hoping that he might consider firing Jimmy.

Baxter listened intently as Jonah described the insults. A small part of him couldn't help but agree with Jimmy's words but looking at the broken human, a small amount of sadness filled him.

After Jonah finished, Baxter opened his mouth and said, 'Jonah, I'm not going to fire him. If that's what you're suggesting, you've got to fight your own battles and fuel your own hatred with a distraction. If I were you, I'd get rid of the problem, and I wouldn't let a child berate me. I'd make it clear that I was the person in charge,' he said carefully.

Jonah looked at him in shock. 'So, you don't think I should go down without a fight, then?' he asked.

'No,' Baxter replied. 'I think you should have a word with him, at the very least,' he said with an awkward laugh before leaving.

II

As the weeks passed, the conversation between Jonah and Baxter replayed in his mind. Taking care of the situation and turning the tide, so to say.

Despite his pleasantry efforts, Jonah didn't win the mind of Jimmy, but still continued his pointless efforts of trying to be friends.

The hate rolled in, and although Miss Sandra continued to bring food to him, which he gladly ate, the likes of Cissy stayed away, much to his sadness. Baxter, too, made infrequent visits like he always did, leaving Jonah alone with Jimmy, with nothing to do but drink and eat, as he said.

Jonah was forced to listen to the drivel, while being made redundant in his bed. He barely did anything but eat, and if anything went wrong, Jimmy would simply blame him, playing on his lack of skill, despite his knowledge and teachings from Baxter.

He was a rogue in disguise, determined to bring Jonah down and corrupt him, all the while convincing those around him of his skill.

Much to his annoyance, Jonah could see that it was working. He heard the compliments from clients, Cissy and Miss Sandra, they showered him with praise. For Jonah it was a kick in the teeth; his life before saw him tall, strong and preparing to be a husband and the trainee of a tailor. That dream had washed away years ago, and now he was old, fat and angry. He envied Jimmy, who was on the path he had once travelled, without the grace of an orphaned life or broken heart.

It began to rile him, the life he was leading; it was slipping away and slowly destroying and breaking him down, yet the words of Baxter echoed around his mind, the thought of him being someone who was left behind to be forgotten.

The days dragged, with Jonah confined to the bed, forever looking at the back of Jimmy's head as he worked, his large hands finely creating a masterpiece. He'd whistle to himself, laugh and berate Jonah, calling him a lazy fat slob, taunting his inabilities, telling him what a wasted and disappointing life he led.

When the days came to a close, he always felt drained after the stream of abuse that he was privy to. He compensated with food and drink, and he happily wolfed down anything Miss Sandra delivered to him.

The evenings bore on, and he dreaded going to sleep and awakening to Jimmy, his patience wearing thin, his anger building as the envy entwined around his heart.

His desires and wants were present, but they weren't available to him; they were all Jimmy's, the cruel and cold-hearted man that made sure to remind him each day.

He'd gone from being a high-ranking tailor with a shop of his own to a dishevelled man who had traded one prison cell for another.

Admittedly, it was cosier and the food readily present, but alas it wasn't enough. He wanted more; he wanted his old life back and the opportunity that Jimmy was currently presented with.

It wasn't right that he was to sit back and watch a man he hated so much achieve the life he should be living.

It was becoming a tiresome task to live through each day, try as he might, to sit beside Jimmy; he couldn't stand one more minute of it, especially when Jimmy began to boast of his new skills and even talk of a local girl that had caught his eye. He had everything that Jonah held dearly, and now his future looked to be a dreary one, bed-bound and meaningless.

Envy rose inside him, and with every moment his urges to rid himself of a wicked man bubbled inside him. He began to spend his days imagining how he might dispose of Jimmy. At first, it started off with Jimmy ruining a dress for one of the more fanciful women in the area and Baxter firing him for his horrid mistake; but as the days continued, his thoughts grew darker.

Next, it was Jimmy tripping and hurting himself, but it soon developed to he himself harming Jimmy, gradually squeezing the life out of him or using the sharper tools to stab him fiercely in the heart, killing him instantly.

It was those thoughts that kept him sane, the thoughts of ending his life and stopping Jimmy from opening his mouth and letting his vile words harm him ever again.

In the beginning, he squashed the thoughts, casting them out as evil; but as time wore on, he found it difficult to ignore them. It soon became a matter of how he would do it — would he clobber him over the head while his back was turned, strangle him with his large hands or stab him to death with the shearing scissors?

He imagined his death over and over, picturing the one method that would be most satisfying. He replayed them, focusing on the heinous comments and maliciously planning his demise. The method he favoured changed from day to day, and he let the darkness absorb him as the temptation peaked.

'If I were you, I'd get rid' — the echoing words of Baxter rang through his mind as he continued to plot Jimmy's death, the harrowing details being filled in by his vengeful and envious mind.

Time dragged, the days stretching out longer than what they should, and Jonah had steadily been gaining more weight as he sat by idly.

The pent up rage and aggression was surging through Jonah. It was the last Wednesday of the month, and he'd been putting up with Jimmy for almost four weeks. It had been busy for the shop, and many orders were due for the coming Friday, with half a dozen still left to complete.

Jimmy was in a foul mood, had been all week and his hatred was only building towards Jonah.

'Look at this,' he called as he pulled material towards him. 'The stitching is pathetic.' He rolled his eyes at Jonah who was looking at the perfectly sewn dress he had completed that morning.

'It's fine, better than most,' Jonah huffed, turning his gaze back to the dress he was fumbling with.

'Better than most? What a load of rubbish, you worthless orphan, forever living off the hands of others while the rest of the world works hard.' He spat venomously at Jonah.

Gritting his teeth and balling his fist, Jonah went to stand but before he could move a blow to his head knocked him back. He didn't see the quick strike from Jimmy, but he did hear the laughter of the young boy who watched the pitiful lump on the bed.

Jonah looked horrified. 'Why?' he asked hysterically. 'Why do you hate me so?'

Through tears of laughter, Jimmy replied, 'Because I can, because you don't deserve more and because I'm forced to be housed all day with a filthy criminal,' he spat.

Jimmy stormed out, leaving Jonah on the bed, his head throbbing from the pain, a tear streaming down his cheek, and before he knew it, he was sobbing like a small child, desperately in need of his mother.

He lay down, pulling the covers over his head, resting on a large pillow, and quietly cried into it. He stayed this way for some time, the sadness slowly transforming into rage as his mind wandered into the darkness again. Finally, he knew how he was going to kill Jimmy.

His breathing steadied as he plotted away, his body relaxing as he calmed down. He pulled himself together just as Miss Sandra walked in, loaded up with beer and food. He smiled warmly and squeezed her hand as she placed it across his lap.

She had made his favourite — beef stew with dumplings — and he was given three times the average portion, while three large slices of buttered bread complemented the dish. She placed a large jug of beer beside the bed, but tonight he ignored it, for he had a business that required a clear head. Instead, he tucked into the stew, the mixture sliding down his throat gently, nourishing him and enticing his taste buds.

Every bite soothed him and he once again let food be the nourishment he craved from people.

Once he had eaten, he lay back on his bed and thought intently. He was going to use the tailor shears to stab Jimmy.

It was easy enough for him to do, simply wait until everyone was asleep to steal the shears and hide them in his room, ready for Jimmy's arrival in the morning.

He paced up and down the room nervously, straining to hear any noise; getting caught would ruin any chance he had. Eventually, he got up the courage to open the door. He pulled it carefully and slowly peered out: everything was dark, and no noise was to be heard. With a deep breath, he quietly stepped out.

He knew the room well, having spent most of his youth there, working with Baxter,

Slowly he crept through the room, heading for the broad set of drawers in the far corner. He knew the spare shears were in the top left box, and very gently, he pulled it open, the wood creaking as he reached in and pulled them out. A wicked smile stretched across his face as he took hold of the cold steel.

He held them up to his face, the moonlight dancing on the shiny exterior. Slowly, his dragged his finger across the shears, stroking the steel until his index finger reached the sharp tip. He winced as it nipped his skin, drawing a small ball of blood. 'Well, well, well, what do we have here?' A voice sounded out in the darkness, causing Jonah to jump and slam the drawer shut as he instinctively hid the scissors behind his back.

'Who is there?' he asked.

A match struck, and the candle on the wall was lit, revealing Jimmy's smug face. He leaned against the wall, his head cocked as he looked at Jonah with curiosity.

Immediately, Jonah's face changed from fear to anger as he watched him standing there freely.

'What are you doing here?' he snarled.

'Me?' replied Jimmy. 'You're the one breaking the rules, out at night in the main parlour, rifling through the private items of your employer.'

Fuming, Jonah exhaled and took a few steps forward, which prompted Jimmy to move quickly through the room, facing him with a smirk.

The anger was seething through Jonah's body; he saw red and revealed the scissors from behind his back, waving them at him with a crazy look in his eyes. He had the satisfaction of seeing the fear spread across Jimmy's face.

A wicked smile curled on Jonah's face, and before he knew it, he lunged forward. In horror, Jimmy stepped to the side and punched Jonah in the face.

He stumbled, grabbing at the furniture, until he was steady, readying himself for another attack.

Breathing heavily, Jonah clasped the shears tighter. He was heaving as his unfit body weighed down on him, but the adrenaline and anger was pumping through him. Whirling around he lunged, the shears held high, but Jimmy was more than prepared.

He was standing tall, his body arched as he awaited the second blow. This time he gripped the shears in his hand and together the men began to struggle.

Punches began to fly as the shears waved in front of their faces. Jimmy was furiously restraining the weaponed hand, the sweat beating down him as he groaned, using his free hand to lay blow after blow to Jonah's body, hitting his face, chest and arms in a bid to survive.

As they struggled, their bodies grappled around the room, the chairs up turning, their bodies slamming harshly into the drawers. During the commotion, Jonah's heel caught against the centre table, causing them both to fall. Their bodies slammed on top of one another, the wooden table crumbling beneath them loudly.

By this point, the sounds of Baxter, Cissy and Miss Sandra could be heard as they frantically began pounding downstairs, their cries ringing out as they poured into the room, their eyes searching for the source of the noise.

It was Miss Sandra who first laid eyes on the pair, a harrowing scream escaping her lips as she shakily pointed to them. Cissy cried out, her hands immediately slapping across her eyes as she turned away from the fight.

'What is going on?' Baxter yelled.

The pair ignored him as they continued to struggle, the shears pushing between the pair. Jimmy, who was crushing Jonah's body into the floor, had the upper hand as Jonah lay like a turtle on its back. Unable to move, Jimmy began delivering punch after punch, furiously pounding his face until he managed to whack Jonah's hand, causing the shears to slip from his grip. Without haste or even flinching, Jimmy grabbed them and plunged them into Jonah's heart.

A gasp escaped his lips, the life leaving his eyes as he made one more feeble attempt to breathe. His face was contorted in pain and shock as he died, leaving Jimmy sat on his still warm corpse.

Screams from Miss Sandra erupted as the blood splattered on Jimmy's face. Cissy buried herself in Miss Sandra as she heard the shears pierce through the flesh. Baxter moved quickly, rushing to Jimmy's side as he lifted him from the body.

Gripping him tightly, Baxter, panic stricken, cried, 'What happened?'

The colour drained from his face as he swallowed, looking at the body. His breathing became harsher, the panic rising in him as the tears welled in his eyes. 'He attacked me,' he said weakly. 'I heard a noise and came down to find him going through your drawers. I challenged him, and then he pulled out the shears and brandished them at me,' he explained, as his legs weakened, causing him to stumble into the closest chair.

Baxter helped him down and looked over at the ladies. He swallowed and looked at Jonah, the shears in his chest, the blood flowing out of his body. He quickly grabbed a sheet of fabric and threw it over his body, before ordering Cissy to fetch the police.

Stepping away from Miss Sandra, Cissy dashed from the room, not looking back at the bloody sheet. Gagging, Miss Sandra backed from the room and into the kitchen, only to return with glasses and a bottle of whiskey. She quietly poured them a hearty helping, before passing them out to Baxter and Jimmy as they awaited the arrival of the police.

Jimmy sat there wide-eyed, his glass loosely held in his hand, as he heard the distant mumbles of Baxter and Miss Sandra, who were quietly talking, continuously glancing at Jimmy, who sat frozen on the very edge of the chair.

Within ten minutes, the police arrived, marching through the shop front and towards the back. There were two large men, one tall and thin, while the other was short, broader and fatter, yet equally as scary.

The tall man had a stern face with steel-cut cheekbones; he was clean-shaven and featured a long and pointy nose, and his beady black eyes were dashing around the room, analysing each person. The larger man had a chubby face that was squished under his hat; he had a big bushy moustache and bright brown eyes, and his face was red from running. He immediately went to the body, examining the wound and bruises that were presenting themselves before sternly looking at Jimmy who had averted his gaze.

He stood up, looked at his partner and nodded towards Jimmy. They each turned to him and took a few steps towards him.

'Boy,' said the tall man in a stern voice, 'I wish for you to follow me. We will then interview each of you separately to get the full story.' He turned as he finished, meeting the eyes of Miss Sandra and Baxter.

Slowly, Jimmy rose, as each man placed their hands on his arms and led him into the kitchen. They spent well over an hour talking with him, during which time the undertaker, doctor and Cissy appeared through the door.

Together they began to tend to the body as Cissy took up conversation with Baxter and Miss Sandra. She was red-faced and Breathlessly said, 'They insisted on taking my statement before they let me go. What's happening now?'

Baxter nodded at her and slowly raised his finger to his lips as he looked at the body.

Both men had set to work, removing the sheet and prodding at the body, before taking the deceased Jonah out on the room on a stretcher. Just as they left, Jimmy walked back into the room, his eyes red as he signalled for Miss Sandra to enter the room. Timidly she walked, greeting the men politely. They could hear her sweet voice, but not quite hear the exact words.

She stayed there for thirty minutes before emerging, her face red and flustered as she nodded for Baxter to enter. He straightened his shoulders and clapped Jimmy on the back before he entered the room, greeting the policemen and taking his seat at the table facing the men.

They each had a warm cup of tea and a plate of biscuits, which he could only assume Miss Sandra had provided for them.

'My name is Constable Johnson,' said the slim man. He motioned to the man next to him and said, 'This is Constable Higgins.' He looked bluntly at Baxter, his eyes cold.

'We need the full story,' Officer Johnson continued. 'I want to know what you saw, who the dead man is and why this act of murder has come to be true.'

Baxter gave a quick smile before introducing himself and beginning to explain. 'Jonah Heizium was once a respectable tailor, born a labourer and trained with grace; but sadly, over the years, he was cruelly ripped of every opportunity.

'Under my wing, I trained him and sent him to a fellow tailor for further training, where he was convicted of theft and later imprisoned. I took pity on him and upon release brought him back here. He was unwilling to work, becoming a sloth and a slob, before Jimmy joined us, and up until today I thought everything was fine.' He paused to take a breath.

'So, you employed a criminal and it backfired?' Constable Higgins said, sarcastically.

Baxter looked at him without blinking. 'Yes,' he said sternly. 'Jonah was a friend; I felt partly responsible, and when I was awoken to cries, I didn't know what to expect. Jonah was disheartened — he led a wasted life, but I never saw him as a threat. His attack on Jimmy seems unwarranted, but his death occurred in self-defence, and that is all I have to say,' he finished, his eyes soft and sad.

The policemen looked at one another as he finished speaking. The tall one pressed his lips together and leaned back in his chair. 'Well,' he said, 'it would seem that the prisoner met a fitting end. Your story corroborates those of the rest of your comrades, and Jimmy Flack has a clean record; he is a respectable and hard-working man, your friend, as you call him, is nothing in the eyes of the law. I think we both agree that Jimmy is a hero who defended all of you. Who knows how far Jonah would have gone if he had succeeded in killing Jimmy.' He looked deeply into Baxter's eyes.

'You think he intended to harm us all, do you?' Baxter asked in shock.

'Indeed,' Constable Higgins replied. 'You can never put trust in men who have seen life on the inside — they are different to us.'

'Indeed, they are, but kind hearts such as yourself find this out the hard way,' Constable Johnson said. 'For now, we will leave you in peace and report back. I don't think we'll be back again; it seems a closed case.'

They left without another word, and the house fell quiet, the last remnants of Jonah stained into the aged rug.

The Sins

Baxter paced around the room, gesturing for Cissy, Miss Sandra and Jimmy to take a seat. He thought intently, his mind reflecting on the life of Jonah Heizium, the man born from the love of two soulmates.

He smiled; his face contorted in wickedness as his eyes darted to the back door of the kitchen. Before long, the door creaked, and three bodies strolled in. First it was the slender figure of Myra, who danced across the floor, her smile wide and gleeful. Next came Sarah; she smiled fleetingly at Baxter as she took a seat besides Miss Sandra. Finally, Mr Bentley came into view, his large body strolling into the room as he clasped Baxter's hand with a smirk.

Returning the smile, Baxter nodded and gestured for the newcomers to seat themselves around the bloody mess.

'The final resting place of our tormented soul, who had the honours in the end?' Myra asked, her voice excited as she studied the large red stain.

'Jimmy, of course. Naturally, it would be Envy who stole from us what we all wanted to do,' Cissy said, rolling her eyes as she poked him in the ribs.

He wiggled away from her bony finger and laughed. 'Please, we all know the instigator and eventual demise belongs to Anger. Isn't that right, Baxter?' He arched his brow as he eyed the tailor.

Mr Baxter smiled. 'I think we can all agree that we each played our parts perfectly,' he said with grace as he turned to look at each individual. 'I must admit, you've been entertaining, somewhat ingenious. You built our little playmate up beautifully and dashed him down just as he believed he had won.' He bowed to them in congratulations, pausing slightly. 'Sadly, our time is up in this festering world. It's time we got back home; but let it be known, my dear Sins, you did so very well.'

Evil smiles spread across their faces as they stood, their bodies becoming fainter as the door to Jonah's old room glowed ominously. Together they marched through, disappearing into the abyss, never to be seen again.

The Watcher

Well, dear reader, the death of Jonah Heizium was an inevitable one; the Sins are dearly happy with themselves. I would love to say that this was it, this was the end, that Jonah died, the Sins returned, and life went on. That the effects the Sins had on others barely rippling through their descendants.

Alas, I'm sad to report this story still hasn't come to an end, for Jonah still had one task — he still had to meet me, make the right choice and move on from his terrible life.

My dear reader, all this time I have apologised for my actions, told you how I slipped up, and up until now, you thought it was allowing the Sins in the human world. My dear reader, I led you up the garden path, or is it the kitchen sink? I can never remember; you funny humans and your sayings.

You see, dear reader, I regrettably gave Jonah an option in which I thought he would choose the sane and right path. Once again, I will leave you, but here is where you will truly see my mistake, my misjudgement of how hate and anger, influences a person.

Dear reader, please try and not judge. You're so complex, so difficult to read, you'd think I'd have a better understanding by now, but each and every one of you is entirely different. You're an unpredictable race!

Jonah

Jonah woke on a dark dirt floor, his chest aching. Immediately, he grabbed it, wincing and gasping for breath, but it was dry, almost unnatural. Groggily, he pulled himself up, staring at the deserted room.

How did I get here, what is here, he wondered, his eyes scanning the place until his gaze was drawn to a bright light that was shimmering from a door at the far end of the room. Without thinking, he slowly got up, his feet stumbling towards the warm glow.

Dust and dirt fluttered upwards with every step he took. A daunting pit formed in his stomach as he finally reached the door, a sense of uneasiness washing over him.

A dark fog had covered his mind, his thoughts blurred as he desperately tried to understand, to remember how he came to be in this room and what he was doing beforehand.

He grasped the door, pulling it gently as the light dowsed him. He paused, momentarily shielding his gaze before shakily stepping over the threshold. Within moments, a bang echoed, and Jonah turned to see the door closed and the dirt room gone. He cried out loudly, his fists pounding the door as he searched for the handle that was no longer there.

Just as he was about to panic, a voice behind him called his name. With calming breaths, Jonah turned to see the outline of a body, the features on his face not quite visible.

'Dear Jonah,' the figure spoke in a tame manner, 'I have been following your story for so long. You've come so far and experienced too much; so much more than what you should have.'

Still confused, Jonah shakily asked, 'Where am I? Who are you?'

'Introductions, I always forget those,' it laughed. 'My name is the Watcher. I watch the souls of the Earth and help them get to where they need to go after they've died.'

'Died? I'm dead!' Jonah exclaimed in horror.

'Forgive me, Jonah, but sadly yes, you are dead; but it gets worse — the evilest force has manipulated your life, the seven deadly Sins positioned themselves rather well in your life; the strongest, Anger, was your good friend Baxter,' the Watcher said softly.

Jonah gasped. 'Baxter? But he was one of my best friends.'

'A wolf in the disguise of a sheep; but, alas, your death has come, and your path is coming to an end. You simply need to follow the way.' He gestured behind him as he spoke. 'You might even see some friendly faces along the way.'

Jonah began to pace back and forth, thinking over his life, the times that Baxter had influenced him, appeared at his side, offering his help, giving him everything he needed, which was inevitably ripped away from him.

If it hadn't been for Baxter, he would have lived a normal life, married and happy, in a well-to-do job, with Rose, his beautiful Rose.

Tears welled in his eyes and the anger seared through his body. 'No, I don't want to just leave, I want revenge,' he said through gritted teeth. 'I want to face him and end him like he ended my life.'

'I would not recommend that,' the Watcher said. 'You'd have to enter the Hollow to achieve that, and, well, I'm not sure what you would find or what would happen to your soul when they won.

'It's out of the question; you can't go there,' he finished firmly.

Jonah looked upon him, his chest heaving, and he noted how the outline of the Watcher turned to the right. It wasn't so much a path, but a tangled web of vines that led to darkness. It was eerie, the type of place a sane man would think twice about entering.

The light to the left of the Watcher was warm and tempting, the promise of seeing those he loved once more was drawing him, but he had to fight back for his honour and that of those they had hurt.

Tears streamed down his face as he fought with the idea. 'Will I see my mother, my father, my loving Rose if I walk towards that light?' he asked with a sob.

'There's a possibility. I've never been; I don't know where you'll go or who you'll see. Of course, the Sins ate up your father's soul when they entered the human world.' He stopped suddenly, moving quickly, as if to cover his mouth.

Jonah looked up, eyes wide with craze, and he laughed maniacally. 'My father's soul was eaten up? They ate his soul?' he screeched.

'No, no, no, I didn't say that. I meant they... well, they did something to someone that resembled your father's soul,' he lied feebly.

Jonah stared angrily, his eye twitching. 'That's it. Let's see how much of a match they'll be now I know what I'm up against.' The venomous tone rang high as he strode confidently towards the darkness, disappearing in an instance.

'No, Jonah, no!' the Watcher shouted hysterically as his figure dissolved into the Hollow.

The Watcher

Oh, dear reader, please, please forgive me. It's all my fault. I should have chosen my words more carefully, had I been more attuned with your emotions. I have messed up here, Death is going to kill me!

I honestly thought that my fears would cease upon the death of Jonah, but now I fear more than ever. The Hollow wasn't created for humans. It's an insidious place, designed solely for the most heinous creatures. It's there to keep them at bay, away from your world.

The Sins' have returned to the Hollow. I felt the unnatural wave enter the realm upon Jonah's demise. Their life-force is limited to the soul they absorbed. Jonah was the last attachment to that world, one linked directly with Frank – the soul they stole. In your world, they would just be someone there one day and gone another. It would raise an eyebrow or two, but for the most part it would be abandonment in light of a shameful and disturbing scene of death. To you humans, how one presented themselves was far superior to their actions; it would be expected rather than questioned.

I very much fear the coming times; just as before, I can only simply watch — watch this fierce battle commence in a world that Jonah couldn't even comprehend.

This fight is to be terrible; the Hollow will be thriving with all the excitement, and that I fear.

Dear reader, how horrible I feel, for I am to blame, I am the one who started this, I am the one that ruined the lives of so many, and now I can but wonder and watch.

My duty to the other souls still lies; now I must abandon Jonah and force him to tackle the Sins alone.

His story continues, and I will continue to watch, but, dear reader, please know I am sorry, I am terribly sorry.